THE FINDING OF DOC JACK

THE FINDING OF DOC JACK

Daniel Jack McDougall

Copyright © 2010 by Daniel Jack McDougall.

Library of Congress Control Number: 2010916590
ISBN: 145652612X
ISBN-13: 9781456526122

All rights reserved. No part of this book may be reproduced or transmitted in any form or by any means, electronic or mechanical, including photocopying, recording, or by any information storage and retrieval system, without permission in writing from the copyright owner.

This is a work of fiction. Names, characters, places and incidents either are the product of the author's imagination or are used fictitiously, and any resemblance to any actual persons, living or dead, events, or locales is entirely coincidental. But you, the reader may wish to read between the lines.

This book was printed in the United States of America.

I dedicate this book to Donna Rose Davidson McDougall, who did pass away on Halloween day as stated and who now rests by Little Lake in the town of Peterborough, Ontario. You are greatly missed.

I will take this time to thank my nurse, Tracy Rowland . . . , of which was supplied to ensure my well-being, not only gave me the insight to write this book while under their care, but also took my words and typed my story word for word for you to read. Many hours she spent getting this story out for me. Thank you.

Special thanks to Drs. Jeffrey D., Paulette W., Virginia S., Christine W., Nicole A. Without you all, this book would not have been completed.

PROLOGUE

Doc Jack was born in 1863, and he disappeared into the Rocky Mountains of Alberta in 1907.

After one year of searching for Doc, the people of the Calgary area presumed that the mountains had taken his soul.

For a doctor who was unfamiliar with winter mountain terrain, the risks were high, and the odds of returning slim, but Doc wanted closure on the last of the six men who had murdered his parents back in Peterborough, Ontario.

In the winter of 2009-2010, a series of avalanches had taken their toll and buried some local snowmobilers.

During the search, all five of the buried men were found alive. But they came across another unidentified body, which was frozen solid. This body was dressed in clothing that would have been worn a century ago. A long caribou coat, which also was lifted from the scene.

On the body, they found handguns still in their holsters, another clue to who the frozen man might have been was a Deputy's Tin Star attached to his shirt.

Finding such a perfectly preserved artifact was a rare gift and opportunity for archeologists. With advances in research having progressed to where they are today, it was prudent to have the cryogenic research team called in secretly to have their findings assessed before the body was turned over to a museum, and then the museum lost their chance to examine it.

The frozen body appeared to have been caught up in an avalanche and then, over time, buried deep below the snow's surface. Only in the researchers' wildest dreams did they ever hope to find such complete specimen.

While examining the corpse, they were able to also perform some tests or experiments that they had never tried on a human body before. The previous results of these tests had been the reanimation of frozen mammals with only some degree of success.

The body known to most Calgarians 102 years ago was that of Daniel Jack McDougall aka Doc Jack himself. How do I know? You'll have to keep reading to find out for yourself.

Cryogenics is the freezing and unfreezing of mammals to be able to perform one day on humans as research, possibly to be able to freeze a human body with a disease that has no cure. Later, once a cure is found, this body could be unfrozen then cured of this fatal disease, giving back its natural life. It could take years to find a cure. Not to mention that, to date, they have never had a body of a human they could perform such experiments to, even bring back a corpse to a living state. (A body of which would have to be healthy at time of passing.) For example, the body of Daniel Jack McDougall.

Not to interfere with ongoing tests of this nature. It was strongly advised to write this book as a fiction considering such new development in progress, we agree not to go into any details of these experiments and developments that may have been performed.

Therefore, this book is written in fiction; for those readers that like to read between the lines, you must read this book.

The author of which writes from the heart from true emotional life experiences that will surely touch your soul. Towns, places of events, as well as names have not been changed as they existed then as well as today. The names written herein are no longer living but may have carried on in the next generation(s). Well, let's just say *most*.

THE FINDING OF DOG JACK

This is the story of Daniel Jack McDougall.

Daniel was born on December 18, 1863, and was raised by his parents, Daniel Leonard and Donna Rose.

His father, Daniel, migrated from Scotland in 1860. He was a very strong man and had the thick Scotland eyebrows, and continuous defiantly not as a downfall, he was quite a good-looking man with a caring and giving character, which was well respected by most. He was astute and was a very hardworking businessman, oftentimes putting as much as twelve hours a day into his business. The business itself was a trading post and general store located in Peterborough, Ontario, which, at the time, was a small village though growing fast. His work was his passion—he loved wheeling and dealing with traders to obtain goods that he could later sell for profit.

While establishing his business, Daniel had developed a steadfast and lifelong friendship with a young man named Barry Davidson, a carpenter by trade along with his brothers Allan and Chuck. Over time, the brothers not only established a name for themselves in the carpentry world but were soon able to pool their finances and their carpentry skills to acquire an acreage on which they built a large log house and a two-story barn. The Davidson boys had one sister, Donna, who acquired a nickname of Rachel. As a young child, her friends figured she was a wild card, unpredictable at times as was an elderly woman, Rachel, who was known in the area. Donna acquired this name as they were one of the same to her friends. Donna, now known as Rachel, was a beauty in her own right. Though Rachel worked as hard as any man on her brothers' farm, she cleaned up well and was truly a warm, elegant woman whose outer strength was easily matched by her inner spirit.

About a year after he established his business, Daniel began courting Rachel. A courtship followed during which they fell in love and decided to wed. As a wedding gift, Daniel bought twenty acres of the Davidson boys' land, along with the log cabin and two-story barn that the brothers built. It was a sturdy and lovely home for the newlyweds to begin their life together.

As much as you would expect any young lady to be interested in decorating her home, it was the barn that was of more interest to Rachel at this time. Rachel had a passion for horses at a very young age. When she was ten years old, her father, an Arabian horse breeder by profession, passed away, and Rachel knew that she would one day follow in his footsteps and continue his legacy of breeding fine Arabian horses. While her brothers were busy establishing their carpentry careers, Rachel had learned all she could about her father's trade.

Her father, aside from breeding Arabian horses, had also established a name for himself as a restaurateur in Nipissing, Ontario. When he passed away, Rachel's mother, Dorothy, raised four children on her own while continuing to run the restaurant business. Dorothy loved cooking as well. She was the best mother any one could have. Eventually, her three sons moved on. Rachel took care of the horses as was her father's last wish. It was a tough job for such a young girl; however, with the help of the ranch hands, Rachel did a good job. Later in her teens, Rachel moved the horses to Peterborough, finding much better pastures for the horses as well better connections for selling and breeding. Her brothers moved years prior, also settling in the same town due to the logging and building of new homes.

While Daniel continued running the trading post and general store, Rachel was content keeping house and breeding her horses, though on busier days, you would find her behind the counter at the store as well.

After only a year of marriage, Rachel became pregnant. It was a very difficult pregnancy, so much so that after only five months, even the most basic of chores became too difficult for her. Daniel brought in a caregiver, Maria, a native women and a healer to the Kawartha Tribe of whom Daniel had met through his trading at the general store. During the uprising of the government and the Natives, Daniel being an unbiased man, gave shelter to Maria and her three children during the war of the two parties, ensuring her children did not get caught in the crossfire. Maria, as well as her family, had great respect for the McDougall family who helped Rachel not only with her daily duties but with the remainder of her confinement as well.

Because of her earlier difficulties with the baby, even the local doctor had his doubts as to whether or not the pregnancy would go to term.

On the evening of December 18, 1863, in the midst of a terrible blizzard, Rachel went into labor. Daniel panicked and didn't know what to do. Fortunately, Maria kept her wits about her and instructed Daniel to go into town and fetch the doctor.

Daniel quickly fetched his horses, hitched them to the wagon, and travelled as fast as the weather permitted. Unfortunately, a trip that would normally take only ten minutes took nearly thirty in the treacherous weather, and by the time Daniel reached Dr. Roy Anderson's house, he was nearly frozen.

Shivering uncontrollably with teeth chattering, Daniel entered the homestead quickly walking to the fireplace where he stood, gesturing that Rachel was in labor. Dr. Anderson only needed a few moments to get ready. After many years of delivering babies, he had the foresight to know that Rachel's due date was soon to come and had kept his medical bag prepared.

While waiting for only a few short minutes, Daniel noticed a pot of hot tea steaming out of the teapot.

"Do you mind, Roy?" He pointed to the teacup on the table. Roy, with a smile, noticed he was dancing all over, trying to keep warm.

"By all means, help yourself." After a few sips of hot tea, they made their way back to the McDougall's log cabin. The trip was quicker this time with few words exchanged by the two. Dr. Anderson implored Daniel to slow down, reminding him that they would be walking through the blizzard if the wagon happened to slide off the trail and into the trees.

When they arrived at the house, Maria seemed to have things under control. She had clean sheets on the bed, water set to boil, and clean linens for swaddling the baby. She was also trying her best to comfort Rachel through each contraction, but judging from Rachel's screams, she was still in unbearable pain.

Dr. Anderson instructed Daniel to wait in the living room. After what seemed like an eternity to Daniel, the doctor, Maria, and Rachel delivered a beautiful baby boy.

Unfortunately, the doctor's work was far from over. Despite the successful delivery, Rachel was not doing very well, which concerned Dr. Anderson as well as Maria. Daniel, already panicking of having his new born about was not told how close it was to losing Rachel, not to panic him anymore. Eventually, a few hours later, Dr. Anderson had the situation under control as Rachel became more stable.

Utterly exhausted, Rachel was able to hold her newborn son for only a few moments before nodding off for some much-earned and—needed sleep while Dr. Anderson stayed at her bedside for the remainder of the night in case he was needed.

Daniel, of course, was still greatly concerned and kept seeking reassurance from the doctor that both his son and his wife would recover from the traumatic experience. The doctor reassured Daniel that all was well for now but that Rachel would need to remain on bed rest for at least two weeks before resuming to any exhausting duties that a mother would have to do. He also advised that Daniel and Maria keep an eye on the baby for a few days to make sure he was thriving.

He then accompanied Daniel to see his newborn son, who was being cradled in Maria's arms in the rocking chair in the spare room.

As Daniel looked down at his son with a soft smile, the baby opened his big blue eyes to stare back at him. Maria offered to let Daniel hold the baby, but as the birth had truly shaken him, he decided it would probably be better to wait until he relaxed a bit more. He asked Dr. Anderson to join him with a small glass of wine. Daniel wanted to celebrate the birth of his son as well as calm his nerves. Doc checked on Rachel to see that she was doing okay and then gladly accepted his offer.

After a quick cheer, it did not take Daniel long to question the health of the two.

"Are you sure that Rachel and the boy will be all right?"

"Yes, they will be fine. However, I wouldn't recommend Rachel having another baby," the doc replied. Though Daniel knew that this may prove to be a disappointment to Rachel, he figured she would nonetheless have her hands full with only one since she had been adamant about continuing with the horse breeding program she had worked so hard to establish.

At noon the following day, with Rachel being stabilized and Maria in possession of all the necessities to tend to the child, Daniel took Dr. Anderson back to town. As they parted ways, Dr. Anderson informed Daniel that he would return to check on Rachel in two days' time.

On the way back to the house, Daniel reflected upon how lucky he and Rachel were to have found such a fine caregiver as Maria. Luckily, she had agreed to stay on to help Rachel with the baby. How she came to be part of the family was indeed through an ironic twist of fate. Maria managed to drop by the house for a few hours each day to help Rachel with the baby. Daniel ensured that Maria and her family were well-paid for their concern, offering them merchandise at no charge from his store whenever they were in need. They felt this was a handout that they did not need and insisted to trade as usual. Respecting their wishes of not giving them free supplies, Daniel was sure the future trades were in their favor.

Daniel and Rachel had discussed many names for their child during the past nine months, and on December 19, 1863, they named their baby boy Daniel Jack McDougall. Dr. Anderson recorded his name for all the appropriate papers when he came to visit and check on Rachel a few days later.

After two weeks, Rachel's brothers Barry, Allan, and Chuck came to visit and celebrate the new year by showering their new nephew with a range of homemade gifts ranging from various toys to a playpen and crib.

During the holiday season, Dorothy, Rachel's mother, announced that she had decided to sell her restaurant in Nipissing and move to Peterborough where she could be close to all her children and, of course, to her new grandson. By the time she arrived, Daniel Jr. was six months old.

Dorothy lived with the McDougalls for three years before moving to Toronto to give the young family more space. Rachel had enjoyed having her company each day, Daniel Jr. thrived on his grandmother's attention, and Daniel Sr. never tired of the home cooking, the baking, and knowing his family and their livestock were being well cared for by his mother-in-law. She worked like an ox as she did in the upbringing of her own children. She was greatly appreciated and missed.

welve years later, Daniel Sr.'s trading post and general store had doubled in size, both in sale and in stock expanding, to include the sale of new and used guns.

Rachel's horse breeding trade had grown to a count of forty-six heads. She had hired local wranglers to help on occasions with the training and care of the horses.

Daniel Jr. became an accomplished rider and a very competent worker. He gained the knowledge and experience needed to perform all the jobs the wranglers did. He seemed drawn to the sick and injured, having a special bond with these animals. They flourished under his care and returned to full health in no time. After a day of school, his first chosen chore was to tend to any of these animals.

He excelled at school and was popular with all the other children. Should any of the children be sick or injured, Daniel Jr. was the first friend to come calling to see if he could aid them in any way. The girls especially appreciated the attention that he gave them and would often come running to have him tend a scrape or pull a sliver from their finger, sometimes put there on purpose. Daniel Jr. was just beginning to appreciate their attention in return.

He also took on the chore of assisting his father at the store three days a week. Between stocking shelves and cleaning, he was a very busy young man and very mature for someone his age. Although he had lots of friends, he preferred to spend his spare time learning a new job or reading.

He did have one hobby. He became fascinated with the firearms in his father's store. Whenever he wasn't working hard, he could be found handling and learning about the firearms. By the age of twelve, he was familiar with each piece and knew how to handle them safely.

Unlike other children his age, Daniel Jr. also had the opportunity to try out all the new models when they came into the store as his father had a target area for customers out back, which was very convenient.

After months of practicing and improving his aim and shooting abilities, Daniel Jr. found a gun belt, which he modified in his spare time to fit his waist. One day, his father found Daniel Jr. on the acreage drawing a pistol from his holster as though he were in a gunfight.

Noting that both the gear and handgun were far too big for his son, Daniel Sr. was unimpressed and lectured him about his equipment. He pointed out that not only was the gun he was using the wrong weight for a boy his size, the gun belt was not secure enough to his waist. And it was far better for him to learn how to handle a rifle expertly. He explained that rifle use was better for distance shooting and taking down larger prey, which would provide food, and to pick off pests, such as wolfs, cougars, not to mention ground hogs. From a distance, they almost looked like large beavers except beavers preferred water where the ground hogs left holes all over the land that other animals could step in and break their legs.

He went on to explain that pistols were fine to use on animals that were caught in traps and mortally injured in order to humanely end their suffering. He also stated that a handgun was used for self-protection, which at this time in his life was not a necessity. Daniel was quite happy with his father as he was not the type of person to yell but to explain why he was not impressed to a point where Daniel could see the reasoning behind it.

"Okay, Dad, I understand. I am sorry."

"Daniel, you're just a boy growing fast. I understand as I was a boy too, and we all make mistakes in our lives. I'm just pointing things out for you to see. I'm not upset with you at all. Come here, I haven't hugged you in long time. I hope you haven't grown up that fast that I can't give you a hug." Sr. laughed. With a big smile, Jr. obliged his dad's request.

"You know, son, Barry and I are going deer hunting in a couple of days. Would you like to join us? It will be great to have you with us."

"Sure, I would love to," Daniel replied with a big smile. However was of two minds on the whole idea. While the thought of heading out with the men folks intrigued him, he was unsure of how he felt about actually killing an animal. He was used to healing them, not hurting them.

The night before they left to go hunting, Uncle Barry came to spend the evening with them so that they could get an early start on the day. There were rifles to be cleaned, skinning knives to be sharpened. Rachel packed up enough food to nourish all of them for the day.

As they regaled Daniel Jr. with stories of past hunting trips, Uncle Barry mentioned that he had seen an eight-point buck a mere two miles from the house on the trail and that he would probably still be around there as the vegetation was plentiful for the deer to graze on. The men agreed that this was where they would first try their hunting the next day.

Uncle Barry looked toward Daniel Jr. and asked him if he was excited for his first hunting trip. In a barely audible voice, Daniel replied that he was and then politely excused himself to turn in for the night.

When Daniel Jr. left the room, Barry asked Daniel Sr. if he was certain that the boy was ready to hunt and still not too young. Daniel Sr. replied that since the boy was old enough to handle a rifle, he was definitely old enough to learn how to hunt. Barry was quick to agree but could tell there was something on the boy's mind but could not place it.

After a toast with some imported wine, which was left from dinner, the two men decided to turn in for the night. As Daniel Sr. passed Rachel in the hallway, he placed a sweet kiss on her cheek. She smiled up at him with a sparkle in her soft eyes and said that she would be joining him as soon as the lunches were packed and after she had checked on Daniel Jr.

From the spare room, Barry called out his thanks and his love for his sister and her family. Rachel replied that housing him was her pleasure and that they should all be quiet and not wake her up when they left in the morning as the opportunity for her to sleep late was a rarity. She instructed them that their breakfast was already on the stove and that the only thing they had to do was to make sure they put the wood in the right place to start the stove.

When Rachel went into Daniel's room, she found him wide awake staring at the ceiling. Sensing that Daniel Jr. needed to talk, she sat on the edge of his bed and laid a concerned hand on his blanket and asked if he was all right.

With a sigh, Daniel Jr. explained the dilemma that had been running through his mind to his mom. He told her that he didn't know if he could actually kill a deer.

With a soft laugh, Rachel said that perhaps the opportunity to actually kill a deer would not even arise, and that even if the opportunity *did* arise, he should follow his heart and not do anything that he really didn't want to do. She explained that hunting was more of a rite of passage for a boy when he was ready rather than something he *had* to do tomorrow.

Daniel felt better after his mother's words, and he sat up and hugged her. She kissed his forehead, and as she turned off his lantern, he fell into a deep sleep.

The next morning, Barry thought he was the first one up. He peeked out the front window and was stunned to see that eight inches of snow had fallen during the night. Shaking his head, he decided to fire up the cast iron stove and put on some coffee. Once the coffee had started brewing, it didn't take long before the aroma filled the cabin as Daniel Sr. awoke to its wonderful scent.

"You're up earlier than I expected," noted Daniel Sr.

"Well, you know how it is when you sleep in a different bed than what you're used to. But it sure is nice waking up having breakfast all set and ready to go. I was just about to start them cooking, but did you want me to wait for a bit?" Barry asked.

"No, you might as well start them up. I'm heading outside for a minute to take care of business, and then I'll wake the boy."

"I looked for him in his room when I got up, but he wasn't there. I was thinking he crawled in with you and Rachel," Barry replied.

Just then, Daniel Jr. came in through the front door.

"I saddled up all the horses except for Uncle Barry's," said Daniel. "I saw movement in the house, so I thought I'd come in and warm up a bit."

Barry and Daniel Sr. looked at each other in amazement.

"Well, aren't you just raring and ready to go," his father said.

"Well, I was up early with an upset stomach. Maybe it was something that I ate last night, or maybe I'm just nervous."

Uncle Barry laughed. "Are you ready for a big day, Daniel Jr.?" Uncle Barry asked.

"I'm not too sure, but I guess I'm ready to go," replied Daniel.

"Hunting deer is really no different than shooting ground hogs. They're just bigger," stated Barry.

"Well, I've never shot one or any type of animal for that matter," replied Jr.

"Really?" said Uncle Barry.

"Why would I?" Junior replied. "They've never done me any harm."

"Well, the time will come when you realize and accept the necessity of hunting," said Uncle Barry gruffly. "In the meantime, just relax and enjoy the day. The weather is perfect for hunting. If you see any deer with big antlers, those are the bucks. So if you don't think you can shoot one, just point them out for us," Barry said with a smile.

As they ate, the men discussed whether or not they would bring the wagon with them or leave it behind. They agreed to leave it at the homestead but that they would bring along an extra horse to carry whatever carcasses they may have at day's end.

Breakfast went quickly, and soon the men were dressed with rifles in hand. The three walked across the freshly down snow in the yard to the barn, and while Barry saddled up his horse, Daniel Sr. prepared Big Hoss, the workhorse, as Daniel Jr. just remembered the food his mother prepared for them was left in the house. It was a good thing too since it seemed no one else remembered. He hurried back to the house, and the other two men went on their way knowing of course Daniel would shortly catch up with them. Rachel was already in the kitchen when Daniel Jr. got back to the house.

"I got up figuring that you boys would forget the food." She laughed.

"Dad and Uncle Barry forgot, but I didn't. I was just coming back in for it," replied Daniel.

"What would they do without you? Now give me a kiss and go catch up with them."

Daniel did just that, mounted his horse, and urged it into a quick trot. It was a little hard for him to see as daylight hadn't quite broken, but with their tracks in the fresh snow, he had their trail and caught up within a few minutes. After thirty minutes of traveling, Barry announced, "Let's cross over this field. Just over the next hilltop is the valley where I saw the big buck I told you about last night. The valley's big. It might be best if we split up. If it's okay with you, Daniel, I'll take Junior with me."

"Good plan. I don't have the chance to hunt often, and he'll probably learn more from you anyway, so go ahead and take him with you. That okay with you, son?" replied Daniel Sr.

"Sure, it doesn't matter much to me either way," said Junior. "I haven't seen Uncle Barry in a while, so I'm okay with that."

It was agreed that the two would round the east side while Daniel Sr. would round the west side of the valley.

"We should meet at the other end. There are three really big maple trees at the far north end of the trail, and it leads into another pasture. Whoever gets there first waits for the others. If any of us makes a kill, fire two quick shots in the air. We'll follow the sound and meet up in the pasture. Everybody okay with that?" Barry asked.

"Okay by us!" Senior was speaking for Junior as well.

As the sun rose on the fresh-fallen snow, the light became very bright, enabling the three to have a better outlook on the surroundings. Being where they were, the area was filled with trees everywhere. As for the valley, it was not that much better. As riding on top of the south ridge was of great difficulties, Junior could now see why the wagon was not brought with them.

"Okay, mates, it's that time to split up," Barry announced. As they parted ways, Barry looked over his shoulder and called to Daniel Sr. laughingly. "Don't forget, we're hunting deer, not mountain goats." Daniel Sr. just shook his head at the comment knowing he was just being smart.

"What's that supposed to mean?" asked Daniel Jr.

"I was just reminding your father that we're in Canada, and in Canada, we hunt deer. In Scotland, where your father's from, there were a lot more mountain goats than there were deer." Barry laughed. "Your dad used to hunt much more when he was in Scotland," Barry explained.

"I've heard those stories from time to time. I don't see Dad much these days because he's so busy at the store, and when he gets home, I'm usually already asleep," said Daniel. "When I'm at the store, Dad's too busy with customers to be able to talk with me much."

Barry took all that in. "Well, my boy, don't ever think that your dad wouldn't love to share stories with you. He works hard to give you the luxuries that many people, including myself, don't have. You're pretty lucky, you know, to have your house and the land it stands on completely paid for.

"Speaking of which, I just realized your dad left you a gift in your saddlebag. He was surely looking forward in giving it to you. I guess we split up a little unexpectedly. Take a look-see," he stated.

Daniel reached into the bag, and his eyes grew big as he pulled out a new gun belt *and* a new Smith & Wesson handgun.

"But . . . but . . . but . . . Dad said . . . ," stuttered Daniel.

Barry interrupted. "Your dad said the gun belt and gun you currently have weren't right for you. They're too big and dangerous. He did *not* say that you couldn't have one at all."

Daniel jumped off his horse in excitement and quickly withdrew the handgun after checking to see if it was loaded, which it was not, then placed the gun back in his holster, and proceeded to strap the belt to his waist.

"Well, I see you were taught with safety in mind. I am impressed. Now look at you. I must say it looks good on you, lad. Now do you know how to use it?" Barry laughed.

"Are you *kidding*, Uncle? I have been practising, you know. With careful aim, I never miss even from fifty feet with a big smile from Daniel. I can really."

"I believe you! Just bugging you, lad." Barry was smiling while watching the excitement on his nephew's face.

"It fits perfectly," Daniel boasted.

"He had to custom order it to fit you and, from the looks of it, did a great job," said Uncle Barry.

"That's not all. I even brought you something myself," said Barry as he handed Daniel a box of shells.

"Wow, thank you very much, Uncle," exclaimed Daniel.

"No worries, nephew," replied Barry. "You see, Daniel, your dad really does love and care about you. How about you load up that spiffy new gun and hop on your horse so we can go?"

Still dumbfounded with amazement, Daniel did as he was told. With the morning being as quiet as it was, you could hear every click of the cylinder as he carefully loaded each chamber. Tucking it back into the gun belt, Daniel was all smiles as he mounted his horse to set off. It wasn't more than fifteen minutes later . . . "Wow! Would you take a look at that buck over there?" Daniel pointed out.

"Quietly," Barry said, "that's the buck I was telling you about. Look, I'm sure that's him, eight pointer but hard to see from here, but he's worthy for my dinner plate." Barry's heart started to pound with excitement.

"Okay, Daniel, you spotted him, you shoot him. Get out that rifle and take the shot, Daniel," Barry whispered. Daniel reached for his rifle, shouldered it, and took aim, not thinking at all as his heart was pounding as he was scared more so because he really couldn't find it in himself to actually shoot the animal.

"Whoa, hold on a minute. Let's take the time to dismount and *then* take your shot," said Barry.

"Sorry, Uncle Barry, seeing that buck so suddenly took me off guard."

Once they dismounted, they quietly made it over to the tree line, and Daniel lifted his rifle again and tried to take aim. But he was shaking so badly he couldn't hold the rifle straight. It may have been from the cold; it may have been from nerves or even a combination of both, but it just wasn't working for him. Daniel met up with his inner self and finally turned to face his uncle.

"Sorry, Uncle. I really think you should take the shot. After all, this is the buck you wanted, you're entitled to take him down."

Barry laughed and said, "Oh, you're such a smooth talker. Okay, let us switch places."

Actually this was sure not a disappointment to Barry. He would have been upset if the shot was taken, and it was a miss.

Within fifteen seconds of switching places, another thirty seconds of setting up his aim, a shot rang out over the valley. The buck bolted into the air and started to run. Within seconds, all you could see was snow as the buck fell into a slide.

"Nice shot, Uncle."

"Thanks," said Barry. "But if it was a *great* shot, I would've killed him instantly, and he never would've had it in him to try and run. He might only be wounded and lying there still alive. Jump on your horse. We will ride closer, let's just keep our distance."

They rode over until they were just thirty feet away, and from there, they could tell that the buck was still alive.

"Okay, from here, we'll walk over to him, but we have to be very careful. We don't want him to suddenly rise up and take off or, worse yet, charge us," said Barry. Barry kept careful aim on the buck with his rifles until he was sure the buck was down for good. It was only then that he lowered his rifle.

When they were both standing next to the fallen buck, Barry sighed and said, "Well, he has to be put out of his misery. You know what that means, Daniel."

"Yes," Daniel replied very quietly.

"He's a big boy," said Uncle Barry. "But you can take him out with one shot if you get him right here behind his ear. And hey, it will give you a chance to use your new handgun. Or I can do it," Barry mentioned.

Daniel, with uncertainty, drew his handgun from his holster and took aim.

"The buck is hurt and in a lot of pain, Daniel." And with that statement, Daniel fired. Barry looked at him and said, "Are you okay?"

Daniel just nodded, arm still at length with his gun still pointed at the deer. Daniel was a little stunned, and Barry noticed that he was deep in thought as he was standing motionless, staring down observing the lifeless animal. "Okay, Daniel! Well, we need to let your dad know that we took a deer down, so before your reholster your gun, fire two quick shots in the air if you don't mind."

Daniel, dazed in thought, quickly heard his uncle's stern but polite voice, did as was requested, and then reholstered the gun.

"Good boy," said Uncle Barry. "Now have a seat here beside me while we wait for your dad."

Daniel imitated his uncle's movement, sitting in the snow with his legs stretched out and his back resting against the belly of the deer.

"It's warm sitting against the deer like this," said Daniel.

"That it is," replied Uncle Barry.

"Seems like this one was meant to be mounted on a wall," said Barry. "I never thought I'd see him again, but I sure am glad I saw him with you.

"Since we've got a few minutes to talk, I thought I'd share a secret with you," said Uncle Barry. "When your dad hunts, he only hunts with me. Truthfully, he doesn't like hunting at all, so don't feel bad as I can see that you really do not like it much either. Your dad knows I like to hunt, so as friends, he keeps me company. More so to spend time with a friend. Your dad would rather buy his meat from the traders that come into his store. So there is no need for him to hunt. Don't get me wrong, he knows how to hunt as he did, at one time, had to kill mountain goats were he came from to put meat on the table. Now let's just say he helps me put meat on my table. As I would rather save my money for other necessities in life. Really that's true about your dad, he doesn't like hunting."

Daniel perked up a little.

"Well, that's my opinion, but I normally can read through your father pretty good. He has a heart of gold. He's a very good friend, and I am honored to have your father as a friend as well as having a great nephew like you. Just remember one thing, you do have to keep in mind that people do have to shoot animals for food, so one day, you have to cross that path. Don't be ashamed or feel guilty. That's why God put these animals on the planet as well as the fruit we grow."

"Thanks, Uncle, I feel better now."

"I am sure you do, son. I want to tell you one other thing too. Your father can't shoot with a damn anyway!" Barry laughed as Junior giggled.

"Are you serious?" Junior said, still smiling and in thought.

"Yes, I am serious." The laugher continued. "In fact, I know your dad so well I made him an agreement that in the normal world, he who kills a deer cleans his own. But knowing your father, the way he shoots, we made a different rule. He who makes the kill does not clean the animal, but the one who didn't make the kill does. That's why I like hunting with your dad."

"That's funny," Daniel laughed.

Quickly, Barry looked around to see if Senior was in sight.

"Time for one more quick story before your dad gets here. And boy, he better hurry too. I have lots of stories." They both laughed.

"Okay, your dad is the best in shooting with handguns that I've ever seen in a man in these parts. As I did say man because your mother, my sister, can even outdraw your dad."

"You're kidding, right? No way! Mom doesn't even carry a gun," said Daniel.

"Hey, believe me, it's true. She is what you would call a quick-draw target shooter as she never found the need to use the gun for defense, but she earned the right to carry one. Nephew, I would not lie to you. It's true," Barry remarked. "She can beat me by miles with a rifle and your dad with a handgun."

"Wow, I guess that saying is true, 'You learn something new every day,' knowing of course that saying is for more of mentally learning something new, such as learning stuff in school," Daniel said with great intellectual skills he has acquired.

"You are pretty smart there, boy, that's pretty accurate. Well, story time's over, here comes your dad. Took you long enough!" Barry yelled as Daniel approached.

"What are you two doing?" Dan Senior said with a smile between the buck and all the laughing.

"We're keeping warm," replied Junior.

"Hope there's room for me. I'm freezing."

"You can take my spot," said Barry. "I need to stretch my legs." Daniel Sr. dismounted and walked around to the front of the buck.

"Hey, this is the buck you were telling me about," Dan senior looked toward Barry.

"Yes, it is," replied Barry. "And your son is the one who killed it."

With shock, Daniel looked over at his son.

"Tell your father you killed it, Daniel. I don't want him to think I'm lying."

"Yes, Dad. I killed it."

Daniel Sr. just sat speechless.

"Wow," said Daniel Sr., "you actually shot this buck. That's great."

"Well, Uncle Barry actually shot him, but I put him out of his misery," admitted Daniel. "When Uncle shot him with his rifle, he didn't actually kill him, so I finished him off so he wouldn't suffer."

With a wide smile, Daniel Sr. said, "Just the same, I'm proud of the *both* of you. Now come here and give me a hug."

"Hey, Little Dan," Barry said, "you have that buck knife in your boot, hand it to your dad."

"Here, Dad. It's sharp, and it's forged steel, your best-seller," Daniel Jr. said with a proud smile as he handed it to his father. Still sitting against the buck's belly, Daniel Sr. suggested that maybe Daniel Jr. would like the honors.

"Oh, but Junior made the final kill, *Dad*!" Barry laughed.

"Tell you what, Dad, I'll give you the same deal Uncle Barry gives you. When I hunt with you, if you kill it, I'll clean it. Barry said you can't shoot very well anyways, so you will be doing a lot of cleaning if you hunt with me," Junior stated with a big smile.

Well, by this time, Barry and Daniel Jr. were laughing uncontrollably while Barry struggled through his laughter to remind Daniel that it was supposed to be a secret.

Daniel Jr. said, "I thought the secret was if you shot it, you're supposed to gut it too, not that part about him being a bad shot, oops."

"I heard that," replied Daniel Sr., trying to hide his own laughter. "But truth be known, I was just pleased to think that your uncle had never figured it out. But just the same, we share the meat so I should help out and contribute to his fine kill since your uncle helps clean my deer. Well, at least two anyway, he said," Daniel Sr. said with a smirk.

"Your uncle tells you a lot, doesn't he?" asked Daniel's father.

"Yes, and he also told me that Mom can outshoot the both of you."

"Your uncle talks too much," Daniel Sr. said as he looked at Barry with a grin.

"Well, he's right, isn't he?" He looked at his uncle with a smile.

"Well! That was then. She's a little out of practice now, I would say. Your mother would have problems hitting a side of a barn. She's so outdated in shooting," Daniel Sr. said with a wink toward Junior.

Senior quickly changed the topic. "I see you got my gift."

"The gun and gun belt I thought were from Uncle Barry." Daniel Jr. laughed. "Sorry, Dad, a lot has happened since he gave it to me that I forgot it was there, thank you so much, I love it."

"Well, I had to talk to your mom about it first, but you can only wear it on our property and when you're hunting with us. That gun is not to go anywhere else."

"I understand," Daniel Jr. said seriously.

"I'd let you practice at the store, but people are starting to complain about the noise of continuous gunfire in town, so best we just keep the noise on our own farm. But *your mother*—"

"Thank you, Barry! I will be happy to show you how to properly draw from that holster. As your mother and I thought you would get a thrill out of that, but your uncle already let the cat out of the bag. Yes, your mother is a great shot as well she's around you more in the day to teach you."

"All right, gentlemen, we'd best get started skinning. Sorry, I meant gutting this deer. Hey, Senior, get over here, and I'll show you how it's done," jibed Uncle Barry.

"Listen to your uncle yammering away about how he think he's been tricking me into gutting all his deer. Let me show you how it's *really* done. Your uncle will probably cut his own finger off, he's so out of practice." Daniel Sr. scoffed to which everyone had a good chuckle.

Daniel Sr. then slid his knife into the groin area of the deer quickly sliding it up toward the buck's chest, and with a whoosh, the deer's innards rolled out onto the snow-covered ground.

"See how easy that was? Now you just have to reach inside and cut the rest out, but I don't think your arms are long enough." Daniel Sr. observed.

"Yes, they are," young Daniel replied.

"If you think you can do it, then get over here and reach in toward the back and cut anything you can't pull out."

"Okay," Daniel Jr. replied, taking out his knife and reaching into the dead animal.

Being so small, he was covered in the blood from his chest down to his knees from having to be so close to the buck. Daniel Sr. and Barry watched as Junior earnestly worked on the deer.

Barry looked at Little Daniel's clothes and said, "Rachel is going to shoot you for this. She'll be washing those all day tomorrow." Both men laughed.

"Well, I guess I taught him two things in one today: how to clean a deer and how to trick someone into doing what you want. Think he'll figure out that I really knew his arms weren't too short?" Daniel Sr. said with a smile.

Daniel stopped what he was doing, looked over the buck toward the two men.

"I heard that, and you didn't trick me. I wanted to do it. And as far as Mom getting mad because of my clothes . . . well, I am going to tell her you made me do it." Junior laughed.

"Daniel, did I ever tell how much I like your son?" Barry was referring to Junior's smart remark and laughed.

Dan Senior just gave a quick smirk as his son just teased him. Barry had picked up the rope from his saddle and placed a hanging noose around the buck's head. Daniel Sr. guided Big Hoss to the front of the buck. Barry handed Daniel Jr. the free end of the rope and tied it to big workhorse.

"Okay, watch yourself, Little Daniel," Barry stated.

"Let's go, Hoss," Daniel Sr. said while making clicking sounds to get the horse moving.

"Let's pull him to that oak tree. There's an overhanging branch right there, and we can hoist up the buck, lay him across Hoss's back. That buck is so big and heavy that I think we will have to tie him on just till we get up the hill, then it's mostly downhill back to flat ground, then we can push him off, and Hoss can drag him the last mile." Barry figured aloud.

"Well, we will see, but Hoss should have no problem carrying him. I really didn't think this buck was so big when you described him to us," speculated Daniel Sr.

The two men and Daniel Jr. put their backs into the task at hand and hoisted the buck up. By using Daniel Sr.'s horse Grey to help pull the buck up and Daniel Jr. guiding Hoss under the branch where the buck was hanging and reaching out to steady the buck, Barry was able to position the buck across Hoss's back and get him tied down.

After insuring the buck was secured, the two men gladly sat down and dipped into the lunch bag Rachel had prepared for them. They had a quick bite and collected their gear to prepare for the ride home.

Daniel Jr. was doing the best he could to use some of the snow to brush the debris and blood off his clothes before he grabbed a sandwich. After a few minutes of eating, he got his stuff together as his uncle and father were already mounted up and waiting for him.

With Daniel Sr. in front leading Big Hoss and Barry flanking the workhorse to watch for any sign of the buck coming loose and Daniel Jr. bringing up the rear to ensure that Big Hoss wasn't faltering, they rode in comfortable silence, each thinking of the day and the hunt before they reached the flatland where they could push the buck off Hoss and let the carcass be dragged the rest of the way home.

Once they were back at the farm, they hung the buck in a nearby shed to cure. Daniel Jr. went in the house to change his clothes and wash up the best he could before his mother saw what a mess he was. Feeling much better in clean clothes, he put his gun belt back on, pulled out his gun, and removed the bullets and cleaned the barrel and gave the outside a quick polish as well.

Barry and Daniel Sr. came tromping in banging their boots on the front-door sill. Daniel Sr. looked at Daniel Jr. and asked, "Where's your mom?"

"Not sure," Daniel Jr. replied. "She's not in here, and I haven't seen her yet. Come to think of it, her horse wasn't in the stable that I recall either."

"I'm sure she'll be back soon. It smells like she did some baking, so she probably took a pie over to Dr. Anderson's," Daniel senior stated.

"Hey, Daniel, I don't suppose there is any milk in the cold room, is there? Would you check and see for me?" Barry asked.

"Okay," replied Daniel who was still playing with his new gun. He placed it in his holster and was about to head off when Daniel Sr. noticed and said, "Yeah, and while you're back there, you can hang up your gun belt as well."

Daniel was crestfallen. "Aww, Dad, can I not leave it on please, just until Mom comes home?"

"Your mother doesn't like loaded guns in the house. She would be angry, don't you think?" asked Daniel Sr.

"I know how she feels, but the gun is unloaded anyway because I just finished cleaning it." Daniel's downtrodden look was enough for Daniel Sr. to concede and say, "Well, okay, but you take it off shortly after she arrives, got it?"

"Got it. Thanks, Dad," Daniel said with a grin. He then ran off to get the earlier requested bottle of milk.

"Let me see that new gun of yours, Little Daniel, I didn't get much of a chance to admire it earlier," Barry said, so Daniel Jr. moved his chair closer to his uncle so Barry could get a better look at it and take it out of the holster himself. Barry pulled the gun out and said admiringly, "Wow, this is a piece of work, isn't it?"

"Yes, it is," Daniel Sr. replied. "There's a fellow that lives ten miles from town who's a very talented gunsmith and leather worker. He comes into the store every now and then, and we got to talking about Daniel Jr. and his homemade too-big gun belt and gun, and he told me that he could redesign it and make a smaller version of both belt and gun, and he did a fine job of it. I will definitely send him some other business."

"How much did he charge you, if you don't mind me asking?" Barry queried.

"He didn't," Daniel Sr. replied. "That's why I'll be sending him more business if this is a sample of how good his work is."

"Well, again, I have to say he does some fine work," said Barry as he put Daniel's gun back in the holster.

"I have a few rifles, as does my brother Allan, that are in need of some refurbishing. I'll bring them in next week, and you can send them over to him," offered Barry.

"I'll do that," promised Daniel Sr. "Where are Allan and Chuck anyway?"

Barry looked surprised. "Rachel didn't tell you?"

"Tell me what?" asked Daniel Sr.

"They took off right before Christmas. They had a deal to build some cabins out of town," Barry said.

"Why didn't you go with them? You normally all work together." observed Daniel Sr.

"Yeah we do, but sometimes everybody's ego gets in the way, and we kind of step on each other's toes, so I thought it was better for me to stay behind this time. Besides, someone needs to look after the acreage and the animals while they're gone."

"Hey, I'd do that for you, Uncle," Daniel Jr. piped up.

"Come here, you," Barry said as he put his arm around Daniel Jr. and hugged him tight. "That's a great idea, and I'm happy that you would step up and suggest taking on that responsibility, and I'd love to take you up on that offer, but I would be gone for a year on this job, and you have school. How is school going anyway?"

"Well, boring, for the most part, but I do enjoy the other kids, and I do occasionally learn something," Daniel Jr. said with a cheeky grin.

Daniel Sr. cut in. "Never you mind the cocky attitude, just concentrate on staying at the top of your class like you have been."

"No kidding? Top of the class, eh? Good for you, Daniel," Barry said approvingly.

"What's that smell?" Barry asked suddenly with a twitch of his nose and a baleful glare at Daniel Jr. still perched on his knee.

"Did you just fart on my lap? That is awful, worse than skunk cabbage." Barry laughed while trying not to breathe in at the same time.

Giggling to himself, Daniel Jr. said, "I didn't mean it. It just slipped out when you put your arm around me and pulled me onto your lap."

"Okay, get off me, by god," choked Barry and unceremoniously dumped Daniel Jr. to the floor. "What do they feed you?" Daniel Sr. bit back his own laughter, watching Barry wave his hand in front of his face in an attempt to get rid of the offensive odor, which promptly sent Daniel Jr. still lying on the floor into great gales of laughter.

"You think I'm bad?" Daniel Jr. gasped in between giggles. "Dad is the stinky one. Mom gives him hell, I mean trouble, every night, and she says he's a stinky son—" Quickly, not waiting for his sentence to continue much further, Daniel Senior yelled, "HEY! Watch what you're saying there, young man."

"But she says it all the time," Daniel Jr. pointed out.

"Well, that's your mom talking, not for you to repeat word for word," Daniel Sr. said pointedly.

"Tell me why she calls him that," Barry prompted, ignoring the glare from Daniel Sr.

"Dad goes to bed, and when he and Mom get settled, he farts, and Mom gets so mad, and she starts yelling at him, even though he tries to tell her that he's being helpful and just warming up the sheets and . . ." Daniel Jr. was laughing so hard at this point he couldn't even finish.

Barry and Daniel Sr. both joined in and roared with laughter until tears streamed down their faces. As the three of them were still winding down from all their laughter, they heard footsteps coming up the steps to the porch and tried desperately to collect themselves, but before they can, Rachel opened the door and stepped in noticing that everyone was red faced and guilty-looking.

Cocking one brow, she takes in the scene with Daniel Jr. lying on the floor. "Looks like you all are having grand time. What's with all the smiles, did I miss something good?"

Daniel Sr. recovered first and managed to look at his wife with a straight face and said, "Oh, nothing, we were just discussing the merits of building an addition on the house to give us more space, yeah, that's exactly what we were talking about." He glared at his son for embarrassing him in front of Barry. Still red faced, Daniel Sr. added, "For your son."

"What do you mean?" Rachel asked suspiciously.

"Tell you later," Daniel Sr. replied, still hiding a grin.

"Really, can you build me a loft? I could actually use a space like that, it would be a good plan, in fact," Rachel continued thoughtfully.

Barry looked at her and said, "It's indoors, so I could get on it anytime. It's up to you and Dan here when you want me to get started."

"We'll talk about it tonight, Barry, and let you know in the next couple days if that's all right," Daniel Sr. offered.

"You're not very busy right now, Barry?" Rachel inquired of her brother.

"No, it's the slow season, and I finished my last job before Chuck and Allan left for Collingwood, so right now, I'm just cleaning up some small stuff."

"How was the hunt?" Rachel asked as she moved to the fireplace to warm up.

"We got a big buck in the shed," Daniel Jr. said, drawing his mother's attention.

"What's this I see you wearing around your waist, young man?" Rachel asked in a teasing voice.

Daniel Jr. walked over to her, beaming brightly, and said, "Oh yeah! Thank you for agreeing to let Dad get this for me."

She ruffled his hair fondly and said, "I'm sure you only have this on to show me, but please remove them. Now you know I don't like guns in the house. But it sure does look good on you. Did your dad go over the rules of having this gun?"

"Yeah, he did, and just so you know, it's not loaded," Daniel told her earnestly.

"Just the same," she said and pointed to the back room.

Rachel turned to go to the sink when her nose was suddenly assaulted with a foul odor. She turned her eyes on the two innocent bystanders sitting at the table and said, "Something stinks in here!" And as comprehension dawned about what they had really been talking when she got home, her eyes lit up with an unholy light as she pinned her husband with a heated glare. "You DIDN'T, DID YOU?"

Barry's laughter cut her off. "IT'S YOUR SON THAT'S SMELLIN' UP THE PLACE. I hear he's taking after his old man." Barry laughed uncontrollably.

Rachel snorted. "I don't know how you boys can think it's funny farting like that. It's always better when it's your own stink you smell and not someone else's. But that's not what I think. The air smells like blood. Did you boys all wash?

"We did," replied Daniel Sr.

Taking another sniff, Rachel asked, "Then why do I smell blood in here?"

"Oh, those are probably my other clothes in my room," Daniel Jr. said.

"I supposed they're on the floor?" his mother asked as she folded her arms across her chest.

"Umm . . ." Daniel hesitated before finishing, "yes, they are."

"Go get them so I can wash them later."

"Okay," Daniel said as he headed down the hall.

Once she was sure that Daniel Jr. was out of earshot, she asked her husband and brother how Daniel had done on the hunting excursion.

"Well, he surprised us. I put down the buck, but unfortunately, it wasn't a clean shot, and it was still alive, and Daniel was with me, so I asked him to try out his new gun and put the buck out of his misery. I could see that he wasn't sure at first as he kept looking into the buck's eyes, and I thought he was going to cry at first, so I distracted him and told him that the buck was in a lot of pain, and no sooner had I finished talking than his gun went off," Barry said, recalling the morning's events.

Barry continued. "I think he was a little shocked himself, but when it came time to the gutting, he jumped right in."

"Yeah, I was a little surprised myself, I really didn't think he would be up for the gutting on his first time out, but we gave him instructions, and he just went at it," Daniel Sr. added.

"Wow, that is something different for Daniel," Rachel said. "I would never think he would do that, let alone shoot an animal even if it was to put it out of its suffering. He loves animals, you know that Barry. He's like a veterinarian, always caring for the injured ones and setting them free when they're healed and bringing home all the strays."

Just then, Daniel returned with his clothes and handed them to his mother.

"My god, you said he jumped in and helped, but I didn't think you meant literally. Did he crawl into it? His clothes are just covered in blood."

"Um, yeah, sort of," Barry stated dryly.

Daniel Sr. spoke up, "Well, his arms are not that long, and that was one big buck out there."

"Well, I guess that would do it, but get him to practice on something smaller till he grows up, or you two boys will be on laundry duty from now on." Rachel warned.

"Sure thing, honey, no problem," Daniel Sr. stated with a wink at Barry who passed the wink on to Daniel Jr.

"Well, Daniel," Barry said, "where are you hiding your playing cards, how about a game of poker?"

"Honey," Daniel Sr. asked Rachel, "can you please pass me the playing cards? They're in the drawer beside you, please and thanks."

"Hey, Little Dan, come on over here, and your dad and I will show you how to play poker."

"Come on, Barry, he's only twelve years old. First you take him hunting, now you want to teach him how to gamble? What's next, teaching him how to drink?" Rachel questioned disapprovingly.

"No no, sis, you don't have good-enough booze for him. Maybe you should import some bourbon, then I might change my mind and give him a mouthful," Barry teased.

"Try it, and I'll give you a mouthful of my fist," Rachel replied unimpressed.

It was well known that Rachel looked out for Daniel's well-being. But leave it to Barry to try to start trouble.

"Hey, sis, Daniel here said you were out of practice with your handguns, said you'd be lucky to hit the side of a barn from ten feet away."

Rachel whirled around. "Excuse me? Daniel, did you say any such thing?"

"Well, honey, you haven't taken your gun out of its holster since Daniel was two, that was twelve years ago, so it would be understandable if you were a bit rusty," Daniel Sr. replied sheepishly.

"It was ten years ago, your son is only twelve now! And what's that got to do with it?" Rachel demanded.

Meanwhile, Barry crooked his finger at Little Daniel to signal him to come over to him while his parents were arguing. Barry reached out to pull Daniel's head closer to his so he was within whispering distance.

"I started this argument on purpose because your mom will never change. She's stubborn, and she would never turn down a chance to prove that she can outshoot him in a draw or contest of skill any day. Now watch what happens, you're about to find out who your mom really is, the way she was before you were born." They both looked on.

Daniel Sr. pointed out. "Well, you would need to practice for at least a month before you could even come close to matching my shot."

Daniel Jr. laughed at this, and Barry whispered "Here we go" and gave Junior a wink.

Rachel's face was flushed with anger at this point. "You think so?" she yelled at Daniel Sr.

Sensing he may have gone too far, Barry said warily, "Easy now, Rachel."

She took a deep breath and let it out. "Yes, sorry, sorry, Daniel. I'm letting your father get me all worked up."

She then looked at her brother accusingly. "Barry, you started this."

The picture of innocence and with a smile on his face, Barry asked, "What? What did I do?"

"Yeah right, you're up to something, Barry, you may as well confess now. You're my brother, and I can tell when you're up to no good."

"Okay, okay, you got me," Barry said. "While we were out hunting this morning, I told Daniel Jr. how you met his dad. Remember that day when you had to pick up supplies, and you two started talking guns and ended up shooting targets all afternoon to see who was the better shot? Poor Daniel didn't even know you owned a gun at the time. That's what this is about."

"Well, Daniel, truth is, your father can't beat a woman in a gun draw, right, honey?" Rachel now addressed her husband with a smile.

"I can now," he replied confidently.

"Well, here's what we're going to do. You said it would take me one month of practice, and I say you give me one hour to get a few shots in before it gets dark. But if you still think that you can beat me, well then, starting *now*, I'm going to the barn to get my stuff cleaned up. By then I should have an hour left to practice, and tomorrow morning, we are all going down to the store, you too Little Daniel and you too Barry, and we'll just see who can shoot. You think I've lost my touch, hah!"

"We all agree," Daniel Sr. spoke firmly.

"Yeah, I want to see this," Daniel Jr. said excitedly. "What about school?" Daniel looked at his mom, thinking she forgot what day it was.

"I guess you can miss the morning being you've never been absent before, and it won't hurt Uncle Barry to get up early," Rachel said.

"Well, I was going to head home later after poker, but I can stay one more night," Barry said agreeably.

"Then it's settled. If you'll excuse me, boys, you play poker, and I'll be back in an hour. Daniel, if you get hungry, get your dad to fix you something to eat, and you'd better get used to his cooking because after, excuse my language, Little Daniel, but after I kick your father's ass tomorrow, he's going to be cooking dinner for us for the next two weeks."

"And *you*, Barry, are staying here for the next two weeks to help him." Rachel finished with a triumphant smile. "So while you're here, you can start that loft as well, and Daniel Jr. can give you a hand when he's not in school."

Rachel thought it was funny how brothers and sisters never changed; Barry always did know how to get her riled.

She grabbed her coat and turned to Daniel Jr. "Make sure you stay in the house while I'm practicing." And then she slammed the door shut behind her.

"Now look what you started," Daniel Sr. grumbled at Barry. "If I lose, I have two cook for two whole weeks."

"You said you could beat her," Barry pointed out. "Can't you?"

"Honestly, I don't know. I really don't shoot that much other than containers in the back of the store with the customers. I was bluffing because I counted on her being out of practice." Daniel Sr. admitted.

"Well," Barry said with a laugh, "I guess I can't complain being I got a job out of the deal."

"Hey, Dad, just so you know, if you lose to Mom, I like my steak medium rare," Daniel Jr. said, trying to hide a smile.

"Oh! You little brat!" Daniel Sr. grouched as he playfully threw a dish cloth at Little Daniel's head.

"Hey, *now* watch those words you're saying. You just about slipped up there, Dad!" said Daniel Jr., laughing even harder.

Barry guffawed. "As I said, Daniel, I like your son, very witty, must get it from his mother. Oh, by the way, Daniel, I like my steak medium."

All three of them laughed.

"Okay, let's play some poker. Grab a seat, Little Daniel," Barry said, pointing to the seat beside himself. Daniel Jr. plopped down into the seat next to him.

"Deal them up, Daniel," Barry ordered.

Daniel started to shuffle the cards. "I hope you know that Rachel is serious. If I lose, she *won't* cook dinner for the next two weeks. I don't know about you two, but I'd rather not poison myself with my own cooking."

"Guess we all better start having big lunches," Barry said with a smile.

"Ah, let her have some fun. What's the problem Daniel, you know how to cook the basics, don't you?" Barry asked.

Daniel Sr. looked at Barry ruefully. "Well, let's just say that was one of the reasons I married your sister. I don't know my way around the kitchen real well, and I don't even like what I do manage to cook."

"Oh, great, we're all going to starve." Daniel Jr. lamented in such a sad tone that both his father and uncle laughed.

"You crack me right up, boy. You're just like your mother. I can see a lot of her in you," Barry said.

"Aww heck, we'll have a fun two weeks. I'll pitch in my cooking skills too. Besides, I can teach Little Daniel how to play poker while I'm here. So let's not worry about tomorrow, just cut the cards."

In a whisper to Daniel Jr., Barry muttered, "I hope you like my cooking."

After about an hour, the boys started hearing gunshots coming from the barn, indicating that Rachel had started her practice time.

Daniel Jr., studying his cards, looked over at his dad and said, "Poker is fun, but can I go out to the barn to watch Mom?"

"She asked for you to stay put while she's out there for your own safety," Daniel Sr. reminded him.

"Oh, just let him go, Daniel. What kind of trouble can he possibly get into out there?" Barry asked.

"Yeah, okay," Daniel Sr. relented. "But you climb up the back of the barn to the hayloft, and you can watch from up there. Don't let her see you either."

"She won't, I'll be careful," Daniel promised as he got up and went to get his coat and boots and headed outside.

Daniel Sr. looked at Barry and said, shaking his head and laughing, "Barry, you are my best friend, but sometimes I don't know why I listen to you. I get into trouble every time or something is guaranteed to go wrong."

"Yeah, but just think of all the stories you can tell your grandchildren or, for that matter, Little Daniel when he's older. I'm sure he would enjoy listening to some of your youthful adventures," Barry said mischievously.

"I suppose you're right." Daniel Sr. conceded.

"Well, look at today for example. Your son will be talking about this for the next fifty years, and his grandchildren will tell it for another fifty," Barry pointed out.

"This is going to be exciting, watching my sister kick your *butt*." Barry laughed.

"You know what, Barry? You are a jackass, now shut up and deal," Daniel Sr. grumbled.

"Well, after you get *your butt* handed to you tomorrow, I'd like to take Little Daniel with me back to the homestead to help me tend the animals, get my tools, and load up the wagon for my little stay if that's all right with you and Rachel. It's an hour and half each way, so I think Daniel will be great company."

"Aren't you forgetting he has school tomorrow?" Daniel Sr. asked.

"Aren't *you* forgetting that he's taking the morning off anyway?" Barry pointed out.

"Yeah, okay, if it's okay with Rachel, it's okay with me."

The two men turned their attention back their card game and tried to concentrate while gunshots still echoed outside.

Daniel Sr. noticed that the sun was going down and thought he may as well start practicing his cooking skills a day early just in case. He put some wood in the stove and lit it then went into the backroom and brought back some steaks to prepare with the bread and vegetables that Rachel had prepared earlier. No sooner had he put the meat on the counter when the door opened, and Daniel Jr. stepped in and with a glance at the stove said, "Hey, Dad, I think somebody better teach me how to cook my own steak."

Unfortunately, at that moment, Barry was in the middle of taking a drink of hot tea, and upon hearing Little Daniel's words, the burning liquid didn't quite make it down the hatch but, rather, sprayed across the room as his uncle burst out laughing.

As the two men were winding down their game, Barry noticed that Daniel Sr. kept glancing at the counter where the steaks were and couldn't help but chuckle.

He leaned over to Little Daniel and whispered, "Truthfully, let's not tell your dad, but your mom's going to win hands down."

Daniel Jr. whispered back, "I think so too. I saw her shoot out there, and out of six shots, she got three of them, and when she did it again, she got five out of six, and boy, is she fast! I was shocked."

"I told you she was good," Barry said proudly, winking at Junior.

"I think you better do some practicing tomorrow morning, old man," Barry said with a chuckle.

"That's what I was thinking too," Daniel Sr. grumbled. "I was also thinking that you and Rachel could stay around the house in the morning, and Junior and I will go into town at eight o'clock as I have to open the store anyway, and while I get a few practice shots in, Daniel can help out at the counter if anyone comes in."

"Good idea," Barry agreed.

Daniel Sr. laughed. "Whatever advantage I can get, I'll take."

Daniel's father caught his eye and said, "Before I forget, you have the day off of school tomorrow. Barry has asked if you could go with him back to his place to pick up the wood, supplies, and tools he's going to need, and he'd like your help. Again though, your mom must approve."

"Great," Daniel Jr. said excitedly. "I'll be a big help."

"Don't get used to missing school in the future. This is a onetime deal," his dad warned.

"I won't, you forget that I like school. It might be boring sometimes, but that's because it's too easy. But I promise I won't start skipping school," Daniel Jr. said, rolling his eyes.

"Hey," Barry interrupted, "I don't hear any more gunshots."

Daniel Jr. looked out the window, and sure enough, his mother was just leaving the barn and making her way back to the house.

"Okay," Daniel Sr. warned, "not a word about me practicing tomorrow morning, everybody, got that?"

"Got it," replied Daniel Jr. and Barry simultaneously.

As Rachel entered the house, she noticed the absence of any smell, more specifically, no smell of dinner cooking. Shooting a look at the men sitting around the table, she said with a laugh, "I thought you would have started practicing."

"Nope, we're doing okay here playing cards, so you go right ahead, honey," Daniel Sr. smirked.

"Okay, gentlemen, I'm going to get dinner started, so start getting your game wound up so we can get the table cleared. Daniel, make sure to go wash your hands before we eat. You've got about forty-five minutes till it'll be ready."

Daniel Jr. nodded and then turned his attention back to his uncle who was explaining the finer points of poker.

They had all worked up an appetite, and dinner was a quick and quiet affair with little conversation. Once they had finished, Rachel stood up and started clearing the table.

"Do you have any studying to do?" she asked Daniel.

"No, Mom, it's already done," he replied.

"Okay, it's an hour till bedtime so keep an eye on the time, please."

"Will do, Mom," Daniel Jr. promised.

"Hey, Daniel, do you still have the Christmas wine in the back? I could use a glass," Barry asked.

"Hey, you two," scolded Rachel, "you don't need to be drinking so much around Daniel Jr. You've gone through almost a whole bottle between you in last day or so," Rachel stated.

"Hey, honey! It's wine, we have a guest, no one's going overboard here," Daniel said in defense.

"Sorry. You're right, there's nothing wrong that. But don't push it on our son. His time will come when he can make his own decisions." Rachel ensured she was well heard.

"Yes, Dear!" Daniel Sr. said as a smart remark as he looked at Barry with a smile.

"You know what, Mr. Daniel McDougall? Keep it up and you're going to get a big surprise, my fist." Rachel smiled, knowing it was of no real threat at all.

"I hardly said a word during dinner. I was busy thinking on how much fun it's going to be tomorrow when I kick your ass!" Daniel Sr. said belligerently.

"That's it! Finish that glass of wine, and then both of you carry yourselves off to bed. you too, barry! Got it?" Rachel demanded.

Daniel Sr. gave Rachel a mock salute. "Yes, dear."

Barry laughed and refilled their glass before handing one to Daniel Sr.

"Bottoms up." Barry toasted, and they continued to finish the remains of the wine.

Barry gave his sister a quick hug and, as requested, headed off to find his bed. Daniel Sr. did the same but gave his wife a longer hug before heading down the hall. Daniel Jr., seeing no one was staying up, gave his mom a hug and a kiss and decided to turn in as well.

Rachel stayed up for another half hour, sweeping and tidying up the kitchen when her eyes fell on the bottle of wine. With a wry grin and a glance down the hall to make sure everyone was asleep, she poured herself a glass knowing that Daniel Jr. was in bed.

"Well, here's to tomorrow." She took a sip then put the bottle in the cupboard and turned in for the night.

It was around quarter after five the following morning when Daniel Sr. awoke. He hadn't slept well as his mind was racing with thoughts of the contest that would take place between him and his wife today. Even though it was all in fun, he knew that Rachel had a very good chance of beating him.

The thought of cooking dinner for the next two weeks was a daunting one, although admittedly, Rachel could use a break from the kitchen. He didn't really have the first clue how to cook anything that would be edible, let alone decent. He smiled silently thinking it wasn't too late for this old dog to learn a new trick if he had to.

Barry walked into the kitchen just as Daniel was putting the coffee on the stove. He had already lit both sides of the cast iron stove, and it was blazing away merrily, chasing the chill from the room.

Daniel cast a look at Barry. "Hungry?"

"Yeah," Barry replied, "but I'll wait for Rachel to get up before I eat."

"I was thinking the same," chuckled Daniel. "Looks like you won't have to wait long."

Barry turned and saw his sister coming out of her room and heading toward them.

"Good morning, boys," she greeted with a big smile. "You're up earlier than usual, honey."

"Just excited about the day, dear," Daniel said with a wink. "Seriously though, Barry started this whole thing so Danny boy could see what we were like when we were younger, before he was born. He wanted him to see you as a strong woman, equal to any man, not just a *mom*. He's proud of you and wanted Daniel to see with his own eyes that you could outshoot any man. That matters more than who wins."

He pulled his wife over and planted a kiss on the top of her head. "Let's just go have fun today."

She hugged him and smiled over at her brother. "Thank you both for that. However," she said with a sly grin, "you two were having fun at my expense, and there's a price to pay."

"Why?" Daniel Sr. asked, laughing,

Sternly, Rachel replied, "Because you insulted my upbringing. Just because I am a woman does not give either of you the right to even fringe on that subject. Women are just as good as men.

"As for you and Barry, cooking dinner the next two weeks, that's just a bonus for me, not to mention a good punishment for you. Am I right, Barry?" Rachel asked, turning to look her brother in the eye. Barry rolled his eyes but nodded his agreement.

"Barry, can you grab some bacon from the cold room so I can get breakfast started?"

As Barry went to the cold room, Rachel went down the hall to go wake Daniel Jr. She opened his door and smiled as she saw him all tangled up in his blanket with one arm over his face and one dangling off the bed. She smothered a laugh at the gurgling snore that came out of Daniel's mouth. She sat on the edge of his bed and gently shook him. "Daniel, time to get up, honey." Daniel just made smacking sounds with his mouth and turned over to face the wall. She leaned over his ear.

"Daniel, can you hear me?"

"Mmmm hmmm," groaned the blanketed heap in the bed.

"Two early mornings are too much for you, eh? Want to sleep a little longer? You don't have to go with your dad right away."

Daniel stretched and yawned. "I want to go with Dad, I will get up now."

He sat up next to his mom and said, "I've seen Dad shoot at the store the odd occasion, but I didn't know that you could shoot so well or even handle a gun at all. Why have you never used a handgun around here before? Uncle Barry says you're the best."

"Daniel," she began, "handguns are mostly for protection, and I haven't had any need to protect myself from anything out here other than getting pecked from the occasional bossy hen, and there are rifles in the house and in the barn in case of any emergency if I needed them. So you see, it's not necessary for me to carry around a gun all the time. Besides, most men don't think highly of women like me. They want a little woman who cooks and cleans and stays home taking care of babies. That's why I love your father so much. He didn't grow up around here, so he's more open-minded and respects and likes the fact that I'm a strong, independent woman. If he wasn't like that, I don't think we would be together, and you would have never been born." She ruffled Daniel's hair.

"Having brothers like mine, I had to stand my ground or be taken advantage off and picked on. I had to help my mom with the washing and cooking, and your uncles would all laugh at me while they ran off to do fun things, so finally, I'd had enough, and believe it or not, I beat them up, both your Uncle Barry and Uncle Chuck."

"What?" Daniel asked shocked.

"Well, I may be their sister, but there's only so much a person can take," his mom chuckled.

"One day, Chuck and Barry were being more aggravating than usual, so I grabbed a rock and clenched it in my fist and took a swing and knocked your Uncle Chuck out cold, then I think I was just running on shock and adrenaline, and I jumped on Barry's back and just kept kicking him and kicking him until he finally just fell down with me still stuck to him. I think he was even more shocked than I was.

"Uncle Barry finally got me to let go and settled me down, and Uncle Chuck was still unconscious, and I was starting to worry that I might have killed him. I was scared and shaking all over, and thankfully after a few minutes, Chuck started mumbling and sat up glaring at me. He was fine, but he did need a couple stitches." Rachel laughed.

"When I got home, my father tanned my backside for fighting and lectured me on my lack of proper ladylike behavior. After that, I decided that I really didn't like men, any man for that matter, not even my father. He treated your grandmother badly, and I swore one day when I got older and bigger that I was going to beat him up too, but the alcohol took him before I ever got the chance. I hate to speak ill of the dead, but your grandfather was a drunk and a mean one at that. That's another reason I would prefer not to have people doing so much drinking in the house. That way, you can make your own decisions in life *later on* that is." Rachel smiled as did Junior.

"Anyway, back to my brothers. They started to call me Rachel thinking it would bother me as there was an older woman around that no one liked, as she also was bugged by people. And one day, she lost it, attacked the people involved. Well, since then I was called *Rachel, the wild one*." Rachel remembered with a rueful chuckle.

Then she leaned in closer to Daniel. "Want to hear a secret?"

"Yes, what?" replied Daniel eagerly.

"Well, my name, when I was born is Donna."

"Mom, if your real name is Donna, doesn't it bother you that people just changed it and gave you a nickname?" Daniel asked.

"No, not really, I sort of like it actually. It makes people stop and think twice before messing with me." She laughed. "Well, back then anyway . . . Besides, there's nothing wrong with nicknames as long as they suit the person and are done in good taste."

"So can I call you Rachel now too?" Daniel asked.

"Um, no, you will still call me Mom as I am your mother, and out of respect, you address me and your father as Mom and Dad, not by our first names," she replied.

"That's not to say once you get older, you may find times it's better suited to call your parents by their given names, but you'll figure that out when the time comes. I have another secret for you," she said. "Are you ready?"

"Yes," replied Daniel with no hesitation.

"I hate to do this, but I'm going to let your father win this morning. But only for one reason, and that's that he doesn't know how to cook, and instead of me getting a break from the kitchen, my time in there would double with having to look over his shoulder every dinnertime," she said with a wink.

"Isn't that like cheating?" Daniel asked. "Kind of like letting another player believe he has a better hand than you at poker when you know your hand can win?"

"Well, that's not exactly cheating, letting someone think their hand is better, that's strategic playing. Strategy is what the game is really all about. In our case, no one really loses by letting your dad win, and you don't have to eat your dad's cooking for two weeks."

"True, but I think it would be fun to see him have to do it." Daniel grinned.

"You do?" his mother asked, surprised.

"Yeah," he said.

"Well, I was just trying to save your stomach, but in that case, hurry up and get ready," she said as she gave him a light slap on the butt. "Let's get moving."

"I'm moving, I'm moving." Daniel laughed as he stumbled to his clothes cupboard.

Rachel left his room and headed back to the kitchen. She saw that the bacon she asked Barry to get was still sitting off to the side not cooking yet, and with a sigh and a shake of her head, she got the rest of breakfast ready and soon had eggs, bacon, and biscuits ready.

Daniel came in and sat down and waited impatiently for the grown-ups to sit down so he could eat. After they all finished, Daniel Jr. cleared the table, and his mom did the dishes while Barry and Daniel Sr. got everything they needed ready for the day.

Daniel Jr. went out to saddle the horses, both his and his father's, so they would be ready to go when his dad came back out. Rachel went out to the barn as well to do the morning chores and to feed and water the chickens.

While out in the barn, Rachel said to Daniel, "Come over here, I have something to show you in the tack room."

Daniel followed his mother into the back where she pulled out a chest. She opened it and showed Daniel her handguns.

"Wow, those are nice, Mom! You've taken really good care of them over the years, I can tell."

She pulled her gun belt off its hook and strapped it low on her hips and then removed her pistols and put them in their holsters.

Daniel, all of a sudden, blurted, "Mom, I saw you shoot yesterday. I came in the back and climbed up to the loft and watched from the upper window."

"I thought I said for you to stay in the house, in fact, I was quite clear, young man."

"Dad and Uncle Barry said it was okay, though," Daniel said.

"Well, your dad and your uncle should know better. What if I would have fired a shot up there, or one of my bullets ricocheted, and I didn't know you were there?" she demanded angrily.

"Listen to me, Daniel, and listen to me well." She grabbed Daniel by the shoulders so that he was facing her squarely. "Please, in the future, if I tell you something, please listen to me, not others, okay? Do you understand me?" Rachel calmed her voice.

Trying to hold back tears at his mother's outburst, Daniel just nodded.

"I'll also be having a talk with your father."

"Please don't, Mom. Dad, and Uncle Barry will think I told you just to get them in trouble. Can we please keep this between us? I don't want them to be mad at me," he implored.

"Fine," his mother sighed. "I understand. But in the future, you need to think about when someone tells you something that they may be trying to tell you something without really telling you. Sounds kind of confusing, doesn't it?" she asked.

"Yes," said Daniel.

"In other words, you have to think of what's right yourself and not listen to others if you think they could be wrong. Sometimes they might be trying to test you to see what choice you would make on your own."

She gave him a quick hug. "Okay, get out of here, and I'll see you guys down at the store."

Rachel quickly finished up with her chores and went to the tack room to load her guns and place some extra bullets in her gun belt. She left the barn and headed back to the house just as Daniel Sr. and Jr. were about to mount their horses. Both of them watched her approach in her cowboy hat, jeans, and duster with her gun strapped on. It was like seeing something out of one of the dime store novels Daniel Jr. read at his dad's store.

She walked up to Daniel Sr. and tipped her cowboy hat back and said with a wink, "How about a kiss before you go?"

Daniel Sr. laughed and presented her with his cheek and then turned quickly and caught her on the lips with a chuckle.

The two Daniels mounted up, and Rachel moved over to Daniel Jr., "You too, mister, lean on down and give me a kiss."

With a roll of his eyes and a laugh, he whispered "Okay, Donna" and leaned over to kiss his mother.

"I'll Donna you," she whispered back, shaking a playful fist at him.

Daniel Sr. watched in amused silence at his wife and son's antics, but he also had a look of confusion on his face. Rachel noticed and mouthed "Tell you later," to which he nodded and said, "I look forward to it."

Rachel took a quick look at Daniel Jr. to make sure he had everything with him and that his horse was ready to go and noticed something missing. "Where's your new gun? Aren't you going to take it with you today?"

"I thought about it, but you and Dad said that the gun had to stay on the farm."

"Yes, we did, but since we're doing some practicing at the store, I thought you could bring it today, and I could show you a few things if you wanted," his mother replied and added. "But I'm glad to see that, even though you wanted to bring it, you listened and were following the rules, good job. Besides, right after your dad and I are done with our little contest, you and Uncle Barry are heading out to his place, which is just over an hour out of town. Being you never know what you might encounter on the road, we're willing to make an exception and let you take your gun with you. But if you'd rather leave it behind . . ." She trailed off as Daniel hurriedly dismounted from his horse.

"No," he called over his shoulder as he raced into the house, "I'll bring it with me."

Being distracted, he failed to notice that the space the door had previously occupied was now filled with a solid flannel shirt and barrelled right into his uncle's chest. His uncle reached out and grabbed him to keep him from falling and said, "Whoa, where's the fire?"

"Sorry, Uncle Barry but I gotta get my gun. Mom said I could bring it, and she's going to show me some stuff!" He slipped under his uncle's arm and hurried to the coat room.

"Well, I'll be damned," muttered Barry when he was sure Daniel Jr. was out of earshot and continued out and down the steps to where Rachel was still standing. He looked at his sister and said, "My, my, how the rules change around here."

"Yup, they sure do, isn't that right, Barry?" Daniel Sr. replied.

"I'm sorry, were you two saying something?" Rachel asked innocently.

"Just that the rules seem to change is all," Barry goaded his sister.

Rachel had had enough. "You boys need to keep your traps shut, especially when you've been drinking."

The two men thought she was referring to the gun challenge, but in fact, she had been talking about their questionable decision to let Daniel Jr. go out to the barn to watch her practice her shooting without her knowledge. She had promised Daniel that she wouldn't reveal that she knew so she kept quiet. Daniel came out of the house buckling his gun belt as he walked.

"Looks like we got us a real cowboy here," Uncle Barry observed.

"I *am* a real cowboy," Daniel said. "I can lasso a horse, a cow, or a bull. I can shoot and hit almost any target, and I can do almost anything else our farmhands do around here."

"It was just a saying, small fry, don't get your dander up," Barry said. "I was only teasing, no harm meant."

"It's okay, Uncle Barry, I'm not upset." Daniel Jr. smiled. "I was just making the point that I really am a cowboy. Even though I'm small, I can still be tough."

"That's my boy," Daniel Sr. said proudly.

"*Our* boy." Rachel put her two cents in with a smile.

"Hey, Daniel, I think Rachel and I are only going to be about fifteen minutes behind you. Sorry, but it doesn't look like you're going to get any time to practice," Barry stated.

Rachel was just walking up the steps to the porch while Barry was standing with the two mounted Daniel's and looking over at the sky behind the house.

"Why, what's up?" Daniel Sr. asked.

"Have a look over yonder," Barry said. "Looks like a snowstorm is coming in, so Rachel and I can't wait around here. We need to get going too. I'd like to get to my place and load up the wood, grab my tools, and get back before it blows in so we don't get stuck on the road in the worst of it."

Barry sighed. "I still wanted to get some measurements before I left, but I don't think I have time now."

"That's okay," Daniel Sr. said. "Hey, Rachel, you might want to pack up some food for your brother and Junior here in case they get caught in the snow later."

Rachel looked at the sky as well and said, "I can pack up some food, or you can just stay here tonight, and you guys can head out tomorrow instead. Either way makes no difference, but I'll pack some stuff just in case." And she headed into the house. She turned in the doorway and addressed Daniel Jr.

"Please make sure your gun is covered by your coat while you're in town. I don't want people to see you walking around with it and have them get the wrong impression or think that your dad and I are irresponsible parents."

"Okay, Mom, I'll make sure it's covered."

"I mean it, young man," she warned.

"Yes, Mom," Daniel replied dutifully.

"Let's go," Daniel Sr. said, wheeling his horse around and applying light pressure with his heels to his horse's flanks to get it moving.

As he moved off, Daniel Jr. was directly behind him, shielding his eyes against the glare of the sun off the early-morning snow. After a few moments, both Daniel Sr. and Junior's eyes adjusted, and they were able to ride more comfortably for the ten minutes it took them to get to the store.

As they arrived, they walked their horses to the town stables where many of the townsfolk rented stalls on a monthly basis to house their horses during the day while they work. There was no one at the stables at this time to greet them, but Daniel Sr. had a reserved stall that he used every day, and they put Little Daniel's horse just across from his dad's in an empty stall. Daniel's father instructed him to leave the saddle on his horse since he and Uncle Barry would be leaving shortly. They left the stables comfortably knowing that the stable boys would show up in the next hour to tend their horses and see to their needs during the day.

They walked across the street and down the boardwalk to a building kitty-corner to the stables. They noticed the blinds being pulled up in some of the windows and a few people sweeping off their storefronts as the little town started to come alive for the day.

"Good morning!" A man's booming voice came from across the street.

Both Daniels turned to see Dr. Roy Anderson waving at them.

"Good morning, Doc," Daniel Sr. replied, and Daniel Jr. waved back.

"I see you have young Daniel with you. Is Rachel okay?" Dr. Anderson inquired.

"She's just fine. She and her brother Barry aren't too far behind us as they're coming into town today too," Daniel Sr. explained.

Dr. Anderson walked across the street to join them so they wouldn't continue to yell across the street.

"So, Little Daniel, you helping your dad today?" he asked.

"Sort of," Little Daniel replied. "My mom and dad are having a shoot-out because Dad said she had gotten rusty over the years."

"He did?" Dr. Anderson queried, somewhat taken aback by the whole shoot-out notion.

Daniel Sr. tried to stop Little Daniel from saying anything more by interjecting "Now, Daniel, we don't need to be telling everyone our business."

"Why ever not, Daniel?" Dr. Anderson said with a gleam in his eye, addressing the elder Daniel. "I've heard that your Rachel is a right fine shot."

Daniel Sr.'s mouth gaped open, but he managed to gain his composure before saying "You've heard that?"

With a hearty laugh and a slap on his back, Dr. Anderson gleefully filled Daniel Sr. in. "Oh, Daniel, the whole town knows all about Rachel. It's a small town, everyone knows everything about everyone, and there are no secrets. You can't even fart in your own house without someone saying 'excuse you' the next day, you should know that."

He winked at Daniel Jr. who was giggling at this point as any mention of farting was apt to do to a boy his age.

"Yeah, I guess so," Daniel Sr. replied slowly, aggrieved at the thought of the whole town talking about his wife.

"You want to come to the store and watch?" Little Daniel asked the doctor.

"Not this time, I'm on my way over to the sheriff's office to check on some rowdies that I patched up after a brawl Saturday night. The sheriff's got them locked up, but I still need to make sure they're okay as they were fair hurting once the liquor wore off," he said with a wink at Daniel Jr.

"There was really a fight?" Daniel Jr. asked.

"Yes, there was really a fight," Dr. Anderson said. "My work here is the busiest on the weekends. You get a bunch of men and booze together, and they're bound to start fighting and shooting up the place and sometimes each other."

"That's what my mom says too, that booze is not good. Can I come with you?" Daniel Jr. asked the doctor, intrigued by the idea of seeing inside the jail.

"If it's all right with your dad, you sure can," the doctor replied.

"Not this time, Junior," his dad replied. "Your mom and Barry will be here soon, and we have other things to take care of this morning, or have you already forgotten?"

"Right," Daniel Jr. said. "Sorry, Doc Anderson, maybe another time I could come because I'd really like to."

"Sure thing, Little Dan," Dr. Anderson acknowledged. "I hear that you're good with caring for animals and tending their injuries. You just might make a good doctor yourself one day."

"I think I'd like to be a doctor," Daniel Jr. said.

"Well, when you get older, come and see me, and we'll see what we can do," Dr. Anderson offered.

"Can you train me?" Daniel asked eagerly.

"Well, I can't formally train you. You need schooling for that, but you can assist me at my office and on house calls if that's what you end up deciding you want to do. Give it some thought, Daniel. If you're still interested when you're finished school here, maybe your mom and dad will send you to the physician's college for four years."

"More school, *really*?" Daniel groaned.

The doctor ruffled young Daniel's hair. "There's a lot to learn, Daniel. I better get over to the sheriff's or he'll be wondering what's keeping me." Dr. Anderson headed down the boardwalk and looked back over his shoulder.

"I'll let Sheriff Rigby know to expect some extra gunfire from your store this morning so he doesn't think there's more trouble."

"Thanks, Doc," Daniel Sr. said. "I don't think it'll take very long, but I appreciate you letting him know."

They continued down the boardwalk while Dr. Anderson walked quickly the other way carrying his black medical bag. Daniel Jr. turned and watched after him until the doctor disappeared into the sheriff's office.

Coming up to the store, Daniel Sr. got out his keys and opened the door. Both he and Daniel Jr. walked in and noticed how cold it was. Daniel Sr. instructed Junior to go out back to get some wood so they could start a fire in the front woodstove to take the chill out of the air and get some coffee on.

The back of the store was still warm as it had a large coal-burning fireplace, which, during the winter months, was always kept lit and left to smoulder through the night to keep some of the goods from freezing and spoiling.

Daniel Sr. had hired Ms. Leighton years ago from Hudson's Haven, the local saloon to come and check on the fireplace every night as he wanted to protect his goods but also didn't want to have a fire breakout in the store. In exchange for Ms. Leighton checking the store every night, Daniel Sr. would give her foodstuffs and also a discount on some of the fancier clothing he carried.

She had been helping Daniel out since he and Rachel moved out of town and into their current homestead. He had heard of Ms. Leighton off and on in the town gossip for years. It was said that she sang and also entertained the men that came through town and visited Hudson's.

Daniel Sr. wasn't one given to gossip, and figured, as long as she took care of his store, then he would help her out.

Daniel Jr. went through the store to the back door to unlock it when he noticed that the door was ajar, and the handle and lock were both broken.

He turned to yell for his dad when he was grabbed from behind, and a hand covered his mouth before he could get any sound out.

Daniel Sr., completely unaware of anything amiss, proceeded to get the store ready for opening. He set out and dusted off the counter displays and counted out change from his pocket to for the till. He then reached under the cash register to get his gun belt and gun and placed them on the countertop.

Normally, Daniel didn't wear his gun in the store, but seeing as Rachel was on her way in, and he wanted to get in some practice, he figured he'd better strap it on now and finish setting up so he'd be ready when she came in. He felt a bit flustered as it seemed he was trying to do everything all at once.

In the back room, Daniel Jr. found himself struggling against a very large man who was holding him tightly. The man turned still holding onto Daniel and keeping his hand firmly against his mouth, and Daniel saw that there were three other men in the back room.

One of the men whispered, "What do we do now?"

"Don't worry, the store owner has a gun under the counter, but he never wears it while he's working so just make sure you don't let him reach under the counter," the man holding Daniel instructed. "But if he does, then shoot him."

Hearing this, Daniel Jr. struggled wildly but was silenced when the man holding him warned, "Move again or make a noise, and I will cut you from ear to ear, got that?"

Daniel froze and then nodded slightly to let the man know he understood.

"Hey, Danny Boy, where's that wood?" Daniel Sr. called from the front of the store.

Daniel's eyes went wide, but he didn't make a sound. He looked around and saw that one of the men was gargling with his dad's imported scotch. The man looked over Daniel's head at the group leader and said quietly "I'm ready" and put the bottle back on the shelf.

"Daniel," his dad bellowed, "where the heck . . . ?"

He didn't get to finish as the three men burst through the back room door into the storefront, and Daniel Sr. instantly realized that he was about to be robbed. Luckily, unknown to the robbers, he was already wearing his guns.

He gave no outward sign of his intent and suddenly dove to the floor behind the counter but managed to fire off two shots before he went down. The first shot found its target with deadly accuracy as the robber fell to the ground, and his second shot went wild as the other two men scattered once they realized that they were facing an armed man.

"Daniel!" A voice boomed from the back room. "I have your son in here, don't shoot as he's about to step into the doorway."

Daniel Sr. raised his head just above the countertop to look toward the back room. A large bearded man appeared in the doorway with Little Daniel held against his chest and a knife still held against his throat.

"Throw down your gun," the man ordered.

Daniel Sr.'s mind was racing. He didn't want to give up his weapon, but he couldn't even begin to imagine what the consequences would be if he didn't. With shaking hands, he tossed his gun over the counter.

One of the men who had scrambled when Daniel fired said, "You said he wasn't going to be armed, Eddy, you idiot!"

"Eddy?" The man rolled over to see Eddy's lifeless body lying beside him.

"Tim," he hollered to the large man holding Little Daniel. "Tim, he killed Eddy!"

Now that Tim knew Daniel Sr. was unarmed, he pushed Daniel Jr. through the doorway and onto the floor off to the side.

"Kill him, Tim," the man said as he saw Tim strap his knife back to his hip.

But Tim drew his gun instead and addressed Daniel Sr. "I may let your son live if you tell me where you keep the guns. Where are they?"

"They're under the floor behind the counter where the till is," Daniel Sr. replied steadily.

"Bobby," Tim directed to the man still sitting on the floor with Eddy, "check it out."

Bobby went behind the counter and pulled up a trapdoor in the floor to expose an armory underneath. He nodded at Tim. "They're here."

"Come over here and get on your knees," Tim instructed Daniel Sr.

Daniel walked over slowly with his hands raised and knelt down on the floor. Fearing the worst, he looked up at Tim as the larger man pointed his gun at Daniel Sr., and a shot echoed. Daniel looked at his assailant and watched in shock as the man's eyes widened, and his head turned to the side to look at Daniel Jr. who was still pointing his gun at him, arm shaking but looking determined.

Tim turned to look at Daniel Sr. again, and as he did so, his legs gave out, and he dropped to the floor.

Bobby, seeing that his friend was dead and his boss injured, panicked and just started firing his gun wildly as he ran for an exit. Daniel Sr. dove across the floor to grab Little Daniel and roll him behind another counter for cover. The third man who had been with the robbers also made a run for it, but they were slowed down as they tripped over merchandise in their haste and stumbled out the front door.

Daniel Sr. grabbed the gun out of Little Daniel's hand and hugged him hard. He stood up and could still see the men through the front window.

Just yards away, Barry and Rachel noticed two men firing their guns and trying to figure out which direction to run from the store. Rachel's blood ran cold, and it felt like her heart stopped when she realized that her son and husband were in that very same store. She jumped off her horse and palmed her gun on the run as Barry grabbed his rifle from his saddle and ran after her.

Daniel Sr., hoping to catch one of the robbers, fired a shot through the already broken window. Hearing the shot, Rachel yelled to the fleeing men, "Stop and drop your guns NOW!"

"Drop them!" she warned a second time.

Neither of the men was inclined to listen, and both turned to fire at Rachel, but before they had even managed to squeeze the trigger, Rachel had fired four shots faster than you could bat an eye, and both men fell to the ground. She turned toward the store, vaguely aware that her brother had been standing behind her the whole time rifle in hand. Barry didn't even have time to raise his rifle by the time Rachel fired all four shots.

"Daniel!" she yelled. "Daniel, answer me, damn it!" she yelled again as she turned back to the store.

"We're okay," he called back.

"Is there anyone else in there with you?" Rachel called, gun still in hand.

"Yes, but it's okay, they're not standing anymore," he replied.

Daniel Sr. made his way to the doorway, and Rachel grabbed him. "Where's Junior, where is he?" she asked frantically.

Putting his arms around his wife, he assured her. "He's okay, honey, he's okay."

Daniel Jr. walked over to the man he shot. He picked up Tim's gun and then noticed that the man was still breathing and trying to move along the floor. He looked up as his mom and dad came into the store and saw that he had his gun trained on the man's chest.

"Son, what are you doing?" Daniel Sr. asked.

Keeping an eye on the fallen man, Daniel said, "He's still alive and trying to crawl for the back door."

"Put down your gun, Daniel," his mother said softly, pleading. "You're making me nervous.

Are you going to shoot him? Please don't, Daniel."

"I'm not going to shoot him unless he wants to hold a knife to my throat again," Daniel Jr. said, sounding far older than his years.

Barry stepped in and made sure that Tim kept his hands away from his knife while Daniel Sr. went to the back to make sure there were no other intruders and to bar the back door until it could be repaired.

"Don't move, mister," Rachel advised as she pinned Tim with a steely glare as Tim continued to struggle.

Daniel Sr. came back in and looked at his son. "Daniel, may I have the gun, please?"

Daniel Jr. slowly handed his gun to his father.

Rachel, realizing that Tim wasn't going anywhere fast with both her husband and brother nearby, reholstered her gun and grabbed her son in a fierce hug. "Are you okay, Daniel, are you hurt at all?" Her eyes raked over him from head to toe and other red marks on his arms and neck; he appeared to be okay.

"I'm fine, Mom." His gaze fell on the man lying on the floor. "Is he going to die?"

"I don't know," his father replied as he fetched tape and gauze from one of the cupboards and quickly brought it over to where Tim lay.

Daniel Sr. bent over the man and pulled his knife out from his boot and cut Tim's shirt open and pressed a wad of gauze over the bullet hole in the side of the man's stomach. He looked up and saw that Daniel Jr. was in tears. "Barry, go get Dr. Anderson. He's at Sheriff Rigby's, make it quick," Dan Sr. stated abruptly.

"Please don't let him die, Dad," Daniel Jr. sniffled.

As Barry ran for the door, he was pulled up short at the sight of Sheriff Rigby pointing a gun at his chest. The sheriff had heard all the commotion, and all he knew was that he had two dead bodies in the street and more gunshots fired, so he was trying to piece it all together. Barry threw his hands in the air and skidded to a stop, but the sheriff quickly recognized Barry and lowered his gun.

"We need the doc now," Barry said.

"He should be here shortly When we heard the gunshots in the street and not in the store, we assumed his services might be needed," Sheriff Rigby said with a look over his shoulder.

They both spotted Dr. Anderson poking his head out from around the corner. As being unarmed, he was in no hurry to come out in the open.

"All clear, Doc," the sheriff yelled. "But hurry, there's a man hit inside."

Dr. Anderson came quickly down the boardwalk and passed the two men lying in the street knowing they were already dead. He walked into the store and looked about cautiously and noted that Daniel Jr. was crying and that Daniel Sr. was kneeling over a man and holding a bloody cloth to the man's side.

"Daniel, what happened here?" Dr. Anderson asked as he put his bag down and rolled up his sleeves.

Seeing how distraught Little Daniel was, Dr. Anderson suggested that maybe he should go outside.

Daniel Jr. shook his head and looked at the doctor with huge tear-filled eyes. "Please help him, Doc. I don't want him to die."

The doctor nodded and turned to Daniel Sr. "Okay, but I need you to stand back, and both of you stay out of my way now."

Both Daniels moved away from Tim, and Rachel motioned for her son to join her near the window. Daniel Jr. gladly went into the safe haven of his mother's arms. She rested her chin on his head and said gently, "People die every day because of stupid choices they make, but be clear, Daniel, those are *their* choices. That man over there woke up today and chose to risk his life doing a dumb thing, and if he dies today, that's his own fault, no one else's.

"Daniel, look at me." His mother put her finger under his chin and tipped his head back so she could look into his eyes. "I know we always talk to you about taking responsibility, but nobody here expects you to stand here and watch this man live or die, do you understand?"

"Sort of, I guess," Daniel said.

"Daniel," his father said, "here, put your gun back in your holster." He extended his arm to hold the gun out to his son.

Daniel turned back from his mother who was ushering him outside and took a step toward his dad. Senior took a step toward him, and they came face-to-face in the middle of the store, and Daniel Sr. dropped to his knees and hugged his son. Overcome with emotion, Daniel Sr. looked into Junior's face and said, "Thank you, you saved my life today, Daniel."

"What's going on?" Rachel asked as she approached the pair.

"If it wasn't for our son, I'd be dead right now. I was looking death in the face down the barrel of that man's gun when Danny Boy shot him. He was just about to pull the trigger, and I heard that gunshot and thought I was about to meet my maker, but it was Little Daniel's gun that went off as he shot the man."

Realizing finally what her son had just been through, Rachel started to cry. "My god, Daniel, I'm sorry, I didn't completely understand what had happened."

"It's okay, Mom, I just want to make sure he doesn't die."

"Okay, can you go to Sheriff Rigby's office just for a minute?" his mom asked. "Please? I just want to talk to Dr. Anderson for a bit."

Daniel nodded and left the store to head to the sheriff's office. He didn't make it far as he saw the two bodies lying in the middle of the snowy road, and he stopped to stare.

Rachel quickly talked with her husband and then turned to the doctor. "I can't have this thief's death on my son's conscience. Is he going to pull through?"

"Truthfully, Rachel, I'm not sure," Dr. Anderson answered her honestly.

"My son shot him, and for my son's sake alone, I don't want him to die," Rachel said quietly.

"What can we do to help?"

"What do you want me to say, Rachel?" Dr. Anderson looked up at her. "I will do my best just the same. Supplies have dwindled to almost nothing in this town. Thief or no thief, I will do everything I can, but to be honest, it'll take the last of my supplies. Just to make him feel comfortable."

"What exactly are you saying, Doc?" Daniel Sr. asked.

"I'm a doctor, and I'd like to think I'm a professional, but sometimes I have to make decisions based on the good of the one versus the good of the many. Do I use all my supplies on a man who probably won't make it anyway and leave all the other people who may need them to suffer? Do I use what's left of my medicines to keep his pain down when they won't even last him long enough to make it through surgery?"

He looked at the trio of adults and asked, "What would any one of you do if you were me? Sometimes it's not clear-cut, and sometimes it's not fair, but that's how it is."

Barry, Daniel Sr., and Rachel all looked helplessly at each other, and it was Rachel who spoke. "How long till you get more supplies?"

"Two more days," replied the doctor. "There's a town about thirty miles from here that might be able to give us some supplies to hold us over, but no guarantees on what they've got either."

"We have to try," Rachel said determinedly.

"Barry, would you go the Lakeview village to grab some supplies?" Rachel pleaded. "Do this for Daniel."

"Absolutely," Barry was quick to reply.

Looking at Dr. Anderson, Rachel said, "We'll go to the next town and get what we can.

Daniel, give Barry some money to buy whatever he can get." The nervousness was quite noticeable in Rachel's tone of voice.

Dr. Anderson nodded and said, "I will write you a letter to take to their physician, Dr. Humphrey, so he will know exactly what I need, and he can help you pick supplies from their general store as well. Daniel, can you get me a pen and paper, please?"

As Daniel Sr. reached for a pen, he stated, "I will cover all the cost of this man's care, you just get him well, Doc, and we'd be much obliged."

Rachel walked over to where the man still lay moaning and looked him square in the eye. "Don't you dare die, you bastard."

"Rachel!" Daniel Sr. yelled.

She stepped away from the man and moved to the doorway.

"Okay," Doc said, "I need some hands to help me get this man back to my office."

By this time, there was a small crowd gathered on the street in front of the store with people gathering around Daniel Jr. to ask what had happened. Daniel Jr. just remained silent as he didn't know what to say. Rachel quickly addressed the small crowd outside the store, which had gathered from all the commotion.

"We need three volunteers to move a body to the doc's office."

Within seconds, three men appeared from the crowd. Two of the men were large men and one not so strong looking but had a bit of height to him to make up for it. They nodded and came up the steps to the store and filed past Rachel. She pointed to the man on the floor.

Daniel Sr. handed the three men a blanket, which they spread out on the floor, and as gently as they could, they picked Tim up and placed him on the blanket as he grunted and yelped with pain. Rachel looked on and secretly wished they'd drop him on his head to shut him up.

She walked out of the store with Daniel Sr., and the men followed carrying the injured man. They saw Daniel Jr. sitting dejectedly on the steps of the sheriff's office with the townspeople milling all around him trying to get information. He wasn't saying anything at all, and Rachel yelled above the crowd, "Get away from him! What's wrong with you people? Leave him alone!"

The people scattered grumbling among themselves to be deprived of some good gossip.

Daniel Sr. said quietly, "What's done is done, Calm down because you're just going to make it worse and give them even more to talk about, and we don't need that right now, especially Daniel."

Rachel took a deep breath and blew it out again. "You're right," she said as she hugged him.

Daniel Sr. stepped up on the stairs near his son with his arm around his wife and addressed the crowd. "Rachel gives you all her apologies. Our family has had an extremely upsetting day, and we would appreciate some time to ourselves. I'm sure you all understand, and the sheriff will probably give you all the details shortly, thank you."

Daniel Sr. herded Rachel and Daniel Jr. into the sheriff's office away from prying eyes where they could sit down and talk in peace. Daniel Jr. was the first to speak. "Is he going to die?"

Rachel looked at her son and said, "Doc is going to look after him, and Uncle Barry is going to Lakeview to get more medicine and supplies to make sure he's in as little pain as possible."

Daniel nodded and was doing his best to be strong but could see his eyes were teary but not falling. Rachel pulled him closer, and he buried his face in her coat. She gently placed her hand upon his head, understanding this was quite a dramatic experience for her loved one. "Everything is okay, dear. You did a brave thing, so it takes a man to make a decision that you did. I am very proud of you." As Rachel kissed the top of his head, she whispered, "I know it's a lot to take in right now, but you're a hero, Daniel, you saved your dad's life.

Just then, Sheriff Rigby walked in and hung up his hat and coat before he sat down at his desk facing them.

"I heard what happened." Looking at Daniel Jr. sitting on his mom's lap, he said, "Your dad was a very lucky man to have you around today, young man. Not so lucky for Tim McNabb, but at least he's better off than the other three."

"Tim McNabb! You sure?" Rachel questioned.

"*Oh yes*," Sheriff assured her.

"But there are eight of them, and all of them are criminals," she pointed out. "This could lead us to all kinds of trouble," Rachel said worriedly.

"Yes, it could," the sheriff agreed. "But hopefully, there won't be any repercussions."

Daniel Sr. interrupted. "Who exactly are the McNabb brothers?"

"They're trouble, thieves, gamblers, and murderers, every one of them," Sheriff Rigby explained. "They live about fifty miles or so from here."

"Big trouble," Rachel seconded the sheriff's opinion.

After about an hour of talking and filing their official statements with the sheriff, a knock came on the door as Dr. Anderson poked his head in.

"Come on in, Doc," Sheriff Rigby invited.

The doctor stepped in and nodded to the sheriff and addressed Daniel Sr. and his family. "Well, Tim's settled, and I've had a chance to clean the wound really good and take a better look at it, and at this point, although it's in God's hands, I'd venture to say that he's going to make it."

It was hard to tell which of the three McDougalls were most relieved to hear his prognosis, and although they still knew anything could happen, it was a small comfort they all needed for now.

The doctor looked at the sheriff and asked, "Did you know that was Tim McNabb that young Daniel here shot?"

"Yes, we did," the sheriff replied,

Doc began. "The other three are Eddy Stanton, one was a drifter named Mike Sanders, and the other was Bobby Brown. And they must have teamed up recently. I have not known them to hang out together."

Daniel Sr. stated that he had heard the robbers use each other's names and that those were in fact the first names they used.

"I honestly don't care who they were, and I can't say that I feel anything but relief that they're gone one way or the other," Daniel Sr. stated.

"Daniel," Rachel began, "I know the McNabbs, and they're like a pack of wolves. When one gets hurt, the rest team up to avenge their fallen, and usually, whoever wrongs them is never seen or heard from again."

"Sounds like I'm in Scotland again," Daniel Sr. replied.

"Exactly," Rachel said. "Your family was always feuding with the Drisdelles. Well, think of it the same here except it's the McDougalls versus the McNabbs."

"Well, if Tim does survive, he will be in jail for at least two, maybe three years," Sheriff Rigby interjected.

"That's all?" Rachel asked incredulously.

"Fortunately or unfortunately, depending on how you look at it, Tim didn't actually kill anyone. Technically, he didn't even fire a shot. All we have on him is possibly an attempted robbery and aggravated assault on Daniel Jr. Your son here foiled his attempt at murder," Sheriff Rigby reminded them.

"But he still held a knife against my son's throat," Rachel replied angrily.

"And that's why I'm saying that he might get two to three years, Rachel," Sheriff Rigby repeated. "Listen to me, he didn't shoot Daniel Sr., and he didn't cut Daniel Jr. What we do know that his goal was to rob the store to get firearms and supplies, but that's it."

"Know what, Doc?" Rachel looked up at Dr. Anderson. "I've changed my mind, let him die."

She sighed and looked at her son and back at the doctor. "I'm sorry, I didn't mean that. It's just frustrating to know that he could have destroyed our family, and yet, he's only going to get a couple years in prison for it. She reassured Daniel Jr., "We'll still do what we can to make sure he's okay, I promise."

They all sat in silence for a minute, gathering their thoughts. The morning was fast becoming noon, and the town as abuzz with news of the attempted robbery as well as the shooting. The sheriff looked over at Daniel Sr. and said, "Why don't you take Rachel and Daniel Jr. on home now, and I'll go clean up the store and take care of it for the rest of the day," Sheriff Rigby offered. "If it's okay for now, I'm going to gather all the firearms and lock them up here in my office until you get the door and the lock fixed. If I may say, Daniel, I had no idea that you had so many rifles and handguns in your store. You've got at least twenty rifles and probably thirty-five handguns under that floor. We'll keep it quiet for now, but I suggest that you get a reinforced metal cage to store them in the future. Maybe tomorrow you can go see the smithy about getting a better storage unit, although I do admit I'm impressed with your current hiding place." He smiled.

"So am I. One of Barry's creative works, he did a good job," Dan Sr. boasted.

"One last thing, Daniel, I know that now is not the time for a lecture, but I think it would be best if you would limit any gunfire at the store for a while. For everyone's immediate safety until things calm down, not because there have been complaints about all the noise. Things could have turned out very differently today because people are so used to hearing gunfire from your store that it could have been a long time before anyone realized that something was seriously wrong."

"You're right," Daniel Sr. replied. "I will be looking to make some changes, just not today."

Sheriff Rigby nodded. "I understand."

Daniel Sr. looked around and noticed someone missing. "Where's Barry? Did he leave town already?"

"Yes, he did," confirmed Rachel. "I don't expect him back before nightfall or possibly by dusk if he makes really good time. If he encounters any problems, he won't be back till morning."

Daniel Sr. reminded her. "There's a storm blowing in so that will hold him up for sure."

"You're right," Rachel replied. "I completely forgot. Damn, Barry's travelling right into it, so there's no way he'll make it back tonight. I just hope he makes it safely both ways," she said worriedly.

"Rachel," Daniel Sr. said, "Barry will be fine. He's a grown man, and if he thought for one minute that he couldn't make it, he would have waited until tomorrow. Besides, I gave him twenty dollars for supplies, so he's extra motivated to get there," Daniel Sr. pointed out.

"Why twenty?" Rachel asked, surprised. "The supplies will only cost around six dollars, and even that's pricey."

"True," Daniel Sr. agreed. "But if he gets stuck in Lakeview for the night, he'll need to pay for a room, stable, and a meal or two. If I know your brother, he'll probably find a poker game to get in on and maybe even find a friend he can cuddle up with." Daniel finished with a wink.

"Daniel!" Rachel admonished. "Not in front of my son, please."

"Rachel, after today, your son is not a boy. He's a young man and should be treated as such." With a proud look at Daniel Jr., he continued, "It was a man, not a boy, who saved my life today."

With a sigh, Rachel conceded the point for now. "Okay, enough, let's go home. I need a drink, and there's a bottle of scotch with my name on it."

Daniel's Sr.'s mouth dropped open. "Scotch? Are you kidding me? You don't even drink."

"Listen, Daniel, I don't want to get into it right now. There is a time and a place for everything. This would be one of those times." Rachel was surely under complete stress as was noticed in the tone of her voice.

"Hey, Doc," Daniel Jr. spoke up, "do you think I can come with you to see that Tim fellow with you tomorrow?"

Before the doctor could answer, Rachel cut in. "I don't think that's a good idea, honey."

Seeing the worried expression in young Daniel's eyes, the doctor said, "Tell you what, Daniel, I'll check on him and let you know how he's doing okay."

Disappointed but understanding, Daniel nodded. "Sure."

As they stepped out of the sheriff's office onto the porch, Dr. Anderson tugged at Rachel's sleeve to pull her back inside the doorway. He slipped a small package into her hand and instructed, "I want you to take this home and give young Daniel no more than an eighth of a teaspoon of this mixed in with his milk at suppertime. He's had a trying day, and this will make sure that he has a really good rest tonight."

Rachel tucked the package in her coat pocket. "Thanks, Doc, I really appreciate it and all you've done today." Indicating her pocket, she laughed and said, "I may need some of this myself tonight."

"That's why I gave you about two tablespoons," Doc said with a wink. "There's enough for you and Daniel as well. Don't take more than a quarter teaspoon each and make sure that you've got all your unnecessary fires out and your coals banked for the night and everything else secured because it'll put the two of you out like a light."

Rachel nodded. "It's just my nerves. Daniel has had to kill to survive before, but as far as shooting a man, this is a first for me and definitely a first for young Daniel." She continued, "I came close when I was younger, but that's a story for another day perhaps."

"No need to explain." He patted her arm.

"Thanks." Rachel gave his hand a squeeze and moved back toward the door.

"I'll drop by the store tomorrow and let Daniel know how Tim's doing so he can tell Daniel Jr. when he gets home for supper after work," Doc promised.

He turned on the stop and added, "I'd probably keep young Daniel home tomorrow if I were you, but that's up to you and Daniel."

"We'll see how the night goes, but that's probably a good idea," she agreed.

She saw that both Daniels were sitting on the bench waiting for her. People were walking by and still looking their way, but at least no one was stopping to harass them with questions. Rachel was pleased to note that her earlier outburst was being adhered to. Rachel knew that there would still be gossip and rumors. That couldn't be helped, but she just wasn't in the mood to deal with it today.

She glanced around and was grateful to see that most of the townsfolk were making an effort to look busy to give them their privacy, so she called out to those within earshot. "I want to thank you very much for your concern for our family, and I apologize for my earlier rudeness. I know that you all want to know what happened, so to avoid any unnecessary speculation, I will tell you briefly so we can head home for the day. This morning, my husband's store was held up by four armed men. If not for this little man"—she gestured at Daniel Jr.—"my husband would be dead right now."

Seeing the avid interest and shock on the faces of the townspeople, Rachel continued.

"My son was forced to shoot the man who is now lying in the doctor's office in order to save his father's life. As you can surely understand, we ask that you please give young Daniel some time and space, thank you." Rachel stopped as she wasn't sure she could say more without giving into tears.

The people around them nodded and looked at Daniel Jr. with a newfound respect, and some of the men tipped their hats in a silent salute while some of the ladies wiped their own tears away as they thought about how they would feel if such an unexpected danger touched their lives.

Rachel addressed her husband. "Are we opening, or rather, are *you* opening the store tomorrow?"

Daniel Sr. spoke loudly enough for the people gathered to hear. "Yes, I am, but for now, I'm taking my family home. I hope all of you who need supplies from the store can wait till tomorrow, but if not, the sheriff has a key if it's an absolute emergency. Otherwise, I'll be open again at around 10:00 a.m. tomorrow."

One of the men gathered spoke up. "Thank you, Daniel, that's mighty kind of you to worry about us, but we'll be okay, you just take care of you and yours."

Several of the other people nodded and murmured their agreement, and a few also thanked Rachel for taking the time to speak to them.

Just then a voice broke above the rest. "Good job, LITTLE DAN!"

This was followed by whistles and waves from the small crowd, and a chorus of "Well done!" and "Good job!" followed, understanding how he must have felt.

The McDougalls acknowledged with a wave and then headed for the stables. After the crowd's reaction, Daniel Jr. wasn't as depressed as he had been, but the fate of Tim McNabb still rolled around in his head. As if reading his son's mind, Daniel Sr. put his hand on Junior's shoulder and said, "We're hoping no matter what, that Tim pulls through. But, Daniel, you had no choice. I would be dead right now if you hadn't shot him. I am very, very proud of you."

"I am too," his mother seconded.

They retrieved their horses, mounted up, and headed for home. Each one rode in silence as they alternately prayed and pondered about the morning's events.

They arrived back at the farm, all three taking a moment to be thankful that they were home all safe and together. They stabled their horses and tiredly walked up the steps to the porch. They looked in surprise at the crate sitting by the door on top of which sat two delectable, still warm apple pies. There was a note attached that read,

We hope that this small token will cheer you up, and know that we love you and we're thinking of you, Ms. Leighton.

Rachel smiled and messed up young Daniel's hair. "I wonder if this pie is really for us, or just for you, Mr. Daniel," she teased. "I'm just kidding." She laughed. "This is very thoughtful of her. We'll have to thank her."

"Apple pie," Daniel Jr. said excitedly, holding up the crate and taking a big whiff. "I love apple pie."

They walked into the kitchen, and Daniel placed the pies on the counter.

"Can I, Mom?" Daniel pleaded with his mom as he couldn't wait to dig in.

Deciding that this wasn't a day to stick with the usual no-dessert-till-after-you've-eaten, she nodded and said, "Go ahead, I wasn't expecting any of us to be home for lunch today, and it's already two thirty. You must both be starving."

"Not really, Mom," Daniel Jr. replied. "But I do love apple pie, hungry or not."

Young Daniel proceeded to get out the plates and glanced back at his parents. "Mom, Dad, do you guys want a piece too?"

Rachel shook her head. "No, honey, none for me, thanks, I have something else in mind."

"Like scotch?" Daniel Sr. asked.

"Yes, scotch," Rachel snapped. "You got a problem with that?"

Daniel Jr. stopped in midslice to look at his mother as her vehement tone had startled him.

Taken aback by her reaction, Daniel Sr. mumbled, "No, I just wasn't expecting you to be serious about the drink."

"Daniel," she began, "for years, I've changed some of my old ways in order to not embarrass you in the town. I don't drink, I don't swear, I usually don't wear my guns in public. But damn it, sometimes I do have a drink every now and then. I'm sure I'm not the only one. There are probably a lot of wives that do it too, and it's funny that you men think we're all at home being perfect angels. Shows how much you all know—Oops, Daniel, what goes on in this house stays in this house, got it?"

"Got it," he replied and turned his attention back into cutting the pie.

"Honey . . ."

"First, there is no scotch in the house. The bottle you're thinking of I gave to Barry months ago. So I will pour you a glass of wine. Will that be okay?" Daniel said with a concerned look on his face.

"That will be fine, thank you." Rachel now started to wind down from all the unwanted commotions.

Once finished, Daniel Jr. took his plate over to the table and sat down to enjoy his treat while it was still warm.

Rachel went over to Daniel Sr. and gave him a hug. Looking up at him, she said, "I love you, and I'm so glad you're both safe."

"I love you too, and I'm glad we're home safe," Dan Sr. replied.

Rachel sat down at the table with young Daniel and smiled at his pie-covered face. "How are you feeling, Daniel, honestly?"

Daniel Sr. took a seat at the table and added, "We both want to know whatever you're feeling or thinking about right now."

Daniel looked up from his pie and said, "Well, I feel kind of shaky, but in my head, I can't find the words to explain exactly how I feel. The pie's good though."

"The pie's good, what?" Rachel asked confused at the sudden change of topic.

"The pie, it's good," Daniel Jr. repeated. "Do you think you could get her to make blueberry tomorrow?"

"What are you talking about?" his mom asked.

"I want more pie," Daniel Jr. said simply.

"Daniel, I'm asking you about how you feel." Rachel was cut off by Daniel Sr., who shook his head and whispered, "It's okay, just leave him be. His mind is stressed, and he's distracting himself the only way he knows how."

Rachel got up and moved away from the table and motioned for her husband to come over to her so Daniel Jr. wouldn't hear.

When they were standing close, she whispered, "This whole ordeal is going to mess with his head and screw him up. We need to do something."

Daniel Sr. put his arm around her and said reassuringly, "He'll be fine, just let him be. His mind just needs time to sort things out and make sense of it in its own way."

"All right, I'll leave him be for now," she said quietly.

She turned back to Daniel Jr. and said, "Blueberry pie, eh? I think I can get around to making you some pie," Rachel stated.

Daniel Sr. appreciated her effort to make Daniel Jr. laugh and admired her resilience and realized that each of the minds and bodies would have a different journey as they recovered from this experience.

Daniel Jr. finished the last bite of pie and shivered. "I'm cold, is it okay if I go lie down for a while?"

His mother nodded. "Sure, go ahead and grab an extra blanket from our room if you want."

Young Daniel stood up and carried his plate over to the counter where he proceeded to place his plate directly into the almost whole pie that was sitting there. His parents just looked at each other and at the now-ruined pie and realized that something was definitely wrong.

As young Daniel trudged off to his room, Rachel looked worriedly at her husband.

"Just let him sleep, honey," Daniel advised.

"We have to do something," she cried.

Daniel sighed. "I think you're in just as rough shape as he is. Listen to yourself today, Rachel. My god, you went against all beliefs not to drink in front of our son. You barely even have a glass of wine on special occasions. Rachel, you're stressed! I see this is bothering you more than I see it in Daniel. Just relax," Daniel said, showing his support.

Rachel looked at her husband and hung her head. "You're right, and I'm sorry."

Daniel reached out and brushed her hair back from her face. "Honey, don't be sorry."

"I embarrassed you today. I shot two men, and I yelled at everyone in town, and not only that, I was openly vengeful and said I wanted a man to die." She buried her face in her hands and sobbed.

Daniel took her hands and put his finger under her chin to force her to meet his steady gaze.

"Listen to me. It's no different than what I told Junior. You did what had to be done. I saw you through the window this morning, and I was terrified, but before I could even get to the door, the two men were already down. I'm as proud of you as I am of Daniel, and no, you did not embarrass me. Daniel's alive, you're alive, and so am I, and I love you more than life itself, don't ever doubt that."

Rachel lay her hand against his cheek and kissed him. "Thank you, Daniel, thank you for loving me and accepting me the way I am, not many men would, you know."

Rachel suddenly remembered the packet that Dr. Anderson had given her. She pulled away from Daniel and went to her coat and brought the medicine back to show Daniel.

"Doc Anderson gave this to me for all of us to take tonight. Maybe I should take some now."

"What is it?" Daniel asked.

"I don't know exactly, he wasn't specific," she replied. "He just said to give some to Daniel at suppertime and for us to take it before bed and that we would all sleep really hard tonight, so it must be some kind of sedative."

Daniel shook his head. "I don't need any of that, but I think it would do you and the boy a world of good. I think you both need sleep more than you need to eat, so go ahead and take it now if you'd like."

Rachel nodded. "I think now is good."

Daniel studied the little packet of powder. "Did he say how you're supposed to take this?"

"Yes, he said to put an eighth of a teaspoon in milk for Daniel, and quarter teaspoon for us in milk or water and then just stir and drink," she instructed.

Daniel Sr. got the milk out of the ice box, poured enough milk for two people in a pot, and put it on the stove to warm up. After a few minutes, he poured the warm milk into tin mugs and carefully measured out the powdered medicine into both cups and stirred the contents until all traces of the powder were dissolved.

Hoping to catch Daniel Jr. before he fell asleep, his dad yelled down the hall. "Daniel, can you come in here for a minute, please?"

They heard Daniel's bed creak and then his footsteps on the floor as he opened his door and came down the hall to the kitchen. His dad handed him a mug and said, "Here, thought you might like a warm drink to wash down that pie and help you sleep."

"Thanks, Dad." An already-sleepy Daniel replied as he took a sip of the warm liquid.

He then handed a mug to Rachel as well. She sniffed the milk and then sipped it slowly, noting that there was no smell from the medicine but that there was a slightly different taste to it. Thankfully, Daniel Jr. was too tired to notice anything different. Daniel Sr. waited a few minutes for them both to finish and said, "I think we could all use a nap, let's go lie down before we fall down."

Daniel Jr. smiled and went back to his room.

"Rachel," Daniel said, "How about you go lie down with Junior? He'd probably sleep better with you there with him, and you'll probably sleep better knowing he's safe and sound."

"Are you sure you're not going to take any?" she asked.

"Yes, I'm sure, none for me," he replied.

"Good," giggled Rachel. "More for me."

Daniel Sr. took her mug and laughed at the obvious effect the drug was having on her.

He tugged her hand so she would follow him. "Okay, let's get you to bed, missy."

They made their way down the hall, and Daniel noticed that Rachel was not particularly steady on her feet. Daniel grinned and said, "I swear you're drunk."

"Yeah right, where's my baby?"

"He's right here, Rachel," Daniel Sr. said as he guided Rachel into young Daniel's room. Daniel Jr. was already fast asleep and didn't budge as Rachel first sat on the edge of his bed and then pulled her feet up and lay down next to him. She pulled him close and stroked his face, whispering, "My baby, my sweet baby."

Daniel smiled as he watched them lying together, burrowed beneath the blanket. "I'll leave you to your nap, but I'll come back to check on you."

He didn't close the door so that he wouldn't make any noise when he came back to look in on them. When he turned for one last look, he chuckled to himself to see that Rachel was also sound asleep, *Wow, that stuff really works*, he thought to himself.

After about ten minutes, he walked back to Daniel's room to make sure that they were both okay. Seeing that they were both snoring, he smiled and went back to the kitchen. His stomach rumbled, reminding him that he hadn't eaten since breakfast, so he got himself a plate and knife and cut himself a piece of the untouched second pie. He used his fork to unwedge the plate that Daniel Jr. had stuck in the first pie and put it in the sink. He was pleased to notice that the pie, although somewhat squashed, would still be edible.

He picked up his plate and went into the living room to relax. Putting his plate on the side table, he went over to the fireplace and stoked the embers back to life to get a little warmth into the room. Once he had a small fire crackling, he stretched out on the couch and reached for his pie. Polishing it off quickly, he set the empty plate back on the table.

With a sigh, he swung his legs up on the couch and put a pillow underneath his head and folded his hands over his now content stomach, and he too fell asleep.

Many hours later, Daniel was startled awake when Barry came walking in the front door. Daniel arose from the couch and stretched to get the kinks out of his back. He glanced out the window and noted that it was pitch-black, and a look at the clock revealed that it was after nine at night. Motioning Barry to be quiet for a minute, Daniel headed back down the hall to check on Rachel and young Daniel. Relieved to see they were still cuddled together and still sleeping deeply, he shut the bedroom door so that they wouldn't be disturbed by his and Barry's voices.

He went back to Barry and said, "I'm glad to see that you made it back. We didn't think we'd see you till tomorrow with the bad weather blowing in."

"You forget that my place is on the way, so I stopped there and took the wagon for shelter," Barry pointed out.

Daniel nodded. "I never thought of that. Did everything go okay in Lakeview?"

"Yeah," Barry replied, "the doctor there gave me everything we needed plus more.

"Did you bring the supplies here?" Daniel asked.

"No." Barry shook his head. "I dropped it all off at Doc Anderson's office on my way back through town."

"Good," Daniel said approvingly, glad that Dr. Anderson would be better able to tend to the injured man right away rather than having to wait another day.

Barry looked around the silent house. "Where's Rachel and Junior?"

"Sleeping," Daniel told him. "The doctor gave them something to help them sleep, and they've been snoozing all afternoon. He thought it would do them good to get a good rest."

"I agree," Barry said.

"Hey, you open the wine here on the table." Barry was asking as he was about to help himself to a glass.

"Believe it or not, it was opened at your sister's request," Daniel stated with a concerned look.

"Wow! That's not like her, she okay?"

"Yeah, I think so. It's been a trying day for her, as with us all," Daniel remarked.

"She's a tough girl. But I am sure this ordeal did give her a good go. I'm sure," Barry stated.

"Daniel? Would you care to join me in a glass?"

"You know what? I think I will. Sure, pour me on too." Daniel had a look of tiredness written all over his face.

Barry poured himself a drink as Daniel once again went to check on Rachel and Daniel Jr. He came back and looked a bit perturbed.

"What?" Barry asked.

"Well, I've checked on them a few times, and they haven't even moved, and it's been more than four and half hours, so that powdered crap Dr. Anderson gave Rachel must be stronger than he thought."

"What powdered crap?" Barry inquired.

"That stuff in the packet on the counter." Daniel pointed at it.

Barry picked up the small packet and smelled it gently then dipped the tip of his little finger in it and touched the powder to the end of his tongue. He looked up at Daniel and said, "Well, they may be out till morning seeing as that powder is opium."

"Well then, maybe put what's left somewhere safe for a rainy day, or for Rachel if she needs it, but I don't think she will want to be giving any more to Junior," replied Barry.

"Yeah, maybe," Daniel said as he refolded the packet and set it aside on the counter for the time being.

"Are you hungry, Barry?" Daniel asked.

"Nope, not at all," Barry said. "Rachel had packed a big lunch for Junior and me for the trip out to my place, so I ate them both on the way."

"Right, I forgot about that," Daniel said.

"When I was dropping off the supplies to Doc Anderson, I asked him about Tim McNabb, and he said he was almost sure that he's going to pull through." Barry smiled as he delivered the good news.

"Good to hear, I'll tell Junior in the morning or whenever he wakes up. He will be relieved to hear it," Daniel said happily.

"Daniel," Barry began seriously, "I got to thinking while I was on the road today that you, Rachel, and Junior might be in for some dire consequences from the McNabbs."

"Yeah," Daniel said, "that's what Sheriff Rigby told us as well, that they will avenge any hurt visited upon their family."

Barry pointed out. "In this case, Daniel, it's your son that's harmed one of their own."

He continued. "I really don't think they would harm him as he's only a child, but as for you and Rachel, I'm not sure how far they would go. They may even target me as I was there too. If he goes to jail, well, you catch my drift."

"What am I supposed to do? I didn't kill him when I had the chance. I made sure he had medical care, I paid for the supplies to aid him out of my own pocket, but I sure as hell am not providing or paying for a lawyer to keep his sorry arse out of jail!" Daniel exploded. "If it wouldn't destroy young Daniel, we couldn't care less what happens to this man," he added angrily.

"Well, Daniel, all I'm saying is that I really think you should take all the necessary precautions to protect Rachel and Junior. Myself as well," he added.

Daniel replied heatedly, "I am not going to live as a prisoner in my own home or in my own town, I won't do it!"

Barry ran his hand through his hair in frustration. "Daniel, I'm just asking you to be more cautious is all. Depending on how long he gets in jail, it will buy you time as they won't come after you until he gets out so he can come after you with them."

"How do you know that's what they'll do?" Daniel asked.

"I know their family, so does Rachel," Barry replied. "When we were younger, we used to hang out with Tim's older brother Billy. Let me assure you, both Rachel and I know enough," he said solemnly. "So trust me when I say that you should have a plan, my friend. Now being Daniel's just a child, maybe they'll let it go as an accident, who knows, or maybe not." Barry shrugged.

"Enough, you've made your point," Daniel said tersely.

Changing the topic, Daniel suggested. "Why don't you and little Daniel head out for your place tomorrow to grab the lumber and tools you need to work on the house? He could probably use the distraction so he doesn't sit around here all day thinking and rethinking everything that's happened. Take your time and keep him busy the whole day if you can, that'll give Rachel and me the day to talk uninterrupted and figure out what we're going on in town and what, if anything, we're going to do about all this."

"Sure," Barry agreed quickly. "I can do that. Do you still want me to go ahead and build the loft right away?"

"Of course," Daniel replied.

"Okay, great, it'll be good to work and keep my hands busy," Barry said.

Barry reached into his pocket and reached out his hand to Daniel.

"What's this?" Daniel asked as he held out his hand.

"It's your leftover money from the twenty dollars you gave me for supplies," Barry said.

"Keep it," Daniel said, taking his hand away. "Consider it a down payment on your work on the loft."

Daniel yawned. "I'm going to bed, so help yourself to whatever you want. You know where everything is. I don't need to tell you where the wine is as the bottle's been in your hand for the last twenty minutes." Daniel laughed.

Barry looked at his left hand, perplexed to see that the bottle was indeed in his grasp, which made him chuckle as well.

"Why, so it is." Barry laughed even harder.

Daniel headed out of the kitchen. "Good night, Barry."

Barry poured another glass and headed for the living room to sit on the couch. He sipped his wine as he stared into the fire deep in thought until his chin hit his chest, and he was fast asleep.

Daniel Sr. lay in bed trying to drift off, but he kept tossing and turning, and after a few fitful hours, he gave up and got out of bed and headed to young Daniel's room. He opened the door and peeked in to see that they were both curled up together, and their blanket had fallen away and only covered half of their bodies.

He bent over to pull the covers back up and noticed that Rachel had her eyes open and was looking around as if in a fog. "Oh, Daniel," she whispered, "what time is it?"

He brushed her bangs out of her eyes and whispered back, "You've been out for about seven hours now, and it's almost two in the morning."

"Why are you still up, is everything okay?" she asked.

"Yes," he reassured her. "Everything is fine, I just couldn't sleep. Too much excitement, I guess."

"I'm going to get up," Rachel said. "He's fine and still asleep, just look at him," she said with a smile.

Daniel looked at his son's sleeping form and smiled himself. Daniel Jr. was sprawled across the bed, one arm over his head and one across his stomach, with his head turned to the side and a faint line of drool tracking down from his open mouth to his chin as he snored lightly.

"You're sure?" he asked his wife. "He may really want you to be here when he wakes up."

Rachel nodded as she swung her legs off the bed and stood up. "Well, let's get you to bed and then let me worry about that, but truthfully, I think he'll be okay after such a deep sleep."

"Well then, let's go get me to bed then." Daniel Sr. chuckled as Rachel followed him to their bedroom.

As they were about to enter their bedroom, she said, "I wonder if Barry is okay or if he's stuck somewhere."

"I totally forgot to tell you when you woke up," Daniel said. "He made it back already, and he's probably asleep in bed. I left him with the wine, so he should be passed out by now as he didn't get in till around nine o'clock. It was a long ride."

"Did he get the supplies Dr. Anderson needed?" she asked.

"Yes, he got everything and took it all to the doctor before coming out here. Dr. Anderson said that he's pretty sure now that Tim is going to make it."

"I'm so glad for Daniel's sake." Rachel breathed a sigh of relief.

"Hold on," Daniel said. "I should check the fire and the door in case Barry forgot before he fell asleep."

Daniel walked quickly back to the kitchen and noticed that the fire was almost out, just embers that could be left for the night. He latched the door, and as he turned, he noticed that Barry hadn't made it to bed at all. He went over to the living room and shook his head at Barry's prone body lying sideways on the couch, no pillow and no blanket in the chilly room.

Rachel had come up behind Daniel to see what was taking so long, and she also shook her head seeing her brother sprawled across the couch with the half-empty glass and bottle rest on the table beside him.

"I suppose we should probably wake him up and send him to bed before he gets stiff from being uncomfortable and cold," she said.

"No, just leave him there," Daniel said. "I'll go grab him a quilt from our room and cover him up, and he'll be fine."

"You're probably right. He had a long ride, he'd probably rather sleep uninterrupted," she agreed. "But it is cold in here, so you get the quilt, and I'll rebuild the fire for him."

Daniel headed off to get the quilt while Rachel added some wood to the fire. He came back and placed the blanket over Barry trying not to disturb him. Rachel picked up the glass and bottle that Barry had left on the table and carried them into the kitchen.

He looked at Rachel. "Before I forget, I asked Barry to take Daniel tomorrow out to his place to get the lumber and tools he's going to need to build the loft and to keep him busy for the day. I figured that would give us time to go to town and see what's being said and to figure out what we're going to do about the McNabb situation."

Rachel shook her head. "I'd prefer to keep Daniel out of sight. It would be better for him to stay here."

Daniel was firm. "Rachel, we need to go into town together, and Barry needs to get his stuff. So he and Daniel are going to continue to take the trip they were supposed to take yesterday. I think it's best for Daniel to go and get away from this for a day while we're in town, and Barry does need the help."

"Okay," she relented, "but only if he's okay in the morning. He's still a child, and he may need the comfort of home and his mom today, so we'll see."

"Rachel, like I keep saying, what's done is done, and we all have to live with it. Besides, we need to talk about possible consequences, and I don't want to scare Daniel. Even though Doc gave him medicine to help tonight, I don't want him stressed and upset to the point that we have to be giving him opium every night. So let's just keep him out of town for a few days, okay?" he asked.

Rachel stared at him blankly. "What opium?"

"The powder Doc gave you. Barry looked at it and said it was opium," Daniel explained.

"Well, that explains why I was asleep as quick as a candle being blown out," she said.

"Barry did mention that it would be best just to set that stuff off somewhere as he wasn't sure you would want to continue to give it to Daniel."

"He's probably right about that," Rachel agreed.

"Put that powder somewhere safe and mark it clearly before someone mistakes it for sugar or something," Daniel requested.

"Good idea." Rachel agreed and put it up in the cupboard for the time being.

"Well, dear, I am going back to lie down. You coming?" Daniel asked.

"I'm just going to tidy up a bit. Then I'll check on Daniel and come join you in bed. I already slept for seven hours, so I'm kind of awake now, so I can listen for Daniel if he wakes up before morning."

"Okay then, give me a kiss here, dear," Daniel requested.

Rachel was more than happy to oblige his request.

"Good night, see you in the morning."

Daniel walked slowly down the hall to their bedroom, leaving Rachel alone in the kitchen. She tidied up, put another small log on the fire for Barry, and checked on Daniel Jr. who was still sleeping soundly before she climbed into her own bed. She put her arm over her now snoring husband and fell quickly asleep much to her surprise.

There were no more sounds or movements in the house until sunrise.

Morning came, and the sun peaked its way through the shutters on the McDougall house. Rachel was already up and had just put breakfast on the table. Barry and Daniel Sr. were also up and out in the barn getting things ready for the day ahead while Daniel Jr. was still fast asleep.

"Good morning, honey," Daniel Sr. said as he came in and kissed her cheek.

"Good morning, yourself," she replied with a smile. "How are you feeling? I'm surprised that you're up this early."

"I feel fine, I'd like to head to town shortly though," he said.

"Morning, Barry, need a coffee?" she asked as her brother came in from outside rubbing his hands together in an effort to get warm.

"Sounds good," he replied and reached for the tin mug she was holding out. "My day wouldn't be the same without coffee." He laughed.

"Daniel Jr. still sleeping?" he asked.

"Yes, he is," Rachel answered.

"I'll go wake him." Barry offered.

"No, just wait a minute as we'd like to talk to you first." Rachel stopped him.

"Sure, what's up?" Barry asked, sipping his coffee.

"We both want to thank you for getting the medical supplies and for taking Daniel today as well," she started, "which is what I really want to talk to you about, so grab a seat."

Barry took a chair at the table and waited for Rachel to speak her piece. "Barry, we would appreciate it if you could keep Daniel busy out at your place and not bring him back till around four o'clock, if that's okay with you. We would like to go into town and talk to Sheriff Rigby about Tim, and we'd also like to talk with Doc to make sure Tim is still expected to pull through. I also have to stop by Daniel's school and talk with Mrs. Morrison about what's happened and about him being absent for two days."

Daniel Sr. wasn't aware of that part of the plan and asked, "What do you need to talk to her for? She's probably already heard everything and doesn't expect him back for a few days anyway."

"That may be true, but I want her to keep an eye on Daniel when he goes back tomorrow and to let us know if she sees him having any problems with the other kids or if he seems distracted or bothered," she explained.

"That's a good idea." Daniel Sr. agreed.

"Anyway"—she directed her attention back to Barry—"if you could do that for us, we'd be grateful."

"Sure, I can do that," Barry said. "No problem at all."

"Now I need to ask you something about Tim as you know him a little better than I do," Rachel said. "I'm considering dropping the charges against him," she said quickly.

"What?" Daniel asked, shocked. "Why would you even consider doing that?"

"I'm thinking that charging Tim would cause even more problems from his brothers and family and that retaliation would be imminent," she rationalized.

"I'm not sure I agree," Daniel said slowly.

Barry spoke up. "Well, you know Rachel could be right, but Tim even by himself might not just be willing to walk away after this let alone his family letting it go."

"That's what I want to find out," Rachel said. "I want to talk to Tim too, depending on what Sheriff Rigby says. I just don't want any problems in the future. I just want it dealt with and done now. I think you're right about Daniel Jr. too. He's no longer a little boy. He's a capable young man now. I think you should start teaching him how to handle a knife and how to fight. You battled for years and fight like an angry bear thanks to your Scottish ancestors. What do you think, Daniel?" she waited for him to answer.

"I think he needs to learn, and now's a good as time as any," Daniel agreed.

"Yeah," Barry said with a laugh, "take the swords out of the barn, put on your metal helmet with the horns and your vest of steel."

Daniel rolled his eyes at Barry's good-natured ribbing about his Scottish heritage, but he also knew that Barry respected the fact that a Scotsman could fight and kill without a moment's hesitation.

"Hmm, helmet with horns, eh? I can do that you know." Daniel pretended to truly consider such a thing.

"One more thing, Barry," she looked at her brother. "Do not give little Daniel any ideas about this shooting. We have to remember that anything we do or say could influence him later in life, and I don't want him to think that it's okay to just use his guns or his fists for anything other than self-defense. No crazy stories, okay?"

"No problem, sis." Barry crossed his heart playfully.

"Rachel, don't you think you're taking this a little to the extreme?" Daniel asked hesitantly.

"Daniel, I just killed two men yesterday, and I don't feel good about it, okay?" she stated.

Daniel moved out of his chair as he saw the tears well up in Rachel's eyes and threaten to spill over and put his arms around her. "Rachel, everything will be fine."

"I'm just worried about Daniel, that's why I want to drop the charges against Tim. Please, can we tell Sheriff Rigby that we don't want to proceed with this?" she begged.

"Okay, let's finish up here and go into town. Let's just take it one thing at a time and see what we can do, all right?" Daniel asked.

Rachel sniffled and stood up. "I'm going to wake up Daniel now, and you boys can start eating."

"I'm all for that," Barry said as he got up and grabbed a plate and headed for the stove and began to fill his plate.

Daniel remained seated at the table and sipped his coffee thoughtfully when Barry's voice intruded upon his thoughts. "You know, Daniel, that it might be my sister who has the issues, not Daniel Jr."

"Yeah, I can see that too." Daniel agreed. "Hopefully, by the time we reach town, I'll have been able to reason with her and calm her down. In Scotland, I had to kill to survive. It's been quite a few years since I was in a lot of fights where I had to finish the job, so I know the stress Rachel's under."

Meantime, Rachel had entered young Daniel's room and opened his curtains and pulled his covers off. She proceeded to give him a light shake. "Daniel . . . honey . . . time to wake up," she said softly.

Daniel stretched and rubbed his eyes groggily and asked, "Is it suppertime?"

Rachel burst out laughing. "No, honey, you had two large pieces of pie, a warm cup of milk, and you went to bed. You've been asleep ever since, it's morning now. Hungry?" Rachel asked and chuckled, hearing Daniel's stomach growl.

"Yeah, starving," Daniel said.

"Well, come on then, sleepyhead, breakfast is ready," she said, ruffling his hair.

Daniel didn't waste any time and was up and out of his room before his mother even got to the door. He didn't even think to ask about Tim as his mind was only on food. Daniel entered the kitchen to find his Uncle Barry already stuffing his face with bacon while his dad was at the stove filling his plate.

"Hungry?" Daniel Sr. asked.

"Sure am," young Daniel replied eagerly.

"Sit down then, and I'll fill a plate for you," his father offered.

"Sure." Daniel Jr. plopped into a chair next to his uncle with a smile. "Lots of bacon please, if Uncle Barry left any."

Barry was just taking another mouthful of bacon, and Daniel Jr. laughed and said, "I think we need a whole pig just for Barry."

"Hey," Barry said in his defense, "I like my bacon, nothing wrong with that."

Daniel Jr. pointed out with a grin. "I see that your belly is bigger than the hogs'."

"Listen to you." Barry laughed as well. "I see you haven't lost your sense of humor after yesterday, killer."

Daniel's expression became defensive. "Oh, did he die? Well, it's not my fault. At first I was worried, but now I realize that he shouldn't have been there, and he shouldn't have tried to shoot my dad. So that's that. I'm hungry."

Both Daniel Sr. and Barry looked at each other in surprise, both at a loss for a suitable reply. Rachel had overheard the conversation from the hall, walked in, and pinned her brother with accusatory glare. "Barry, I already talked to you about this, don't be starting stories, and don't be calling Junior a killer either."

Barry turned to Daniel Jr. "Sorry, small fry, I was calling you killer in response to you being very strong and brave yesterday. I didn't mean killer literally. Tim hasn't died, and in fact, Dr. Anderson strongly believes he's going to make it."

Rachel walked over and put her hands on young Daniel's shoulders. "But I'm glad that you're okay with what happened, and you know that what you did was the right thing in the situation you were in."

Daniel nodded. "I do, Mom."

He looked up at her and asked, "Can I go into town with you and Dad today?"

Barry looked at his nephew. "Well, actually, killer—"

"Barry!" yelled Rachel.

"Sorry," Barry said quickly and then addressed Daniel Jr. again. "Actually, Daniel, I could use your help today. I thought you could come with me back to my place as we still need to pick up the lumber and tools like we were going to yesterday. We can stop in town on our way back as I'll need to pick up supplies from your dad's store, or we can stop there tomorrow if we're back late." Barry suggested. "Rachel, Daniel, what do you think?"

Rachel replied first. "I'm not sure about today, but tomorrow sounds better."

"Yes, it's fine." Daniel Sr. countered. "Bring Junior back to the store when you get back, but just make sure to give us enough time like we discussed last night."

Daniel Sr. placed a heaping plate on the table in front of Daniel Jr., which included an extra large portion of the requested bacon.

"Great! Extra bacon," Daniel exclaimed and swatted away his uncle's hand as Barry pretended to try and swipe a few pieces.

"Hands off, chubby," Daniel Jr. squealed, trying to keep his plate covered.

Daniel Sr. laughed at Barry's antics. "He's got you pegged."

Barry smiled and playfully shook a warning finger at young Daniel. "It's a long ride back to my place, and I'll show you just how chubby I am when I sit on your head and fart."

Rachel cut in. "Barry, enough, that's just gross."

"That's okay, Mom, he wouldn't be able to catch me anyway." Daniel Jr. pointed out.

Barry smiled at Junior while his father laughed from his spot by the stove.

"What is it with you men and farting? It's not funny, it's disgusting, and the horse manure in the barn smells better," Rachel said, making a face at the three of them.

Daniel Sr. saluted Rachel with his coffee cup while trying to smother his laugher. "Nothing like catching someone a little off guard is there, honey?"

Rachel scowled at him. "You boys are sick. I'm going out to take care of the horses."

She headed for her coat and shrugged it on and slipped her feet into her boots when Barry leaned back on his chair and let out a long, loud, vibrating gaseous release deliberately so that Rachel would hear it.

"Oh, you bunch of pigs! You're lucky I'm on my way out, Barry. If I were staying, I'd hit you over the head with that bloody frying pan." Rachel turned on her heel and stormed out, slamming the door behind her.

Both men and young Daniel were all laughing so hard that tears were rolling down their red faces. Junior was laughing so hard he started to choke on his food, which prompted them to catch their breaths and try to calm down again though the lingering odor brought out the occasional snicker.

Daniel Sr. shook his head at Barry. "I think you really got under her skin with that last one."

"Just a little," smirked Barry. "She doesn't like it because Allan, Chuck, and myself used to always fart around the house and drive her crazy."

"So you were just bringing back fond memories?" Daniel Sr. asked with one eyebrow raised.

Then he looked at his son and warned. "Just so you can't say I never told you, it's impolite to fart when there's a lady present, or at the table, so don't take any lessons from your uncle."

Before Daniel Sr. had even finished his sentence, he was laughing again. "But that was funny. I normally only catch her when we're in bed."

"I know." Daniel Jr. smiled. "I can hear you all the way to my room."

"Well, you won't have to hear it for much longer." Daniel Sr. reminded him, referring to the loft they were going to build, which would put more space between their rooms.

"Listen, your mom and I are going to see Sheriff Rigby today to see about dropping all the charges against Tim. That's another reason we wanted you to go with your uncle today."

"Why?" Daniel Jr. asked.

"We think it might be best. Besides, Tim learned firsthand what could happen if he continues his current profession and will have plenty of time to think about it while he's laid up recovering from his bullet wound.

"To avoid any future problems with him and his family, we think it might be better to let it slide this time, but we need to talk to him first to try to ensure he's not going to be looking for trouble after he recovers," Daniel Sr. explained.

"Will I be able to see him?" young Daniel asked.

"I'm not sure about that yet," his father replied. "We'll let you know after we talk to him. But for now you need to help your uncle go get his stuff."

"Speaking of stuff," Barry said, "I'll need to buy more lumber on our way back through town."

Daniel nodded and reached into his pocket and tossed Barry a small pouch. "Here's twenty dollars in gold nuggets that one of my customers paid me a while back. It should cover the extra wood easily."

"I'll say," Barry said, catching the pouch neatly.

"Okay, I'm going to give Rachel a hand and then we'll head into town," Daniel Sr. said as he came over to the table and ruffled Daniel's hair. "Be good to your uncle."

Daniel Jr. nodded. "I will."

"I'm off then." He put his boots on, grabbed his coat, and walked outside.

Barry smiled and winked at Junior. "You're all mine now, killer."

"Whatever, chubby," Daniel Jr. said with a snort.

Daniel bolted out of his chair as he saw his uncle jump out of his own chair to chase him around the kitchen table. "What? Am I too fast for you, Uncle?"

As they both dashed the opposite way around the table, Rachel walked back in the house to get her gloves she'd forgotten earlier. Watching the two boys, she shook her head at the sight of the two chairs toppled over, lying on the floor. "What's going on in here?"

"Nothing," Daniel Jr. replied innocently. "Uncle Barry here was just trying to lose some weight."

Barry shot Daniel a look that promised retribution at a later time and waggled his eyebrows.

"Make sure you clean up," Rachel said. "Barry, remember what I said yesterday."

Barry waved her away with a smile. "Yeah, yeah, just go back to the barn."

Rachel rolled her eyes and went back outside.

Daniel Sr. watched her approach with a concerned look on his face. "What were you yelling about in there?"

Rachel smiled and said, "The boys are horsing around, so I told them they'd better clean up before they leave."

Daniel Sr. laughed as they mounted their horses and headed for town. The two guilty parties were indeed at that moment setting the kitchen to rights and tidying up so as not to incur the wrath of Rachel again. Barry looked around and, seeing they were almost done, said to Daniel, "I'll finish up, and you go get dressed. I'll go saddle the horses, so just meet me in the barn when you're done."

Daniel went to his room and quickly dressed, so he wouldn't keep his uncle waiting. Barry, not enthused by cleaning on the best of days, swiped a rag over the counter and threw it in the sink, figuring it was good enough by his standards. He put on his boots, grabbed his coat and rifle, and headed out to the barn.

Coming into the kitchen, young Daniel looked around and shook his head with an exasperated sigh at his uncle's so-called cleaning. Knowing his mother wouldn't be impressed with Barry's tidying, he put the dishes in the sink, wiped the table, and gave the counter another once-over before deciding it would do for the time being.

He headed for his coat but then remembered the leftover apple pie and went back to pack it up for him and Barry to enjoy on their trip. He also remembered to bring along the lunch that Rachel had prepared for them earlier.

He headed out to the barn and proceeded to put their lunch in the wagon and saw that Barry was just walking his own horse out of its stall. Barry looked at young Daniel and teased, "What took you so long? Still filling your face in there?"

"No, I was cleaning up. Mom wouldn't have been happy with the way you left it, if you know what I mean," Daniel Jr. stated.

"Truthfully, I do know what you mean. Don't forget that I grew up with her, and she was my sister before she was your mom." Barry chuckled as he was hitching the horse to the wagon. "You know we used to mess the house up on purpose when we were kids because we knew that Mom would make Rachel clean it up. Come to think of it, we did a lot of things to your mom just to get a rise out of her. She was no angel either mind you." Barry smiled. "She would get us all into trouble with our dad, and he would bend us over the water trough and kick us each in the ass. Needless to say, that was our way of having fun, by picking on each other."

Barry finishes securing his rifle inside the wagon and hefted himself up onto the bench seat. "Well, jump up and let's get going."

Daniel Jr. stepped up sitting down beside Barry's horse, and the two rode off in the bright sunshine thinking what a beautiful day it was. As nothing new with the storm, the night before left a blanket of fresh snow, which covered all tracks made the days before buried underneath.

By this time, Rachel and Daniel had already arrived in town and stabled their horses. They walked down the street to their store, and not long after opening, people started coming in. They noticed that most people were just puttering about buying small things and were more interested in gaining information about the shooting than about their purchases. Rachel began to get annoyed and said to Daniel Sr. "I'm going over to Dr. Anderson's office" as she headed for the door.

One of the ladies that frequented the store, Mrs. Whitehead, heard Rachel and stopped her. "The doctor's not at his office right now, he's at Sheriff Rigby's. They moved that fellow your son shot over to the jail so Doc's over their tending him."

"Thanks for letting me know, Mrs. Whitehead, thank you very much," Rachel said graciously and shot a look at Daniel Sr. that said "Oh, here we go."

Mrs. Whitehead clutched at Rachel's arm. "Wait for me, Rachel, I'll just go with you."

Daniel Sr. interrupted to gain the elderly woman's attention. "Is there anything I can get you, Mrs. Whitehead?"

"Oh, well. Yes, please, I'd love some tea, one of those new flavors you brought in, if you don't mind, Daniel," Mrs. Whitehead said as she headed to the counter.

"Sure thing," Daniel said as he put the tea packets in a small paper bag. "Anything else?"

"No, dear, that's fine for now," Mrs. Whitehead answered. "I can come back later for whatever else I was looking for. I just can't seem to remember what it was, but I'm sure it will come to me."

Rachel mumbled under her breath. "I'm sure it will, but the only thing you really came here for was information."

Thankfully, Mrs. Whitehead was hard of hearing and didn't hear Rachel, but Daniel did and subtly shook his head at her to keep her from saying anything else.

"Have a nice day," Daniel said as the older lady turned to leave.

"Thank you, Daniel, you too, bye for now." She gave him a little wave.

"Are you coming, dear? I will walk with you," Mrs. Whitehead said, looking at Rachel.

"Oh! You go ahead, my dear. I just remembered I had to talk to Daniel here about something. You have a nice day."

Once she was out of earshot, Daniel turned to his wife. "Rachel, you have to understand these things are going to happen now. People are going to come in from town, from out of town wherever they've heard the story. We're going to have more people coming in."

"They're nosy . . ." Rachel began.

"Rachel," Daniel sighed, "it's curiosity. They don't mean us any harm. Please try to be patient. It's up to us what we tell people, so we'll only tell people what we're comfortable with, and they'll need to respect that. If you think about what's happening, you will see it will work out to our benefit, as more people coming into the store will increase our business opportunities. It's more important than ever for us to be over helpful and courteous."

Rachel couldn't argue her husband's logic and asked, "Why is it that you always find the good in a bad situation?"

"Well, the way I see it is why stress myself over something I can't control? My father used to say that we can't control the direction of the wind, but we can adjust our sails, so that's what I'm doing, and you should too, honey. Folks are going to look at you differently, that can't be helped, but some of those people are going to be looking at you with respect, and those are the people that matter, the people that knew you even before you knew me," he pointed out.

With a mischievous smile, he said, "But now they *know* not to mess with you Rachel *the wild one*!" He laughed. "So do us both a favor and don't scare all the customers away. Some of them will be coming to try to comfort you as well, as they have children of their own and can't imagine how you must be feeling right now."

"Let's lock up for a few minutes and go see the Doc with you at the sheriff's office," they both stated at the same time, prompting a smile from each of them.

They stepped out onto the boardwalk, and as Daniel turned to lock the door, they noticed a couple of people were crossing the street in their direction.

"Daniel, you open?" one of the two men yelled, accompanied by Mrs. Sweeting just behind them, who was one of Daniel's best customers. She loved to sew and came in every week at least two to three times once, but now her husband has become *ill*, she doesn't make it into town much these days.

"Sorry, folks, can you give us a half hour? We're on our way to see Dr. Anderson over at the sheriff's office," Daniel told them.

"Sure thing, we can come back a bit later, thanks." One of the men tipped his hat, and the two men continued to stroll up the street.

"Daniel?" Mrs Sweeting inquired, "did my order of knitting materials come in last week? I don't get into town very much these days as you know."

"Yes, Shirley. Do you need them right now?" Daniel asked.

"Well, honey, if you don't mind, I need to get back. Leaving the twins with Charlie in his condition, I would like to get back soon as possible."

"Sure, I'll do that for you. How about you just wait here? I will run in and grab them for you."

Daniel went back inside.

"So how are you, Shirley? And how is Charlie doing anyway?" Rachel asked as she always did like her.

"I am doing good but . . . Charlie, he has developed some sort of breathing problem. Doctor doesn't know what it is, so he's not doing much work right now. He has a lineup of wagons to fix but is always running out of breath when he gets started. Doc is trying new medication thinking it may help."

"And the twins! They are in good health, are they?"

"Warren and Wendy. They're definitely a handful but in good health . . . ," Mrs. Sweeting replied.

"You decide to have any more kids, you going to have a handful in no time, especially if you have another set of twins." Rachel laughed.

Daniel emerged from the store.

"Here you go, Shirley. I just put that on Charlie's bill."

"Thank you, Daniel. Nice to talk to you again, Rachel," Mrs. Sweeting said with a smile and a nod of her head as she turned to cross the street.

"Nice lady, she is," Rachel commented as Daniel agreed. "One of best customers, especially Charlie always in looking for new gadgets he can use to alter or fix his wagons."

Daniel and Rachel proceeded on to the sheriff's office and walked in.

Dr. Anderson looked up at the sound of the door opening. "Well, this is a bit of a surprise. I didn't think you'd be here so soon."

"We weren't going to be here till a bit later," Rachel said. "But we wanted to talk to you and get things sorted out sooner rather than later."

The doctor nodded in understanding at the couple's anxiousness.

"So how is Tim doing?" she asked.

"He'll live," Doc answered. "But he may not have complete use of his left arm for the better part of a year or longer. The bullet went through his left arm and then entered his chest. If not for it hitting bone first, I wouldn't be attending to him right now."

"Is he awake?" Daniel asked.

"No, I gave him enough pain medication to keep him asleep for at least another three hours," Dr. Anderson advised them.

"Good, that give us a chance to talk without Tim hearing us," Daniel Sr. said as he pulled up a couple of chairs for him and Rachel to sit in.

"We've thought this over, and we've decided not to charge Tim," Rachel said in a rush before she could change her mind.

Doc raised his eyebrows in surprise as did the sheriff who's listening on. "He robbed your store and held your son as a hostage and tried to kill you. Two to three years in jail wouldn't hurt him none," Doc Anderson replied.

Rachel said, "Two to three years isn't very long, and we don't think it's worth the possible repercussions to our family. We believe that being wounded is enough of a lesson."

"What's done is done," Daniel affirmed. "How long before he'll be well? Capable of movement, I mean."

"Probably about a week," the doctor replied.

"Okay, we'll cover his medical costs like we said before, and we'd like to be notified when he wakes up," Daniel stated.

"I'm not too sure I can allow that, Daniel," Sheriff Rigby finally spoke from his desk in the corner.

"He's still a prisoner, and he committed a crime in this town. Whether you press charges or not, he still has to answer to his actions, or I'll have every criminal sniffing around, robbing stores, and causing havoc thinking they'll just get away with it," Sheriff Rigby pointed out. "Your store could even get hit again, Daniel, and if Tim here doesn't try it again himself, someone else will."

Rachel leaned forward in her chair and suggested, "Then charge him with breaking in the store, as you said yourself, he didn't leave with anything he didn't pay for."

Shaking his head, Sheriff Rigby reminded her. "That's because we carried him out."

"Whatever," Rachel cut in impatiently. "Charging him could cause us more problems, so can we please agree to just charge him with trespassing and let the rest go?"

"Fine." Sheriff Rigby conceded and then added, "And on top of that, he is not allowed back in this town *ever*. If I ever see him within the town limits, I will prosecute him for robbery."

Rachel and Daniel nodded in agreement. "So be it, and thank you. Will you please tell us when he wakes up then?"

Doc Anderson glanced at the sheriff and then replied, "Yes, I'll send word when he's conscious."

Daniel reached into his inside coat pocket and pulled out a pouch of gold dust and handed it to the doctor. "Here, this should more than cover all the medical costs for Mr. McNabb and leave you a little something extra for yourself."

Daniel then addressed Sheriff Rigby. "We'd like to give you a gift as well. Come on over to the store when you have time and pick out your choice of any rifle I've got in stock."

"You don't have to do that, Daniel," Sheriff Rigby said quietly.

"There's a lot I don't *need* to do, but I would *like* to do it, is that okay?" Daniel persisted.

"Yeah, sure thing, Daniel, thanks," the sheriff acknowledged. "By the way, all your firearms are here locked up in the back."

"Oh, that's right too. Well, just pick one out for yourself, and I'll take the rest back to the store," Daniel instructed.

"Well, I do like that Winchester lever-action repeating rifle you brought in a few months back," Sheriff Rigby admitted sheepishly. "May I?"

"Absolutely, it's yours," Daniel promised.

Remembering another commitment to the sheriff, Daniel said, "Can you send the blacksmith over to the store if you see him? I want to go over some plans with him to build me a cage to store the guns in more securely."

"I sure will," the sheriff responded. "He'll build a perfect storage cage for you. He built all the ones here in the office as well and did a great job."

Daniel nodded, "Our thanks to you both again."

He and Rachel stood up and left the office to return to the store. As they walked, Rachel rolled her eyes at Daniel and said sarcastically, "Why don't you just buy the whole town a rifle? What was that all about anyway?"

"Actually, it's business," he explained. "His service anniversary is coming, and the town was going to buy him either a rifle or a pocket watch. The pocket watch is worth more than a rifle being it's made of almost pure gold. So now that I've given him the rifle, the town can spend the money to get the watch," he said with a wink. "Besides, he's a good guy and deserves both."

Rachel smiled, feeling foolish for doubting her husband's business savvy. "I guess that's why I deal with horses, and you run the business." She looked thoughtful. "You should become a lawyer."

Daniel laughed. "No time for that, and to be honest, Rachel, I have enough problems reading as it is, I can barely make it through the newspaper when it comes."

Rachel was surprised. "Are you telling me the truth, Daniel?"

"Yes," he admitted, looking embarrassed. "I hide it well, but I can only read and write very basic words and sentences. Not enough to become a lawyer that's for sure."

Rachel patted his arm and said, "Well, I guess your son will have to give you some lessons."

Daniel looked at her sharply. "My son doesn't need to know."

Rachel sighed. "You're too proud."

"No, I just don't want him to think that he can get by in life without a decent education, Rachel. I was lucky, but it doesn't work out that way for everyone," Daniel said.

"He only has one year left of school, honey, he's turning thirteen soon, and his grades are outstanding." Rachel tried to reassure him.

"But what happens in one year when he's done?" Daniel asked.

"Well then, we'll send him to some college or finishing school, and he can be a lawyer if he wants, but the bottom line is he needs to further his education." She was adamant.

"Maybe we should sit down and talk to him and see what he wants to do," Rachel suggested.

"I agree. We should do that," Daniel said as he unlocked the door to the store. They stepped in and shut the door behind themselves, but it didn't stay closed for long. As Daniel had predicted, people were in and out all morning long. Rachel followed Daniel's earlier advice and bit her tongue and did her very best to be cheery and helpful, and it wasn't long before conversations turned toward the robbery.

The general consensus without a doubt painted Daniel Jr. as a hero who had saved his father's life, which pleased his parents immensely.

At this time, Daniel Jr. and Barry were almost at Barry's house, which was a beautiful three-bedroom log house. The barn was a large dwelling that didn't house any large animals such as milk cows or horses, only a few cats and a pregnant dog. The rest of the space contained two good-sized wagons as well as all the brothers' working tools, saws, and other carpentry items.

Sectioned off in another room were various trapping equipment—beaver and rabbit snares, steel bear traps—and piled on a work table were fur pelts from cougars, grizzly and black bears, and a wolf as well.

As they approached the homestead, Daniel looked around to take it all in as they directed their horses to the barn. They dismounted and tethered their horses and entered the barn.

"Can I look around?" Daniel asked.

"Sure," his uncle answered. "Just don't touch any of the equipment, or your mom will have my hide if you accidently get hurt and lose a finger or two."

Daniel walked around and found the room with all the traps and furs and became quite amused with the bearskins. He looked at his uncle and asked, "Did you shoot all these animals?"

"No, only a few are mine. I did the black bear and one of the cougars," Barry said.

"The grizzly is one your uncle Allan shot while he was building a cabin just north of here, and the other wolf your uncle Chuck took down with just his knife and has plenty of scars on his arm to show for that little fiasco."

"No way," exclaimed Daniel.

"Yup, your grandfather liked to hunt mostly for food, but now we hunt for both food and necessity. That's one thing he did pass on to us boys. Cattle in this area are prey to these beautiful creatures, and it's very costly for a rancher to lose a cow to a pack of wolves on a regular basis, so when we spot one around any of the grazing pastures, we take them down."

Noticing that Daniel couldn't take his eyes off the wolf pelt, Barry said, "You like that wolf, do you?"

"Yeah," Daniel answered.

"Well, tell you what, it's not mine to give you, but if you like, I got something over here you may like just as much," Barry said, leading Daniel over to a tarp that was covering a large object.

Barry whipped the cover off and underneath was a bobcat lynx mounted on a log, posed to look like it was about to leap off. Daniel took a step back, eyes wide as he looked at the lynx. "Whoa, Jesus, it looks like he's still alive, Barry, that's awesome!"

Barry chuckled at Daniel's enthusiasm. "Then it's yours on one condition, don't ever use the Lord's name in vain again, as there's no need to address the Lord. He is quite aware of this animal. If you're saying Jesus, you had best be praying, got it?"

"Sorry," Daniel said abashedly.

"That's okay, just show some respect for your elders as Jesus is an elder. Not living but in spirit he is."

"My elder?" Daniel said in confusion.

"Sure, no matter what one person or one church says about how we got here, I personally believe we started from two people, one man and one woman. You can do the math from there, we are all related and one big family," Barry explained. "Others may believe differently, but I believe in God and Jesus and that Jesus is no different than you or I, just no longer in a living body as we are today.

"Just the same for years to come, the stories of God, Jesus, Mary, and all the disciples will change with what people believe and how they interpret it in their own minds, and people will always fight for their beliefs. That's why there's always fighting between the white man and the natives, but believe it or not, I see them as family. They are like brothers or cousins who speak a different language. Jesus spoke a different language than we do today, but we don't fight him, so why do we fight against the Indians?"

"Why are we fighting them, Uncle?" Daniel asked.

Barry shook his head. "That's a good question, Daniel, and this is just what I believe. You'll make your own opinions when you're older. It's a fact that our population is getting larger and larger, and more people means we need more land. A lot of that land belongs to the Indians, and they're being forced off of their lands and sometimes killed in order for the white man to have it. They need to realize, though, that the Indians need that land for their people to build on and survive.

"When one side started killing people on the other side, the fighting escalated to where it is now, and both sides are enemies. They're going to keep fighting until both sides come to their senses. Now the white man are rounding up more men to fight the Indians, but don't worry, Danny boy, you're too young to be enlisted, but if I were you, when that day comes, I'd stay out of it if you can.

"Just look out for yourself. As for your father and myself, we're too old now, and they don't want us as soldiers. But if you have no choice and you have to fight, then your first priority is your own life because they won't hesitate to kill you given the chance," he said grimly.

"Anyway, those are my beliefs, not anyone else's. So in life, young Daniel, fight for what *you* believe in, and that doesn't always mean physically fighting but, rather, standing up for your beliefs."

Barry patted Daniel on the back. "So we have a deal on the lynx?"

"Yes, we do," Daniel agreed.

"Then give me a hand, and we'll load him up," Barry said, reaching for one end of the log. Daniel quickly grabbed the other end and, between the two of them, got it out to the wagon and put the tarp back over it.

Barry then put their two horses in the corral so they'd be out of the way while they were loading the supplies. They put all the tools in the front of the wagon and all the wood planks in the back until there was no more room in the wagon.

"Grab the lunch your mom packed and come on into the house, I'm hungry," Barry said as he headed toward the steps.

"Sure," Daniel said and retrieved the lunch from his saddlebag and ran to catch up with his uncle.

Daniel took a really close look at his uncle's house and fell in love with the look of the building. "It really is beautiful, Uncle Barry."

His uncle smiled. "Glad you like it."

As Junior walked in and took a look around the inside, he noticed right away that it was not the cleanest place he had ever seen. In fact, it was worse than his bedroom got at times. But dirt aside, all the woodwork that graced the cabin was incredible, and Daniel was in awe of its workmanship.

"Did you make everything in here?" Daniel asked.

"Well, not by myself. But yes, Allan, Chuck, and I made everything you see by hand," Barry said proudly.

"Wow, do you think you could teach me how to work with wood?" Daniel asked hopefully.

"Yes, I can," Barry assured him. "We're going to start soon. In fact, that's why we're here getting all my tools and wood."

"Oh yeah, right, but I meant show me how to do all the carvings like over on that chair back and on the arms."

"Well, that's your Uncle Allan's doing, but I can show you how to use all the tools for now," Barry said.

"That would be great," Daniel said enthusiastically.

"Okay, enough gabbing, let's eat," Barry said, grabbing some plates from the cupboard.

They sat down to eat and polished off the lunch quickly as they were both hungry from the ride and from loading the wagon. Giving the dishes a quick rinse and grabbing a few final supplies, they hitched up the wagon to the two horses that had been in the corral, and the horses they had ridden in on were tied to the back of the wagon so they could follow and were ready to head back.

"You're a smart kid, Daniel, I've got to hand it to you." Barry observed and then gave the horses a gentle slap with the reins. "Hyah!" And they headed back to town.

Back in town, Dan Beard, the blacksmith, had stopped by Daniel Sr.'s store. He looked around at all the goods and tipped his hat to Daniel. "I hear you need a gun cabinet built."

"Yes, I do, and Sheriff Rigby said you built the gun cage at his office and that you do really good work," Daniel acknowledged.

The two men went over some design ideas and where the ideal place would be to put it and settled on a fair price when Dan Beard said "Oh, by the way, the sheriff told me to tell you that the guy who robbed you yesterday is awake now."

"Thanks for telling me. How long will it take for you to have the cage ready?" Daniel asked.

"I can have it for you in a week, maybe sooner," the blacksmith advised.

Daniel nodded. "Thanks, a week will be fine."

The two men shook hands, and Mr. Beard tipped his hat to Rachel and shook Daniel's hand before he left the store.

Daniel looked at Rachel. "Well, you ready to go see Tim?"

"No," she said, looking down at the floor. "Do you think you can handle it, and I'll watch the store? I just don't think I'll be able to keep my head together."

"Sure, I'll go," he said as he leaned over and placed a kiss on her cheek. "See you in a while."

"Wait." She grabbed his sleeve. "I've changed my mind, and I'm coming with you. Sorry."

Daniel blew out a frustrated breath and rolled his eyes. "Okay then, let's get going."

"I just have to grab my coat," she said as she went to the back room.

They walked to the door and flipped the door sign to read Will Be Back Shortly and locked the door behind them. In a few moments, they were walking into the sheriff's office. Sheriff Rigby looked up from his desk at the couple as they entered. "Hello, Rachel, Daniel. I didn't think it would take you long to come over. Just so you know, I haven't said anything to him," he said as he stood up and took his keys off the hook. "He's in the back. I'll take you to him."

Daniel and Rachel followed the sheriff to the first set of doors and waited anxiously for him to unlock them. They proceeded past a row of cells to another door where the sheriff stopped and announced, "Tim, you have visitors."

Tim was lying flat on his back, staring at the ceiling while Daniel and Rachel stood looking at him through the steel bars. Tim glanced toward the door, and his eyes widened at the sight of the couple standing outside his door. "What's going on here?" Tim demanded.

"Shut up, Tim," Sheriff Rigby ordered and then motioned to Daniel. "There are two chairs over there if you want to grab them so you two can sit down outside his cell while you talk. That would probably be best."

Rachel shook her head and implored the sheriff. "We need to go in there. We need to look straight in his eyes to make sure he understands this arrangement."

"What arrangement?" Tim tried to yell and sit up but fell back due to the pain.

Sheriff Rigby was losing patience. "Shut up in there, or I'll come in there and finish the job!" he yelled back as he looked at Rachel and Daniel, hesitating on their request to open the door. But finally, he muttered "Well, I guess he can't really go anywhere in the condition he's in" as he unlocked the door.

The sheriff addressed the couple and said, "But I will be taking any guns you have on you."

"We're not carrying any, Sheriff," Daniel assured him.

"Okay then." He opened the door and gestured for Daniel and Rachel to go in and said "I'll just be in the other room if you need me" and walked away.

Rachel stood aside as Daniel grabbed the two chairs and brought them into the cell and placed them across from the bed where Tim lay. Daniel proceeded to sit down and looked at Rachel. "Are you coming over here, or are you going to stand over there?"

"No, I'm coming over there," she said from where she was standing with one shoulder leaning against the cell door and proceeded over to the empty chair beside her husband and sat down.

Tim eyed them both suspiciously. "So tell me why you're in my cell, to scorn me? I think the judge will do that, so why don't you two just leave?"

"Listen for a minute," Daniel began, "there isn't going to be a judge in this case."

"What are you saying? Are you going to take me out back and shoot me?" Tim demanded.

"It's crossed my mind," Rachel replied seriously. "But no. We've talked to the sheriff, and you're facing two to three years in jail. We're willing to drop the charges from robbery to trespassing. Once you're healthy, probably ten days from now according to the doctor, you have to leave town. According to the sheriff, you will not be welcome here ever again, and if he catches you here, then he will proceed to charge you with robbery."

"You're kidding me, right?" Tim asked incredulously.

"No," Daniel replied. "We're not. We are peaceful people, and we don't wish to be looking over our shoulders wondering when revenge is coming our way from your family while you're in jail. Truth be told, we will be securing the store better to try to ensure that no one else attempts this kind of thing again."

Still stunned, Tim inquired, "What about the other two men that were with me?"

Both Rachel and Daniel looked at each other as they had assumed he already knew what had happened.

Daniel quickly replied, "They're both dead. I'm sorry, I thought you knew."

"No," Tim shook his head. "But I didn't know them that well anyway. I only just met them."

Tim asked for clarification. "So you're telling me that I'm free to go?"

They both nodded. "As soon as you're capable, if you agree to this arrangement."

"Well, I really don't know what to say. I mean, yes, of course, but I'm just . . . I don't really know why . . . well, I guess I do, but you two are something else," he said in shock, amazed at his good fortune. "I accept, and thank you." Tim nodded his appreciation.

"Okay, now the doctor tending you will continue to do so until you're ready to leave, and then you'll be on your own, you understand?" Daniel explained.

Tim nodded. "Well, I hope he doesn't charge a lot because I don't have anything to pay him with except maybe my horse in trade."

Daniel and Rachel were secretly impressed that Tim was honest enough to even think of trading in his horse to pay for his treatment, but Daniel stopped him. "No, you keep your horse, you'll need it. Dr. Anderson has already been paid for your care, and we'll continue to pay the bills until you leave town. We also took your horse to our farm to care for it until you're able to travel. We'll bring him in to you when the doc and Sheriff Rigby clear you to leave."

Tim was completely dumbfounded. "You're covering my doctor's bill, you're taking care of my horse, *and* you're dropping the charges and all this so I will leave town and not return? I think the punishment is me not returning, this town is nuts. I'm feeling very guilty for what happened."

"As you should," Rachel stated boldly. "So we have a deal?"

Tim had already accepted, but with the new information about his horse and bills, he wanted to make sure he was clear. "Yes, absolutely."

"There's one other thing we want from you," Daniel said. "Our son, Daniel, has been asking to see you. It's important for him to know that you're okay."

Tim tensed. "Your son that shot me?"

"Yes, he's the only son we have. If you don't want to see him, that's okay, but as you can probably surmise due to his age, he has never shot a man before, and it's been very upsetting for him."

Tim was feeling generous. "Sure, send him in. I'll be glad to see him."

"He's out of town for another two to three hours, but maybe later this afternoon, we'll bring him by if you feel up to it," Daniel offered.

"I'll feel up to it, you just bring him by whenever you can. For what it's worth I'm sorry, really sorry for what happened," Tim admitted.

"That's all I needed to hear," Rachel said and added as an afterthought. "Do you know who I am?"

"Besides Daniel here's wife?" Tim replied.

"My name is Donna Davidson, but people call me Rachel. My brothers and I grew up not that far from you," Rachel informed him.

Tim looked thoughtful. "Your brother, is his name Barry?"

"Yes, it is," Rachel said.

"He used to hang around my older brother. I met him a few times though." Tim recalled.

"Well, you're going to meet him again because he's coming into town with Daniel Jr. this afternoon, and I'm pretty sure he wants to talk to you," Rachel said with a hint of warning in her voice.

"Is that right," Tim replied. "Well, maybe you should keep that door locked then."

"I don't believe he's going to retaliate in this case, but I'm sure he would if the situation was different. So you get some rest." Daniel and Rachel stood up to leave.

"Hey," Tim said. "Again, thank you. Can you send the doc back in? And if it's okay with you, can he give me more stuff to help with the pain? I'd really appreciate it."

Rachel nodded. "We can do that, get some rest."

Daniel and Rachel walked out and found Dr. Anderson waiting on the front porch talking with Sheriff Rigby.

Sheriff Rigby looked up at the couple. "How'd it go?"

"It went really well. He accepted our terms and seems very thankful. I think we hit a few nerves, and he is genuinely remorseful, which is enough for us," Rachel said.

"Just to let you know, a reporter came in here asking questions, but we didn't say anything at this time," the sheriff advised. "But they're hanging out around your store, and there's more than one, just so you know."

"What do you want us to say if they come back?" Sheriff Rigby asked.

"Better leave that up to Daniel," Rachel decided, figuring her husband would have more patience than she would.

"Well, Daniel?" They looked at him in askance.

"Okay, this is what we'll do," he said as he walked to the steps and whistled sharply in the direction of his store where he saw three men loitering outside the shops door. The men looked quickly in his direction, and Daniel motioned them over with his hand. Hoping for a good scoop for their headlines, the men ran over eagerly to where Daniel was standing. He invited them into the sheriff's office to talk; they all walked in followed by the sheriff and Dr. Anderson.

One of the men blurted out, "Can you tell us what happened?"

Daniel replied dryly, "Well, if we don't, you might not get the right story."

He continued. "Yesterday, an attempt was made to rob my store by four men. They were looking for firearms. Hold on, let me rephrase that, three men died attempting to rob my store."

Another reporter interrupted. "And two of those men were shot by your wife, right?"

"That is correct," Daniel affirmed.

They quickly turned their attention to Rachel. "Rachel, tell us, how does it feel to be the woman who shot those two men?"

She looked at the reporter solemnly. "It doesn't feel very good, but I did what I felt I had to do with my family being threatened. I was brought up by my brothers and can handle a gun as well as any man. Believe it or not, women can do more than cook your dinner."

Seeing that Rachel was getting agitated, the reporter backed down and said, "Sorry, ma'am, the question wasn't meant to upset you or infer that women weren't as capable as men."

Rachel nodded, acknowledging his apology and continued, "In my family, we work together, we cook, clean, and do the chores equally, although some of us may cook better," she said with a smile at her husband. "It's about time men started respecting that. There is no reason why a woman can't have or learn to handle a gun for self-protection. All you men out there can't be around us all the time, can you? So why shouldn't we be able to defend our homes, or our family, and ourselves?"

She wagged a finger at the reporters and warned. "But don't be writing stories on why a woman should or shouldn't have a gun. Those are my opinions and have nothing to do with yesterday's incident, all right?"

"No, ma'am." The reporters nodded their agreement.

"However," Rachel added, "I would be willing to teach any woman that wanted to learn for the purpose of self-defense only. Lucky for me that my husband, Daniel, and I have the same beliefs, which is part of the reason I married him."

"What about your son?" one of the reporters asked. "Does he have the right to carry a gun too?"

Rachel nodded. "If he's old enough to shoot one, then he's old enough to carry one. We were lucky yesterday that he had access to a gun when we were being robbed."

"So he did shoot Tim McNabb then?" one of the men asked.

Daniel stepped up and stated, "Tim McNabb was shot, that is true. And yes, by my son as well. One by myself. Both were shot inside the store. The other two men were accomplices as Tim was the leader of the group. Those two men started firing wildly in the store and ran out empty-handed. At that time, they were asked to drop their guns, which they failed to do and turned their guns on my wife and her brother. Rachel was forced to fire on them in order to protect herself and her brother."

Daniel continued. "As my wife mentioned already, she was raised with three brothers and fortunately was taught well. Before you ask, Tim McNabb is being charged with trespassing."

"What about robbery?" one of the reporters asked in confusion.

Another reporter chimed in. "I heard he held a knife to your son's throat."

"Listen," Daniel cut in impatiently, "you're going to hear a lot of things and a lot of exaggerations. Like Rachel killed four men single-handedly in a gun draw in the middle of the street at high noon. Come on, fellows, I hope you're smarter than that. Tim had no knife, and he did not leave my store with anything that he didn't come into it with. We see no reason to push this issue any farther," Daniel finished.

The sheriff then added his two cents. "Tim will serve ten days in jail for breaking into the store, which is the standard punishment."

Daniel cut in. "And we, as the victims, are content with the punishment Sheriff Rigby has meted out."

He put his arm around Rachel and said, "Thank you for your time, we have nothing more to say. So if you will excuse us, gentlemen, we need to get back to the store. We also need a moment to speak with the doctor if you don't mind." And he opened the door and indicated they should take their leave.

The men thanked them for their time, walked out the door with Daniel firmly closed behind them.

The sheriff patted Daniel on the back. "Well done, Daniel, well done. I'm impressed."

"So am I," Tim yelled from his cell in the back.

Sheriff Rigby rolled his eyes. "Shut your trap back there!"

Dr. Anderson smothered a laugh, which caught Daniel's attention. "By the way, Doc, I almost forgot, but can you give Tim some more pain medication, please? He was asking for some earlier."

"Sure thing, you're the one paying for it," Doc Anderson agreed quickly.

Turning to the sheriff, Rachel said, "My son may come by later. If he does, please let him go back to see Tim. Barry will be with him, so it'll be all right, and Tim knows he's coming."

Daniel and Rachel left the sheriff's office, and the doctor shut the door behind them.

Sheriff Rigby walked Dr. Anderson to Tim's cell and opened the door. The sheriff shook his head at Tim and said, "You know, Tim, you are one lucky man."

Tim looked up and nodded. "Yeah, I see that now."

"Just don't be causing any more trouble while you're here," the sheriff warned.

"Honestly, Sheriff, I was wrong, and whether you believe me or not, I am sorry for the commotion I caused here in your town."

The sheriff just turned his back and left as the doctor started getting his supplies ready. "Don't worry, he'll come around," Dr. Anderson said, referring to the sheriff's brush-off.

Tim watched the doctor pull out ointment and strips of cloth and said, "Hey, tell me about this kid Daniel."

The doctor looked thoughtful. "Daniel? He's a good kid. He's a born caregiver that's for sure. He's thinking of becoming a doctor someday."

"Really?" Tim asked a bit sarcastically. "But yet he managed to shoot me."

Doc chuckled at his patient's disgruntled tone. "The last we spoke, he was indeed interested. Now roll over on your side very carefully, I need to have a look at your wound and change your bandage."

With a grunt and much discomfort, Tim managed to turn over onto his right side with assistance from the doctor.

"So the kid wants to be a doctor," Tim continued, trying to distract himself from the pain. "Whoa easy, Doc!"

"We need to get more ointment around the bullet hole. Sorry, but the gauze is sticking to the dried blood," the doctor informed him as he continued to tend the wound.

"So how old is Daniel?" Tim hissed as the doctor hit a particularly sensitive area.

"He's twelve years old and very smart lad," Dr. Anderson said. "You know, Tim, I hope you realize what the McDougalls did by dropping the charges and reducing them to breaking in as well as standing up and lying to the press on your behalf."

Tim scratched his head. "Well, that's what I don't understand. Help me out, Doc. Why did he tell the press that there was no knife? You got any ideas?"

"Tim, you robbed their store by force and threatened the life of their child. If the press found out the truth, it would just invite other bad elements into town to rob every store thinking they would just get a slap on the wrist and be set free," the doc explained.

"The way Daniel explained it, it didn't sound so bad, and it shows that your intentions weren't honorable but that you didn't actually succeed in the robbery, which makes it easier for the public to accept. It was the only way to set you free and hope they wouldn't face retaliation from your family either."

Tim pondered this. "Smart, I guess. I can see his reasoning now. Maybe it's not too bad having a family of criminals."

Doc snorted at Tim's revelation. "The McDougalls are a good family, and Daniel is a very smart, fair, and well-respected businessman around here."

"I can see why," Tim said.

"Okay, take a big breath on the count of three as I need to get the rest of this packing off the wound. One, two, and three . . . big breath . . . hold it . . . ," the doc said as he pulled the rest of the soiled gauze away.

"Oh. Doc, my god," Tim hollered.

"Easy does it, just give me a second and keep taking deep breaths," Doc said as he quickly cleaned the wound, covered it with ointment, and placed fresh bandaging over it.

"Damn it, Doc, are you trying to help me or inflict more injury?" Tim yelped. "Damn, that hurt."

Doc rolled his eyes. "It's not like you haven't been shot before, Tim, and I can see other bullet scars, so you've been shot at least two other times."

"Yeah, many years ago, and it was a lot more painful when all I had was whiskey to dull the pain. Speaking of which, can you give me some more of that pain medication now?"

"Yes, I spoke with Daniel, and he mentioned that I was to give you a little more when I came in," Doc said. "Again, you are very lucky. Rachel sent her brother Barry to the next town yesterday to buy more supplies, including pain medication, as we were running low here. We definitely wouldn't have had enough for you, but Daniel paid for enough to stock my shelves for the next three months, so I can give you a little extra when you need it," Dr. Anderson told him.

The doctor handed him a small tin cup. "Here, drink this." Taking back the cup and packing up his bag, he said, "Okay, we're done here. You're going to get sleepy pretty quick, so don't fight it."

"Hey, Doc," Tim said, "thank you, and you have my apologies as well."

Doc nodded. "No problem, Tim, rest."

He shut the cell door behind him and proceeded down the hall and knocked on the main door, and Sheriff Rigby opened it and passed the doctor to go and lock Tim's door and came back and locked the main door as well.

"Okay, Don," the doctor said to the sheriff. "I'll come back in about four hours, but in the meantime, I'll arrange for some food to be prepared for him at the hotel, and I'll bring it with me later."

"Sounds good, enjoy the rest of your day," Sheriff Rigby walked him out.

By this time, Barry and Daniel had purchased the extra maple wood Barry needed for the loft project from one of his friends who ran the local lumber mill. Having everything they needed, they started back on the final leg of their trip. Looking up, Barry noticed that a few snowflakes had begun to fall, and he reached behind the wagon seat and pulled out a bottle of whiskey. Pulling the cork out with his teeth, he took a draw and offered it to Daniel.

"Here, have a swig. It'll warm you up," Barry said.

Daniel grasped the bottle, studied the thought, then . . . "Thanks anyway, Uncle, I'll pass." He remembered his mother's words that alcohol is not good, especially for someone of his age.

"I am only offering it as its cold out here, it will warm you up."

"I appreciate that, but I'm not that cold. Must be your age, Uncle, that is why you're cold. I would think all that fat on your belly would keep you warm, *chubby*!" Daniel said, laughing.

"Hey, what did I say about that? You do know no one is here with you to protect you," Barry said with a mischievous smile.

"Listen, when we get back, maybe we'll go directly to your dad's store and find out what's happening with everything," Barry suggested.

"You know, Uncle Barry, I really don't think that Mom should worry so much about me. I really don't feel much different than I normally do," Daniel stated.

"The worry here is about Tim and his family members. They're quite a wild bunch, and even though Tim was in the wrong, they could retaliate against your folks or even you. I do know Tim's older brother, and I would say but we're more acquaintances than friends. They were too wild even for me, but I haven't seen Billy in ten to twelve years," Barry explained as he took another swig of whiskey.

"Last chance," he said as he offered the bottle to Daniel.

"*No*, thank you." Daniel once again refused.

"You know, Daniel, I am very impressed with you. There is nothing wrong in saying *no*. Besides, I was just testing you to see how strong your willpower is," Barry replied with a smile and a wink.

Daniel looked at his uncle and with a smile said "Yeah, okay!" and winked back.

Daniel did not believe that at all.

"I understand the respect you have for your mom, and it's a good thing. Truthfully, our father would get drunk and beat up our mom, and when we tried to interfere, we got it just as bad. He drank himself to death. He wasn't a very likable man, and he just couldn't stop. But that's enough said, you don't need to hear any more about it."

All of a sudden, Barry yelled "Whoooo there!" as he pulled back on the reins, slowing the wagon to a slow pace. "The right wheel seems to be grabbing. Daniel! Lean over and tell me if that axle is sticking or coming loose. Something's not right here."

Daniel carefully stood up and then kneeled toward the floorboards and leaned out to get a better look at the wheel. "It seems fine," he replied.

Just then, Barry lifted his foot and shoved it hard against Daniel's backside and pushed him off the wagon directly into an approaching snowbank.

Covered in snow and sputtering in shock, Daniel rolled over and pushed himself up out of the snow while Barry brought the wagon to a stop.

"What the—"

"NOW! NOW!" Barry quickly interrupted.

"What did you do that for?" Daniel demanded.

Barry was laughing hysterically and couldn't even speak as Daniel grumbled "It's already cold enough out here."

Daniel stood and brushed his clothes off the best he could when Barry finally found his voice and looked Daniel straight in the eye. "That'll teach you for calling me chubby!"

Daniel's mouth dropped open before he too burst out laughing and said, "You know what, Uncle? You just started a war between us. So I hope you sleep with one eye open as I will get even with you."

Barry held out his hand and pulled Daniel back up into the wagon. As Daniel got settled, he noticed that his uncle still had big grin on his face.

"Yeah, keep smiling. You just wait. Now where's that bottle of whiskey? I'm freezing."

"Sorry, lad, you're too young to drink this stuff, didn't your mother teach you anything?" Barry said, laughing.

"She did actually, I was just going to rinse my mouth with it. So when I get back, I'm going to give Mom a big hug and kiss so she can smell this crap on my breath."

Barry grinned and said, "Yeah, you do that!"

"I'm just kidding." Daniel gave his uncle the wink. "But just you wait, your turn's coming."

Barry nodded. "I'll be waiting, lad," he said as he snapped the reins, setting the wagon in motion and jolting Daniel in his seat.

They continued to ride in silence, each happily plotting their next move in their little war and were soon pulling into town. Daniel noticed that school had already been let out when he saw a couple of girls wave and call out "Hi, Daniel!" from across the street.

"Hi, Victoria, hey, Elisabeth. How are you?" Daniel responded as they drove slowly by.

"Fine," the girl named Victoria replied quickly with a smile.

Barry turned to Daniel. "I thought that you weren't into girls yet."

"Doesn't mean I don't talk to them or be polite," Daniel answered.

"That Victoria there is a good-looking girl," Barry noticed, watching for a reaction from Daniel.

"She is," he agreed. "You should see her in the summertime when we all get together and go swimming. She is definitely good-looking."

"I think she likes you," Barry said.

"Yeah, well, her dad doesn't," Daniel pointed out.

"Not many fathers would approve of their daughters having boys as friends, but if you like her, don't let that stop you," Barry advised.

Daniel nodded. "In time, in time."

They pulled up in front of the store, and Barry pulled the wagon to a stop as Daniel jumped down onto the snow-covered street. Barry also stepped off the wagon and walked over to Daniel as they went into the store together.

Rachel looked up from the counter and smiled mischievously at her son. "Daniel, there were two girls here a few minutes ago looking for you."

Daniel rolled his eyes at his mother. "Yeah, it was probably Victoria and Elisabeth."

She nodded. "It was, how did you know that when I didn't even tell you what they looked like?"

"We just saw them down the street when we drove in," Daniel said.

"They dropped off some homework for you," Rachel told him, indicating a book and some papers on the counter.

"So what's happening with Tim, sis?" Barry asked, eager to hear what had transpired.

She looked at her brother and smiled.

"Everything's fine. The sheriff just charged him with breaking into the store, so Tim is going to be serving ten to fourteen days in jail or until he recovers enough to travel, then he has to leave town. If he ever comes back, then the sheriff is reserving the right to charge him with robbery."

Barry nodded as Rachel continued. "He also agreed to see Daniel Jr."

She looked at her son. "Do you still want to see him?"

"I don't know," Daniel said slowly.

"Well, I'm going over," Barry replied.

"Okay, I'll go with you," Daniel Jr. said, feeling more assured that his uncle would be there with him.

Barry took off his gun belt and motioned Daniel Jr. to do the same. They handed them to Daniel Sr. who had just come in from the back room.

"Best we leave these here," Barry said as he looked at Daniel Senior.

Daniel Sr. agreed, putting the fire arms behind the counter.

Both Barry and Daniel left the store and walked over to Sheriff Rigby's office. As they entered, the sheriff greeted them. "Hey, Barry, Daniel, you come to see Tim?"

"Yes, we did," Barry responded.

"Leave your guns with me, please," the sheriff instructed.

Barry moved his coat out of the way so the sheriff could see he wasn't armed. "We left our guns at the store."

Sheriff Rigby stood up and grabbed his keys. "Here, I'll show you to his cell." He opened the main door and proceeded to lead them to Tim.

"There you go. Tim, wake up, you have company."

Tim slowly opened his eyes and tensed his body to try and stretch a little and noticed that Barry and Daniel were standing there. He immediately addressed the older man. "Barry, I'm sorry, I didn't know it was your sister's store."

Barry countered. "Would it have stopped you even if you knew?"

"I don't know. I was pretty deep in the drink, so I wasn't thinking clearly, but I'm real glad that they weren't hurt."

"Me too," Barry agreed. "I guess you've met my nephew."

Tim glanced at Daniel and said with a small chuckle, "Yes, we were acquainted yesterday."

"How are you doing?" Daniel finally spoke up.

"Well, I should be up and around in a week, maybe two according to the doc. I'm in a lot of pain. but I deserve what I got plus more, so I'm very grateful to your mother and father."

"Well, I'm glad you're going to be okay," Daniel said solemnly.

Tim nodded. "Hey, son, I'm sorry for what happened—"

Daniel cut him off in a burst of anger. "I am not your son!"

"Hey, ease up there, cowboy," Barry interrupted, putting a hand on Daniel's shoulder.

"No, that's okay, Barry, let him speak," Tim said.

Daniel continued. "I won't apologize to you for what I said or for putting that bullet in your side either."

"I don't expect you to," Tim replied.

"Truthfully, I never wanted to cause harm to any living thing, but yesterday, you sort of changed that. I realized that there are some bad apples around, and I really hope that I don't run into anybody like you again."

"Well, Daniel, there aren't a lot of people like me. I'm taking this opportunity to change some of my ways. That may not mean anything to you, but it does to me, and I have the utmost respect for what your mom and dad are doing for me. Barry, again I apologize to you too."

Tim started to cough and grasped at his chest to brace himself. Daniel noticed a pitcher of water sitting on a small table beyond Tim's cot. Daniel went over and poured a tin of water and handed it to Tim. Tim gratefully accepted the water and looked at Daniel. "Doc is right about you."

Daniel was taken by surprise that the doctor would have said anything about him to this man. "Why, what do you mean?"

"He said you're a natural caregiver, and I can see that he was right," Tim observed.

"Let's go now, Uncle Barry," Daniel said, ready to leave and go back to his parents.

"Well, I'll see you around, Tim." Barry nodded to the man on the bed and put his arm around Daniel and walked him back to the store.

While they were there, Barry stocked up on nails and a few other items he was going to need over the next few weeks.

"Well?" Daniel Sr. asked. "Are things all looked after?"

"Yeah, things are fine," Barry replied. "Daniel Jr. and Tim had a good talk I'd say. Where's Rachel?" Barry asked, realizing he hadn't seen his sisters since he and Daniel returned from the sheriff's.

"Rachel already left to put dinner on. We were really busy today," Daniel told him.

"I can imagine," Barry replied as he picked up his supplies and headed out to the wagon. "Hey, Little Dan, can you grab that bag of nails for me? I want to get the wagon loaded up and get going so we can get it into a covered barn before the weather changes again."

"Sure thing," Daniel Jr. said, lifting the bag and heading for the door but then stopped and faced his dad. "Hey, Dad, do you need me to do anything before I take off with Barry?"

"No, I'm good, thanks for asking," Daniel Sr. replied. "Get going."

Barry was already in the wagon waiting when Daniel came out. He put the bag of nails behind the seat and climbed into the wagon himself, and the two headed for the farm. They made the trip quickly and got the wagon into the barn and unhitched the horses before unloading. They put everything away and headed for the house.

They walked in to the welcome smell of a roast in the oven as they put away their coats and boots.

Rachel was setting the table and smiled at the two of them. "Hungry?"

"Yeah, but we'll be okay for a bit while we wash up," Barry offered.

"Well, hopefully you can wait for Dan Sr. to get home," Rachel said.

Barry shook his head. "Daniel Jr., Daniel Sr., it all gets so confusing, why don't you just call Junior here by his middle name? It's Jack, isn't it? Besides, he's not that junior anymore."

"That's up to Junior, I guess," Rachel replied.

Daniel pondered this for a minute and said, "Yeah, I like Jack. Uncle Barry's right. You yell out Daniel, and both me and Dad answer, and every time we go somewhere and someone says, 'Daniel,' we don't know who they're talking to."

Rachel agreed. "Well, Jack it is then, son."

Rachel finished getting everything ready for dinner, and they went to sit in the living room to go over some of the plans for the loft. They had decided that the loft would go above the living room and would include a vaulted ceiling to give it the illusion of even more space.

"Your dad has a surprise for you, Jack," Rachel teased.

"What is it?" Jack asked eagerly.

"If I told you . . . ," she trailed off and looked at the ceiling with great concentration.

"Yeah, what?" Jack badgered her.

"Then it wouldn't be a surprise," his mother burst out, laughing at his expression.

"So why'd you tell me in the first place?" he asked, disgruntled.

"To get you wondering about it. Didn't anyone ever tell you how mean I am?" She continued to laugh.

Jack glared at her. "I know a lot of things about you."

"Like what?" she asked.

"Like you almost took Uncle Barry's eye out by throwing rocks at him and that you would lie to your dad about your brothers just to watch them get their butts kicked. That you put manure in Uncle Allan's sandwich."

"Barry!" she yelled, outraged.

Barry laughed and held his hands up in supplication. "What? What'd I do?"

She eyed Jack and Barry suspiciously. "What other tales did he tell you?"

"Oh, that your dad—" Jack paused to look at his uncle who was shaking his head no.

Daniel quickly changed the subject. "I mean that you don't like people farting because your brothers would sit on you and fart when you were little, which I think is funny," he added.

He raised an eyebrow, which made him the spitting image of Rachel. "Should I go on?"

"*No*, that's fine. Barry, I hope you know that I would like to keep some things private." She scowled at her brother.

"Hey, sis, I just got started," he said with a laugh as she reached over and punched him in the arm.

Unaware of the chaos in his own home, Daniel had just finished at the store. Before locking up, he pushed a shelf full of goods over about two feet to reveal a loose floorboard. He knelt down to pull it open to reveal two swords, pieces of leather armor, a large shield, and leather helmet decorated with Scottish knot work.

The equipment was his own from his life in Scotland where he'd been trained as a soldier. He was taking the items home for Daniel Jr. so he could teach him the skills of a fighter and how to use a knife and sword. Daniel himself was an expert in the handling of all blade weapons, as well as hand-to-hand combat. He also wanted to teach him that, along with being able to fight, being able to defend himself was the very most of importance.

He rolled his gear into a tarp then recovered the hole in the floor, pushed the shelf back in place. He gathered up his things and locked up the store for the night. Anxious to get home after a long day, he galloped his horse all the way and reached home within minutes where he headed straight for the barn to unsaddle his horse and unload his gear.

He walked into the house. "Smells good in here, my dear." He placed a kiss on her cheek and noticed Barry was in the living room tending the fire.

"I see you have all your wood and tools in the barn. Are you going to start tomorrow, or would you like a day to relax as you've had a busy few days as well?" Daniel Sr. asked.

"Nope, I'll be starting tomorrow," Barry said.

"Where's Junior?" he asked.

"He's in his room doing his homework," Rachel replied. "By the way, Barry suggested that we start calling him Jack as his old brain is finding it confusing between you and Daniel Jr., so your son agreed he likes Jack better. Are you okay with that?"

"Yeah, that's fine," Daniel replied.

"Hey, did you get your equipment to give Dan, I mean Jack, a demonstration?" she asked.

"Yes, I did," Daniel confirmed.

"I've to see this." Barry laughed.

"You will, right after dinner," Daniel said. "Once we eat, I'll go to the barn and gear up, and you can bring Jack out about fifteen minutes after I go out."

Daniel had also brought in a bottle of imported wine and joined Barry on the couch in front of the fireplace. He handed Barry the bottle. "Here, Barry, something for your travels. Thanks for helping out."

"Wow, I've never seen that label before," Barry said as he examined the expensive bottle.

"Trust me, you'll like it," Daniel said.

Barry wasted no time in opening it. It was obvious that Barry loved his wine, and he eagerly poured two glasses for himself and Daniel. He sniffed his glass. "Whoooeee, that smells good!"

"For you," he said as he handed a glass to Daniel.

"Here's to you, here's to me, friends indeed," Daniel toasted.

They clinked their glasses together, and both sat back sipping their imported wine.

"Daniel," Rachel said, "I think we need to discuss with Jack the physicians college if he's still interested so we can organize our finances to pay for it."

"Yeah, we can talk to him over dinner, and then I can go talk to Dr. Anderson about it tomorrow," Daniel agreed. "But right now, I'd like to do as we discussed and teach Jack how to fight two or three evenings a week."

"I have never even seen you in your battle gear. Can I watch as well after dinner?" Rachel asked.

"Sure you can, let's just eat for now. I'm starving," Daniel said.

Rachel yelled, "JACK, DINNER!"

Jack came out of his room and sat at the dinner table with his father and uncle while his mother dished up their plates. While they were eating, Rachel asked, "So, Jack, now that you've changed your name, maybe you can give us an idea of what you're planning to do at the end of the school year. Have you given any more thought to becoming a doctor, or is there anything else that you're interested in?"

"Actually, Mom, I would like that. I think the number one reason I want to do it is because I believe this is what you want me to do," Jack replied.

"Jack, don't do things that you yourself don't wish to do. It's your life and your decision, not ours," his mom said.

"I'm not, I'd be happy to become a doctor. I just meant that it's even more appealing because you and Dad would approve," Jack clarified.

"Well, then that's settled," Daniel said.

"Hey, what's wrong with being a carpenter?" Barry asked indignantly.

"Nothing, I'd like to learn that too. Just because I wish to be a doctor doesn't mean I can't swing a hammer," Jack said with a smile.

"He's got you there," Daniel said, chuckling.

After dinner, while Rachel was tidying up, "Well, if you all will excuse me, I have some things I have to do in the barn." Daniel then left the table.

"Why don't you give your Mom a hand with the dishes, Jack?" Daniel said.

"Just what I was about to do," Jack replied.

Just before he went outside, Daniel retrieved a small box from his coat pocket.

"Jack, come here for a minute, this just came for you today."

"What is it?" Jack asked.

"Open it," his dad instructed.

Jack opened the box to find a harmonica. "Right on!" he exclaimed as he blew into the side of the wooden piece and let out a loud racket.

Barry chuckled. "You're going to be true-blood Davidson there, Jack."

"Why's that?" Jack questioned.

Barry reached into his shirt pocket and pulled out a harmonica and started playing, but it wasn't racket that came out. He played incredibly well.

Stunned, Jack demanded. "Show me how, show me!"

Barry laughed and started to show Jack some of the basics while Daniel slipped out to the barn.

Once he got out there, he donned his kilt, leather armor armbands, vest, and helmet. It was a good thing for Daniel that the weather was fairly mild as his kilt left his lower legs and arms bare. When he was ready, he grabbed one of Rachel's handguns, which was stored in a chest, and fired off a shot. This startled the three in the house.

"What's going on out there, I wonder."

"Jack, Barry, grab your coats! See why Daniel shooting his gun, will you? Please. Actually I think I will go with you."

Of course, Rachel and Barry knew there was no emergency and that Daniel had fired the shot to get Jack's attention and add to the excitement of his surprise. They all dressed quickly and ran to the barn. Jack ran in first, and Rachel and Barry followed.

"Dad? Dad, are you in here?" Jack called out.

Finding it very hard to see, Jack called again as he found the lamp and turned up the flame.

"Dad, you in here?"

His eyes were just adjusting to the dim light when Daniel jumped down from the railing he'd been standing on to land right in front of Jack.

"Holy crap!" Jack yelped as he stumbled backward.

Everyone was laughing except Jack. He couldn't figure out what was in front of him at first as he was lying on the ground squirming to get to his mother and uncle.

"Hey, watch what you're saying there," Rachel remarked, knowing that all kids eventually have a slipup in their words here and there. But she was adamant on staying on top of the situation as not to let Jack think it was okay to use such words.

Jack focused more intently on the figure in front of him. "Dad? You're kidding me! Wow, that's pretty neat, I like it."

"These are warrior clothes for when we went into battle in Scotland," his father said proudly.

"We took Scottish history in school last year, and we saw pictures of gear like in our picture encyclopedias, but if I would have known you had the real thing, I would have asked to take it to school to show everyone," Jack said excitedly.

Barry was standing off to the side laughing like crazy. "Hey, I have to ask, are you wearing anything under that dress of yours?"

"Tell you what, Barry. First, this is a kilt, *not* a dress. But if you think you're man enough to lift this kilt that you call a dress, then come find out yourself," Daniel taunted.

Barry cocked a brow. "Is that a challenge, my friend?"

"No, because you won't be able to do it so not much of a challenge, I'm thinking." Daniel goaded him even more.

"You don't think so?" Barry asked, taking the bait.

"Nope, I don't, in fact. I've known you for some time, Barry, and I'll tell you what, I have twenty dollars above the stove in the house that says you can't," Daniel said.

"Twenty dollars, your money, your loss." Barry shrugged. "But it's mine now!" He lunged toward Daniel.

Within seconds, Barry's feet were swept out from underneath him, and he was flat on his back with a sword held to his throat. Being it was all in play for Jack's benefit, Daniel offered, "Want to try again?"

"Sure," Barry said as he held up his hand for Daniel to assist him to his feet. Knowing that Barry was going to try to catch him off guard, Daniel gamely held out his hand. As Barry took it and rose to his feet, he attempted to grab the kilt with his free hand, and in one twisting motion, Daniel grabbed his arm and tossed Barry over his shoulder and onto his back and had a knife against his neck while Barry lay on the floor motionless except for his stomach jiggling with laughter as Rachel and Jack laughed as well.

"Okay, okay." Barry conceded as he got up slowly and dusted himself off.

"You okay, Uncle?" Jack asked a bit concerned at the hard falls his uncle had taken.

"I'm fine. I just didn't want to embarrass your dad. I let him do that, you know," Barry reassured him.

"Yeah right," Jack said. "I could see that," as he looked at his mom, and she rolled her eyes.

"Oh, by the way, Uncle, he's not wearing anything under his kilt," Jack laughed.

"We could see his naked butt when you went over his shoulder."

"Dad, that was great! I didn't know you could fight so well." Jack was a bit awestruck.

"Years of practice, son," Daniel said, patting his head. "Now it's your turn, come at me."

"No, I think I'll just pass, thanks," Jack answered, and everyone chuckled. "But you will teach me right?"

"Well, I believe I can do that starting this weekend. Consider yourself in training and keep in mind it's for future purposes and self-defense, not for you to be showing off to your friends, got it?" Daniel asked.

Jack nodded, and his father added, "Your mother's going to teach you how to shoot better as well so your accuracy will be improved a lot."

"Great," Jack agreed, "I like that idea, and Uncle Barry's going to teach me how to play poker."

Barry laughed. "That I will. Let's go back to the house, I really need a stiff drink now. But yes, I will be more than glad to teach you how to play. I am one of the best in these parts," Barry boasted.

"By the way, Dan, you look kind of pretty in that dress, but now I know for sure who wears the pants in this family," Barry remarked as he tried to work the kinks out of his back from the recent tumble he took. He tried to loosen the affected muscles as they started to aggravate him.

As Dan changed back into his regular clothing, the others headed back toward the house.

"Wow, I didn't think that could fight like that. He is very quick with the knives, and boy, did you look funny flying over Dad's shoulder, Uncle Barry," Jack said with a laugh.

"Yeah, I'm glad you were impressed. I knew your dad was going to give you a demonstration, so honestly, I didn't put much effort into it," Barry replied ruefully.

"But I can see or, should I say feel, that he put lot of effort into it. But I will admit I didn't think your dad could even get my butt off the ground, let alone over his shoulder. That surprised me without a doubt," Barry noted, still rubbing his back.

"I'll say," Rachel noted with concern. "Are you all right? You're walking like you were run over by a horse."

"It definitely feels that way." Barry grunted as he bent over to touch his toes trying to stretch out his lower back.

As Barry was bending over, Jack was standing directly behind him and noticed that he did not appear to be overly injured. Not one to resist temptation, Jack quickly placed his hands on Barry's rear and gave him a healthy shove. Barry quickly put his hands in front of him to break his fall but was not quite quick enough and landed face-first in a foot of snow.

"Oh, you little bugger!" Barry hollered as he pushed himself up onto his hands and knees.

"Daniel!" Rachel yelled. "That wasn't very nice. Now help your uncle up!"

Jack quickly retorted. "First, it's Jack, and second, what I just did is nothing compared to what he did to me earlier. He pushed me right off the wagon while it was still moving," Jack said with a smile as he saw that there was a smirk on Barry's face.

"That was funny, wasn't it?" Barry chuckled as he rolled over onto his back and held out his hand for Jack to help him up.

"Well, in the future, I will stay out of your play. But the two of you be careful. Someone's going to wind up getting truly hurt, and you'll only have yourselves to blame," Rachel warned.

Jack held out his hand to help his uncle up. "Need a hand up, chubby?"

Rachel struggled to hide a smile as Barry retorted. "That's what I'm holding my hand out for, come on, one, two, three, up. And did you just call me chubby?"

Barry looked straight into Jack's eyes, and Jack noticed his uncle's eyes held a gleam of what was to come as he tried quickly to pull away but was too late. Barry grabbed Jack and quickly dropped him into the snow. "You called me chubby again, you little pest!" He grabbed handfuls of snow and gave Jack a good face washing.

"Hey that's not fair, you're sitting on me! Mom, Mom! Get Barry off me," Jack howled at the cold.

Rachel turned from where she stood on the front steps of the cabin. "Hey, I said I wouldn't get involved. Sorry, honey."

"Mom, he's putting snow in my pants." Jack gasped as he tried to squirm out of his uncle's hold.

"Okay, okay, I'm sorry, Uncle. I won't call you chubby anymore. I promise, I promise," he yelled.

Barry was quite satisfied and not because of the promise but because he knew that that promise wouldn't be kept. But it was satisfying nonetheless to have filled his nephew's pants with snow. Barry felt like a kid himself all over again.

Barry released his nephew and got up and brushed himself off. He started walking toward the house smiling as he turned to look back at Jack hopping up and down to get the snow out of his pants.

Just then, Dan came out of the barn smiling to himself. It was dark out, so he hadn't seen the commotion, but he had sure heard it. As Daniel approached Jack, he noticed that he had pulled his pants down to get the last of the snow that Barry had shoved down the back of his pants.

"You know, if you wanted to wash yourself, there's hot water in the house," Daniel said with a chuckle.

"Very funny, Dad," Jack snorted.

Jack shook the rest of the snow and pulled his pants back up. They walked the rest of the way to the house together. "Hey, Dad, just to let you know, that demonstration was pretty good. You're quick."

"That's from many years of practice, but I'm getting a little rusty, but I still have enough left in me to teach you." Dan reached out and tousled Jack's hair.

"Whenever you're ready, I'm ready." Looking ahead to make sure that Barry was in the house already, "I'd like to give chubby in there a taste of his own medicine."

Dan laughed. "I'll tell you one good lesson, Barry's twice your size—"

Jack interrupted. "Yeah, that's because he's got a big belly."

"That is true," Dan chuckled, "but if you ever come across a man bigger than you, move fast. Don't ever let them get a hold of you, or you're finished. It's best to wear your opponent out, bigger men run out of breath quickly. Just remember, no breath equals no energy, and no energy means no swinging. He'll be so tired he'll have a hard time even trying to throw a punch. Now I showed you quickly how to use knives as well as how to use your opponent's weight against him. That's why Barry went flying over my shoulder. Take your opponent off balance, bend your knees, then tuck yourself under and stand naturally so his weight is behind you and then push up with your legs and over they go. It's not strength that wins a fight, its technique."

Daniel continued, "I can assure you, if Barry and I ever got into a fight, I would be black and blue. That is if I had ever let him get his hands on me as he is a very strong man. Anyway, part of your upcoming training will be technique. Hands, feet, and knives, are you ready for that?"

"I am," Jack replied.

"All right then," Dan said. "Let's get you inside and get those wet clothes off. It's getting late."

Dan and Jack entered the house to hear Barry say, "Well, well, looky here, Mrs. McDougall and the snow boy."

They both glared at him as he laughed while sipping a freshly poured drink, sitting on a couch by the fire.

"You just wait, Uncle, you just wait," Jack muttered as he hung up his coat.

Daniel smiled. "Mrs. McDougall, is it? How's your back feeling there, old man?"

Rachel interrupted, "Jack, once you change your clothes, why don't you fix your uncle's back for him?"

Barry looked over wondering just how Jack was going to accomplish that.

"Yeah, I guess I could," Jack said as he headed for his room.

"Rachel, how is Jack contending to fix my back?" he asked.

"Just trust me. Take your shirt off and lay on the floor stomach down. Do it quickly though because Jack has school tomorrow."

Barry stood up, took off his shirt, and laid it on the couch. He then proceeded to stretch out on the floor, which is where Jack found him when he returned from his room.

"Okay, what's the plan here?" Barry asked.

"Jack is going to walk on your back," Rachel replied.

"Are you serious? He'll snap my spine in two," Barry said worriedly.

"He's not going to walk on your spine, Barry, but beside it."

Jack carefully stepped up, placing one foot between his uncle's shoulder blades, and the other foot on the other side of his spine. He then slowly inched his way down his uncle's back to his waistline. Barry tried to speak as he was having all the air pushed out of him. "By gosh, you're heavy," he grunted as Jack continued to work his way back up again. Both Barry and Jack could hear little popping noises.

"Oh my god, this feels good." Barry sighed.

Jack continued for five minutes and then stepped off.

"Wow, that was great," Barry said.

"I'm not done yet, just hang on a second," Jack said as he went into the kitchen cupboard and pulled out a bottle of horse liniment oil. He put them on his hands and proceeded to rub them together to warm it up before rubbing it on his uncle's lower back. Jack's job was done.

"There you be."

He stood up and looked down at his uncle's lower back near the top of his pants and noticed that he could see the crack of dawn. Jack picked up the oil and contemplated about pouring it down that crack and was just about to . . .

"Jack!"

He looked up at his mother to see her pointing and shaking her head no when she saw what he was planning to do. "Now, now, that's enough excitement for you for one day."

"Okay, Mom, okay," he grumbled, but Dan Sr. had no such hesitation and proceeded to take the bottle from Jack and did the honors himself.

Within seconds, Barry jumped up in the air. "Holy—aw, aw damn . . . that's all the way down to my . . . oh . . . oh . . . oh . . ."

Barry was jumping around and trying to strip his pants off at the same time while Rachel grabbed a towel and threw it at him as he cried, "That's burning and stinging!"

At this point, everyone was laughing except Barry, who was pretty much naked and rubbing himself with the towel. Dan laughed as he sat down to take a sip of wine that he poured while Jack was working on Barry's back. He held out his glass in a mock salute to Barry, "Who wears the pants in the house now?"

This caused even more laughter.

"Funny," Barry muttered.

"I thought so," Jack seconded.

"All right, I guess the jokes on me." Barry sighed in defeat.

"Okay, Jack, time for bed," Rachel said.

"Okay, Mom."

"Hey, Jack, my back feels great. Seriously, thank you," Barry said as he stretched again.

"You're very welcome. I do it for Mom and Dad all the time. Doc Anderson was here once, and I did it for him as well. He told me not to tell too many people, or I'd put him out of work," Jack stated.

"No doubt," Barry agreed.

"Okay, bed," Rachel ushered Jack out of the kitchen.

"Good night, Uncle, good night, Dad." He tiptoed and gave Rachel at kiss on the cheek. "Night, Mom."

"Night, dear," she said as she hugged him.

After Jack was out of earshot, Barry marvelled, "That is really something. My back feels great. I notice that he's very careful about putting his weight on my back and knew to not apply to much pressure. I'm impressed."

"I'm pretty sure we'll be sending him to the physician's college," Rachel advised her brother.

"What do you think, Dan?" Barry queried.

"Sure," Dan agreed.

"It's settled then. I'll go into town with you tomorrow as I'd like to talk to his teacher. Firstly for him missing school and, at the same time, ask her opinion if she feels that Jack can do it, and then I'll go visit Doc Anderson to get the rest of the details if that's okay with you, honey."

"Fine by me," Dan replied.

Rachel finished tidying up the kitchen, said good night, and headed off to bed. Barry lay back on the couch while Dan threw a few more logs on the fire before they turned in for the night as well.

orning came, and Rachel was in the kitchen cooking breakfast for everyone. She had wisely thought to make extra bacon. Breakfast passed quickly, and everyone was full, but even so, Barry was eyeing the last piece of bacon on the serving platter as was Jack.

"Not this time, tubby." Jack quickly grabbed the bacon off the plate and shoved it in his mouth.

"I thought you made me a promise," Barry reminded him.

"I did promise. I promised I wouldn't call you chubby, and I didn't. I called you tubby." They both chuckled.

Jack quickly left the table before his uncle could retaliate.

"Let's go, Jack," his dad said. "I have to get into town and get the store opened."

"Wait for me," Rachel said.

"Why are you coming, Mom?"

"I would like to talk to your teacher, and I have a few errands to do."

"Oh," Jack said, "if it's about missing school, I don't think it's going to be a problem."

"Just the same, I'd like to see how things are going there, if that's okay with you?" She arched her brow at him.

"Well, just don't embarrass me, Mom."

"I won't embarrass you, don't you worry," she reassured him.

They all finished dressing and headed out to the barn. They saddled their horses quickly and headed into town. Barry finished his coffee and headed out to the barn to gather his tools.

Arriving in town, Dan took his horse to the stables as usual, as did Jack, while Rachel rode on to the schoolhouse to talk to Mrs. Winger.

Rachel opened the door to the schoolhouse and poked her head in. "Good morning, Mrs. Winger."

"Good morning to you, Rachel," Mrs. Winger greeted back cheerfully.

"I just stopped in to see how Daniel is doing with his schoolwork," Rachel explained.

"He's doing really well," Mrs. Winger confirmed.

"Before I forget, Daniel has decided to be called by his middle name, which is Jack. There is less confusion at home this way. But in school, you can still call him Daniel if you wish."

Mrs. Winger nodded. "I can completely understand that. I have another student named Daniel as well. It's a very common name. Well, it would be easier here too if he doesn't mind being called Jack of course."

"I would also like to apologize that Jack was not in school for the last few days."

"No need, we all understand. Daniel is quite the hero in our town now," the teacher said proudly. "I know the other students are excited for him to return. Will he be back soon?"

"Yes, as a matter of fact, he will be back in class today. He's just at the stables with his dad taking care of the horses, and then he should be here."

"That's great, I've been looking forward to his return as well," Mrs. Winger said.

Rachel smiled and said, "There are two things I would like to ask you, if I could?"

"Of course, Rachel, what is it?"

"I'm sure things will be okay, but would you keep an eye on Jack? Right now, it's like nothing happened, but just the same, I don't know how this shooting episode will affect him over time. Can you just . . ." She trailed off as she was politely interrupted by the teacher

"I will absolutely keep an eye on him, Rachel, you have my word. Jack is very smart and has a lot of friends, so I'm sure he will be just fine."

Rachel nodded. "Thank you. Speaking of smart, how are his grades? I mean I know that he is above average in his learning capabilities, but do you think he would make it into the physician's college for a degree?"

Mrs. Winger nodded enthusiastically. "His reading level is by far exceptional, and your request doesn't surprise me in the least about the college."

"Why is that?" Rachel asked.

"Here, come with me," the teacher instructed as she let Rachel to Jack's desk. "Open up the top and look inside."

Rachel opened the top of his desk and looked in amazement as she took out a pile of medical books. She gazed in amazement at *Diagnosis of Illnesses*, *The Skeletal Structure*, *The Muscular Structure*, and a book covering medical terminology as well. She looked up at Mrs. Winger with a puzzled expression on her face. "Where did he get all these?"

"He bought them himself. He spoke with Dr. Anderson some time ago and had the doctor order them for him," Mrs. Winger explained. "I thought you would have known about this."

Rachel shook her head. "No, I had no idea."

"To be honest, he's one of the smartest kids I have ever had the privilege to teach. He's never caused any problems for me or the other students. He does advanced work as well as the regular work that every other student does, and I told him it's not necessary, but he insists on doing the same as everyone else to not cause any hard feelings. The other kids know he's smart, they just don't know how truly gifted he is. I put your son in the back of the class so that when he has time, and the other students are working, he can sit back there and study his medical books. When he first got them, I quizzed him just to be sure that they were too difficult for him, and believe it or not, Rachel, Jack answered all my questions as well as I could myself, so I would absolutely say he would be capable of excelling at the physician's college."

Mrs. Winger paused for a moment before continuing. "If I may say, Jack is very humble and just wants to be like every other child. If he ever realized how intelligent he really was, he probably would've rebelled. He doesn't want to be the brainy kid, just a normal one."

"Thank you so much, you have answered all my questions," Rachel said as she turned and walked out of the school building.

As she stepped out into the bright daylight, she noticed that many of the kids were playing in the snow and throwing snowballs at each other.

"Hi, Mrs. McDougall," the girl Rachel recognized as Vicky called out. "Is Daniel coming back to school soon?"

Rachel smiled at the girl's obvious interest in her son and replied, "Yes, he is, he's coming back this morning. He's just at the store with his dad right now. He should be here in time to catch the school bell though."

Vicky beamed. "Oh great!" she said and ran off to tell her friends who hadn't heard the news. "Daniel's coming back today!"

"Where is he now?" Elisabeth asked.

"He's at the store with his dad," Vicky informed her. "Come on, let's go over. We still have twenty minutes before Mrs. Winger hits the cowbell. Let's go!"

The two girls began to run down the street right past Rachel as she laughed and called out, "Where you girls off to in such a hurry?"

Both girls stopped running and slowed down to a quick walk. "We're going to go see Daniel if that's okay, ma'am."

Rachel was still smiling. "You girls go ahead but don't be late for school."

"We won't," they promised as they both broke into a full run again only to come skidding to a stop on the unshovelled boardwalk that was placed them directly in front of the store.

"Okay, you go in first . . ."

"No, you . . ."

"Not me, this was your idea, not mine," Elisabeth replied.

Vicky blew out her breath in exasperation and rolled her eyes. "Fine, let's just go in then," she said as she pushed the door open. As the two girls walked in, they noticed that neither Daniel nor Jack seemed surprised at their arrival and would have been mortified to know that everything they had said had been heard through the door.

"Good morning, Mr. McDougall," both girls chorused together.

"Hi, Daniel," they greeted him as well.

Vicky stepped forward and quickly offered. "We thought maybe we could walk you to school your first day back." A blush stained her cheeks as she waited for Daniel's reply.

"Umm . . . sure. I'm ready," Jack responded slowly. "Okay, Dad, I'm leaving for school now."

His father laughed at the young people's awkwardness. "Okay, you kids have fun," he said with a smirk.

The three turned and walked out of the store. They had only taken a few steps when they bumped into Rachel on the boardwalk. She nodded her head in greeting, "Girls, Jack. You girls sure getting your exercise this morning," she said, holding in a grin.

Both girls lowered their heads shyly and mumbled "Yes, ma'am" as they hurried off.

Vicky turned to look at Jack with a puzzled look. "Did your mom just call you Jack?"

"She did," he affirmed. "Jack's my middle name."

"I like it," she stated.

"Me too," piped in Elisabeth.

Vicky could no longer contain herself and blurted out, "So tell us how you shot this guy, tell us everything."

Jack thought about it for a moment. "Truthfully, I don't know what to say . . . really."

"We heard that he was going to cut your dad's throat when you took the man's gun away and shot him. Is that true?" Vicky asked.

"Not exactly, but I don't really want to talk about it right now if that's okay," Jack responded.

Vicky put her hand on Jack's shoulder. "That's okay."

Impulsively, Vicky leaned over and quickly kissed Jack on the cheek and then pulled away just as quickly, looking stunned. "I can't believe I just did that," she said somewhat bewildered as her face turned red as did Jack's.

Both of them blushing, they continued to walk toward the school completely oblivious to Elisabeth's presence. Jack realized that he did like Vicky, perhaps a little more than he thought. Elisabeth was a little taken aback by Vicky's bold action as she also had feelings for Jack and was proud to be seen walking with him but was a little offended that his attention seemed to be centered on Vicky.

As they walked closer to the school, the other kids noticed Jack as well, and within minutes, he had a handful of his schoolmates surrounding him all clamouring for the details on what happened. Jack just stood there in silence, uncomfortable with all the attention. Mrs. Winger had been watching the commotion from the window and could see Jack's discomfort, so she decided to ring the school bell a few minutes earlier than normal.

The kids disbanded and walked past their teacher into the schoolhouse, and as they filed past, Mrs. Winger took Jack aside. "Jack, can I see you for a minute?"

"Yes, ma'am," he said and came to her side.

"You do realize that the kids are going to keep asking you what happened. They've heard lots of rumors and want to hear it from you. It's natural for them to be curious. If I may make a suggestion, if you feel up to it, you could address the whole class and tell the story just once. They may stop them from bombarding you with questions," she offered.

Jack thought about it for a moment and nodded. "Well, I guess, but that's like saying that I'm proud of shooting someone, and I'm not, so I don't want to glorify the event."

Mrs. Winger looked sympathetic. "I understand that, and I will tell the class that I am the one asking you to do it not that you volunteered to tell them."

"Okay, I can do that," he agreed.

Mrs. Winger walked him into the classroom where the other students had already taken their seats. Jack glanced at Vicky and saw that she was still blushing and looking at him with undisguised interest. The teacher proceeded to the front of the classroom and turned and addressed the class.

"I know we all want to welcome Daniel back to school as well. Rachel and Daniel McDougall have decided that Daniel will start going by his middle name, which is Jack, so going forward, please make every effort to honor their wishes. I have also asked Jack to speak to you all about the events that took place earlier this week."

Hearing this, the whole class cheered, and one enthusiastic pupil piped up, "All right! No test this morning!"

Mrs. Winger laughed and wagged her finger. "There's still a test."

"Awww . . ." came a resounding whine from the class.

"However," she continued, "Jack prefers to not tell the story."

"Oh, come on, Jack," one of the other boys wheedled. "Please," he added as an afterthought as he caught a disapproving look from Mrs. Winger.

She cut in. "Wait a second here, everyone. Jack has said that this is not something he is proud of, and I for one respect that. But as we all know, every one of you were going to badger him until you get all the details. Subject will tell us the story once, and I expect for him to not have to repeat it again, understood?"

There were many nodding heads and murmurs of agreement throughout the class followed by "All right, Jack, let's hear it."

"Hold on now, quiet please, everyone. I want to teach you all something. I'm going to whisper a sentence in Jack's year, and he in turn will whisper that exact sentence into Vicky's ear, and she will pass it on to Elisabeth. You will all whisper the same sentence to the person next to you and will carry on to all the students in the room until it reaches Robert here in the front. Once Robert hears the sentence, he will stand up and tell everyone what that sentence was. Does everyone understand?" Mrs. Winger asked.

The class unanimously replied, "Yes."

She then proceeded to walk back toward Jack was still standing and whispered this sentence, "Big Bob was six feet in height and was fishing, caught a seventeen-inch pike in the brook."

"Now you tell Vicky what I just said," she instructed.

Jack leaned over and whispered this sentence at Vicky's ear, and she turned and proceeded to tell Elisabeth, and for the next ten minutes, everyone took a turn whispering into someone's ear. It finally reached Robert after passing through fifteen other children. Robert stood up and said, "Big Bobby was seven feet tall and caught at six-inch fish and was a crook."

The class laughed, and Mrs. Winger said, "Thank you, Robert. Now Jack stand up and tell us the sentence that you were told."

Jack stood up and recited the sentence Mrs. Winger had told him. "Big Bob was six feet in height and was fishing, caught a seventeen-inch pike in the brook."

"Thank you, Jack, you may sit down." She turned to the rest of the class. "Now see what just happened here? When things travel from mouth to mouth, the story progresses and changes, and by the time it reaches the end, it's all wrong. We should take a lesson in this to not spread or believe stories secondhand as there's probably not much truth to it. That's how rumors get started, and rumors do nothing but hurt others, so in the future, you should all be cautious of what you think you've heard and be careful of what you say because it may not be worth repeating. Now with all that being said, Jack, would you mind coming up here and telling us what really happened?"

"Yes, I will. But in all seriousness, I'm only going to tell it once, and after I tell my story, I'd prefer not to talk about it ever again. I hope that's okay with everyone here," he said as he walked to the front of the room.

The class all agreed, so he proceeded to tell them the events that took place that day, and as hard as it was, he left nothing out and told them everything. They were an avid audience, and no one made a sound as he made his way back to his seat.

When Rachel returned to the store, there were few people inside talking with Dan as well as a few shoppers already knowing about. Rachel went to the counter to assist the customers that were waiting. After the rush was over, and the last customer had left the store, Rachel started to sweep the floor. Dan looked over and asked her the meeting went with Mrs. Winger.

Rachel replied enthusiastically, "Mrs. Winger says Jack's skills are way above average as well. She mentioned that Jack had ordered some medical books from Doc Anderson so he could study them and do some research. So I would say he's definitely interested in taking steps on his own to learn about the medical profession. Mrs. Winger is quite sure that Jack would be a success in medical school."

"Well, I guess it's a good thing that I set some money aside so paying for college won't be an issue at all, and if we continue to be as busy as we have been, I'd be able to send another child to college too," he said with a wink at Rachel.

"Well, in that case." She moved a little closer to Daniel and hugged him with a smile on her face.

"You think! Well then, maybe we should put out the Closed sign," Daniel said as he waggled his eyebrows at her.

Rachel laughed and immediately said, "Don't even think about it."

Dan smiled innocently. "Me?"

Rachel laughed. "Anyways, I'm going to go home and put some lunch on and do some chores."

"Come here, give me a kiss first," Dan replied.

Rachel wrapped her arms around him and kissed him soundly.

Just as Rachel was leaving, the blacksmith entered the store. "Hey, Daniel."

"How's it going, Mr. Beard?"

"Good, thank you. The sheriff had me put a rush on your gun cage so I'll be able to install it for you two days from now. Which is why I came by your shop and have a second look at it."

"That's okay, but I'm sure it will be one of your best works. I've never seen any work that you've done that wasn't great," Dan complimented him. "So two days from now?"

"Yeah, I might even have it done by tomorrow night. I just came to get a spare key from you as I will be working late tonight, and I may need to get in here to double-check some measurements. You know the old saying: measure twice and cut once." Mr. Beard chuckled.

"Sure, hold on at second, and I will get you a key," Dan said as he walked into the back room where he lifted up an empty can and took a key from underneath it. He walked back out and handed the key to Rick. "Here you go, but I should probably check if it still fits and that it's the right key."

"I'm sure it probably does," Mr. Beard stated.

"Hey, I'm just ensuring you have a key that works," Dan said as he tried the key, and sure enough, it was the right one. "Here you go, Mr. Beard, and thanks again for all you've done. I forgot to tell you that I did notice you fixed the back door, thanks again."

Mr. Beard laughed. "No worries, it's on your bill."

"Yeah, okay." Dan laughed. "You have a good day."

Back at the farm, Barry was working steady on the loft. He estimated three weeks to complete the job, and he was usually very accurate. He just hoped that Jack would love his new room. He even went out to the barn and brought in the lynx bobcat and mounted on the top railing so it would peer down over the railing into the living room area.

Tim eventually healed from his injuries but took longer than expected to be up and about. Prior to leaving town, the sheriff took him over to the store so that he could apologize again and thank the McDougalls for the care they gave him and to also thank them for looking after his horse during his convalescence. Tim had about eight dollars on him and handed it over to Dan, but he politely refused it and stated that a man with no money in his pocket was just asking for trouble.

The sheriff had already received permission to retrieve Tim's horse from the McDougalls property and also had possession of Tim's guns, tackle, and saddle which he now handed over. The sheriff stood with Dan and Rachel on the boardwalk as Tim saddled up his horse and got his gear ready. They watched as he mounted his horse and tipped his hat as a sign of his gratitude and also farewell.

Tim rode out of town that day and never returned to Peterborough as agreed with the sheriff and the McDougalls as part of his ongoing punishment.

The next four years progressed rather uneventfully, which suited the McDougall family just fine after all they had been through. Jack grew until he reached a height of six feet tall and now weighed close to two hundred pounds, most of which was solid muscle. Between his remarkable physique and bright blue eyes, he soon became the talk of all the ladies in town with many hoping to catch his notice.

Jack was finally ready to leave home to attend the physician's college where he would stay for the next four years to complete his medical degree.

During his time away, Jack also became a master at hand-to-hand combat both from the early teachings from his father and from his own interest and practice of different techniques he found in books at the college library. He also loved to show off his prized handguns, many of which he had had custom made by Smith & Wesson that were designed especially for quick drawing and trick shooting. Jack would amaze his friends with this trick-shooting abilities;

it was quite a show to watch Jack perform, and he often did so to entertain the local students as well children in the town of Toronto.

Two years into college, Jack had three weeks off for a break, so he decided to go home to see his family. He had decided to travel by stage coach instead of by train as Jack was more used to the coach than to the modernized train that ran the same route.

During the four-hour coach ride, Jack read two books in order to continue with his studies and noted that his eyes were aching from trying to read on such a bumpy journey. He was relieved when the coach stopped for the night and the driver announced, "We're stopping here, my friend, so be back in the morning at nine o'clock sharp. The hotel's across the street there, and the saloon is just up the road if you're interested in cards. There's always a poker game to get in on although you don't really look like much of a poker player, but you can get a decent beer there too."

Jack smiled and looked up the road and then back at the driver. "Tell you what, if I'm not here at nine sharp, then come pick me up at the saloon, I'll be playing poker. Here's a dollar to look after my stuff, can you do that?"

"For a dollar? Are you serious? I only make a few dollars a week, so sure and thanks, I'll come and get you. Heck, I might even check in to see how you're doing," the man exclaimed.

"You do that." Jack invited as he grabbed his sidearms from the hanger in the coach, strapped on his gun belt, tied his leg strap, and as he bent over to adjust the strap again, he backed right into a group of young ladies around his own age coming out of a milliner's shop.

He stood up quickly and turned to face them. "Oh, excuse me, ladies," he said, only to lose his balance again and almost trip over the boardwalk curb but regained his footing quickly. Looking at three fine ladies, Jack was a little embarrassed but stood straight and tipped his hat.

One of the ladies whispered to her companions, "Isn't he a handsome one?" She turned to Jack directly. "Do you have a girlfriend?" she asked with a laugh.

He smiled. "No, can't say that I do."

"Where are you from?" she asked.

"Peterborough originally, but I'm just on a break from college in Toronto and heading home to visit," he explained.

"What college is that?" the young lady persisted.

"The physician's college," he replied.

"You're a doctor? You're kidding me . . . you look like you're only nineteen," she said in disbelief.

"Yeah, whatever," Jack said impatiently. "I'm one of their top students, and I've been going there for two years already."

One of the other ladies asked, "Where are you going now?"

He glanced at her, insinuating poker. "To the saloon for a game or two."

"You better be careful in there, there's always trouble of one kind or another. My older brother gets into fights there all the time," the second lady spoke up.

Jack grinned, giving her a rakish look. "I'm used to trouble. Any of you girls care to join me?"

This prompted them all to giggle. "Where *did* you come from? You're crazy! They don't allow women in the saloon unless they work there as the entertainment, which I assure you we do not," one of the ladies said huffily.

"My apologies, ladies, I meant no offense at all." Jack blushed a bit. "In Toronto, there are some places where they do allow women, and they're allowed to drink too, not in all the saloons but some for sure."

The second lady spoke up again, "I've never heard of such a thing. Besides, my brothers are in there."

"So are mine," the first girl confirmed.

The most brazen of the bunch chimed in, "My brothers would kick my butt just for being outside the door, let alone setting a foot through the door." She looked Jack over and offered, "But if you're interested, there's a barn up the road there about a mile from here. It's the only barn on the left side of the road. There's a dance tonight, and you're welcome to come by. There'll be a lot of people our age there."

"I just might. What are your names? Mine is Jack McDougall," Jack inquired.

"I'm Sarah, this is Christine, and this is Roberta," the first girl introduced them all, and Jack, being ever the gallant gentleman, took their hands and kissed the backs of them after each introduction.

"My god, a real gentleman." Roberta was quick to note.

Jack tipped his hat again. "It's been my pleasure, ladies, and perhaps I will see you all later," he said as he turned and walked down the street but couldn't resist looking over his shoulder to have another look at the ladies, and when he did, he was pleased to see that they were all still watching him walk away. He smiled and waved, which caused the girls to blush and look away quickly, but he was feeling mighty fine at having three pretty young women checking out his posterior.

Jack was starting to think that maybe he had missed out on a lot by being in college but realized that they just didn't have the same rules in Toronto. He walked up to the saloon and pushed the doors open, noticing as he entered that it was full of locals, mostly farmers and ranchers by the looks of them. There was a woman entertainer playing the piano and singing in the corner, and otherwise, it was indistinguishable from all the other saloons he'd ever been into. Being a new face, he garnered some stares but paid them no attention.

He walked directly to the bar and leaned back against it with his elbows so he could observe the activities going on around him while waiting for the bartender to notice him. He looked around and his eyes settled on the poker tables, and he considered heading over to get an early start on the evening.

The bartender was now directly behind him, and he addressed Jack, "Excuse me, son, but does your father know you're in here?" The other six men lined up at the bar burst into laughter as did the barkeep, and Jack fought to keep his irritation from showing as he said, "Hey, I've had a long drive in on the stage coach, and I'm going to assume you meant no offense because all I really want is to sit and have a quick beer and play some poker." He placed his money on the counter.

The bartender took in his dusty, weary appearance and said, "Sure, sorry, I was just giving you a hard time."

Jack sighed. "It's okay, I get it all the time."

The bartender handed him his beer. "Your name is?"

"Jack, Jack McDougall," he replied as he took a long drink.

The bartender looked at him closer. "You related to Daniel McDougall in Peterborough?"

Jack was surprised. "Yes, he's my father."

"What are you doing here so far from home?" the bartender asked.

"I'm on a break from college and heading home to visit, I'm going into my third year."

The bartender pointed out. "The only college out there is the physician's college."

Jack raised his brows. "There you have it."

One of the men sitting at the bar listening to their conversation cut in, "So, Jack, what would you do if the bartender here was serious when he asked if your father knew you were in here?"

Jack retorted, "Well, he wasn't, and so I do not see in the point in answering the question. So let's not worry about it, shall we?"

The man grunted. "Snappy thing, aren't ya . . . young gun?"

Jack chose to just ignore him as he had a mouthful of beer, so he couldn't say anything right away anyway.

"Hey, I'm talking to you!" the man yelled, causing everyone else in the bar to look their way.

Jack looked at the man coldly. "You've got to be kidding."

"Those toy guns on your hips, Jack?" the man taunted.

Jack rolled his eyes. "Listen, I don't want any trouble here. I just came in here to play poker and have a drink, so why don't you have one too and relax?" Jack motioned to the bartender. "Get this man a beer, it's on me," Jack stated graciously.

The barkeep nodded and scooped up his money. "Sure thing."

Jack noticed, as did everyone else, that this man was not going to let things go, and sure enough, the man swung his coat away from his body to reveal his sidearms, thinking that the sight of them would make Jack hightail it out of the saloon.

Jack just looked at him expressionlessly. "Mister, you don't want to do that." Jack really didn't want to get in a gun fight. "Tell you what, do you play poker? Gamble?"

The man looked confused but answered. "Sure, who doesn't?"

"Good," Jack said. "I'll make you a bet. Let's put these on the counter." He unstrapped his gun belt and placed them on the bar and looked expectantly at the other man. "Now you do the same."

"For what purpose?" the man demanded.

"Well, why shoot someone because you're offended, or because I may be offended for that matter, so here's your bet. I have five dollars right here." He placed his money on the counter so the man could see it and then continued, "Now you come up with five dollars of your own or combine with your friends," Jack stated with a stern voice.

"What's the bet?" the man asked, getting more impatient.

"The bet is that you and I will go outside, and if you think you can beat me in a fair fight, no weapons, the five is yours," Jack explained.

"You kidding me?" the man asked incredulously.

Jack smiled. "Makes you wonder, doesn't it? But I'm sure it's better than having to prove yourself with a gun."

"I'm in." He turned to his buddies. "Hey, lend me some money." The other men obliged and scraped enough to make up the difference to meet the required amount and handed it to him as he was six feet four inches tall and weighed a good two hundred fifty pounds, so they weren't about to say no.

The man handed the money to the bartender. "Here's my five."

The bartender took the money, and Jack reminded the man. "And your guns too."

He took off his coat and left it and his guns on the counter. Jack decided to have a little fun, and he hollered across the bar to the entertainment girl who was playing the piano. She stopped playing and swivelled around on her chair to see what he wanted. He smiled at her and held up a dollar. "Here's a dollar for you if you'll come over and check my friend here for any hidden weapons, can you do that?"

The woman stood up and walked toward them with a mischievous gleam in her eyes and replied "Sure, honey" as she plucked the dollar from Jack's hand and tucked it into her bodice then proceeded to pat down Jack's opponent who didn't seem to mind the attention one bit. She nodded to Jack. "He's clean."

One of the other men pointed out. "What about you?"

Jack replied, "Well, I paid her a dollar to search you, so how about you pay her a dollar to search me?"

Everyone in the bar had their attention focused on the scene being played out before them, and Jack laughed out loud. "Never mind, I'll pay my own dollar," he said as he reached into his pocket for another dollar. The woman gave him a saucy wink and said, "That's okay, I'll check you for free."

Jack obligingly held his hands above his head but then stopped. "Wait, let me give you my knives first." He pulled one out of a scabbard on his hip. "Oh, here's another one," as he pulled one out of a sheath on his left arm. "Oh my god, here's another one," he said as he took the one from his right arm. "Wait, I think I have one more." He reached down into his boot and pulled out another. After placing them all on the bar, he nodded to the woman. "Okay, I'm clean. You can check me now."

Jack knew he was being cocky, but he was getting tired of people underestimating what he was capable of just because he was young and having them assume he didn't know any better.

The woman came close and started to run her hands over Jack, and she met his gaze and said quietly, "I can see you've got money, and the confidence, but do you know what you're getting yourself into, honey? This guy you're about to fight is a big troublemaker, and he knows a thing or two about fighting."

Jack replied, "You know, I don't get out often, but I can tell you that I definitely know what I'm doing."

She finished with her inspection. "This guy is built like a bull, so be careful."

He tipped his hat. "Ma'am, thank you for your concern and kind words. I just figure this is the best way to deal with this. Everywhere I go they have to pick on the new guy, so I have to stand my ground, and maybe they'll start to leave me alone."

Jack was ready. "Let's take it outside then."

The bartender stepped in and offered. "Listen, if you guys are going to fight, then do it in here, not on the street. At least in here, no one will interfere, and I mean no one." He pulled a shotgun out from behind the bar and looked at the men who had been sitting with the man that Jack was about to take on. "Am I understood?"

He looked around to see nodding heads and continued, "Now clear a spot."

While some of the other patrons moved chairs and tables to accommodate him, the bartender hollered, "I put a dollar on that kid Jack, any takers? I'll match every dollar bet."

Jack heard this and came up with another wager. "If I lose, I'll cover 50 percent of your loss, and if I win, I get 50 percent, so take all bets dollar for dollar."

The bartender nodded. "You're on." He started to gather the money. "Place your bets, gentlemen."

As he collected the bets, Jack and his opponent started to warm up by rolling up their sleeves and stretching. The other men rushed to the bar to get their bet in as the female entertainer wrote down names and wagers.

At this point, Jack looked at his opponent and raised his brow. "You know, I do know how to fight." He smiled. "It's not too late to change your mind."

The other man snorted. "Let's get this over with."

All the bets were collected, and the bartender came over and stood the two men face-to-face and raised his hand in the air between them. "When my hand falls, get started." He looked at both men and then let his hand drop. The bigger man wasted no time and took a jab at Jack but got nothing but air. Jack laughed. "You'll have to be a little quicker and maybe next time you'll hit me."

Another swing sailed by but didn't connect. "Wow, that was close. Try again." Two more attempts met nothing but empty space as Jack was nothing if not fast. "You know I never did catch your name," Jack said as he noticed that the other man was huffing and puffing already.

"Joe," the man grunted as he took another poke at Jack and still missed.

"What's the matter, Joe? Too quick for you?" Jack taunted.

Joe scoffed. "When you going to start fighting, Jack?"

"I am," Jack replied. "Fighting also involved moving, doesn't it?"

"Enough of this," Joe said as he charged at Jack.

Jack used both hands to grab Joe by the shirt as he leaned back pulling Joe's weight toward him and raised his foot so that when his back touched the floor, the momentum carried Joe over his head and sent him crashing to the ground. The move not only took Joe by surprise but also those crowded around them and even those who bet against Jack began to cheer him on.

Jack got up quickly and waited for Joe to regain his footing as he would never hit a man while he was down. Jack, being the savvy fighter that he was, knew the only way he could be an equal match for an opponent as big as Joe was to wear him down, which he did. Joe rose to his feet still short of breath while Jack hadn't even broken a sweat and wasn't out of breath at all.

Joe said, "I came here to fight, not to chase you around the room."

"But it's so much more entertaining this way," Jack pointed out as everyone gathered around laughed.

"Are you going to fight or what? Maybe we should call your mother to chase you home," Joe taunted.

This comment infuriated Jack. "That won't be necessary. Have a good night's sleep." He jump and turned in the air so that both feet connected with the side of Joe's head knocking him out instantly.

Jack and the others watched the scene as if it were in slow motion as Joe's head twisted from the blow while he fell to the floor.

The bar was completely silent, and no one was even cheering as they all stood there in shock.

"Sweet Jesus and God above," the bartender stated as he stared at the fallen man.

"I don't believe that just happened," one of Joe's companions said while people rushed over to where Joe lay and checked him to make sure that he was only out cold and not dead, and sure enough, he was only unconscious.

"Wow," the bartender said as other gathered around and one let out an appreciative whistle.

One man well into his cups approached Jack holding his fists up in front of him and said, "Hey, I'm next." Jack turned, and the patron quickly held up his hands in surrender and laughed. "Just kidding."

The saloon girl interrupted all the revelry and pointed out loudly to be heard above the crowd, "Somebody better find the doctor quick," as she bent over Joe.

"Don't bother," Jack yelled over to her after taking a sip of beer. "I am a doctor, well, in a manner of speaking." This only made everyone in the bar gape at him as if he had sprouted two heads.

He addressed the bartender. "Can you please get me a cloth and some water?" The bartender fetched the requested items and handed them to Jack who walked over to Joe and knelt beside Joe and dabbed his mouth with the cloth. He looked him over quickly and lifted his eyelids to check his pupils before announcing, "He'll come around in a minute or two." Jack stayed by his side and waited for him to regain consciousness.

Joe's eyes slowly fluttered open as his eyes fell on a man kneeling by his side and knew that the man looked familiar, but he didn't realize immediately that it was the same man he had just fought with as his head was still fuzzy from the blow.

"You okay?" Jack asked.

"I think so, who are you?" Joe answered slowly.

"I'm Jack, nice to meet you. But you forget we've already met," Jack stated, waiting for recognition to dawn in the other man's eyes.

Joe looked around, taking in his surroundings when all of a sudden he realized that he had been fighting with Jack and that it was he who was lying on the bar floor. He quickly tried to take a swing once he figured out that it had been Jack he was fighting, but the bartender grabbed his fist to stop him.

"Easy, Joe, enough! You just lost a fight and lost badly, I might add, so just take a breath and stop." The bartender held out his hand. "Here let me help you up."

Jack stepped away and headed back to the bar and picked up a beer, which he held up in salute to Joe as he watched the other man struggle to his feet. "You know, there's a cold beer here for you if you want it."

Joe looked at Jack and then looked around at the people watching him and didn't know what to say or do. He knew if he didn't that he would be the talk of the town, but it felt damned odd to get into a fight and then have your opponent buy you a beer afterward. He made no reply but walked over to the bar and looked at Jack. He was still bleeding from his mouth when he finally spoke, "Well, since you took my money and all my friends' money, I guess I will accept that beer."

"You're making me feel bad," Jack said and turned to the bartender. "Give him and his friends all a beer, and I'll cover it."

Joe picked up his beer while the bartender filled the other glasses, and he and Jack clinked their glasses together, and both took a healthy swig of beer. The patrons clapped and calls of "Good fight" rang out as the crown dispersed.

The bartender caught Jack's eye. "You know, we made a few good dollars from this fight, and as agreed, 50 percent of it is yours."

"Tell you what, I can't take Joe's five, so give it back to him." He continued talking to the bartender.

"Well, maybe you should give it to him." The bartender thought it would be better for Jack to do this.

Jack held out the money. Joe shook his head. "Well, thanks, I appreciate the gesture, but I did make the bet so you keep it, you earned it."

Jack still held it out. "Seriously, take it back. I've been well-trained since I was twelve years old, and not to say that I can't be beaten, but everywhere I go, someone seems to feel the need to challenge me. So today I'd just had enough, and I owe you an apology for taking all my frustrations out on you when I normally have much better self-control."

Jack stood up and held up his glass again. "Cheers. Now if you'll excuse me, I think I'll go play some poker."

His comment was overheard by the men sitting at the poker table closest to the bar, and one man called out, "Hey, I'll take some of those winnings from you. Come have a seat."

Jack grinned at the man's enthusiasm. "Sure thing." He turned to hold his hand out to Joe and shook the man's hand. "It was good to meet you, maybe we'll meet again. No hard feelings and keep some ice on that cheek, it'll keep the swelling down."

Joe smiled. "I will, thanks." And he returned his handshake and nodded, and Jack walked over to take a seat at the poker table. Noticing two empty seats, he asked, "Are either of these seats taken already?"

The man who had called him over shook his head. "Nope, they're both open so pick whichever one suits your fancy."

Jack pulled out the closest chair and sat down. "Listen, gentlemen, as with Joe over there, I only feel it's fair to warn you that, young or not, I play a mean game of poker. Still want me to join you?"

A few of the men chuckled, and one added, "Looking forward to the challenge, make yourself comfortable."

Jack played his first few hands conservatively in order to gauge the skills and telltales of the other players. He deliberately lost a few hands, so they would think he was all talk and underestimate him as it would benefit him later.

A few hours later, Jack was well up in the game and raking in large amounts of money.

One of the other players acknowledged, "You do play very well, either that or you've got some really lucky cards hidden up your sleeves."

Jack met the man's gaze evenly. "I warned you ahead of time that I was good, and I do not cheat nor do I care for the comment."

The man seemed to recall who he was talking to and what Jack was capable of as he backed down quickly. "No, no, I'm just kidding. It was a bad joke, I apologize. No offense intended."

"Apology accepted," Jack said, relaxing back into this chair. "Other hand, gentlemen?"

"Not for me thanks," the first man declined.

"Nor me," added another. "You've just about cleaned us all out."

"Sorry to hear that," Jack said. "Well, it is getting late, it's been a pleasure." And he stood up and pocketed all his winnings.

He walked back to the bar and briefly considered going to the barn dance but decided not to. He noticed that Joe was still at the bar. "How you feeling, Joe?"

"Not too bad, you're quite a fighter," Joe answered.

"Well, I did try and warn you," Jack reminded him.

Joe nodded. "You did that."

Joe had a thought. "Listen, if you're up to it, there's a dance down the way. I'm going over there myself if you want to tag along."

Jack shook his head. "I heard about that dance from some girls I met earlier today when I got into town. But I really don't know anyone, so I wasn't going to go."

Joe laughed. "Well, you know me, so let's go."

Jack grinned at the man's audacity and changed his mind. "Sure, why not."

Joe and Jack left the saloon together and headed down Main Street. Jack confessed that it was not very often that he had the opportunity to dance, and Joe laughed and replied, "Neither do I. But I always just tell the girl I'm dancing with to follow me because most of the girls at these dances don't know how to dance either, so if something goes wrong, and they step on my toes, then they think it's their fault not mine."

Jack also laughed. "Hey, that's a pretty good idea, Joe, but I think I'll stick with telling them the truth."

Joe shrugged. "Each to their own. So how'd you hear about this dance again?"

"I ran into three girls when I got off the stage coach and they invited me," Jack said.

"Did you catch their names?" Joe asked.

"Yes, they introduced themselves to me. They're Sarah, Christine, and Roberta."

Joe looked surprised. "You got to be kidding me. Roberta's my sister. Listen, Jack, I would really appreciate you not saying anything about the fight, okay?"

"My lips are sealed," Jack promised.

Within minutes, they were at the barn and walked in. There were about thirty people gathered inside, and it didn't take long for them to realize that there was a new face in the crowd. Roberta quickly spotted them and made her presence known by pinching Jack's butt as she walked up behind him. "Hey there, handsome, I didn't expect you to come escorting my brother." She took a closer look at Joe. "What happened to your face?"

Joe rolled his eyes. "What do you think happened?"

She turned toward Jack. "See what I told you about that saloon? Did you get to see my brother in action?"

"I sure did," Jack said with a smile. "Thank god it wasn't me," he added with a smirk at Joe.

Joe snorted. "Yeah, he was the lucky one, but he was gracious enough to tend my cheek, that's how we met."

Roberta nodded, remembering their earlier conversation outside the store. "That's right, you're a doctor, or about to be. Would you like to dance, Jack?"

"Um . . . sure, but I should tell you that I really don't dance well," he admitted.

"That's okay, at least you're honest unlike my brother here who lets the girls he dances with think it's their entire fault when they step on each other's toes. Isn't that right, Joe?"

"Whatever," Joe grumbled at his forthright sister.

"C'mon, Jack, let's dance." Roberta tugged at his arm to lead him to the middle of the floor where they arranged themselves in the proper dance position. Jack hesitated a moment before Roberta started counting out the steps for him. "One, two, three, and step back, one, two, three, and step back . . . that's right, you've got it," she encouraged.

The rest of the dance went relatively smoothly, and he escorted her back to the side of the floor where he was instantly surrounded by other young ladies wanting to dance with him. Jack held up a hand to calm them down. "Tell you what, I'll dance with every one of you if you get my friend Joe here up on the dance floor as well." He motioned for Joe to come over. "Joe, get over here, we're going to the dance floor."

"Sorry, Jack, I only dance with women." Joe attempted to keep a straight face as all the ladies around them giggled.

"Smart-ass, I wasn't talking about me," Jack retorted with a chuckle.

"Well, in that case, I'm in," Joe agreed naturally.

Jack excused himself from Roberta who didn't seem to mind sharing him at all. After all, she did dance with him first. Jack had a full evening of dancing, and much to his surprise, it was one of the most enjoyable nights he could ever remember having. It was getting uncomfortably warm in the barn, so Jack found Roberta, and they left to take a walk and get some air. They returned about twenty minutes later.

The first person they saw was Joe who didn't seem pleased. "Jack, can I see you for a minute, please?"

"Sure." Jack followed him a few feet away from Roberta so they could have a little privacy.

"Listen, I don't know what you were doing with my sister, and I'm sure I don't want to know, but you're walking on thin ice, so be careful and remember that's my sister, okay?"

Jack was quick to reassure him. "Hey, Joe, we just walked and talked, that's it."

"Just remember who she is, okay?" Joe looked him directly in the eye and apparently was satisfied that Jack was telling him the truth and held his hand out to Jack.

Immediately Jack took it. "Sure, Joe, no problem."

Jack and Joe returned to Roberta who was waiting for Jack. "Everything okay?"

"Sure is," Jack replied lightly. "Want to dance again?"

"Of course," she said with a bright smile.

Jack eventually got tuckered out and excused himself to leave as he really was exhausted between the long coach ride, the fight, the gambling, and the dancing. It had been a very full day. He decided to get a room after all just so he could rest for a few hours in a real bed before getting up to catch the stage again.

"Joe, Roberta, ladies, it's been a pleasure. Thank you for the invite. It has been a great evening, and I appreciate the dance lessons." He gave them a small bow of his head and turned to leave when Roberta quickly blurted out, "I was just leaving as well. Let me walk with you to the hotel."

Joe caught Jack's eye over her head and waited to see what Jack's reply would be. "Some company would be very nice, why not. Hey, Joe, you may as well come for the walk too so your sister doesn't get into any trouble on the way back."

"Well, since you put it that way, how I can refuse," Joe said, grateful for Jack's understanding, trying not to notice his sister's look of annoyance.

Joe added, "Truthfully, nobody would touch my sister if she was alone . . . so I'm sure your intentions are honorable, so you two go ahead. I'll wait for her here."

"Well then, this is good-bye, Joe, nice to meet you. Maybe we'll cross paths again," Jack said.

"Maybe." Joe clapped him on the back with a smile.

Jack held out his arm, and Roberta slipped her hand through his elbow, and they left the barn to head back to the hotel. Jack kept his word about keeping his hands off, but he hadn't said anything about his lips, so it didn't stop him from kissing Roberta about every twenty feet until they reached the hotel where he took her hand. "Thanks for a wonderful evening, Roberta."

She gazed up at him. "The pleasure was mine, Jack. I truly hope we meet again."

Jack was noncommittal. "We might. I will be travelling back this way, but I think I'll probably take the train next time, but if I don't see you again, it will always be my loss." He dipped his head and gave her a firm, lingering kiss across her lips. "Take care."

"You too, Jack," she said as she slowly turned and walked away.

Jack checked into the hotel extremely pleased by such a perfect night, a sentiment echoed by Roberta as well. It didn't take Jack long find himself in dream land.

Morning broke, and Jack was wide awake. UN rushed took his time to wash up and have a shave. Then he went down to the restaurant attached to grab some breakfast. While eating breakfast, he started to think again of a wonderful night he had as well wondering if he would ever see Roberta again. After finishing the last piece of bacon and his last sip of coffee, Jack was on his way to meet the stage.

Jack was only too surprised to find Roberta at the stage coach platform. "Roberta, what are you doing here? I mean, were you looking for me?"

She appeared a little embarrassed. "Sort of, yes." She hurriedly continued. "I'm going to ride the stage coach with you for an hour as I have to stop in the next town anyway. I've already talked to the driver, and my horse is tied behind the coach for me to ride back. Do you mind?"

"Not at all," Jack replied. "I've been the only passenger so far. Well, until now."

"Good!" Roberta replied. "Then it's settled, and I'm ready to go." She looked up at the driver. "Are you, sir?"

The driver laughed and winked at her. "I am, and I'll try not to take any sharp corners."

"You do that." She laughed as Jack gave her a hand up into the coach and jumped in behind her. They settled into their seats, and Jack smiled over at her. "Well, I must say that I wasn't expecting this."

She smiled at him. "You know, Jack, never have I been treated with as much respect and manners as I have been by you last night or, should I say, early this morning, and I have to admit that at some point, I wished you weren't such a gentleman," she added, lowering her eyes quickly.

Jack burst out laughing, and he mumbled "Yeah, me too," which made Roberta laugh as well.

The coach was moving at a steady pace through the town when Roberta looked at him expectantly. "So, Jack, how about another one of those kisses?"

Not a man to be told twice, he moved over to her side of the stage and kissed her soundly before pulling away and held on to her hand as they continued to talk.

For the next forty-five minutes, they did some serious talking about their lives, their interests, and just enjoyed learning about each other. They exchanged addresses so they could write to each other when time permitted.

Jack decided to be completely honest with her. "Roberta, I have to tell you, you are an amazing girl, but truthfully, I think I'm going to stay single at this point in my life. I can't say what the future will bring, but that's how I feel right now, and I hope that doesn't hurt your feelings."

Roberta thought about it for a moment and then shook her head. "No, it doesn't bother me, Jack. I like you, and I've enjoyed spending time with you. I'd rather you be honest and upfront like you have been than lie to me. You had the guts to tell me in advance, so I appreciate that, but just the same, should you change your mind, you know where to find me."

"Oh, trust me, if I'm by this way again, I will find you." And he kissed her again.

They were interrupted when the driver yelled out, "Next town in five minutes, folks!"

"Well, Jack, I guess this really is good-bye this time," she said as she hugged him tight. He held her for a moment then pulled away and yelled back to the driver. "I'll get out here."

They could hear the driver bringing the coach to a halt. "Whoa, there, whoa!"

Jack got out and held up his hand to help Roberta down, and they walked around the back to where her horse was tied. She was untying her mount when Jack stated, "I thought you had to go into the next town."

She was already in the saddle when she looked down at him with a big grin on her face and said simply, "I lied. Take care, Jack."

"Take care," he replied and waved as she wheeled her horse around and rode off in the direction they had just travelled.

Jack turned just in time to see the driver also watching Roberta ride away. "Well, well," the driver said with a smile, "nice girl."

"Yes, she is." Jack smiled back and got back in the coach to finish his journey and spent the next few hours pondering what a memorable trip this had been.

That evening, the stage coach finally made it to Peterborough. As it passed the McDougall Trading Post, he glimpsed his father inside the store. The coach stopped at the station, and Jack unloaded all his stuff and thanked the driver. "It was a great ride here."

The driver nodded with a knowing look on his face. "It was, wasn't it?"

Jack blushed. "Yeah, yeah, you take care."

He picked up his bag and his books and headed down the street for his dad's store and walked in and hollered, "Anybody here have a room to rent?"

His dad poked his head around the shelf he'd been cleaning, and his face lit up at the sight of his only son. "Jack, Jack! Why didn't you tell us you were coming home?"

"Then it wouldn't have been a surprise, Dad," Jack pointed out.

"And a great surprise it is. Your mother is going to be so excited to see you," Dan said excitedly, "Hey, how about a haircut? Your uncle has a barbershop, you know."

"Yeah, I heard. Okay, I'll go," Jack agreed.

Dan patted his son's shoulder affectionately. "I'll go with you."

"What about the store?" Jack asked.

"We're closed now anyway," Dan replied. "So let's go catch your uncle before he locks up too. Leave your stuff here for now."

Dan locked up, and they walked down the boardwalk together. Jack put his hand on his dad's arm holding him back. "Dad, let me go in first."

As he walked into the barbershop, he said, "Hey, old man, think you can cut my hair without that belly of yours getting in the way?"

"Well, I'll be damned," Barry whooped. "You sure grew a bit, didn't you?"

"I sure did," Jack said proudly. "How about a haircut, Uncle?"

Dan walked in and took a seat into barber chairs to wait.

Barry replied, "For you, a haircut, shave, and the finest cologne money can buy, and it's on the house, so sit down, you little bugger."

"Okay, okay." Jack laughed and sat down while Barry cleaned him up.

He looked at himself in the mirror and was more than pleased to see that he had the best haircut of his life and smoother shave he couldn't have asked for. "Damn, Barry, this is one fine haircut, nice job."

"Thanks," Barry beamed. "Now let's go get a beer."

Jack looked over to his father. "Do we have time, Dad?"

"Sure, why not?" Dan said. "Let's all go."

As they were walking, Doc Anderson spotted Jack. "How are you doing, Jack?"

"Great, Doc, thanks for asking," Jack replied.

"Good to hear," Doc continued. "Listen, I won't keep you, but while you're in town, I'd like you to come by my office when you get a moment in the next day or two."

"I'll do that," Jack said, and the three of then continued on to the saloon. They walked in, and Barry asked, "So how was the trip home?"

Jack, trying to be humble, said, "Very, very eventful," with a smile on his face. "One bar fight and met one great gal."

"Who won the fight?" His father asked.

"Well, there aren't any marks on me, thanks to your great teaching," Jack grinned at his dad.

"And . . . what about the girl?" Barry wanted to know.

"I'll leave that for another day," Jack said as the bartender came over.

"Three beers, please," Barry requested.

"Three beers coming up," the bartender acknowledged and set them up.

Well, after those three and another three and yet another round:

"I think we should get going," Dan suggested. "Ready, son? We're about to suffer the wrath of your mother. It's in your favor that she hasn't seen you for two years, but we're still going to get it."

The three of them stepped out, and Dan and Jack decided to just leave his stuff at the store as Dan hadn't brought the wagon into town that day. Barry waved them off as he headed off and told them he'd catch up with them the next day.

Dan looked at Jack and said ruefully, "Well, if you're not in too much of a rush, we can walk home, and your mother may not realize that we were in the saloon."

Jack chuckled. "I'm in no rush. Let's walk, it'll do us good."

On the way, Dan told Jack that Barry's girlfriend was pregnant. Jack was a bit stunned. "Wow, a lot's happened since I've been gone."

"Not much, just that really," his dad assured him. "Your mother misses you a lot, you know. How's your grandmother doing?"

"Very well, actually. I see her every weekend, well, almost every weekend. She's so much like Mom, which is probably why I haven't been that homesick," Jack said.

Dan smiled and warned. "Well, you better tell your mother that you were. She cries herself to sleep sometimes because she misses you so much."

"I like to hear that, well, not that she cries, but . . . well, you know what I mean," Jack stammered.

"I do, son, it's okay," Dan reassured him.

They continued on enjoying each other's companionship as they caught up on lost time. They stopped a few feet from the door when Dan put his hand on Jack's shoulder. "Hey, before you go in, it's great seeing ya . . . I love you," Dan declared as he pulled Jack into a bear hug.

"Love you too, Dad," Jack replied, clasping his dad tightly.

They let go, and Jack opened the front door and saw his mother cleaning an unlit lantern glass. She glanced up having heard the door open. "Jack! My god, Jack!" She ran to the door crying and threw her arms around him. "You didn't tell us you were coming home!"

"Well, we had three weeks off to study for exams, so I thought this would be a good surprise for you since I am pretty much well caught up on my studying," he said, laughing as his mother was covering his face with kisses.

"Next time, you tell me you're coming. Look at me, I didn't even fix my hair . . . ," she fretted.

He stilled her hands. "Mom, I don't care what you look like."

"I do," she said and then looked at the two men suspiciously. "You two have been drinking. You look and smell like beer. I know that smell well. Jack? You been drinking?"

"Mom, come on now, I am twenty one years old. There's nothing wrong with having an occasional beer now, is there?" Jack replied

She sighed. "Well, you're right. I was still thinking that you're still a boy. You are old enough to make those decisions on your own. Sorry, honey. Are you hungry?"

"Not really, Mom, thanks though," Jack answered, stifling a yawn. "It was a long drive, and I had a few beers with Dad and Barry, so I'm more tired than hungry."

"Oh, so you were with Barry too, were you? That doesn't surprise me," she stated.

"Yeah, he cut my hair too. Looks good, doesn't it?" Jack asked, trying to divert her attention.

She nodded. "He always was one that took pride in any task he sets his mind to and cutting hair is no different." She reached up and ran her hand through his hair.

"So, Jack, tell me, how's school? Sorry, college, do you like it?" she asked.

"I love it, Mom, I really do, and before I forget, Nanny sends her love," Jack replied.

"How is Nanny doing?" Rachel asked anxious for news of her mother.

"Healthwise, she'll probably outlive us all. I told her she should write a book as she's after me every weekend telling me that food's not good for me, that all you need is one glass of juice, or you're just wasting all the good proteins and vitamins. I think she should have been the doctor. She's a funny gal, but I must say, she's right in her statement as she eats a very healthy diet. I like seeing her on the weekends. It keeps me from being homesick with her being so close. She mentioned that she was coming for a visit in two weeks, and we could catch the train back together after she visits for a week. But I'm not completely sure that I'll take the train as I sort of like the coach better. That's how I came home."

"Why did you take the stage? The train is much faster," Rachel asked.

"I needed some time to relax and time to study as well," he explained.

"Yeah, and he met a girl an hour from here," Dan said, finally getting a word in edgewise.

"Dad . . ." Jack rolled his eyes as his dad continued. "Well, you did."

"It's nothing serious, Mom. She's just a friend, but yes, I was considering stopping by that way again on my way back to school, we'll see."

"So tell me about her," Rachel asked.

"Mom, it's nothing. I have more friends just like her in Toronto . . . a few actually," he stated.

"Jack, you're going to get yourself in trouble, so you better be careful," his mother admonished.

"Mom, I know what I'm doing. Thank you though." He tried to glare at his father but ended up smiling.

Jack looked mischievous. "Any chance there's any pie? I'm getting hungry but not dinner food hungry but sweet food hungry."

Rachel huffed. "Well, if you don't want my dinner, and I guess I'll fix some pancakes. I don't have any pie that should cure that sweet tooth of yours."

"Sure, I could go for pancakes. You do have syrup?" Jack asked.

"Since when would we not have syrup?" his mother retorted.

"Okay, pancakes will be good." Jack laughed as his mother pretended to cuff him.

Rachel looked over at Dan. "Honey, you want pancakes too?"

"What about dinner?" he asked.

"We were only having leftovers from yesterday, and I already ate while you were obviously getting a beer, *at the saloon* I might add, with your son. I knew something was going on. It's not like you to stay at work this late," she said as she turned toward the kitchen.

"Sure, I'll take pancakes too then," Dan agreed as he winked at Jack with a smile.

Rachel looked around and asked, "Where are your bags, dear? You are staying for three weeks, aren't you?"

"Yes, Mom, three weeks. We left them at the store as we walked home, but we'll take the wagon into town tomorrow and pick them up."

His mom glanced up from preparing the pancake batter. "Your girlfriend or, should I say friend, Vicky, is getting married."

"Great, good for her," Jack said.

"You should drop by and visit her while you're home." Rachel suggested.

"I just might," Jack replied.

In no time, Rachel had whipped up a batch of pancakes along with a heaping plate of bacon knowing how much Jack liked both. Jack looked down at his heaping plate. "This is excellent, Mom, and bacon too. Nothing like a late-night early breakfast, eight hours early that is." He laughed.

He continued on between my mouthfuls. "Wow, I miss Barry. He's not here to fight me for the bacon."

Rachel looked up from her plate. "Yes, he's started a family of his own."

"Kind of a late start, I'd say," Jack replied.

"Your uncle never wanted to be tied down," Rachel defended her brother.

"Well, I kind of agree with that myself," Jack stated.

After their late breakfast or, rather, early being it was eleven o'clock at night, the three of them retired to the living room. Dan looked over at Jack. "Here is something for you to try." He got up and went to the kitchen cupboard and pulled out a bottle of bourbon. "Now if you want a good drink—"

Rachel cut in. "Honey, if you open that bottle, there'll be three of us drinking it."

"I'm not going to argue with that," Dan said as he opened the bottle. "We have a new importer coming in, and he always gets me a couple bottles of the really good stuff, very well aged but a little too expensive for some. Here, try this," he offered a glass to Jack.

"I don't really drink that much, but I will try a small bit," Jack replied.

"Hey, you ever hear of ladies first?" Rachel demanded.

"Sorry." Dan rolled his eyes at Jack and handed a glass to Rachel. "Here, dear, just for you."

"There you go calling me dear again, do I look like a deer to you?" She laughed, and Jack smiled with her.

Jack took a slow sip of his drink and sighed. "This is good, Dad."

"You know, I always waited for the day to come that you would be old enough to have a drink with me both in the saloon as well as here at the house, and that day has now come, so cheers to my son and future doctor." He held up his class. "Cheers."

After talking a while longer, the three retired for the evening.

The following day, Rachel went into town with her son while Dan opened the store. Rachel was so proud of her son that she started talking to everybody they passed, and it wasn't long before Jack tried to duck away but was unsuccessful and spent the whole morning talking with everyone. He had finally had enough.

"Listen, Mom, how about we go to the restaurant for lunch? Then I would like to go visit a few people and stop in to see Barry, if that's okay."

"Sure, I'll come with you," Rachel said, not anxious to be parted with Jack after he'd been away from home so long.

"That would be great, Mom, but I'm going to see if Barry wants to go to the saloon to play poker," Jack explained.

"Oh, okay then, I guess," Rachel said dejectedly.

"Mom, come on here, you know I love you. But truthfully, I think I talked all morning. I just need a couple hours to unwind if that's okay," Jack said as he took her hand.

She sighed and nodded. "Yes, it is, Jack, and I'm sorry."

"Are you kidding me, Mom? I can see you are proud of me, and I like that because I do want you and Dad to be proud of what I'm doing. How about we all go to the hotel tonight for dinner? I'm buying, and we'll invite Barry too. So how about we meet at Rowland's restaurant say around six. Better yet, six thirty. That will give Dad time to close the store."

"You're going to buy dinner?" his mom asked, surprised.

"Yes, me," he confirmed.

"Have you been withdrawing extra money from your bank account while you've been at school?" she asked.

"No, Mom, here look." Jack took out a wad of bills from his coat pocket.

"Okay, mister, where did you get all that money?" she asks suspiciously.

"Mom, I do play poker, and I'm pretty good at it. I've been playing weekly since I've been in Toronto, and I've made some pretty good money." Jack told her as he pocketed the money again.

She smiled. "Well then, maybe you should go play poker with your uncle then."

"Just for a while, Mom, then I'll be back. Love you." He gave her a quick hug.

"After lunch, and you're buying, Mr. Poker." She laughed.

They had a great lunch then Jack proceeded to see Barry.

"Okay, I will see you later, Mom." Jack stated quickly kissing his mother's forehead.

"You make sure Barry doesn't get you in trouble," Rachel remarked.

"I'm sure everything will be fine. See you later. Thanks for understanding, Mom."

Rachel was a little distraught that her son needed a break, but could see his understanding.

Jack went into the barbershop to collect Barry, and they both headed to the saloon. Barry just sat back at first and just watched Jack play. "Well," Barry said, "I think I'm going to go play at another table," he whispered in Jack's ear. "You play a little too well for my liking. I think my odds are better playing over there." Jack just laughed.

After a few games, both Jack and Barry had cleaned up at their tables and were ready to leave. Jack walked over to the Rowland's Hotel to meet up with his mother and father for dinner. Barry had gone back home to collect his girlfriend and met up with them a few minutes later and very quickly made introductions. "This is my nephew, Jack, Jack this is my girlfriend, Trudy."

"It's a pleasure to meet you, Trudy, I hear you're expecting," Jack said. "Congratulations."

"Yes, indeed," Trudy confirmed. "And I hear you're about to become a doctor."

Jack nodded. "Only two more years to go."

"Great, now let's eat," Barry said, rubbing his hands together. "I'm going to try to break my nephew's bank account."

"Barry!" Trudy exclaimed, embarrassed.

"I was just kidding," Barry chuckled.

They all sat down and had a beautiful dinner, lots of laughs, and great conversation. Keeping in mind Trudy's delicate condition, Barry said, "I think we're all getting tired, I think we should call it a night."

"Yes, I agree," Jack said, understanding his uncle's wish to take Trudy home so she could relax. Jack flagged down their waitress so that he could take care of the bill, but she shook her head and said, "Sorry, someone already beat you to it."

"*Mom,* I said I was buying."

She shook her head. "I didn't pay for it."

"Neither did I," his father said.

Barry smiled. "I think that just leaves me. It's good to see you, nephew."

They all stood and hugged and shook hands. "You didn't have to do that, Uncle Barry," Jack said.

"I'm quite aware of that." Barry smiled.

"Thank you," Jack said seriously.

"You're very welcome," his uncle replied.

"Well, I guess this is a good night. Shall we all head back home?" Daniel Sr. stated

"Yes, I think we are," Jack replied, putting his hand out to his mom to assist her up and out the door.

"You know, I can walk just fine by myself, but you can walk me out any time, Sir Jack." His mother and father smiled with Rachel's words.

"It's my honor, ma'am," he joked

"Oh, aren't you the gentlemen? No wonder the girls like you . . ." Rachel was impressed with Jack's manners.

A short ride home on a beautiful summer night, Rachel being so happy raising such a fine boy. The night ended once inside the home dwelling. Everybody jumped into bed.

The following morning, Jack went to see Doc Anderson, stepping into his office.

"Well, I'll be damned," Doc Anderson said with a smile. "Look at you. You grew up to be a handsome devil, didn't you?"

Being a little modest, he said, "Well, I don't know about that but definitely grew."

"How about a checkup? You are qualified to do that, are you not?"

"Well, yes, of course," Jack replied.

"Well, would you mind?" Doc requested.

"No, I don't mind at all," Jack replied.

"Great. Let's get started." He lead Jack to a treatment room.

After approximately ten minutes into the exam, Jack stated, "You seem to be having some abdominal problems here. Are having some issues, Doc?"

"I am very impressed, Jack, very. To answer your question, I have a disease, cancer that is. It's new apparently. You know much about that, Jack?"

"Yeah, a fair bit, I'd say, but not enough to do much at this time. I will check into it for you though."

"Really, that won't be necessary, Jack. I already seen a doctor. One of your teaching colleges, in fact. The outcome isn't going to be good."

"I am sorry to hear that, Doc," Jack replied.

"Anyway, Jack, I asked you here the other day to ask you if you would continue your practice, once you graduate of course, here in Peterborough. The town is going to need a good doctor. Before you ask any more questions, it would be an honor if you would do that for me."

"Well, Doc, that's quite an honorable statement. I don't know what to say."

"You can start by giving me some peace knowing the town will be looked after and say yes."

"Yes then, yes, I was looking forward to working with you anyway as we talked when I was a kid.

"Well, that part now all depends on my health. But they say I will be around for a few years yet, so we will see."

"Well, you have my word, but don't you dare think of leaving too soon. When I get back, I will put full concentration into your situation, and we will see what we can do."

"I'm sure you will, son Thank you." The doc smiled at Jack's helpful thoughts. But he knew this time in the world, there is no help for this condition as it was being newly researched. Jack wanted to give Doc hope but also knew the same.

"One other thing, you have to promise not to say a word of this, even to your folks. Will you do that for me too?" Doc wanted some peace without the town concerned with himself.

"You have my word truthfully. Not a word, promise. Besides, you just became my patient. That's confidential information." Jack smiled.

"That's my boy. Told you that you would make a great doctor, didn't I?" Doc replied.

"That you did, Doc. Thank you for giving me the encouragement."

"You're one of a few, Jack, that you are. Now get out of my office," Doc said jokingly.

"Okay, Doc," he said with a smile. "I will see you before I head back to college."

"Don't worry about me, just spend some time with your folks, got it?" Doc demanded.

"Got it. See you in a couple of years, you hang in there. Have a good day," Jack said with a smile as he walked out of his office.

With that bit of info, it didn't make Jack feel very good, but as Jack knows, everybody can't live forever. But he did keep the agreement not to tell anyone.

The next two weeks passed by quickly and were enjoyed by all. Jack's grandmother, Dorothy, arrived in Peterborough to stay with the family of Rachel as well as to visit with Barry for a few days.

It was finally time for Jack to go back to college as almost three weeks had passed since he left, and he decided to go back by train after all. After seeing his family and seeing everybody else getting married and having kids, he was a little hesitant to see Roberta again so soon.

Once he arrived back in Toronto, Jack continued with his college degree.

Barry came out to visit Jack over the next two years and had many occasions to regret ever teaching Jack how to play poker as he had become a very masterful player and had taken more than a handful of coins from Barry's pocket much to his dismay and Jack's amusement. More often than not, they would go to the saloon together but sit at different tables as they each knew how the other played and didn't give each other as much of a challenge as they could get challenging players they didn't know.

Well, graduation day came. All Jack's family came, including Barry, Allen, and Chuck and their young kids. Dorothy, his grandmother who lived in Toronto, had a real good go housing her complete family, but it all turned out to be a great success. Jack was thrilled the whole family was present. Jack set up practice joint with Dr. Roy Anderson

After a week, Dr. Roy Anderson had the doctor's office changed from Dr. Roy Anderson's Office to Doctors Roy Anderson and Jack McDougall

Dr. Jack McDougall was well loved and respected by everyone in town, especially the older folks as most of their kids have moved out of the area when they came of age.

The younger kids in the area were always coming into his office to raid his candy jar as he was known to keep some of the best candy in the area, not only just for treats but as a reward for all those who sat bravely through various medical procedures. Being so close to the schoolhouse that he had once attended, it was not uncommon for two or three of the kids to pop in every week as Jack always kept a jar of candy on the counter and made it well known that any time anyone wanted some, they were welcome to just walk in and say hi and get some. This caught on quickly, and normally, the kids would drop by after school to take advantage of his offer. This did not bother Doc Jack at all as he looked forward to them coming into his office, and he never scheduled any appointments between three thirty and four thirty to make sure he had time to visit with them. So that he could give his offerings as well as have fun with the kids.

Once a week, usually on Fridays, as the children only had a half day of school at the end of the week, Doc would schedule a day off to watch over the kids as most of their parents were working, and they looked at Jack as a babysitter of sorts, and he enjoyed it and felt it was good practice and felt good about helping out in his community.

Doc was always a daydreamer and a fantastic storyteller. He could hold the children enthralled for hours at a time, making up stories and acting them out at the same time. He loved to find ways to entertain them, including putting on trick-shooting show with his handguns. They would sit in silent amazement as they watched him quick draw and hit all his targets faster than most men could even pull their guns out.

Being a doctor, he was naturally concerned with everyone's welfare, but he was especially cautious when it came to his guns, never forgetting the rules from when he was a young man. He always kept them unloaded to avoid one being accidentally fired, especially as most children like to paw at his guns when they were in his holster. Live rounds were only in the chambers when targets were being shot, but at that time, all children were well behind him during this performance.

People often questioned why Doc would wear guns in town and in his profession anyway and also why one gun was reversed in its holster on his left hip. They soon figured out that he loved the attention and the rapt audience that the children made whenever he pulled his guns out, and he couldn't very well do that if he wasn't wearing them.

The reason that Doc wore his gun in reverse on his left hip was because his little finger developed a curve at the middle joint, not only could he not straighten that finger but it would get in the way when drawing. After years of practice, he still couldn't draw and shoot accurately with his left hand but that he was able to reach across his body with his right hand and draw and hit a target as quickly as he could straight shooting with his left.

He was a gifted entertainer in many ways and also enjoyed using his knives to put on a show. At any given time, you could find three knives on Doc's person, and he could pull one out from any of the three areas he had them hidden and hit any target with deadly speed and accuracy, which also kept the kids wanting to see more. Hearing the excitement and laughter in the kids' voices always astonished Jack, and it wasn't unusual for some of the parents to leave work a few minutes early to avail themselves to a few candies and part of a story or show.

Dan McDougall often joked to his customers that he was not going to stock candy in his store anymore because his son would hand them out for free across the street and was going to put him out of business. It really didn't bother Dan in the least, in fact, kids that would come in with their parents asking for candy and when the parent's sometimes denied their requests, saying quietly, "We can't afford any today, but maybe another time." Dan would tell them that his candies were stale anyway as they'd been sitting on the shelf a while and would taste better if they were fresher and that they might want to try the candy across the street at the doctor's office because they were always fresh, and he would whisper conspiringly to the parents, "Doc gives them away for *free*." He would add with a wink.

They all knew that candies didn't really go bad, but they appreciated his understanding and respected him for supporting his son as well when they went over for candy. They were also offered a free checkup by Doc Jack himself, and he acquired many new patients that way. Being the only town doctor, Jack was easily able to make very good money, but when needed for someone less fortunate, he would provide his services either for less than the usual fee or for free, no one was ever turned away.

On some occasions, he and his father would make house calls to those who were either physically or financially unable to make their way into town to give them medical aid, as well as medicines. Every second Sunday, Rachel would join them, and she would pack extra food as well as fresh pies to drop off to some of the poorer families while Jack gave them free checkups. The townspeople greatly admired and respected the McDougall family for their generosity and kindheartedness.

Dr. Roy Anderson passed away being with Jack McDougall for just over a year. Prior to his death the day before, he had told Jack he was very impressed with his newfound business and thanked him for taking over. This was a great honor to Jack that these words were spoken.

As Peterborough grew, other stores opened, and some carried the same items as the McDougalls store, but none could truly compete. Some of the townspeople would go to the new store and buy a few things to help out the store owners, but they always saved the majority of their shopping for the McDougalls. It had always been Daniel Sr.'s belief that to get good business, you had to have respect, and that respect would come from helping and caring for others, which was one of the reasons all the McDougalls were so well liked.

Being they were so well thought of it often begged the question as to why Jack didn't seem to court any woman with serious intent and seemed to show no sign of being marriage minded whatsoever. He could have had his choice of women as you would be hard-pressed to find a single young lady who didn't look up to Doc Jack favorably. He was kindhearted, intelligent, and well-mannered, and he loved children. He was close to his family, and being a doctor didn't hurt his reputation any either. Combining all that with his good looks and charm, it was surprising to not see him with a steady lady on his arm. He was always impeccably dressed, and with Barry owning the barbershop, he had access to the best-smelling colognes that none of Barry's other customers could afford, but he would order it in special for Jack.

The ladies loved to flirt with him, and truth be told, he loved to flirt back, which made many of the other men in town jealous. More than a few envious looks were tossed the way of the handsome, financially secure, well-spoken doctor. It amused him to see that occasionally a gentleman escorting a young lady would see him coming and lead their ladies across the street, not intending any disrespect to Jack but nonetheless not taking any chances that their female companions might give Doc the eye.

Jack had many girlfriends as you could well imagine, but he was not cavalier in his relationships. He was a true gentleman and respected women greatly. He also respected the other men in the town. He always looked at a woman's ring finger before engaging a woman in conversation. He would still talk to them, but he wouldn't flirt or encourage them in any way. If a lady was single, then he would turn on the charm full blast, and he was interested in many of them, but he was not interested in marrying, just the same as he enjoyed spending time with all his girlfriends and didn't want to give that up just yet. He knew that the day would come when he wanted a lifetime companion, and marriage was important to his future plans, but he wanted to wait to commit until he was sure that his eye wouldn't wander as he had a healthy sensual appetite like any other man but respected the sanctity of marriage once vows were taken.

Saturday afternoons would often find Jack in the saloon enjoying a game of poker. He knew that the weekend would always bring in some new faces to town and into the bar, and he liked having new players to challenge his skills. Even better than poker were the saloon girls who provided many forms of entertainment and were a big attraction for all the local ranchers and wranglers after a hard week's work.

Jack would run into his uncle frequently Saturday nights, but for the most part, they sat at different tables as it was more fun to win money from friends and strangers than to take money from a family member.

One such evening brought a few wranglers into the bar that seemed intent on causing trouble. This wasn't uncommon, but occasionally, it could get out of hand. Jack remembered one time when a group of four men slammed open the doors to the saloon and barged in already liquored and yelling at the bartender to hand over a bottle of his finest imported whiskey. Drunk or not, a paying customer was a paying customer, so the bartender put a bottle down on the counter and lined up four glasses beside it and opened the bottle and poured for them. No sooner had he done that, the men started yelling and cursing, drawing the attention of everyone in the bar.

"Did I ask you to open and pour this whiskey?" one man demanded.

"No, sir," the bartender stated.

The drunk snarled. "You just grab us another bottle, and this time, keep your bloody hands off the cork."

"Well, sir, you have my apologies," the bartender said, not wanting to cause any further problems, and picked up another fresh bottle and gave it to the man unopened as the other three men downed the glasses he had already poured. He then went to pick up the opened bottle to put it back behind the bar. He faced the man again and said, "That'll be three dollars."

"Three dollars? Are you crazy?" the man yelled, his face turning red in anger.

"No, sir, I charged you for the four glasses of whiskey you fellas just drank as well as the bottle," the bartender replied, trying to keep his own temper in check.

The group of men laughed before the leader pointed out. "You poured it, and I didn't ask you to now, did I?"

"No, sir, but you did drink it," the bartender stated the obvious.

This triggered one of the men in the group to pull his gun on the bartender, which drew the immediate concern and attention of everyone present, including Jack who, unsure of the gunman's intent, yelled "Whoa, hold on there" as he stood up and left his poker game.

Barry was also keeping an eye on things and readied himself to take action by unlatching the strap on his holster to give him quick access to his gun if the need arose. Being at another table, no one would see him coming.

Jack approached the bar and heard the man slur loudly. "I do believe that the bartender has made an error." He slapped a dollar down on the counter and slid them to the bartender. "This should cover your four drinks."

Jack put his hand over the man's money and slid it back to him. "Now, sir, you just pay him for the bottle."

The man glared at Jack as did his three companions and demanded. "Just who the hell do you think you are?"

Jack met his stare directly. "My name is Jack McDougall, and I often frequent this establishment, and I'd have to say that you boys are causing a lot of unwelcome commotion tonight."

"I don't really give a damn what you think," the man said as he drew himself up to his full height and faced Jack squarely. "Maybe I should teach you not to stick your nose into other people's business." He swung open his coat to reveal his guns.

"Wow, I don't think we need to go that far," Jack said quietly, trying not to rile the man further as he was realizing the potential of other patrons getting hurt if things proceeded on this course.

"Well, Jack, maybe you just might not have a choice in this case." the mouthpiece stepped back. "C'mon, open your coat. I want to have witnesses when I put a bullet in you."

Jack sighed. "You're really not going to give me a choice, are you?"

The man smiled smugly. "Nope, don't believe I am." And he turned to give one of his cohorts a knowing look indicating that he was going to jump the draw. At this point, Jack quickly decided that he needed to get these men unarmed and fast.

He eyed the men and said, "You know that fighting with guns causes some pretty severe injuries." He directed to the man holding the gun on the bartender. "It would be pointless to have someone killed because of some cheap bottle of whiskey, no offense." He nodded to the bartender.

"None taken, Jack," the barkeep replied.

"I'll tell you what," Jack offered, "I'll make a bet with you. Pick your two most experienced men to stand with you." He saw that the forth man was young and didn't want to have to worry about him being jumpy and grabbing for a gun. The young man met his glance and looked sheepish as if Jack could read his mind.

"And," he continued, "I challenge all three of you to a fight. If I lose, there's about twenty dollars in this pouch, it'll be yours to take. And if I win, you put the bottle back on the bar and leave."

Jack waited. "So what's it to be?"

The man thought about it for a moment and nodded. "You know what? Beating the crap out of you does sound like more fun, you're on." He nodded to the two other men behind him.

"You'll have to take your gun belts off," Jack reminded them as he turned to remove his own and was pleased to see the man who threatened the bartender lowering his gun and put it down as well the younger man taking off his belt too, no doubt, so he could join the fight if needed to help his buddies.

Jack, being well trained in hand-to-hand combat, took on all three men and, having no choice, took out one opponent by a sweep of his leg as he approached, leaving him to face off against only two men who were shaken by the sight of their friend so easily downed and now lying on the floor clutching his leg.

The two men spread out a bit to approach from different sides to get the advantage, but Jack was too fast for them, and within fifteen seconds, he disabled one with a quick hit to the nose and a side kick to the head and then focused on the one left standing. The man realized he had made a serious error in judgment in challenging Jack and was shocked as were many of the bar's patrons who had never seen their Doc fight. With his two friends already down and doubting his abilities to get out of the situation relatively unscathed, he yelled at the younger man, "Shoot him! Shoot him!" as he watched Jack approach.

The man hesitated but then started to reach for his revolver, but before his hand could touch the weapon, he felt something cold against his head and heard the click of a trigger as Barry, who had approached from behind, held his gun against the man's head. Barry reached over and took his gun out of reaching distance in case the man decided to try and make a grab for it.

The man in Jack's sights panicked, knowing it was just him and Jack and, in desperation, pulled out a knife at which point, the bartender pulled out a gun from behind the bar and trained it on the man and said, "Drop it."

Barry looked over at the bartender and shook his head. "Put the shotgun away, trust me."

The bartender knew that Barry and Jack were family, so he did as he was told and put the gun back behind the bar.

Jack looked at the armed man and grinned. "So we want to play with knives, do we? I have one of those too." The man went pale as Jack reached behind his back and pulled two eight-inch knives out. Jack was truthfully just playing with the fellow at this point to put on a show for the other patrons as Jack seriously did not want to cause any life-threatening injuries but did want to teach this man a lesson.

His opponent lunged at him repeatedly, but not once could he get a clear strike, and as he tried, Jack took advantage of the openings he was given and inflicted several minor wounds on the other man's arms and chest that produced a lot of red staining to his clothes but were not life threatening.

The man staggered back against the bar where he noticed that his sidearms were still lying on the counter within his reach, and he quickly reached out his hand for them.

Barry yelled, "Jack!" This action was also seen by Jack. Within a second, he threw his knife, which impaled the man's middle hand, forcing him to drop the gun to the floor. He then strode over and knocked the man unconscious with one hard blow to the head.

The whole saloon went wild and erupted in cheers while Barry winked at Jack then stated, "This was more fun than playing poker."

Just then, the sheriff entered and took in the three wounded men on the floor and Barry's grinning face and Jack standing in the middle of it all and rolled his eyes. He questioned a few people at the bar and the bartender and quickly got the story that it had not been Jack's fault. Jack took a step and bent over his opponent, who was starting to wake up, and pulled his knife out of his assailant's hand, wiped it on his opponent's pants, and returned it to its sheath. He stood up and placed his hands on the bottle of whiskey. "I do believe this is now yours again," he said as he handed the bottle back to the barkeep

"What's going on here?" Sheriff Rigby asked.

"These gentlemen were just leaving," Jack informed him.

"They need some medical attention, don't you think?" the sheriff asked.

"I would say so," Jack said, hiding a smile. "The office is open, and the doctor is definitely in."

The sheriff had a few of the other men in the bar gave them a hand to escort the three wounded men over to Jack's office where the new physician that Jack had been training was on duty. The sheriff walked in and jarred the door open and motioned to Dr. Gordon Munroe, the attending physician. "Doc Jack sent you some patients, and I sure hope he doesn't make a habit out of it."

"What do you mean by that?" Dr. Munroe inquired, being confused of his statement.

"It was Doc that caused their injuries," the sheriff clarified. "I didn't get the whole story yet, but he apparently took on all three of them."

He patted down the three men and made them empty their pockets on the doctor's side table. "Well, well, look at this." The sheriff looked at their wads of cash. "It doesn't look like there are going to be any issues with these fellows paying for their treatment."

Gordon was still gaping at the wounded men. "You said that Doc Jack did all this?"

"I did," Sheriff Rigby confirmed. "It doesn't surprise me. His parents are very well-trained in self-defense of all kinds. What does surprise me is that this is the first time I have ever had to witness the aftermath. Anyway, I'm sure these gents won't cause you any problems, but I will drop by later to see how they're doing. As soon as you're done, let me know though as I think these three have worn out their welcome in this town."

With that statement, Gordon nodded. "By the looks of things, I'll be about three or four hours."

"Right, well, I'll check in soon then." The sheriff took all their firearms and took them to his office for safekeeping. He dropped the guns off and locked them up before heading back to the saloon where he pulled up a seat and sat behind Jack who was busy playing poker.

As Doc continued to play, the sheriff leaned forward to whisper in his ear, "Listen, Doc, I appreciate you giving your assistance, really I do, but if you don't mind me saying so, you're the main doctor in this town, and it doesn't look good for you to be acquiring new patients by putting them there by your own hand."

The sheriff leaned back a bit and continued. "Now on the other hand, if you're interested in becoming a deputy sheriff, you wouldn't have such a conflict of interest."

"Well, Don, thanks for the offer, but I am truly busy with my practice, and I do enjoy being a physician. I do thank you for the advice, but tonight was not my doing."

"I'm quite aware of that, Jack. Just try to do your best to stay clear of trouble. It's not good for your practice as many people won't come in from out of town to see you if they keep hearing stories like this." Then he stood up and patted Jack's shoulder and left the poker area.

As he walked to the bar, the young chap that had been with the other three was sitting, drinking a beer. The sheriff approached him and confirmed, "I take it you were with those other three men?"

"Yes, I was. We work together and drift from ranch to ranch," the young man explained.

"Where are you working now?" he asked.

"We work for Mr. Roberts, Ted Roberts, about five miles out of town," he answered.

There sheriff nodded. "Well, your friends should be out of the doctor's office in about four hours. When they get out, I would suggest that you leave with them since you're all together, understand?"

"Sure, no problem, Sheriff. I just came for the drinks and the entertainment, so four hours is plenty for me," the young man affirmed.

"Well, I guess we're in agreement there, chap, so enjoy the rest of your stay. Hope you boys have a wagon with you," the sheriff stated.

"We do, why?" the wrangler asked.

"Your friend with the leg issue won't be able to ride a horse with a splint on, so he's going to have to lie down or sit in a wagon to go back with you." He tipped his hat. "Good night, stay out of trouble." And he walked away.

Barry and Jack spent the rest of the night playing poker, which actually extended into the wee hours of the morning when Barry finally walked by Jack's table. "Well, I'm done here. I'm heading out."

"Hold on, Barry, I'm done too," Jack said as he excused himself from the table and put his winnings in his pocket. He and Barry walked over to the bar and ordered a shot for both of them. Now that they could talk alone, Barry commented on the fight. "Nice job taking care of those rowdies tonight."

"Yeah, and listen to you telling the bartender to put away his shotgun and letting this guy pull his knife. What's with that?" Jack ribbed his uncle.

"Entertainment." Barry laughed.

"At my expense," Jack grumbled.

"Hey, you knew as well as I did that you could handle it," Barry said with a grin.

"True, very true," Doc replied.

They finished their drinks and put their money on the bar and put their coats on. They exited the bar into the crisp fall air and stood for a minute watching the leaves blowing down the street. It didn't take long for them to feel the chill. "Damn, it's starting to get cold out," Barry said, pulling his coat a little more closed. "Is your mom getting everything ready for Halloween?"

"Of course." Jack laughed. "It's her favorite day of the year. She wouldn't miss it for anything."

"It always has been," Barry said. "She offered to decorate your office and my shop as well. She wants to put a skeleton in one of my chairs and put it on display in my front window."

Barry paused to think about it for a second. "I like the idea, I just hope that people don't think the skeleton is me due to lack of clients." He laughed as they both knew how busy his shop had become.

"Yeah, that's Mom. She loves to scare kids at dad's store too," Jack said. "It's really quite something to watch."

"Well, it's only three days away, and I've never had a Halloween that wasn't eventful," Barry said as he parted ways with Jack to get his horse from the stables. "Good night then."

Jack walked into his office through the side door, which was also the entryway to his suite. He saw Gordon, the other physician that was staying with him while the practice picked up, sitting in the living room. Gordon looked up with a wry smile. "Thanks for sending me some patients over. It kept me busy for the rest of the night. So you really took all three of them down by yourself?"

Jack nodded. "I really didn't have a choice, and it was either shoot all three of them or immobilize them."

"Why didn't you just shoot them?" Gordon asked.

"Couldn't do that, I promised my parents, especially my mother, that if at all possible, I would never shoot another man, so I do my best to keep my word."

Jack yawned and stretched. "I'm going to bed. Good night, Gordon."

"Good night, Jack, and by the way, thank you for having me in your home and your practice," Gordon said sincerely.

"No problem," Jack replied. "I really don't classify this as my home as one day I want to open my own saloon and have my own ranch to live on. All in due time though."

"A saloon?" questioned Gordon. "Why a saloon?"

Jack looked at Gordon. "Well, one, I like playing poker, and the other reason is I do not expect you to understand this . . . But I do not like the way they treat the female staff. I feel they're treated unfairly. So I thought one day I could change the way the normal saloon operated."

"Okay . . . And what would you name that saloon if you decided to do this escape?" Gordon was asking in curiosity.

"Well, I haven't really given it much thought, but I was considering calling it Saloon of Doc Jack's."

"Well, that's a catchy name for sure. At least the patrons will know they wouldn't have to go far for medical aid." Gordon smiled.

"Yeah, well hopefully that won't be required. It was just a thought just the same. Well, I think my bed is calling my name, I will see you in the morning. Good night," Jack stated.

"Good night, Jack."

Well, a few days past Halloween day came, and Rachel was running around collecting items she could use to put the final touches on her decorations for the store. True to her word, she would have Barry's shop decorated by the time the children were out early from school. The first place they would notice would be the barbershop. She finished by propping a skeleton head and boney arms in a barber's chair, with an apron on and ready for a trim The kids would especially love the barber's blade in the skeleton's hand.

Rachel stood back and admired her work. It was quite a spectacle, but then, she always took time for Halloween. If there was anything she could do to scare the kids or turn their stomachs, she did it. She got into her costume, which was a male trapper, realistic to the point of gluing real hair onto her face to resemble an unkempt beard. To test her ruse, Rachel left and wandered over to visit her son at his office. "Hi there," she greeted her own son in as low and gruff a voice as she could muster while hiding a suspicious grin. "I've got this awful lower back pain, can you help me out?"

Her son glanced up and replied with something that Rachel was far too entertained with herself to hear, and as he turned away to grab the trapper some medicine, she couldn't contain herself any longer and erupted with laughter.

"Mom?" Her son gazed at her quizzically. "Is that you?"

Rachel wiped the tears of mirth from her eyes and nodded. "Where's your costume?" she asked her son, still chuckling. He shook his head. "Wow, that is amazing. Nice job. I don't have a costume, but I'll let you fix me up later if you want. I'll stop by the store." Rachel nodded and, heading out, called back to him not to be too late, that she would have something ready for him around two-thirty or three o'clock.

Jack did enjoy Halloween as his mother made it hard not to get in the spirit, and she always ensured that they had a good time. He especially liked handing out candy (as he was already accustomed to from his own practice), and he did find dressing up in costume appealing.

It was almost an hour later when a group of men rode up to the town. There were six riders in all, one man drove a covered wagon and the other five were on horseback. The wagon and one single rider broke from the group to pull up behind the buildings. Four were on horseback and riding down the middle of the street when two others broke off from the group to circle around from the end of the street. The remaining two trotted along pausing to look around, something one might find suspicious if they had noticed the men instead of the flashy saloon decorations. Upon nearing the center of town, the two riders continued down the street where the sheriff was just stepping out of his office.

The sheriff noticed the two riders, tipped his hat to them, and greeted them with a polite "Good afternoon."

They tipped their hats in kind, and the taller of the two inquired, "Is the saloon very busy today, Sheriff?"

The sheriff shook his head. "Not normally at this time, though I assure you, it will be busier later tonight."

The rider tipped his brim in thanks as the other chap drew out his weapon. The sheriff started and reached for his own, pausing, guarded when he began speaking, "Where can I get my gun repaired?" he asked, motioning to his weapon. The sheriff calmed himself and chuckled. "You want McDougall's Trading Post and General store just farther down the road. McDougall will help you out, but I am not sure you will get your revolver fixed today."

The riders tipped the brim of their hats.

What the sheriff didn't notice was the two riders smiling to each other like they had a secret, like they knew exactly where they were going and what was about to happen.

Now that the children had cleared out and were home preparing for the night ahead, Rachel was in the back quietly adding an old, inoperative rifle to her ensembles while Dan, behind the counter, was greeting his two new customers. "How can I help you, gentlemen?" He smiled.

"I'm looking for a new rifle, and my friend here is looking for a handgun." Dan nodded and reached for his keys.

"I'm happy to say I can help you both. Let me unlock the gun cage, and you can take your pick." At about this time Rachel, who had gone unnoticed by the riders, was still in the back putting the final touches on her costume.

Dan unlocked the cage and swung open the doors, giving a clear view of thirty different makes and models of rifles. "This one is our most popular model," he started and turned to face them and found himself at gunpoint. His heart skipped a beat. "Take it easy there, don't do anything stupid. I'm unarmed, so take what you want and leave." It was unfortunately at that moment that Rachel strode out of the back in full trapper regalia looking pleased, waving a rifle and hollering in a gruff voice, "Hey, how's this?" The riders were as startled as she was by them as they weren't expecting an armed trapper to burst out of the back room. They reacted by taking aim, one fired and hit Rachel, taking her to the ground.

Dan heard his own voice screaming "No! No! Rachel!" as he tried to push by his assailants to get to her. He didn't even feel the pistol against his chest before it fired. He fell hard, gasping, and realized that his eyes were closed and opened them in time to see the pistol pointed at him again, and then blackness took over his sight.

Moaning on the floor, Rachel bit her lip until it bled to keep the screams from escaping her as she watched, helpless, as her husband's life was ended. She could see his face against the shop floor, lifeless. She panicked but couldn't move. He was standing right above her, looking at her with a puzzled expression. He holstered his revolver and grabbed at her whiskers as it didn't take much at close range to see that they were fake. The rider swore and stood up still watching her. "Hell, this isn't no man. It's a lady dressed up like a damned trapper."

The other man started to walk over. "You're kidding me, right?"

Rachel could do nothing. She was hurting and tired, and she couldn't move. The man who shot her opened his mouth again, and she heard, "No man, I'm serious. It's a woman," and then the other man spoke up, "Damn, shooting a man is one thing, but a woman . . . aw, hell."

She couldn't keep her eyes open anymore. She started to fade but could hear the back door swing open and feel herself being dragged to the side by more than just two men. There were at least three more arguing over the shots that had been fired. "The whole town will be here soon," one said, and another,

"Never mind that now. Grab the guns and load the wagon, you two take it, we'll follow." And then she heard nothing more.

Jack heard the shots but thought nothing of it and carried on his way to see his mom as he was late to his agreement. Just as he stepped off the boardwalk, two riders raced past him heading out of town in a hurry. Jack felt a foreboding, tingling sensation of worry and walked steadily to the store, barely slowing to push through the door. His eyes found the body immediately, his father, his usual white shirt stained with red, two dark holes in his chest and a look of terror on his lifeless face.

Jack already knew in his heart that it was too late, but he had to check. He knelt beside his father and held two fingers to his neck. He was gone. Jack cried out a battle cry, angry and loud, and then he saw a set of feet sticking out from behind a counter.

"No, no, no!" He heard himself yell as he left his father and ran around to find his mother bleeding badly and unconscious but still breathing. He yelled out, "Someone give me a hand in here!" It wasn't uncommon or worthy of notice when gunshots were heard, to hear yelling, but yelling for help was a different story.

Three men came barging in from the street and came through the door and helped Jack lift the trapper and carry him across the street to his office. Halfway across, the men realized that it was Rachel they were carrying, and when they got into the office, they lowered her onto the table. The other physician, Gordon, came rushing in to see what the commotion was only to find Jack in a panic, pulling the office apart and running. His bloody hands glided through his hair as he was, for the very first time, confused looking for cloths and bandages to stop the bleeding.

Gordon grabbed him, "Jack, you have to calm down."

"You bloody well calm down!" Jack roared back.

Gordon stepped away and over to Rachel and went straight to work while Jack started cutting the clothes from her chest and applying pressure to what was a very severe wound. Gordon handed him a towel to try to stop some of the bleeding.

The street outside filled quickly, and the sheriff was already at the McDougall store. Looking around, he avoided stepping in the fresh-staining floor as he gazed down at Dan and shook his head. "I told you this would happen one day, my friend," he murmured sadly and knelt, placing his hand on his friend's chest. He stood and turned as a man ran into the store. "The other one, Sheriff, it's not one of the robbers, and it's not a male." The sheriff felt his chest tighten. He knew before it was said that it was Rachel.

The sheriff ran to the doctor's office, pushing and yelling to get spectators to move. "Get the hell out of my way!" he yelled, and he missed the door hitting the door frame and smashed the glass as he forcefully opened the door and yelled behind him. "No one comes in here!" He looked around at the damage he'd caused in his haste. "No one."

He hurried into the medical room as Jack was administering a strong measure of medicine to ease Rachel's pain. Jack glanced up at the sheriff who looked anguished. "Jack, Jack, I'm so sorry." The sheriff noticed the tears in Jack's eyes.

Jack turned to Gordon. "Get out," he said quietly and lowered his head.

"Jack," Gordon protested, "let me help you."

"Get out!" Jack yelled as he shook his head and pointed at the door, turning abruptly when his mother turned to her side, blood gurgling up her throat.

The sheriff looked at Jack. No one could do anything, and Jack knew it. He turned toward Rachel as Jack moved to stand beside her. She gasped for air and rasped, "I'm not going to make it, am I, son?"

Jack grabbed her hand and held it between his, tears running down his face. He didn't answer.

"Don't talk, Mom," Jack pleaded.

The sheriff could barely hear her, but what she said brought tears to his eyes. "Son, I'm proud of you, and I always want to be proud of you. Don't rebel and be like them, don't use your guns on another man for revenge." She coughed and spewed onto the pillow. Jack was nodding his head.

"Only in self-defense, Mom, I know. Hush now." He bent down and hugged her.

Jack could feel her weakness. "Jack, look at me." He heard her whisper into his shoulder. He didn't want to, but he pulled back and did as he was told. "Promise me," she said and squeezed his hand. He held hers tight. "I promise, I promise, Mom. Only in self-defense as I was taught. Yes, Mom, I promise." He gasped as her hand went heavy in his, and her chest fell for the last time.

His eyes swelled, and they flowed, unstoppable spilling onto her body as he stood over her.

The sheriff and Gordon pulled him away, and he didn't fight them as they helped him to his office and sat him down, promising to return very shortly. Jack stood up with shaky legs and went to his drawers pulling out the two guns that he often used to entertain folks, mostly kids. He loaded both and holstered them as the sheriff came back into his office just as Jack was tightening the gun belt to his waist. "I've got men being assembled to go after them, Jack, they won't . . ." He trailed off seeing Jacks weapons. "Jack, no, stay here please. Let us deal with this, you promised." Jack stared at him. The sheriff held out his hands. "Give them to me, Jack." Jack slowly handed them over and then fell to his knees and wailed. Everyone on the street outside could hear and feel his sorrow.

Gordon, inside the store, watched carefully as men lifted Dan McDougall to take him to lie beside his wife.

Barry tried to stop guessing what had happened as he made his way to the doctor's office. It didn't matter once he stepped inside and found Jack in tears. He looked up, and Barry went to him, wrapping his arms around his nephew's shoulders. "They're dead, Uncle, they're dead," he sobbed into Barry's chest, and Barry choked on his own emotions, letting tears fall unchecked down his cheeks. "Where is she?" He heard himself say and released Jack to follow the direction Jack had pointed.

Barry found his loving sister next to her husband, covered in a white sheet stained in red.

He pulled back the edge of the sheet and had to chuckle through his tears as he took in her costume and mumbled, "You outdid yourself this time, dear. Great costume." Her trapper look had definitely fooled someone. His throat burned as he spoke to her. "I love you, sis. We've had so many good times, and I'm going to miss you so much." Barry turned heavenward and clenched his eyes shut. "May God be with you and watch over you both. As you approach the Pearl Gate, may you be as loved there as you are here."

He opened his eyes and looked down at her. He smiled, wrought with emotion, and kissed her forehead before turning away and walking out. Barry entered Jack's office to find him sitting crouched in a corner shaking like a leaf.

The sheriff informed them that a group of men had volunteered to go after the robbers right away and would handle it. He looked at Barry and said, "I would suggest you both stay here." Barry helped Jack up and then turned to the sheriff and growled and met his gaze. "I don't think so," he muttered.

Barry left the office, retrieved his horse before heading back to McDougalls store, and helped himself to a couple of decent rifles that were left behind, some shells, and bullets for his handgun. He exited the store and stood next the sheriff who was addressing the small band of men who would ride with him. Barry quickly stated, "Take bullets if you need. The door's open." And some did go in to restock.

The sheriff, joined by Barry, led at least a dozen men out of town the same way the robbers headed. After riding hard until late in the day, they found the wagon empty and abandoned in the middle of nowhere. There wasn't much light left, and the wind was wiping any tracks that might be helpful, though the sheriff surmised that they must had met up with other riders and dispersed the weapons based on what tracks they could still see. Barry and the sheriff decided to call off the chase as none of them were prepared to stay the night, and they couldn't carry on in the dark.

It was very late, and with heavy hearts, they met up with their awaiting wives and children at the church, which was their designated waiting place, where it was apparent by the men's faces that they had not found what they were looking for. After all checked in with their families, which were concerned of their loved ones on the chase, the men went to the saloon to find out what was the next course that would be taken.

The sheriff headed to a table where Barry was already seated with bottle and shot glass. He turned to the bartender and proclaimed, "These guys are on my tab tonight." He motioned to Barry and the men trudging in behind him. The bartender nodded and started to set up drinks.

Jack had heard the riders come back into town and charged into the saloon and walked up to the sheriff. "Anything?" he demanded, and the sheriff and his uncle both shook their heads. "No luck, Jack, I am sorry." Jack hung his head and fell into the seat beside Barry and then looked up at all the men, thanked them for all their efforts before he got up and went back to his office.

The funeral took place early in the morning a few days later, and Jack stood silently with the rest of the town, dressed somberly in black until he was motioned to speak. He stepped forward and said a few words.

"I like to take this time to say by the size of this funeral setting, I can see there are people from miles away as this must be the largest funeral attendance I have ever seen. I thank you all for coming. As it is with no doubt these two people here, Daniel Lenard McDougall and Donna Rose Davidson McDougall, also known to most as Rachel, my parents will be greatly missed. And I do know they are with God and at peace. Thank you again for coming.

"One last thing, I do realize that I may not be thinking straight at this moment, but the next statement I make, I have thought it through completely. As you are all aware, Dr. Gordon Munroe has joined my office. He is a great doctor and will be happy to tend to you all. At this time, I am resigning as the town doctor. I leave the practice to Dr. Gordon Munroe. My apologies to all, but this I am final on. I will not even consider a change to my thoughts till every person that was involved sees a jail cell or a box to lie in."

Hearing this, the town quietly whispered to each other, understanding his sorrow and rage inside the well-mannered doctor.

After the funeral, the sheriff approached him. "Jack, we still need you here. Gordon can't take care of everything, and I urge you to reconsider." Jack smiled calmly and rested his hand on the sheriff's shoulder. "I am sorry. There are other doctors looking for work too. Gordon can make the decision if he requires another."

At this time, Jack turned and looked at Barry and stated "I am sure with your new family, you will take over the store. It's yours. I already signed it over to you. Here are the documents. It only has one other request set off, 20 percent just in case I may require it one day. As far as my parents' house and land, please see over it for me. You can even move your family in. It's too big for me. If something happens to me, the land is yours. It's all written. Take this please."

"Jack, now I can't do this," Barry remarked.

Jack turned away as his uncle called after him. "What are you going to do, Jack? Talk to me," his uncle pleaded. Jack turned to face Barry and the sheriff. "I need to find them." He stared down at his shuffling feet. "They killed my family." He felt himself growing angry.

The sheriff shortened the distance between them. "You can't go shooting people, Jack, not for vengeance, not for your parents. They wouldn't want that." Jack looked him in the eye; he could hear his own voice was cold. "I never said I was going to shoot them but for them to see a jail cell."

The sheriff's raised eyebrow demanded an explanation, and Jack sighed. "I made my dying mother a promise that I would not shoot any man unless it's in self-defense. I will keep that promise."

Jack had no thoughts of ever returning to his home and sat down in the saloon with his uncle and insisted that Barry would inherit the store and hold title over the farm. Jack, feeling confident that he was leaving things in good hands, was surprised when the sheriff interrupted their discussion. Jack gazed behind him to see the mayor and four others with him. "What is this, Sheriff? Am I under arrest?" Jack was confused and amused at his own thought.

"Not at all," the sheriff replied. Jack looked to Barry and realized that he was not at all curious as to what was happening, meaning he already knew. Jack shook his head at his uncle.

The sheriff spoke again, "As a sign of our respect to you, we have decided to do you a favor, which I strongly suggest you accept graciously and use wisely." Jack cocked an eyebrow. He was very interested to know what was going on.

The sheriff continued, "Please raise your right hand." Jack did it instinctively but still questioned the validity of the request. "You're kidding me," he scoffed and was ignored. "I, Sheriff Don Rigby, with the blessing of the mayor and town council, which are present here today to witness my swearing you in as a full deputy in the County of Peterborough—"

Jack interrupted him, "Wait a minute, what . . . ?"

"Wait until I'm done please," said the sheriff calmly, and Jack obediently shut his mouth. "We swear you in amongst these witnesses who will testify to the validity of this oath and with a signature on this paper, which states you are a deputy of Peterborough. Your assignment as written here is to find the men responsible for the robbery of McDougall's Store and for the deaths of Donna Rose Davidson McDougall and Daniel Lenard McDougall, killed on October thirty-first of this year. Will you swear amongst witnesses that you will do everything in your power to bring these men to justice?"

Jack scanned the room. "I do, most certainly." As the badge was placed in his hand, the sheriff leaned in to whisper, "This should help you if there's any issues. It gives you the right to go after these men, but it doesn't give you the right to commit murder."

Jack looked down at his badge and then into the old sheriff's eyes. "I promised someone I wouldn't do that." His heart welled at the memory of his mother's dying words. She couldn't have known that her dying would lead to this, but she would be proud.

"Jack, one other thing." He was pulled from his thoughts. "I would like you to meet someone before you go. A fellow in the next town overheard what happened. This person purchased a rifle off a rider yesterday, one from your parent's store. He didn't know, Jack, but he's seen these guys, chatted with them, and thinks he can help."

Jack nodded. "Where is he?" He looked around the room and found an unfamiliar face of a man standing in the corner. The sheriff nodded. "That's him. His name's Tim McNabb, and he was going to go after the fellows himself when he heard but figured he would check in here to see if there was a posse that would be heading out soon."

Jack knew that name. He wandered over and asked the man to have a seat as Jack joined him. Now seating across the table from him, Jack said, "I put a bullet in a man by the name of Tim McNabb when I was twelve years old."

The man hesitated to give a smirk. "That would be me." Jack didn't know what to think.

Tim broke the silence of his racing mind. "Listen, your parents gave me an opportunity for a different life, I daresay a better one, and I took it. For so many years, I wanted to return to thank them, but now I can't anymore, I'm sorry about your folks."

Jack nodded, his mind still processing.

"I picked this rifle up from a group of men, 'bout ten of them, and after, they started talking about where they got them and how they robbed the McDougall store and shot a man and a woman there.

Seriously, if at that time I was not outnumbered, I would have been bringing a few bodies back here with me. So the least I can do is to come here in respect of your good-natured parents and offer my assistance if you will allow me. Surely, I can be of some use."

Jack nodded, understanding the man's position. "Gather your gear, you can stay at my parent's house with me tonight. I have some things to take care of before we leave. And it will give us some private time to talk. Is that okay with you, Tim?"

"My gear is already outside on my mount whenever you're ready," Tim replied.

The next day Jack went to the bank and took out a large sum of money.

Then he met up with his uncle, Tim already at Jack's side.

"Barry!" Jack explained, "I sold half horses on the farm to Mr. Charles Sweeting. He will be by to take his pickings in a few days. I gave him very cheap rate. I talked it over with his banker knowing things are tough over there, and at this rate, he has equity for his small loan."

Upon returning to the house, Jack took Barry's hand and placed the money from the horses in it. Barry fought him and tried to give it back, but Jack insisted, "You will need some money to keep the stock going, and I'm your business partner, so this is for the business, mind you. I did take some out of here. Do what you think is best."

Jack knew this wouldn't make his uncle happy. "I don't think I can live in this town anymore, Barry. Everyone, everywhere, and everything reminds me of my parents, of what I've lost. I can't be happy here. Besides, I've got my own money as well. They left me more than I even thought was in the bank. I will be fine."

That night, as the three men sat in the saloon, Tim informed Jack that the robbers knew that someone would come looking for them, so they were heading to Calgary. "Alberta?" Jack started. That meant they were already a week behind.

"Well, that means we leave in the morning. I have done what I needed to do." Jack in thought as to leaving the next morning.

After a few good-byes to those in the saloon, Jack and Tim headed for his parents home for the last time.

In the morning, Barry assisted Tim with the wagon and horses while Jack raided the store for supplies, apologizing profusely for taking it. Barry laughed at him and slapped him on the back.

"I'll just take it out of your 20 percent, partner, and you know, Jack, if you ever change your mind, it's all here waiting for you. I will rip this all up, you know, the ranch, the store. Whenever you come back, they're yours."

Jack dropped his supplies into the wagon and turned to hug his uncle. "I need a change. I've needed one for a while, and I just didn't have a reason to go until now. You take care, Barry." Jack hopped up next to Tim and waved as they rode off.

The sheriff met them on the road prior to exiting the town standing with his rifle in hand. Tim slowed the wagon as Jack hopped out. The sheriff shook his hand. "I've got a favor to ask, Jack."

Jack nodded. "What's that?" The sheriff handed the gun out to him. "This gun was given to me by your father. It would be a great honor if one day I got this rifle back. Knowing it has assisted you in some way would be an honor."

Jack smiled. "Ah, but I thought I was supposed to let the courts do that." The sheriff tapped his left breast pocket where the badge rested.

"Didn't you know? That badge you're wearing *is* the court." Jack nodded and thanked him for everything. Shouldering the sheriff's rifle in the wagon, Jack asked Tim, "Are you ready? Let's go before I change my mind," Jack stated.

"Good day, Roy. Take care of this town with a smile."

With a snap of the reins, they were off.

They travelled west by railcar and on horseback and as a month had passed; they'd made it to Saskatchewan. During one of their discussions, Tim informed Jack that he was originally from Calgary and knew the town quite well, which would hopefully be to their advantage.

Tim made a good companion to Jack during their journey, and they enjoyed each other's company, and with the exception to Tim being a little cocky when he drank, they travelled well. They slept under the stars for most, but when available, in some of the finest hotels, enjoyed good meals, and stopped to play poker in many small towns, which helped Jack keep his mind off his troubles.

They spent the night in Saskatoon, and Tim was his usual self, shooting off his mouth a little too much as Jack could hear him from where he sat playing a game of poker. Tim, continuing his loudness across the pub, put an end to Jack's game. Then decided it was time to take him to the hotel. Jack glanced over to the bar and caught sight of part of Tim wedged between four other guys, not seeming to be in a fair situation—four on one.

Jack strolled up and stated, "Looks like your mouth got you in some trouble here," he said with a smirk. "Need a hand?" He was not getting a reply from Tim being wound up with these men.

One of the men fighting looked at Jack and asked, "This your friend?"

"He is, and I'd appreciate you letting him go while he's still somewhat standing," Jack replied dryly.

"And if we don't?" one of the men taunted before he turned and punched Tim again, causing him to hit the floor hard.

Jack shrugged. "Then you will have to deal with me." And before the men could heckle him any further, Jack turned and swung hard, connecting with a jaw and again with a cheekbone. It went on like this for several minutes. Tim being wholly unable to help, watched from where he was lying on the floor. Fortunately, Jack didn't need any help and took only a few very minor hits before all four men were down. Jack lifted Tim to his feet and sighed. "What was that about? When are you going to learn to keep your mouth in check?"

The bartender came over with a chair. "I don't get it," he said. "Your friend just asked about the sidearms they were wearing, told him he thought they may have been stolen, and they just got into it."

Tim was still having trouble talking clearly, but he pointed to the revolver that had fallen on the floor next to one of the men.

Jack propped the man up against the bar and showed him the revolver that he'd dropped. "Where did you get this?" he demanded as he took note that the revolver was indeed from his parents' store. The man spat blood out and wiped his swollen lip. "Bought it from a group of men when we were out of town the other day," he remarked.

Jack nodded. "Okay, how many men?" The man seemed to ponder for a moment, and Jack found himself losing patience when the man finally blurted out, "Seven, seven for sure." Jack patted his cheek to keep his attention. "How much did you pay for it?" Jack demanded an answer. The guy smiled and said proudly, "Five dollars."

"Just five bloody dollars? This gun's worth thirty at least," Jack yelled.

Jack had stopped listening at this point, so he took five dollars out of his wallet and threw it in the man's lap. "There, I just bought it from you. Now get out of here before I use it on you." The bartender stepped up, not wanting to see one of his regulars ripped off, and pointed out, "You just said that gun was worth thirty, not five."

Ready to snap at this point, Jack pulled out his deputy's badge and placed it forcefully on the table. "Either he can accept the five, or I can arrest him for suspicion of being an accessory to the murder of my parents, so pick one."

The bartender looked shocked; the man took the five and raised a finger quickly to indicate option 1.

The bartender nodded. "Since you put it that way, I do believe he just sold his gun to you."

"That he did," Jack agreed. He looked at the man as he took the gun. "You have problem with that?"

"Nope, not at all." The man shook his head.

Jack stowed the revolver in his inside coat pocket and turned to haul Tim to his feet.

"C'mon, Tim, I'll fix you up at the hotel," Jack said as he shook his head at the damaged man. The bartender helped lift him over a chair, and they walked toward the door cautiously as the other downed men were starting to stir.

The bartender looked at Jack and asked, "So who was murdered again?" Jack clenched his teeth only partly from the weight of his drunken companion.

"My parents," he muttered, which caused the bartender to stop.

"What's your name?" He sounded genuinely sorry, and Jack appreciated the man's assistance so he answered, "Doc Jacks."

"You really a doctor?" the man asked.

Jack nodded. "I am, but for now, I have also been appointed a deputy, and I'm looking for the people who murdered my parents in Peterborough."

"Well, good luck to you," the barkeep said as he walked them out the door. Behind them, the entire saloon was bustling with talk of Doc Jack McDougall, now acting deputy.

A couple of men who had overheard Jack left the saloon in a hurry as they had been a part of the group the new deputy was looking for. But lucky for them, they went unnoticed.

The two outlaws rode for a full day, meeting up with several men at a campsite where they informed the rest that the son of the McDougalls they'd killed was on their trail.

One man spoke up. "I thought he was a doctor."

The two men looked wary. "I don't know about that," one of them said. "He took out four men at the bar single-handed, and he had a deputy's tin star in hand. Took a revolver off one of the guys he beat, who told him he bought it from a group of men for five dollars."

"Damn." The leader of the men frowned. "They won't be far behind. Let's leave now and ride until we hit Calgary." The two men who had ridden out shook their heads. "We weren't in town when this took place. We didn't participate in the killing. We all rode together for some time, but I am heading a different path. Sorry, guys."

"That goes for me too!" the other rider agreed.

As they left, the remaining six men sat down and tried to figure out the best course of action. They argued and decided they would all continue on to Calgary together.

Jack and Tim rode for a good hard two days before they reached Calgary. Completely exhausted and tired the last few miles, both Tim and Jack were pretty much letting the wagon of lead horses steer them into town. Without a thought, a bed was in both their minds. Jack even paid for someone he passed on the street to take the wagon and horses to the stable, not paying much attention but paid the man a petty penny just so they could get in and get some sleep. And that's exactly what they did.

Tim woke up earlier than Jack but still was late around 10:00 a.m. Tim went to Jack's room.

Knock knock

"Jack, you awake in there?" he yelled through the door. "Jack!"

"Yes, I am just getting in a shave. Come on in, the door's open," Jack stated.

"Man, I am starving, Jack," Tim mentioned.

"You're not the only one," Jack agreed.

"Let's grab some breakfast. They have a great menu here in the hotel," Tim stated.

"I'm with you on that. Let's go. I am ready." As Jack opened the room door, they both exited.

In no time at all, they were sitting at the table; service was quick.

"Good morning, gentlemen. What will you have?" the waitress asked.

"Everything you have!" Jack stated jokingly.

"Hungry, are we?" the waitress replied.

"Ma'am, I am so hungry, I could eat my horse." Jack laughed.

"That's a good one, never heard that line before. You're not from around these parts. If I may ask, where are you two from?"

"Peterborough, Ontario," Jack replied.

"That's a long way from home. Anyway, you boys look hungry. What will you have?" the waitress stated with a smile.

"Well, I have an odd request just the same. I will have half of a pound of bacon, three eggs, and four pieces of toast. Oh, the odd part is do not overcook the bacon. I mean that I just like it extremely hot, that's it. And yes, I am aware the bacon will not be cooked. But that's the way I like it," Jack said, knowing she was going to mention the uncooked bacon.

"All righty then . . . Coffee with that, sir? And would you like that coffee hot? Or should I just give you the coffee grounds on your eggs?" The waitress laughed. So did Jack and Tim.

"Yes! Hot and in the cup please." Jack smiled back.

"For you, sir, what would you like?" The waitress was addressing Tim.

"The same, but I will have my bacon normally cooked, thank you," Tim replied.

"Oh, and I will have a *hot* cup of coffee too." Tim smiled as did Jack and the waitress.

"Okay, gentlemen, be right back with those coffees." The waitress gave a smile to both.

"I like her. She has a good sense of humor," Jack replied.

"Well, Jack, I say we go to the saloon after breakfast, nose around a bit, take it from there," Tim replied.

"Your coffee, gentlemen. Nice and hot." The waitress winked at the two men.

"Thank you," they both replied.

Enjoying their fresh hot coffee, Jack quickly takes a sniff.

"Ahhh!"

"Well, that hits the spot," Tim replied.

Minutes later, "Bacon, eggs for you, and raw bacon and eggs for you." She paused to be sure this is what Jack ordered.

"Great, thank you," Jack replied.

"I'll just grab your toast. Be right back, gentlemen," the waitress stated.

"And here is your toast. Anything else, gentlemen?" the waitress asked.

"Ummmm yes," Jack said, trying not to talk with his mouth full. "Two glasses of milk, please."

"Be right back."

"This is a great breakfast, and it defiantly beats your cooking, Jack," Tim remarked.

The two men ate quickly. Jack was finishing his last mouthful of bacon and washed it down with a swig of coffee then swallowed a glass of milk in one shot. "You ready?" he asked.

"I am," Tim said as he put his hat back on. Jack stood to get the waitress's attention so he could pay their tab. The waitress spotted Jack on the rise and made a quick wave to insinuate "I see you be right there." She then came over with the bill. Jack handed her a generous amount. "This should cover it."

The waitress looked at the money in her hand and said, "I'm sure it will." Being modest as to be unsure if Jack required change, or the balance was a tip, she said, "I'll grab you some change."

"No," Jack stopped her, "that's fine."

"Thank you," she said as she slipped the money into her apron pocket. "That's very kind of you. Are you boys staying in town for long?"

Jack nodded. "Yes'm, for the time being, we are."

She smiled. "Well, please do come back."

"We just might do that," Jack said.

"Thanks a lot for the tip, it means a lot to me," she said earnestly. "My son has been sick, and we've got quite the stack of medical bills, so I'm trying to pay for those as well. He still needs a few more treatments, so this really helps. Sorry, I know it's not your problem, and I'm babbling, but I just wanted you to know that my thanks are sincere."

"Jack," Tim interrupted, "we need to go now." But Jack, being the kindhearted man that he was, wasn't inclined to leave yet after hearing the woman's plight. Tim, knowing Jack as he did, knew that Jack would assist in some way. Jack held out his chair and asked the lady to sit before sitting back down himself, leaving Tim sighing and standing alone.

"Now tell me what's happening with your son. I may be able to help," Jack instructed.

"Jack, I'm going outside to get the horses from the stables," Tim advised as he started to walk away.

"Okay, Tim, I'll only be a few minutes," Jack said as he turned his attention back to the waitress. "Sorry, go on. What's wrong with your son?"

She clenched her apron tightly in her hands as she spoke, as if it was difficult for her to retell. "Last week, my son, he's thirteen years old, was trampled by a herd of cattle on the farm he was working on. He was in bad shape, and the doctor's bills got so high that I couldn't afford for him to come out as often, and now my son has a fever and is getting worse."

Jack was thoughtful, "Where is your son now?"

"He's at home with his sister," she replied.

"Ma'am, let's go see him. Can you leave now?" Jack asked.

"If it's regarding my son, then yes. I can get someone to fill in for me. I'm sorry to look a gift horse in the mouth, but I'm not sure if I understand how you can help us," she said hesitantly.

"First, let's go take a look at your son. Second, I will take care of all your doctor's bills. Third, let me introduce myself. My name is Dr. Daniel Jack McDougall, but people call me Doc Jack, so I may indeed be able to offer some much-needed assistance," Jack reassured her.

Upon hearing that he was a doctor, the waitress's face lit up as she rushed to the back to tell her boss what had happened, and he followed her back out to the table where Jack was waiting. The man looked Jack up and down. Noticing he was very clean-cut from of most men in the area, he took a silent sniff, knowing the cologne Jack was wearing was a very different brand, to tell it was of an expensive taste in the cologne products.

"You are a doctor?"

Realizing that the man was just being protective of one of his staff running off with a strange man, Jack answered easily, "I am."

"Where do you practice?" the man asked.

"I just left my practice for personal reasons in Peterborough, Ontario," Jack explained. "I have studied medicine as a doctor for twenty-seven years."

The man was satisfied with Jack's answers and said, "If you can help her and her son, we'd all be grateful." Turning to the waitress, he put out an extended arm to take her apron from her,

"Take the rest of the day off." Then with a positive high tone voice, he said, "Go! I can handle things here."

"Thanks, Bill," she said excitedly as she turned to face Jack, and they walked outside before she turned to Jack and said, "I'm sorry, I just realized that I haven't even introduced myself or told you my name. I'm Laura, and my son's name is Jonathan."

Tim was waiting with the horses saddled and ready to go when he saw Jack and the waitress heading toward him. He looked at Jack. "Don't need to tell me you're going to be tied up here, aren't you?"

Jack nodded. "Sorry, Tim, but yeah, I will be for a bit," Jack said and reached into his pocket and pulled out a wad of bills. "Here, go play some poker." And he took a few steps back and opened the hotel door and yelled "Excuse me" to the clerk. "We'll be staying tonight as well, I'll pay up when I get back."

"Sure thing," the clerk replied. "I'll keep your bags till you come back."

"Give me some time if I'm late though and don't rebook the room, I will be back," Jack promised.

He stepped back out and joined Laura and Tim. "Tim, you mind if I borrow your horse?"

"Sure, Doc, go ahead," Tim replied as Jack offered Tim's horse to Laura.

Jack, looking her fabrics over, said, "Sorry, I can't offer you a sidesaddle. Are you able to ride astride with your dress?"

"Yes, I can," she assured him. "I do not much care for the sidesaddle anyway. They're not much to my liking." Jack offered her a hand up as she mounted Tim's horse. Jack then adjusted the stirrups on the saddle then mounted his own horse. "Ready?" he asked, and with a nod from Laura, they rode out of town. It was about a ten-minute ride when they came upon a small, run-down house where Laura turned her horse into the yard. Jack dismounted and helped her down.

They tied the horses and walked toward the house. As soon as they entered, they could hear the moaning sounds of Jonathan's, and his breathing could be heard from the doorway as he was wheezing heavily. Laura led him into the bedroom where Jonathan lay in the small bed with an obviously broken arm and his face still swollen from multiple head injuries.

"Hi, honey. I brought a new doctor here to take a look at you," Laura stated to Jonathan.

Unable to talk all that well, Jonathan just in nodded agreement.

Jack sat on the edge of the bed and gently parted the boy's nightshirt and leaned over to place his ear directly onto the boy's bare chest and listened. He glanced up to see a nervous young girl sitting in the corner of the room. "Is this your daughter?"

Laura looked over having forgotten all about the girl in her worry over her son; she nodded. Jack asked the girl, "Can you ride a horse?" Jack did not even ask the child's name first.

The girl stared at him eyes wide and whispered, "Yes."

Jack looked at her intently. "Listen to me carefully, it's really important. Take the brown horse outside and ride into town and get the other doctor that's been attending your brother and tell him to get out here now, can you do that?"

"Yes, sir," she said solemnly, determined to carry out his words exactly. Jack quickly penned a letter, folded it, and handed it to her. "Give this to him, and he'll understand."

"Yes, I will," the young girl replied.

"I am sorry. What is your name, dear?" Jack inquired.

"Tina," she said.

"Okay, Tina, you go now and do not come back without him unless you are unable to find him, understand?" Jack directed.

"I understand," she replied and left the room.

Within a minute, Tina was on the ride into town.

Laura looked at Jack. "What's going on?"

Jack took a deep breath not wanting to be the bearer of bad news. "Your son will not survive another forty-eight hours. He has internal bleeding, and his lung is filling with blood, that's why he's struggling to breath, and he has a fever. I'm sorry to stress you more than I already have, but while we're waiting for the other doctor, we have things to do. Go out and get my saddlebags, please."

Laura gathered herself, knowing she needed to be strong, and hurried outside to get the requested bags. Jack went into the kitchen and cleared the table to use as an operating surface. Laura came in carrying his bags, an immediate look of concern on her face as she watched Jack making room.

"This is quite serious to what I was told," Laura stated.

"It is, and we're running out of time," Jack confirmed quietly. He stirred up the fire and pumped water into the large pot and placed it on the wood stove and started pulling out his tools so he could sterilize them.

He then went into the bedroom where Jonathan had awakened but was not completely alert. "My name is Doc Jacks, and you're going to need to trust me. I'm going to give you something to drink, it'll help. But I won't lie to you, what I need to do will be painful at first but just for a short while then I can give you more medicine that will make you sleep, and you won't feel anything, do you understand me?"

The boy looked at him with feverish bright eyes and slowly nodded his head. He was incredibly nervous but, on a subconscious level, knew that his life was in jeopardy, so he agreed. "Yes," he croaked through his hoarse throat.

"Do you mind me calling you, John? We might as well get to know each other," Jack said, just trying to keep the boy's mind occupied.

"John's fine," he stated with a breathless speech.

Jack mixed some liquid and powder in a cup and tipped it to Jonathan's lips and made sure that he swallowed it all. He went back out to the kitchen and prepared his instruments and, after about ten minutes, went back in to check on Jonathan. He asked him how the pain was, and the boy said it was a little better.

"I have to move you to the table now, and it's going to hurt when we carry you," Jack warned. He picked up the bedsheet on one side and told Laura to grab the other side. "Okay, on the count of three, lift. One, two, three, now," he said as they both pulled up the sheet and struggled to get Jonathan to the kitchen table. Jack looked down at the boy and tried to make light of the situation. "How we doing, John?"

"I've had better days," he moaned.

Jack smiled. "Understood." They set him on the table. Jack then centered him, moved his arms by his sides. Looking up at Laura, he said quietly, "We need to wait for the other doctor, and hopefully, he'll be here shortly. But if not, I'm going to have to go ahead without him."

Laura looked fearful but nodded. She went to the bedroom and got John's pillow and placed it under his head and tried to keep him comfortable as Jack cut through the boy's shirt and poured alcohol liberally over the boy's whole chest to clean it. He had just finished when they heard riders approaching. He breathed a sigh of relief when Tina came in leading the doctor.

The other man took in the boy lying on the table and Jack's instruments spread out. "I got your letter here. You're a doctor from down east, eh?" the doctor inquired.

"I am. My name is Doc Jacks . . . sorry, Dr. Daniel Jack McDougall. I have been practicing this field for twenty-seven years. I became a doctor when I was just twenty-one."

"My name is Dr. Robert Williams."

"Well, Doc Williams, I need to talk to you in private for a moment if you would," Jack requested. He glanced up at Laura and Tina. "Ladies, if you'll excuse us, please."

Laura put her arm around her daughter and led her outside.

Jack looked at Doc Williams and asked, "How long have you been practicing medicine?"

"About two years on my own," Doc Williams replied.

"Okay then, let me explain something to you. When someone falls from a height or is hit with a blunt force, there's more to check for than broken bones. You've heard of internal bleeding, have you not?" Jack questioned.

"I have, but I've never seen a case of it," the other man admitted.

"Well, you're looking at one right now. Look at his chest and the side of his body, what do you see?" Jack demanded.

"I see purple and red contusions from where the cattle stepped on him," Doc Williams pointed out logically.

A little frustrated, Jack pointed out. "If that were the case, you would see markings from the hoofs, would you not? There are no marks like that in this area, are there? So that would lead me to believe that he was hit with something blunt like the animal's leg or head, so these marks are from bleeding on the inside, which is spreading into his right lung. Which I would say a rib has punctured the lung as well and that is why he can barely breathe."

Jack took a breath to calm down before continuing. "Now I'm not blaming you, but I want you to pay attention to these kinds of things in the future. Someone's life could depend on it."

Doc Williams looked grim, realizing what his lack of experience could have resulted in, and he nodded. "I will."

"Now I need your help. I need to make an incision in his side between these two ribs. I'll need to push all the way through to the lung. When I do, I want you to insert this tube in until you see blood pouring out of it, then we're going to suture the tube in place and bandage him up. Be prepared as he's going to do a lot of yelling and thrashing, but no matter what, that tube has to go in, got it?" Jack instructed.

Doc Williams looked shaken then nodded. "I do. Just let me wash up here."

A minute later, Jack looked down at Jonathan, who had been trying to follow the doctors' discussion.

"Okay, John, one more sip here. Are you ready for this?"

"I don't think I have a choice, do I?" he said with the ghost of a smile.

Jack smiled back. "No, you don't, sorry. But hang in there, okay?"

Jack went to the front door and opened it and yelled, "Laura! Tina!"

He spotted them returning from around the barn, and he took Laura aside and whispered, "You may want to take Tina for a walk. Your son is going to do a lot of yelling, and I don't want either one of you to come running in and distracting us at a crucial moment. Trust me, he will be fine if I have anything to do with it."

"Okay," she said, wiping tears from her eyes. She walked up to the door so that Jonathan could hear her and said, "It's okay, Jonathan, I'll be right outside okay, honey?"

"Okay," he mumbled, already lulled by the medication he'd been given.

"Go now," Jack ordered her as he could tell that John had barely been able to get those last few words out. He stepped back in and closed the door and walked over to the table and picked up his scalpel. "Here we go, John," he said as he placed his fingers on the boy's ribcage finding the gap between where he would have to cut. Not wanting to prolong the boy's pain, he pushed his blade quickly and firmly through the boy's side, causing Jonathan to cry out in agony. He pushed as fast as he could with precision then pushed his fingers into the incision to widen the hole, which caused even more hoarse screams to erupt from the boy's throat.

Laura and Tina hadn't made it far enough to block out the sounds from inside the house. Laura held her daughter tightly and tried to cover her ears so she wouldn't hear her brother scream. All the while tears poured down Laura's face as she fought the urge to run in and be with her son.

Satisfied that there was enough room for the tube and no internal tissue in the way to cause any blockages, he nodded at Doc Williams to insert the tube.

The other doctor started pushing the tube into John's chest, which caused the boy to thrash even more. Jack held him down and spoke to him encouragingly as Doc Williams got the tube in all the way and blood starting pouring out. He looked at Jack, who nodded for him to continue, and started taping the skin around the tube to hold it in place.

Jack smoothed the boy's hair back from his face. "John, John, listen to me. It's done, we're done."

He stepped back to grab a pot to place on the floor under the tube to catch all the blood that was draining from the boy's lung. Doc Williams watched the blood flow and was amazed. "Wow, that's a lot of blood."

"It is," Jack agreed as he bent over the boy again. "Try to calm down, John. It'll make it easier."

The boy was shaking, but Jack was pleased to see that he wasn't moving or fighting it any longer. "You're okay. You did well, and I'd say you'll live long enough to pester your sister for a good long while, sound good? Now I need you to drink this. It is much stronger than the last that I have given you."

John nodded with a smile and slowly drifted off to sleep as the medicine Jack had given him kicked in fully.

They watched over him for the next hour until the fluid in the tube went from a dark red to bright brilliant red then eventually nothing. Finally, the tube was removed. Jack stitched the punctures in his lung wall and his flesh. When they finished, Jack gathered up his instruments to boil them and looked at the other doctor. "Well, you've just assisted with your first lung drainage, congratulations."

He went on as he wiped down the table and the floor. "Now in the future, he may need this done again. I hope not, but you never know. His care is in your hands, and I trust that you'll know what to do."

"I do," Doc Williams said humbly. "Thank you, he would have died without your help."

"Yes, he would have," Jack confirmed. "But it's not your fault. You can only do what you've been trained for, and you did your best. I need to ask you a favor."

Doc Williams looked surprised. "What's that?"

"I'm going to pay Laura's bill myself," Jack informed him.

"That won't be necessary," Doc Williams said. "She has no bill, not anymore."

Jack grinned and slapped the Doc Williams on the back.

"Now that's what I like to hear. You're a good man!"

Jack had finished cleaning up and gave his hands a final rinse. "Well, I'm going to leave you with your patient. I have things I have to do and someone waiting for me in town."

Doc Williams held out his hand. "It's been a pleasure meeting you, Mr. Doc Jacks."

"The pleasure is mine," Jack responded and picked up his bag and stepped out onto the porch where Laura and Tina were huddled together at the end of the porch. Seeing him, Laura jumped up and approached him with an unspoken question in her eyes.

Jack smiled. "Your son will be fine now. Doc Williams knows what to do and will handle it from here."

She squealed and threw her arms around him before stepping back and hugging her daughter who was all smiles at the news her brother would be okay. Laura looked at Jack and stated, "I'm not sure that I want him to attend to my son any longer."

Jack was startled. "Wait a minute here. You saw that it took two of us to do what had to be done. If he had attempted to do this by himself, your son would have died on that table. He did the best he could with the training and experience he had, okay?"

Laura still didn't seem pleased but acceded. "Oh, all right then," she said in a quiet voice.

Jack hadn't told the whole truth, but with being a physician comes experience of which Doc Jacks had lots, but Jack didn't want to see a potentially great doctor get blamed for his lack of it as it would come in time.

Laura and Tina went inside to be with Jonathan.

Jack packed up his bags, mounted up, and rode back to town. He arrived back in town around the same time that Laura realized that he had left. Jack looked up at the sky and saw that dark clouds were blowing in, and a winter storm was imminent. He kept his gaze on the sky, smiled, and uttered a personal prayer to his parents above. "Dad, Mom . . . it's days like these that are the most pleasing. Thank you for putting me through college." With a proud smile, he lowered his head back to the trail, patting his horse on his side of his neck as if to congratulate the horse for a job well done.

He continued to ride into town and stabled the two horses then went back to the hotel, knowing that Tim wouldn't be far as it was only two o'clock in the afternoon. He went to the clerk to get his room key and bags as he needed to change his clothes before going anywhere. The clerk eyed his bloody shirt.

"I heard you are assisting Laura with her son. Everything go well?" The clerk was still staring at Jack's shirt.

"I would say yes, *yes it did*. Thanks for asking," Jack, very proud of the events, stated with a positive, firm voice.

"I need that room key, please," Jack stated.

"Oh, sure thing, sort of got tied up in the conversation. I was instructed to give you another room as well, much fancier and bigger. There won't be any extra cost. In fact, I am not to take any money from you today. The owner wants to talk to you in the morning as he is already gone for the day."

"That will be fine. Thank you very much," Jack replied.

Jack then proceeded to his room. "Wow this is some room," he said quietly to himself thinking the bed alone could easily sleep four people. Wash basin was of great art details, towels were like new, room smelled like it never been slept in or smoked in, very clean. Jack was very impressed.

He stripped off his shirt and stretched then poured fresh water into the basin on the washstand and quickly splashed water on his chest and face. He dried off and ran his fingers through his hair. Feeling a little more human, he grabbed a clean shirt and put it on then headed to find Tim.

Jack approached the clerk and gave him his shirt, asking, "Could have this sent to your cleaners here?"

"I can do that," the clerk replied

"By the way, thank you for the room. If I knew this room was available when I came here yesterday, I would have rented it. Thank you very much," Jack stated as he was very pleased.

"Actually, we are not allowed to rent that room. The owner only allows certain people that he knows use it, and occasionally, the owner once in a while. Other than that, it's never used," the clerk advised.

"Well . . . I am very honored. Thank you again."

The clerk gave him a smile with a polite nod as Jack walked out.

With Jack's surprise, there was a snowstorm taking place outside. He turned up his coat collar and walked to the saloon to find Tim.

It didn't take Jack very long to walk to the saloon. Once inside, he brushed the snow off his clothes as the snow was wet and heavy. Then he heard Tim being his obnoxious self telling jokes.

Tim looked up and saw him come in. "Well, I'll be damned. It's Doc Jack, the great doctor, deputy . . . what else are you, Jack?" Tim hollered with the slightest tone of sarcasm in his voice.

"Hey, Tim, I think you've had enough, so simmer down," Jack warned, knowing that Tim wasn't a good drinker at the best of times.

"Come on, Doc, take out them guns and show these good folks how they work. C'mon, Jack . . . ," Tim yelled.

"Enough," Jack growled.

The other men around Tim were just as inebriated, and one put in, "Hey, he's already told us all about you, no harm done, but we'd like to see what he's been talking about. Your friend Tim here actually was speaking very highly of you. He states that you are an entertainer for kids with your handguns. No harm intended, could we see how you entertain these kids?"

Jack raised an eyebrow. "You would, would you?"

He rolled his eyes and drew his guns, unloaded them and, for the next three minutes, proceeded to entertain the group of men while Tim bragged to anyone who would listen. "Yup, that's my friend Doc Jacks."

"Wow." Patrons cheered. "Jack, that was something else. Thank you. Can I buy you a beer, sir?" the man asked.

"I thank you, but I am hungry, actually. So I will pass on that beer. Maybe another time."

The gentleman accepted his refusal with "Okay, another time it will be."

Jack reloaded and holstered his guns. "Okay, Tim, that's enough. You need some food in that belly of yours too," Jack stated with concern of his being more than half cut.

"Gentlemen, it's been a pleasure," Jack stated.

Tim and Jack proceeded to get something to eat then returned for some poker playing for the rest of the day and evening as well. Tim continued to run off at the mouth and was having a blast. Jack, as usual, walked out with far more cash than he'd walked in with. Jack may have walked but not easily as he had Tim thrown over his shoulder and was carrying him back to the hotel where the clerk rushed up the stairs ahead of them to open Tim's door so that Jack could dump him on the bed before retiring to his own room. Giving the clerk a small tip, Jack thanked him and went to his room two doors down.

The next morning, Jack was not up early 7:00 a.m. Jack quickly washed, dressed, and went to knock on Tim's door. As he was walking to Tim's room, he came face-to-face with a man he had seen Tim having a drink with the day before. The man had been knocking on Tim's door.

"I don't want any trouble, see? It's just I heard what you did for Laura and her son. I actually know Tim. I tried his room but didn't get any answer. He mentioned yesterday that you were looking for six men," the man stated with a look of nervousness.

"Well, seems they are all in town. Well, four of them now. Two just left to head for British Columbia. Actually they left prior to sunrise, I tried Tim's door early this morning around 1:30 a.m. to tell you what I overheard. Sorry, I thought I would give Tim this info."

"What about the other four?" Jack asked.

"They're staying to confront you if you make this far. At this time, they are unaware you're here. And no one knows either." The man, feeling more relaxed, could tell he was sincere with his words.

"Thank you," Jack replied. "Here, you saved me much time." He place five dollars in coins in his hand.

"If you hurry off, you're sure to catch up with them. Just don't mention to anybody you got your info from me, please. And thank you, sir."

"You're welcome. And I never heard anything from you. Good day, sir," Jack announced.

The man quickly left.

He continued to the next few steps to Tim's room and knocked on the door.

"Wake up, Tim."

After the fourth knock and still no answer, he tried the door only to find it locked. He banged on the door until Tim crawled out of bed and over to unlock the door.

Jack looked down at Tim in amusement as he was still on the floor. "Well, are we going to try this again with no interruptions today? I am sorry, Tim," Jack stated.

"You know, Doc, it's just what you do, no need to apologize," Tim said.

"I wasn't sure as you seemed pretty pissed with me yesterday when I came into the saloon," Jack pointed out.

"I was sort of," Tim admitted. "I am proud of you, Jack, really I am. I wish I was as talented as you. Everywhere you go, people love you. You have women chasing you, you have money, and you play poker like you invented the game. You can fight, you can shoot your guns just as well as you can entertain children, which they just think you're the best. Every time I'm with you, your talent comes out. I'm impressed and jealous all at the same time. So I'm sorry for being an ass."

Jack digested this for a moment. "Well, Tim, I respect you for being there for me as a friend. As I've told you before, I don't really don't have male friends, probably for all the reasons you just mentioned.

"It didn't come naturally though. I was brought up from a young age with good training, so I have an advantage," Jack said. "But, Tim, you will always be my friend." He reached out to shake Tim's hand and help him up from the floor as seemed to be their habit every morning lately. Jack thought with a chuckle.

Tim started to wash as he heard a very loud gas sound escape from Jack's butt. Being men, this was common; however, when he saw Jack go over to open the window, knowing quite well that meant, there was a linger about to take over his room.

"Nooooo! Jack, tell me that you did not." Tim was afraid to breathe through his nose but decided it was infinitely better than through his mouth. "My god, get out of my room!"

Jack laughed and held his hands out. "But I opened the window! What more do you want?"

"How about not passing gas in *my room?*" Tim grumbled,

"Hey, c'mon, Tim, it smells like roses," Jack said, sniffing the room with more laughter. "Just call that the wild rose scent. Isn't that what they call it in Alberta?"

"Wild rose?" Tim declared. "Well, I'm sure the wild roses around here don't smell like that. Damn, Jack, you stink," Tim retorted.

Jack was just wasting time so that Tim couldn't escape the room too quickly. He raised his nose in the air and sniffed loudly. "See, it's gone already." Then deliberately raised his leg and did it again just to aggravate Tim, and it worked.

Tim just shook his head. "Okay, I'm ready. I'll shave tomorrow. I can't stay in this room another minute. Damn it, Jack."

Jack was in tears of not just the smell but watching Tim's expression heading for the door, his shirt still not down up pulling the other suspender over his shoulder.

Once out of the room, Jack was still laughing.

"Man, Jack, you have to stop eating raw bacon," Tim demanded, shaking his head from side to side.

They went downstairs and met the clerk at the counter. The clerk noticed Jack was all smiles.

"I see it looks like you're in a great mood this morning, Mr. McDougall."

"I am in a great mood," Jack replied. "Best morning I had in a long time." Jack laughed.

"I'm glad you think that's humorous," Tim stated angrily.

The clerk, looked uninformed as his eyes squinted slightly one more than the other, looked at Jack like "What is he talking about?"

Jack just raised his shoulders and raised his eyebrow as if to say no idea.

"Here, I'll pay for last night. *My room,* that is." Tim glared at Jack.

This started Jack laughing again.

The clerk stopped him. "No need, I've been instructed that there's no charge for the two rooms and that I am to inform you that you're welcome to stay another few nights at no charge."

"Okay," Tim said, looking confused. Then they saw Laura come around the corner and walked straight up to Jack and kissed him. "Good morning," she said brightly.

Slightly bemused, Jack replied, "It is, isn't it?"

"Good morning, Tim," she said and kissed him on the cheek.

"Hey!" Tim complained playfully, "If you're going to kiss me, at least do it on the lips too."

Laura laughed and gave him a quick peck on the lips, and Tim smiled. "Now I agree that it's a good morning." All four of them laughed.

"Breakfast is in five minutes," Laura informed them as she headed toward the restaurant.

"Now this is good service," Tim said.

The two men sat down and Laura came over. "Coffee?"

"Yes, please," both men replied.

Jack inquired, "How's Jonathan doing?"

"Very good, actually. He's breathing well again, and his fevers broke," Laura informed.

"Here comes my boss. He wants a word with you."

Bill came over to the table. "Mr. Doc Jacks, I really appreciate what you did for Laura's son. Just because I'm honored to have you in my hotel, I'll cover the costs of both your rooms for another three days, and that includes breakfast too."

Jack nodded. "I appreciate that, but I have my own money."

"This is my request for what you did yesterday. Please, I insist," Bill stated.

"Thank you," Jack replied.

"You're always welcome here," Bill said.

"Much obliged, sir, thanks again." Jack felt a little embarrassed to be given such a reward for something he would have done for nothing.

Laura came back to their table with breakfast in hand. "Half pound of bacon barely cooked and three eggs for you, and bacon cooked with three eggs for you." She set down their meals.

"Dear GOD NO!" Tim spoke. "I mean the raw bacon. This guy has to start eating cooked food." He shook his head.

Laura looked at Tim with a smile but was waiting for the main reason of his comment.

Jack quickly changed the subject. "So tell me again, how's Jonathan? We got sidetracked there when Bill came over." Jack, with a smile, knew Tim was going to let the cat out of the bag.

Laura hesitated to answer and then said, "Doc Williams told me that it was you that saved my son's life and that he felt it would be wrong to charge me and cancelled my bill that I owed him. But this doesn't come close to covering what you did," she said, meaning the hotel and breakfasts being paid for.

"Hey, stop right there. I don't need anything but a thank-you, and that's plenty," Jack assured her. "Got it?" Jack said with a stern but polite voice.

"Got it," she said with a smile. "But I will always be indebted to you."

"How about you both let me fix you dinner one night?" she offered.

Jack was noncommittal. "Maybe some night. We're still going to be in and out of town, so we'll see. If you don't mind me asking, why are you not at home with Jonathan?"

"You never gave me a chance to thank you yesterday, so I came in to see you," she replied.

"So Doc Williams is still there from yesterday?" Jack asked.

"Yes, he said he'd stay till I got back," she said. "I told him to expect me back by noon, and my boss gave me a few days off, which I took now that I'm not as stressed about the money, so thank you again, Jack."

Jack and Tim finished eating and got up to leave. They walked outside, and Tim looked at Jack knowingly and said, "See what I mean? Everybody loves you."

"C'mon, Tim," he said, smiling. "I only have one friend though, and you're it," he said as he put his arm around Tim and pulled him off the boardwalk. They walked over to the stables and saddled up their horses.

"Hey, Tim." Tim turned to face Jack. "I would have told you this during breakfast, but we had company around our table." Jack continued, "Some guy was knocking on your door this morning. You didn't answer, but it was an acquaintance or an old friend. He came by to tell you that all six of the men were in town. However, two left around sunrise heading for British Columbia."

"Great! What now?" Tim replied.

"Well, I say we go after the two that left this morning. The other four apparently don't know we're in town and intend to stay. So let's just hope they stick around," Jack mentioned.

"All right then. We should grab some supplies. We could be gone a while. As for the wagon, it won't make it where we are going," Tim mentioned.

"Well, let's get on our way then. And Tim, you are a friend. I appreciate what you're doing for me, and my parents really thank you," Jack announced.

Once supplies were gathered, horses mounted, Jack and Tim rode out of Calgary in a fairly quick pace. As they got to the outskirts of town, they slowed down as they realized that the two men ahead of them would probably travel until dark, and they didn't want to risk winding their horses too early in their pursuit.

"We can cut through here and end up in front of them," Tim pointed out a spot on a map he was carrying. "Or we may come in just behind them. There's a lot of brush and trees through there, but it will save us a few hours of time. It will take a few good hours cutting through though."

"Well, Tim, that's why I pay you the big bucks, so lead the way." Both men laughed.

Tim wasn't kidding about the bush and trees. It was slow going at some junctures, and they were both fighting their way through.

"Look out!" Tim yelled as he let a branch go, and it swung back. Jack looked up in the nick of time, ducked just before the branch would have taken him right off his horse.

"Watch what you're doing up there, Tim!" Jack bellowed, hearing Tim's laughter.

"Sorry, Jack. My eyes are not very good, still watering from when you were in my room this morning." Tim was getting a kick out of Jack not paying attention.

"Yeah, whatever," Jack replied with a frustrated frown.

They worked their way through and emerged out the other side into a pasture where Tim stopped to wait for Jack to catch up.

After another hour, Jack was furious, mostly at Tim thinking he was getting even for passing gas in his room. It was of great joy to see the clearing just yard ahead.

"See, that wasn't so bad," Tim said, trying not to laugh at the whipping marks, and the frustration that was on Jack's face was priceless. "Okay, the road they're on is about a half mile to our right, which will bring us to the same trail that they're on."

They rode on for about ten minutes until they arrived at the path in question. When Tim looked down and remarked, "Well, look at this, Jack. You can thank the Lord that it snowed yesterday. Here are their tracks. We are behind them."

As they rode forward, Jack thought about how very mild the weather conditions were. The Peterborough area was usually buried under two feet of snow at this time of year.

About fifteen minutes on the new trail, Jack and Tim heard a woman's screams coming from farther up the path. The men both looked at each other and nodded in agreement. They urged their horses forward into a gallop, charging up the snowy trail. Around a small bend, they came upon a wagon and two horses, but no one in sight.

Another scream from the trees and bushes on the left broke the silence. Tim drew his rifle from its scabbard; Jack drew his pistol. They quickly dismounted their horses and moved forward toward the desperate sounds.

Several moments later, they spied a clearing ahead and could see movement in the brush beside. The scene before them sickened and appalled both men, and they stared in disbelief at what they saw.

Once getting a better view of what was happening Jack was outraged.

"Hold up right there. Don't make another move. Don't even as much as to scratch your ass as I will put a bullet in you faster than you can blink. Now *very* slowly unduo those gun belts with one hand, just let those belts fall to the ground," Jack ordered.

Tim quickly let them know Jack was not by himself. "You heard the man. Drop them." He cocked the lever-action rifle, putting a bullet in the chamber.

The two men hesitated but did as they were told when they saw that both Jack and Tim had their guns trained on each of them. Jack motioned with his gun for the men to move away from the woman. She looked up hopefully at Jack, and he spoke softly to her. "Ma'm, if you can get on your feet, it's best that you head back to the wagon," Jack stated with a calm voice.

She struggled to her feet and held her head high as she stepped carefully away from the men, moving quickly back toward the wagon.

Jack kept his gun centered on the two men while Tim moved in to collect the sidearms that each of them wore. Tim collected the guns slowly, walked backward till he was close to Jack's side then turned his back on the men, whispering to Jack, "This is the two we're looking for, Jack."

Jack drew in a sharp breath. "You sure?" said Jack in an eerily calm voice.

"I'm sure. There's no question in my mind. It's them. I am not blind. They were with the guys in Peterborough. Jack, I am telling you," Tim replied.

"Okay. Go attend to the woman," Jack ordered.

"What are you going to do, Jack?" Tim asked

Jack whispered, "I'm not sure yet. *Go.*"

Tim headed toward the wagon to assist the woman, leaving Jack to his deliberation.

Jack stood and stared at the two men, men who had, in all likelihood, murdered his parents or at least assisted in the murder. He came to a decision at last. "The two of you start walking out toward the wagon and get yours going." Jack followed with his gun still trained on the two.

Just as they got close to the wagon, Jack stated, "This is your lucky day. It's a good thing this lady didn't suffer any serious injuries, or you wouldn't be standing right now. I suggest the two of you mount up and get on your way."

Tim threw them their guns.

Tim eyed Jack because of what he was doing but did as he was asked and tossed their guns to their feet.

"Now pick up your guns and go," Jack said as he reholstered his gun.

"Noooo! You can't let them go! Look what they did to me!" screamed the lady, who had paused to listen to Tim's words.

"Hush, ma'am," Tim whispered in the woman's ear. "These men helped to kill Jack's parents. He won't be letting them go free."

The two men watched Jack warily as they holstered their guns and headed for their horses.

Just as they were both thinking this was their lucky day, strapping their guns back to their waist, "Hey," Jack yelled. Startled, both men whirled to face Jack. "I forgot to tell you who I am."

Both men were wondering.

"My name is Daniel Jack McDougall Jr., now also known as Deputy Jack McDougall from Peterborough, Ontario," Jack replied in a menacing tone.

The two men's faces instantly drained of color upon hearing this pronouncement. Their hands flashed down to draw their guns. Before either man could clear their holster, two shots rang out from Jack's handgun. Each now had a neat hole in their chest, Jack watched as the both hit the ground.

One of the men died within seconds after hitting the snowy ground. The other opened his eyes, and Jack looked directly into them. The outlaw still had enough strength to slowly take his revolver out of the holster so slow it was not of any threat. Jack stepped to his side and placed his foot on the hand in question.

"That's for Daniel and Rachel McDougall," Jack said as the life faded from the outlaw's eyes.

Jack confirmed that they were both dead by placing his fingers on each of their throats. Then he reholstered his own gun.

Jack walked back toward Tim and the woman waiting by the wagon. The woman had wrapped herself in her shawl, which had lain, discarded by the outlaws, on the ground by the wagon.

"I hope they rot in hell," said the woman. "Thank you to both of you." She smiled of gratitude.

"Ma'am, just glad you're okay," Tim replied.

"Ma'am, I'm a doctor. They call me Doc Jack, Dr. Daniel Jack McDougall that is. Can I clean up your injuries and then we'll escort you to wherever you're headed?"

"Please!" Being a little stunned from Jack's words. "Yes . . . I'd be grateful . . . ," she said taking a breath. "Thank you, you surely saved my life. My name is Susan West. Thank you again," she stated.

Jack poured some water from his canteen onto a clean handkerchief then carefully wiped away the dried blood and dirty handprints from Susan's face and arms. Their eyes met for a brief moment.

Jack saw something that he never seen in a woman before. Her beautiful blue eyes just made Jack speechless, her hair was the color of a ripe wheat field in the fall, and her skin, where it wasn't bruised and scraped, was soft and unblemished.

He also took note of the wedding band on her left ring finger then quickly changed his direction of thought.

"There, all done. Now let's get you back to your husband," Jack said.

"I'm a widow. My husband died two years ago," replied Susan. "But I'd greatly appreciate it if you could escort me back to my home. I'm feeling quite shaken by this whole experience. I dread to think what may have happened if you hadn't come along when you did!"

Jack took the hint when she mentioned that she was a widow.

"Just the same. We will be honored to escort you home. Let me help you up," Jack replied.

Jack helped her up onto the wagon and tied his horse to the rear. Just then, Tim cleared his throat, calling attention to himself.

"What about the bodies? We can't just leave them here for the coyotes, although I would like to," Tim stated.

"Right!" Jack remarked. "Mrs. West, would you mind if we put them in your wagon, and once we've seen you home, we'll take them into Calgary, turn them over to the sheriff?" asked Jack.

"You mean Brian Smith? That's the sheriff of Calgary. As for those jackasses, I much prefer you just left them, but I understand. Yes, you are more than welcome to put then in the back, whatever makes it easier for the two of you."

Tim and Jack proceeded to carry the bodies of the two outlaws, placing them in the back of the wagon.

"Hey, Jack, look here," commented Tim, pulling two rifles out of the scabbards of both horses. They were in fact the rifles that had been stolen from the McDougall store. He found another two rifles wrapped in the blanket roll strapped behind the saddle.

Jack looked at the rifles but didn't say a word. He helped Tim load them onto the wagon, and when all was secure, he climbed up onto the front seat beside Susan, released the side brake, shook out the reins, and proceeded to turn the wagon around on the trail.

Jack need no directions as he followed the still fresh wheel marks of the wagon made prior. Jack, who was in deep thought of his parents as well what just happened, did not say much at all.

"You okay, Jack?" asked Susan in a soft voice.

Jack then released an uncontrollable tear that followed quickly with a few more tears now slowly falling down his face.

She reached over and gently wiped the tears from his cheek. "Your friend, Tim, told me a bit about what happened. Sorry to hear about your parents."

"Thank you, Mrs. West. That's kind of you. Truthfully, I think it was you that slowed my reaction to my thoughts," replied Jack. "You are okay, aren't you?" Jack was now refocusing.

"I am, Jack, thanks for asking, and please call me Sue."

"So, Sue, tell me what happened back there besides what we saw." Jack really just needed her to talk some to keep his mind from thinking too much.

"I was heading for Calgary, going to see about hiring a couple of ranch hands for my spread. I saw those two coming toward me from the side. So I slowed down thinking I might ask them if they were looking for work. Figured it might save me a trip. Guess I need to use better judgement, maybe be more cautious. My husband used to look after most of our dealings with other people. What about you? What brought you this way, Jack?" Sue asked.

"They did," said Jack, jerking his thumb at the two dead men in the back of the wagon. "I've been tracking six of them for just over a month, all the way from Peterborough, Ontario, to Calgary. We left the town of Calgary knowing that two of them came this way. Tim has seen them before and clued me in to who they are. Tim's been with me since I left Peterborough. And that's about it," Jack stated

"Did you two grow up together in Peterborough?" Susan asked in a curious manner.

"Well, that's a long story. We met a long time ago and haven't seen each other since. The sheriff in Peterborough hooked me up with Tim just before I left town. He figured I could use the help in tracking the men who killed my parents. He also made me a deputy sheriff so I could legally chase after them," Jack continued. "I'm a doctor by profession, so Tim's been a great help. He knows a lot about tracking. I'm a bit of a green horn at it, like I never left Peterborough or, should say, Ontario. There was no need," he stated.

"So you've come a long way," Susan remarked

Jack, thinking hard, then stated, "I did, and I'm not sure if I'm going to return."

"Why's that?" asked Sue.

"I've lived in Peterborough my whole life. I thought about leaving from time to time, but with my parents there, I never wanted to live somewhere they didn't. Now, I can't think of one good reason to go back, other than my uncle. He was close to me, but I need to get on with my life," Jack said with sadness in his voice.

"That's some story, Jack, really. I hope things work out for you," Susan stated with a caring voice.

They continued on in silence when the wagon rounded a bend through tall cottonwood trees coming out on a clearing beside a quiet stream that opened up in the distance to a large pond. Cliffs rose on two sides of the pond towering at least thirty feet in the air.

"This is my place," Sue said with pride. "I sold off a quarter sections last week. So I have the funds to expand the cattle business, that's why I need the hands. I just can't manage the place and grow the business without help."

In the foreground was a large house with smaller outbuildings and a large barn and paddocks set back toward the stream. Behind the barn, Jack could see cattle grazing and drinking from the pond. A fence surrounded the house and buildings, and the name Hidden Valley Ranch was spelled out on a sign above the main gate.

"I'd like to invite both of you in for lunch. Those two ruffians won't be going anywhere, and I'd like to repay your kindness," offered Sue with a hopeful look on her face.

"That's mighty kind of you, Mrs., I mean, Sue. I'd like that a lot." Jack looked down and away as he felt the color rise to his cheeks. *God, I feel like a damn school boy again*, Jack said to himself.

"Tim!" Jack hollered back to his friend. "Sue here has invited us in for lunch. Let's get the horses and wagon settled. We've got time for a quick bite and still get into Calgary before dark."

Jack, stepping down from the wagon, quickly went to the other side to assist Sue.

"Thank you, Jack. See you boys in a few minutes, the door's open. Don't dawdle now!" Susan smiled.

Jack drove the wagon around to the barn and unhitched the horse. With Tim's help, they removed the tack from all the horses and settled the animals with water and feed in a large paddock beside the barn.

After washing up at the well, the men hurried to the house and in the back door through which they had seen Sue moving back and forth preparing a meal for them. They entered the kitchen, and Sue motioned for them to sit at the table. Jack noticed that Susan had changed her clothes and cleaned herself up. She was a beautiful woman.

Sue had laid out two heaping plates with thick slabs of ham and fried potatoes. Fresh biscuits that were obviously made earlier that day sat in a basket, steam rising and mingling with the smell of brewing coffee, making the men's mouths water.

"Would you men like milk with your meal?"

"Yes, ma'am," said Jack and Tim in chorus.

She got both glasses and a pitcher of milk, and once the milk was poured, she sat down with Jack and Tim. Without another word, Jack and Tim began eating, trying at first to be polite as they wolfed down their meal.

Jack wiped the last of the ham grease from his plate with a final bite of biscuit, pushed his plate away from himself, and sighed contentedly. "I must say that was one heck of a feast, Sue. I haven't had home cooking in quite some time."

"You're not kidding. May I have the last biscuit?" Tim said around a mouthful of food, trying to smile at the same time.

"It's been a while since I had someone to cook for. I'm glad you enjoyed it, and yes, Tim, please eat up! I want to thank you both again for saving me. I truly am grateful. You know that I am looking to hire a lead hand and a couple of wranglers. I've found a couple of young men to help with the general chores, and they'll be here next week. I intend to keep all the hands well fed. If I don't have to ride one more fence line, I'll cook day and night!" Sue hesitated and then asked in a rush, "Do you gentlemen know the cattle business? I'd like to offer the jobs to you if you'd be interested."

"Yes, ma'am," Tim replied. "There isn't much about ranching I don't know. But at this time, I am committed to give Jack a hand."

"The offer is mighty tempting, Sue . . . but I have to deal with the other four men who murdered my parents. I just can't let it go. I feel that neither my parents nor I will rest until I do. I shouldn't take more than a week or two to finish this business. Then I'd be honored to come back and help in any way I can. Although I think what I'd find most satisfying would be to continue as a physician. I may even open a saloon, well, seriously considering it any way," Jack replied

"You never mention this at all to me," Tim replied.

"Well, that's because there's no sense talking about it till I was sure, and I do like it out here. So I don't know right now. It's in my mind," Jack stated.

"Just so happens that there is a small town near here that is looking for a physician. You'd need a place to live, and I could use the extra board money, so you could stay here!" Sue was beside herself with glee at having come up with this thought that quickly left her mouth. Jack was a mighty handsome man. Who knew where this would end, she was still thinking.

"You are a quick thinker, Mrs. West! Let's see how this matter pans out, and then I'll come back and may take you up on your offer. As for Tim . . ." He eyed his friend, whose attention was still riveted on his last biscuit, savoring each bite.

"I think he's already made up his mind and will be staying with you. I believe it's best that you stay here, Tim, when I return with the bodies to Calgary. I'll be contacting the sheriff and asking for his help to arrest the other four outlaws."

Tim, looking confused and just a bit hurt, wiped his mouth with his napkin and laid it on the table. He looked across the table at Jack and raised his eyebrows in askance. "I was under the impression that you wanted to deal with these outlaws yourself, but you still need me, Jack."

"Truthfully, I do, but this whole situation with the two men lying dead outside has made me ill, Tim. I deliberately returned their guns, so they could draw on me. I knew they didn't have a chance. I don't think my parents would be proud of me, and I want to do what's right from here on out. I need to do this, Tim," Jack stated.

"Well, Jack, then a couple of things. First, however it went down, those two men deserved to die. I believe they had as much chance as you did, no matter how fast you think you are with a gun. Either one of them could have been faster, you don't know, so get off your high horse, young man! Second, I promised you I'd see this through to the end. You're my friend now, Jack, and I am going to be with you. So thanks for giving me an out, but I'm coming with you."

Jack chuckled and held out his hand in a peace offering. Tim took his hand, and they shook, smiling at each other. "Thank you for your help and loyalty. Now, why don't you head out and start getting the horses ready, Tim, and I'll have a proper look at your injuries, Sue. Sue's been guarding her side since we have been in here, I have been noticing. Would you mind, Tim?"

"Not at all, Jack. Mrs. West, thank you. That meal was the best."

"You're welcome, Tim. And thank you," Susan stated.

"Well, let's take a look. You may wish to grab a covering . . . uhm for . . . uhmmm." Jack actually was embarrassed. "I am sorry, my head's not clear at the moment. Can you get a towel please?" Jack's face was a thousand shades of red.

Sue's face was just as bad, thinking what a true gentlemen he was.

"No problem, Jack." Sue stepped away to grab a towel, smiling, then slipped in the next room to return with her hands holding the towel up.

Jack slowly palpated the side of her rib cage, which was exposed.

"You have a fractured rib. You're going to be really sore for the next couple of days. I can give you some pain medication, and I'll wrap your ribs," Jack advised.

"Great," Sue replied. "I still need to go into town for supplies."

"I would not advise that. You will be in a lot of pain. Rest those ribs for at least three to four days, I am serious." Jack reinforced his advice.

"We'll get these bodies back to town and talk with the sheriff, and I'll make a quick trip back here in two days to check on you and bring you more medication. I only have enough with me to last for a couple of days, and I think you will need to have the painkiller for at least a week. So at the same, I could bring back your supplies. That is if you can wait two days."

She smiled. "Yes, I can wait." Then she lowered her eyes and in a quiet voice said, "I'd like to see you stay, Jack. It feels nice having you worry about me, and I'd like to get to know you."

Jack reached out and covered her hands with his. "I can't make you any promises, Sue. We'll see what happens."

"Well then, you should leave the bodies in the wagon and take it to Calgary. It'll make your trip easier. I'll give you a list and money, if you really don't mind? It would save me the trip later. I'd be grateful."

"Of course, and I don't mind at all." Jack felt a curious sense of pride that she would feel comfortable enough with him. He gazed at her, again noting just how attractive she was.

"You are a beautiful woman, Sue," Jack blurted, and immediately, his cheeks flushed to a crimson red.

Sue blushed as well then said, "Thank you! It's been a long time since a man has even looked at me that way. Besides, I think you're mighty handsome, so we thought of the same, Jack." They each had big smiles

Jack spied movement through the window and saw Tim near the barn leading their horses from the corral.

"I'd better go tell Tim about the change in plans," remarked Jack, glad for the distraction as he hurried to put his coat on while heading for the door.

"We'll speak before we leave, and I'll collect the list and money from you," said Jack as he pulled his boots on and exited as quickly as if he was too excited with their words.

Sue stood and watched them as they talked for a moment and proceeded to switch horses and hitch Sue's to the wagon. Tim tied their horses on behind and threw their tack into the bed of the wagon. She wrapped her arms around herself, thinking how such a bad day had ended up as maybe the start of a really good change in her life.

When Jack and Tim were prepared to leave, Tim climbed up onto the seat of the wagon, and Jack came back to the house.

Sue had interrupted her gazing long enough to get the list of supplies she needed and handed it and a packet of money to Jack as he mounted the porch.

"I'll expect you back in two days then," she said as much a question as a statement.

"I will be back, Sue, I promise," Jack said solemnly.

He turned to go, quickly climbing up onto the wagon. Tim shook out the reins, and the horse pulled against its harness, moving into a steady walk.

"Good-looking lady," remarked Tim with a smirk on his face.

Jack looked back to the porch where Sue stood. She looked so small and alone. Sue raised her hand in a farewell gesture, and Jack did likewise.

"Sure is mighty fine," responded Jack. It occurred to Jack then that the outlaw's horses weren't tied to the wagon. "What did you do with the other horses, Tim?"

"I left them for Sue. After what they put her through, she deserves to keep them."

Jack smiled at Tim. "You really have changed your ways, getting all soft and considerate. I'm mighty impressed, Tim!"

Time passed swiftly as they enjoyed the scenery, and soon, they arrived in Calgary and went directly to the sheriff's office.

Tim had drifted off to sleep while sitting up, and Jack nudged him awake as they pulled up to a stop.

"Tim, you awake there, buddy?"

"Yah, I hear ya," Tim grunted, opening one eye.

"We're here, my friend."

They stepped down from the wagon stiff and cold from the long rough ride.

Jack and Tim eyed the bodies in the back of the wagon, and with a heavy sigh, Jack headed up the steps and into the office. There was a deputy seated at a desk reading a dime-store novel, and he looked up when the two men entered.

"Good evening, deputy," said Jack, taking note of the deputy's badge. "Would the sheriff be around?"

"Not at the moment. He's down at the saloon checking on a couple of rowdies. He should be back shortly. Anything I can help you with?"

"I think it's best if we just wait on the sheriff, if you don't mind," Jack responded as he opened his overcoat to reveal his deputy's tin pinned to his vest pocket.

"Name's Daniel Jack McDougall. From Peterborough, Ontario. I've have a couple of bodies in the wagon outside. Both men were wanted for murder."

"You're a long way from home then. My name's Rick. Deputy here. Would you like to explain?"

"It's a long story, and I'd really like to wait and tell it to the sheriff."

"I think I'd best go get the sheriff for you then. You can wait right here," said the deputy.

"That is probably best. We'll just sit by your stove and warm up. We've been on the trail for quite some time." Jack moved toward the stove, Tim at his side.

"Pour yourself a cup of coffee if you'd like. It's a fresh pot. It won't take me long to fetch him."

The deputy bundled into his coat and set off, while Jack and Tim wasted no time in getting a cup of coffee poured. The warmth of the coffee settled into Jack's stomach and spread through him, enabling him to think again, thinking of what the sheriff was going to think. He sighed deeply and, as was his way when relaxed, passed gas noisily.

"You rotten, stinking, no-good . . ." Tim gasped, glaring at Jack.

"What, can't a man relax a little?" Jack laughed.

"You better hope the sheriff doesn't come back too quickly! You'll kill him and his deputy just by them having to breathe this air!"

Jack relaxed even more now that he'd had a bit of a laugh, albeit at Tim's expense. Unfortunately, the deputy did moved rather quickly, and within a minute, both he and the sheriff came stomping up the steps and into the office.

The sheriff walked right up to Jack and extended his hand. "You must be Dr. McDougall. I'm right honored to meet you. I heard what you did yesterday helping Laura's son. Everybody in town is talking about you. I'm Brian Smith, the sheriff here in Calgary. My deputy here is giving me quite a little fill-in as we were walking back here."

"Well, first, this is my friend Tim McNabb. He's travelled with me from Ontario. Has my back, you could say."

The sheriff shook hands with Tim and, motioning for them to sit, moved to pour himself coffee. "Well! So tell me what—" then stopped in mid conversation sniffing the air around himself, lifting each of his own boots on his feet, and having a look at the soles. Then looked to the other three men and commented, "There's a boot scraper just outside the door. I think one of you has stepped in something that I'd rather not have tracked into my office.

Jack's face turned a dozen shades of red. Tim pulled his hat down over his eyes and covered his mouth, laughing behind his hand, but he just couldn't contain himself. He burst out in a belly laugh that made Jack feel like crawling into his boots to hide. "No, sorry, Sheriff, our boots are definitely clean," chortled Tim.

Jack blushed even harder. The sheriff, beginning to see the light, stomped over to the door, coffee in hand, and opened it wide, even poking his head out to escape the stench.

He looked back, first at Tim, who promptly pointed at Jack, and then at Jack and said with a smirk on his face, "These two men that are out here in your wagon, did they die of asphyxiation by any chance?"

Jack threw his hands in the air. "It's not that bad!"

The sheriff chuckled and closed the door, having aired out the small office.

"Let's hope that will be the last unfortunate thing we have to smell for the next while." The sheriff directed that comment directly at Jack.

"I'm positive it will be, Sheriff." Quickly changing the subject, Jack stated as for Laura's son. "Jonathan, I'm just glad that I could help."

"Don't be so modest, I heard you saved his life!" The sheriff sipped his coffee. "What I don't get is why a doctor is wearing a deputy sheriff's tin. Do they do this a lot back in Ontario? Making doctors deputies doesn't sound right to me," the sheriff questioned. "And we're all ears for a reply."

Jack spent the next half hour explaining his reason for being there and why he wore the deputy sheriff's tin. Jack continued, "Knowing that two of the outlaws had left town this morning, we headed out after them. We caught up with them a couple of hours out of Calgary. They had attacked a woman on the trail and were roughing up the lady. Susan West her name is from the Hidden Valley Ranch," Jack announced.

The sheriff gasped at this news as he knew Sue well. He had been a good friend to her deceased husband, and he worried often about her being alone out so far from town.

With concern, the sheriff asked, "Is she all right?"

Tim spoke up at that point, continuing their story. "She was after Jack shot them both. In self-defense, I might add. She invited us back to her ranch. Jack tended to her injuries, and she made us the best ham and biscuits I've had since my mamma passed away!" Tim said, still thinking of his belly and great food.

"She has a fractured rib and a lot of bruises. She'll be mighty sore for the next few days or so, but she seems to be made of tough stuff. She'll be fine," Jack said.

"Seems I need to thank you again, Deputy Doc," he said with a smirk from the sheriff as he was staring at Jack. "That woman is a very good friend," the sheriff continued.

"So these two men out in the wagon are in fact the ones you were looking for? Are you sure of that?" the sheriff questioned.

"That's right," Tim confirmed. "I was a witness to purchasing a rifle from them in Peterborough. They talked about it as I am talking to right now, face-to-face that was two of them out of six. No question."

The sheriff stood and pulled on his coat. "I'm just going outside to take a look. Jack, Tim, stay here and finish your coffee. Rick, come with me," he said, referring to his deputy. They went out and lifted the tarp back that covered the bodies. Sheriff realized that they looked familiar.

"Rick, look at this," the sheriff spoke. "These two were with four others that came into town a few days ago. I was just at the saloon calming down those same men."

"So what now?" asked the deputy.

"I'm not sure yet, let's just play it by ear. Don't mention a word to Jack and Tim about this."

They went back into the office, and the sheriff remarked lightly, "Well, they're definitely dead! So, Jack, what are your intentions now? I mean with the other men, if you find them," the sheriff questioned with some concern.

"I came out here to see that all six men paid for what they did. I believe that they should be arrested and sent to jail. Maybe it's not for me to judge them as much as my thought sometimes wonders." Jack continued with short hesitation. "But that's why I am in your office. I just want to put this all past me so . . . if they're here as I was told the other day, well, you tell me now *what?*" Jack raised his shoulders in question.

"You'll be satisfied with them being in jail?" the sheriff responded.

"I am, sir. I don't believe my parents would want me killing anyone, even in self-defense. They certainly wouldn't approve of revenge. If the remaining four outlaws will come peacefully, I'll even escort them back for trial," Jack stated with all honesty.

"I'm glad you feel this way, Jack. I won't tolerate a vigilante wandering the streets of my town. I know where the four men are or, rather, were an hour ago. They were the reason I was down at the saloon when you two arrived in my office. I saw them with the two dead men in your wagon a few days ago. I'd like you and Tim to join me and my deputy to round them up tonight. But remember, we do our best to bring them in alive. If you give me your word on that, we'll get going."

"You have our word, Sheriff," Jack replied solemnly. Tim nodded his agreement.

"Do either of you need a rifle?"

Jack opened his coat, revealing his handguns. "I prefer these," he said.

"I've got my rifle outside," Tim responded.

The sheriff and his deputy retrieved rifles from the gun rack and loaded them, putting spare rounds into their coat pockets.

"Well, gentlemen, unless you'd like to leave it to us that is," teased the sheriff. "Shall we?"

"No! We are right with you," said Jack and Tim in unison.

"Normally I wouldn't invite you along, Jack, but your story touched me, and you've travelled a long way to get to this moment. I don't want to deny you some sense of satisfaction at the end of the trail. You probably don't even have any jurisdiction here in Calgary but . . ."

Tim slipped outside to retrieve his rifle as the other three men continued to load and check their firearms. He returned after a moment with the rifle that had been meant as a gift to Jack from the sheriff in Peterborough. "Jack, I hope you don't mind me using this. I'd like to try to honor Sheriff Rigby's request. Even if it just helps bring the men to justice and not to shoot them, I believe he'll be satisfied."

Jack nodded his agreement. "Of course, Tim. You're becoming a very thoughtful soul in your old age!"

"Old! Why I ought to—!" grinned Tim.

"Okay, gentlemen, as long as you don't start an all out gunfight in the saloon, I suggest we make our stand outside of the saloon. Just too many innocent people in there tonight. It's Saturday after all," cautioned the sheriff.

"Here's how I'd like to see this played out: Jack, you, and Tim head out and down to the saloon, staying on this side of the street. The deputy and I will leave a couple of minutes after you and cross over to the far side of the street. There's a wagon parked directly across from the saloon at the barbershop. It should be there all night, so I will take up a position beside it. My deputy will take up his position in the small walkway beside the barbershop. We'll both be able to see you if you take up positions near the front door of the saloon. When you see any of the four men heading for the door, wave to us, and we'll make the first contact. Maybe luck will be on our side, and they'll come out one at a time and just give themselves up. But . . . well anyway, we all understood." The sheriff met the eyes of each of the men in the room. "Any questions?"

"We understand, Sheriff. Thank you," Jack replied.

With that, Jack and Tim exited the office and turned left along the boardwalk. Darkness was nearly upon the town, and the kerosene lamps were being lit.

Jack took note that the lamps did not run down the far side, so the sheriff and deputy would remain in the dark in their chosen hiding spots.

They walked casually down the boardwalk, Tim ensuring to keep his grip on the rifle very casual, looking to anyone who may take notice of them.

After a few moments, the sheriff and deputy came out of the office and crossed over to the far side of the street. Talking softly between themselves, making it appear that they were just checking that the doors to the closed shops along the boardwalk had been secured for the evening.

The streets were beginning to empty except around the saloon as Jack and Tim neared the front door. Jack realized that the night door had been closed to keep out the cold, which meant that they wouldn't be able to see inside until someone was on their way out. Just then, a man stumbled out of the walkway between the saloon and the next building, doing up the buttons on his pants. Jack figured the patrons must use the alley as their washroom from time to time instead of the outhouse in the back.

Jack looked across the street and saw the sheriff and deputy exiting the doctor's office a few doors down. The sheriff had warned the doctor to stay close by in case this whole situation ended up with gunfire, and someone was injured.

The sheriff and deputy took up their positions as had been outlined.

Just then, Tim, who had been taking a look around the side of the saloon, beckoned to Jack in an exaggerated whisper. "Come over here, Jack." Jack moved over beside Tim, who pointed to a small window on the side of the building. Jack carefully looked in through the small spot that Tim had apparently wiped clear of grime.

Tim mentioned a far table in which he was instructing Jack to look at. There was something familiar about one of them, and it took Jack a moment to realize that this one was the man he had seen riding hell-bent passed him in Peterborough just before he found out his parents had been shot.

"I can stay here and keep an eye on them, Jack. You stay over by the door, and I'll whistle to you if any of them are heading for the door."

"Okay, sounds good, Tim. And, Tim, be careful," Jack said with sincerity.

The sheriff watched this interaction from across the street, wondered if he had made the right decision in including these two. Maybe they were a couple of crazies! *Oh well,* he mused, *just have to hope they can keep it together long enough to get this done!*

Jack returned back to his position beside the door, leaning up against the wall like he was just getting some fresh air. About twenty minutes passed, the sky fully dark now, the only light being cast was by the street lamps and the glow from the saloon windows spilling out across the snow-covered road.

Jack started thinking that maybe they should barge right in and catch them off guard, but he didn't think that the sheriff would want to change the plan. It really was better to have the confrontation outside than in a crowded bar.

Tim whistled at that moment, catching Jack attention, and whispered to Jack, "One's coming out!"

Jack waved his hat to the sheriff and deputy, who immediately moved forward to the middle of the street, rifles raised and ready.

The lone outlaw exited the saloon, turning as he did to shut the door behind him so he didn't see the lawmen right away. As he turned away from the door and took a couple of steps forward, he spotted the sheriff and stopped dead in his tracks.

"Hold up right there, mister!" called the sheriff.

Jack and Tim stood slightly behind the outlaw and to each side, unnoticed as yet, Jack with his handgun drawn and Tim with his rifle at ready.

"Sheriff, I don't know what's going on here, but you must have the wrong guy. I ain't done anything wrong here. I'm just stepping out to take a leak," he said, keeping his hands in the air.

Jack stepped out from the shadows so the man could see him. "Maybe not *here* but how about back in Peterborough?" Jack stated.

The outlaw turned toward Jack seeing the handgun pointed at his heart. He'd heard stories of just how fast Jack was with his guns. But just the same, he was thinking if he threw himself to the right and drew at the same time, Jack wouldn't be fast enough to take aim and fire first.

Unbeknownst to him though, Tim now stood behind him and could read his body language, so as he tried this manoeuvre, Tim raised his rifle butt and clipped the outlaw in the side of the head hard, causing the outlaw to pitch forward into Jack's arms.

The sheriff and deputy moved forward to the steps of the saloon, rifles still trained on the outlaw as they ran closer. Just then the door to the saloon burst opened. A customer staggered through, leaving the door wide opened, the two lawmen in full view of all inside the saloon. He saw the lawmen with their rifle ready and hurriedly retreated back inside. This odd movement was noticed by many near the door, and those customers scrambled immediately to get away from the door, knowing that if there wasn't already trouble, there soon would be.

This reaction, the outlaws spotted the sheriff and deputy through the open door and saw the boots and legs of their comrade as he was being dragged away from the door. Sheriff looked up from his position at the bottom of the saloon steps and met the eyes of one of the outlaws staring at him through the open door. "Damn, somebody close that door!"

Tim stepped forward and quickly drew the door closed, but as he did, all three of the outlaws inside drew their guns and fired shots. One of the bullets ricocheted off the door and hit Tim in the thigh. Tim fell to the boardwalk in front of the door, dropping his rifle in the process. Clutching his leg, he rolled himself under the railing and onto the street, taking shelter under the edge of the boardwalk.

Jack stumbled under the weight of the unconscious man in his arms and fell backward to the ground.

"Tim! Are you okay?" he called to his friend as he pushed the outlaw off himself.

"Got hit in the leg," he said as he drew his sidearm. "Doesn't seem to be bleeding too much, so I guess I'll live." The pain from the gunshot was more than apparent in Tim's voice, even though he was attempting to make light of the injury.

Jack stood and with the help of the deputy, dragged the outlaw across the snowy street to the cover of the wagon.

"Well now, At least we got one out of the way," said the sheriff.

Meanwhile inside the saloon, the shooting had caused chaos.

The leader of the three outlaws, Cliff, quickly surveyed their options. "We have to get out of here before they reorganize out there. Let's make a run for it. On the count of three, we will run through the door. That'll make them duck for cover, and we head around back for our horses and head for that little town out toward the mountains. We can get supplies there in the morning and catch up to Carl and Bill by tomorrow night. Sound good, men?"

Being slightly gullible when it came to their leader and not realizing that Carl and Bill lay dead in a wagon parked at the sheriff's office, Joe and Bob nodded vigorously in agreement. Cliff actually had no intent to go out that door. He was using his own men as a decoy.

"Go on three," sighed Cliff. "One, two, *three go go*."

The door flew open, and two men burst through the door, guns blazing, bullets flying in every direction. Immediately, Cliff ran through the saloon, jumped through the glass windowpane as did patrons in the bar to get out of the way.

Jack dropped to the ground and fired back. Tim could hear the men on the boardwalk above and behind him but could not yet see anyone and struggled to roll over and peer over the edge.

The sheriff took a bullet to the shoulder, dropped to one knee to steady himself as he shot back. The deputy accidently moved in front of the sheriff's line of fire just as he pulled the trigger. The bullet from his rifle tore through the deputy's lower back, dropping him to the ground face first where he lay motionless. The sheriff watched in horror as his comrade went down with his bullet.

Jack took aim on the outlaw who was drawing a bead on the sheriff as he sat frozen in place, stunned by what he had done. Quickly, before the outlaw could fire, Jack squeezed the trigger on his gun, sending a bullet to ripe through the outlaw's heart, dropping him dead where he stood.

Tim, having managed to struggle up high enough to see over the edge of the boardwalk, was just in time to see the second man heading straight for him. The outlaw was stooping, clutching at a bullet wound to the stomach. It never was determined who had shot him, but someone's shot had taken to him during the gunfight.

Tim raised his revolver and shot finishing the outlaw. Silence filled the air as the gunfire ended, and the smoke from the shots fired drifted away on the brisk evening breeze.

Jack called to Tim. "Did you see the other one come out?"

Tim responded, "No, but I heard a window break shortly after these two came out, and I saw a few men run off down the street. Could be it was the one we're looking for."

"Jack! Jack, please, come help me!" cried out the sheriff.

Jack turned to the sheriff and saw the deputy lying in the snow facedown, the sheriff bleeding from a wound on his shoulder. "Let's get him off the street. I can't do anything for him here." He looked around and saw that some of the saloon patrons where spilling out into the street, curious now that the gunplay had ended.

"You men," he called urgently to them, "three of you come help us over here. Get the deputy to the doctor's office quickly," Jack stated.

Jack assisted Tim. The sheriff managed on his own to walk while stating, "Here's my key to the jail. Someone come here, grab it, put that other one on the ground that's still alive in a cell."

Quickly, someone ran over, took his key to do just that.

Once the deputy was in the doctor's office, Jack and Dr. Williams worked swiftly to remove the bullet and stop the bleeding from the deputy's back. Luckily, the bullet had missed the spine and kidneys but had lodged itself against the deputy's hip bone. He would be laid up for quite some time but should recover full use of his hip.

Jack left Dr. Williams to stitch up the sheriff and Tim. The bullets had gone clean through both of them, so they just needed some stitches. Once this was done, and Doc Williams was finished with his patient, Doc Williams produced a bottle of fine scotch and passed it around, each of the men taking a long, well-deserved pull from the bottle to settle their nerves.

"I think we could all use some sleep now," said Dr. Williams. Rising from his chair, he helped Tim to his feet, and between him and Jack, they walked down the boardwalk to the hotel, checked in, and put Tim to bed. Before they made it to the door, Tim was snoring. The combination of the pain medication and the scotch was too much for his constitution at that point.

Jack, returning to help the sheriff home, said goodnight to the doctor, who would stay at his office on a cot to keep an eye on the deputy.

He walked with the sheriff to the jail, and once they had determined that the prisoner was conscious and secured and that the mortician was notified to come get the bodies of the two dead outlaws, they continued on the two blocks to the sheriff's house.

"I wish this evening had gone as planned, Sheriff Smith," Jack started. "But it's not over for me yet. I intend on following the last outlaw first thing in the morning."

The sheriff was silent for a moment as they continued toward his home. Pausing at the gate to his yard, the sheriff turned to Jack. "Look, Jack, I can't stop you from going. I'm not sure I even want you to go after Cliff, but promise me you'll wait for me to see you off. I have some things that will help you on your trail."

Jack gave a tired smile and held out his hand to shake the sheriff's in an act of comradeship. "I'll be up and ready to get my supplies as soon as the mercantile opens. I promised Sue that I would pick up supplies for her, and I need to drop off some medication for her as well, so once I'm finished, I'll stop by your office. I'll appreciate any information you can give me about travelling the mountains west of here too. Thank you for your help tonight. You and your deputy paid a high price."

With that, Jack turned away and made the trek back to the hotel and his room where he lay on his bed fully clothed, exhausted from the day's events.

He drifted into a dream of the outlaw stealing off into the night, sorely unprepared for the hard journey before him. Jack was struggling through chest-high snow as if swimming through it, trying to catch up to the outlaw but never really gaining on him.

Jack awoke with a start, sun streaming in the window, the morning more than just begun. *Damn, of all the days to sleep late!* Jack thought as he jumped up from the bed. He splashed some water on his face at the washstand, ran his fingers through his hair before placing his hat on top of it, and hurried out the door.

He knocked softly on Tim's door and entered the room when he heard Tim's voice.

Tim was sitting up in bed fully dressed, and he looked Jack over as he entered the room. "'Bout time you got up, Jack. I was waiting for you for since sunrise. Thought maybe you'd run off without even saying good-bye. Guess I should have known better."

"How'd you know I'm going anywhere?" asked Jack.

"I just know you'll be after that last outlaw. You aren't put off that easily. You'll go off on your own. I bet you planned on leaving this morning, didn't you?"

"That was the plan. Now I don't think I can get supplies, stop by Sue's, and be on the trail by dark, so I'll use today to get myself properly prepared for a long cold journey and head out to Sue's. I'll leave from there in the morning. Besides, the sheriff told me last night that he has something to help me on my way, so I want to see him before I go too."

Tim, with a look of grave concern on his face, said, "I hope you're not thinking of going alone. I know I'm not in any shape to go with you, but surely, the sheriff can find someone willing to go along."

"I think I'd rather do this alone, Tim. I'll be fine on my own. After all, I've had the best teacher show me how to survive on the trail." Jack gave Tim a meaningful look. "I want to thank you, Tim, for everything you've done for me. You are a good friend, maybe the best one I've ever had. When I get back, maybe we'll both stay on at Sue's. Semiretire. I'll go back to being a physician, and maybe I will make you a partner in Doc Jack's Saloon," Jack said, boasting and with a smile.

"Doc Jack's Saloon! You are serious. You actually came up with a name for it now," Tim replied.

"Yeah, I thought about it more, why not? I sure am not the type of person to take advantage of people, so the staff will be more than happy to work for me than any other saloon around. I still want to be a doctor, so that's where you come in. You manage the saloon, I put out the money."

"Well, I'm in," Tim replied.

"Well, come on, Tim, let me help you downstairs and grab some breakfast."

"All right then. Help me up and hand me those crutches over there, I'm starving. Let's go get some breakfast!"

"Before I forget," Jack opened his coat took out an envelope, "this is for you." He handed the envelope to Tim.

"What's this?" Tim inquired.

"Your pay. You deserve it even though you did this for my parents. This is something from me," Jack said with sincerity in his voice.

Tim opened the envelope. "Damn, Jack, there's a lot of money in here, like *a lot*. Are you serious, Jack? This is mine?" Tim asked.

"Tim, *shut up*," Jack said jokingly.

"Let's go for breakfast, Jack."

"Thank you, Jack. You really didn't have to this."

"*Tim*, let's go." Jack smiled.

During breakfast, Jack added some pain medication to Tim's coffee and handed him the packet. "One fourth teaspoon two times a day is all you need of this. Too much can kill you, so be careful. If you have trouble sleeping because of pain, you can take another dose, just not every night. Try not to do too much walking around for a couple of days. Best to have some bed rest and keep your leg elevated for a week, which means you need to stay here. Then you can head out to Sue's. Just make sure to keep the wounds clean and have the doctor check it before heading out."

"Yes, mother," Tim joked.

Jack smiled back and chuckled along with Tim. They both looked up as the sheriff approached their table. "I thought you'd left without seeing me! Thought I'd come see for myself."

"I guess I needed the rest more than I thought. It's been a trying time. I guess it's caught up with me," Jack replied. "I've decided to use the rest of today to get the supplies and get out to Sue's. I'll leave from there at first light tomorrow. I hate to lose the entire day, but I want to be well prepared for whatever may happen out there. I've heard some stories about travellers being held up by the weather out west for weeks, so I guess rushing off was my heart talking, not my brain."

"Glad to hear that, Jack. I'm beginning to like you. I'll look forward to your return. Maybe while you're gone you can consider becoming my deputy when you get back. The town's growing fast. I'll need more than one deputy soon enough."

"Thanks for the offer sheriff. I won't promise anything until I get back. I've really had my heart set on a few other ideas I just don't know."

"Well, you think about it. Either way, before you go, I'd like to deputize you. Make you official so there will be no question that going after this man is within your rights as a lawman in Alberta. We've had enough vigilante justice out here in the past, and we've managed to change peoples' way of thinking finally. Most times they come to me if there's a problem, so I'd like you to do this the right way. I can now see why the sheriff of Peterborough did the same for you. You're a good man, Jack McDougall."

"Whatever you think is best. I don't want to cause any trouble for you, Sheriff," said Jack.

"You just let us swear you in. You don't have to keep the job when you get back but consider it. Once you've been sworn it, I'll take you down to the mercantile to pick up your supplies. The town will pay for them since you'll be on official business. I'll also give you a map of the trail to the other side of the pass. Up at the top of the pass, there's a trapper's cabin. You can take shelter there, use what you need and leave your supplies when you go. The trail down is a tough one. You don't want to carry too much with you, just the basics.

"If you get that far without catching the outlaw, you'll come to a small mining town where you can stock up again. Although I expect you'll find his body frozen along the way somewhere. He's left town without being kitted up right, and I've just had a rider come back from Cochrane telling me that the outlaw didn't stop there. A few of the townsfolk's dogs set to barking last night, and there were fresh tracks through town, one horse. Otherwise, no one has seen him. Dumb fool." The sheriff looked right at Jack and caught Jack's eyes in a hard stare. "You're sure you're ready for this, Jack? Once you get to the other side of the pass, if you make it that far, you'd best not plan to come back until spring. There have been some lives lost in recent years up along that route. Why, the railway even lost some men to avalanches up there. It's not an easy journey you're undertaking, so don't take my warning lightly!" admonished the sheriff.

"I guarantee you I'm not taking this trip lightly, Sheriff, and I truly appreciate your advice."

"All right then, I'll say no more. I wanted to be sure you understood what you're getting into. It takes courage and conviction to do what you're doing and that, combined with good planning and advice, is what you need to survive out there alone, winter or summer." The sheriff conceded at last. "Now, where's the waitress?" He waved the waitress over to their table. "I'll have some coffee while you finish eating, and then we'll make you one of our own!"

An hour later, after seeing Tim back to his room to rest, Jack emerged from the sheriff's office with a shiny new deputy's tin pinned to his chest. As promised, the sheriff had given him a route map and had gone over every detail and marker he would find along his route to the other side of the pass.

The sheriff and his new deputy, Jack, gathered Sue's horse, wagon, and Jack's horse from the stable and purchased both Jack's supplies and Sue's from the general store. Jack took his leave from the sheriff thanking him again for all the help he was providing and promised to let him know the moment he returned.

"Just do me a favor and give my job offer some thought. I think you'd make a fine lawman, Jack," he said as he shook Jack's hand in farewell. Clapping Jack on the shoulder, Sheriff made his way back to his office.

Jack watched him go, realizing how fortunate he was to have met some fine people on this journey of his. He really liked the people in this area and was thinking more and more seriously of staying put here, setting down some roots, so to speak. His face broke out in a grin as he thought of starting a family, maybe with Sue.

He headed off to check on Tim one last time before he left town. Knocking quietly on Tim's door, he entered without waiting for Tim's answer. Tim was snoring softly on the bed, leg propped up as Jack had instructed.

Jack watched his friend for a moment, thinking back to the first time he had met him and how different their lives were now. The leniency his parents had shown Tim, albeit for reasons not to do with kindness but protection of their family, had touched Tim's core and helped him to live a better, decent life. He had become Jack's closest friend and companion, and Jack would miss having him there on this part of his journey.

Tim must have sensed Jack in the room as he stirred and opened his eyes. "Ready to hit the trail?" Tim mumbled.

"That I am," replied Jack. "How're you feeling?" he asked as he approached Tim and felt his forehead with the back of his hand. "No fever, so that's a good sign."

"I'm doing okay, just tired and a bit groggy. I think it's the medicine you gave me. I'm feeling like I could easily sleep the day away."

"Good, good. Just what the doctor ordered. Well, my friend, I'm off then. I'll try to send word once I get to the first town on the other side of the pass. Tim, I wish things were different. I'm going to miss having you at my side." He held out his hand, and Tim offered his. They shook, and suddenly, Jack pulled Tim into a bear hug. He squeezed Tim till Tim pounded him on the back, and when Jack released him, he gasped for air, breaking into a fit of laughter.

"Miss me! You nearly squeezed the life out of me!" Tim sputtered. "But seriously, Jack, I wish I could go too. I feel like I'm letting you and your parents down."

"No," Jack started to protest.

"I know I'm not. It's just the way I feel. Now get out of here before you relax and stink up my room again. You never can make it past about five minutes without a big fart, so get out. I'll expect you back in two or three weeks or not till spring, if it's longer than that."

Jack smiled at his friend and as he opened the door, lifted his hand in farewell. Tim nodded and watched Jack close the door behind him. But not before Jack release the silent air that was stirring in his stomach. Knowing that Tim would not be impressed as he was in no shape to move quickly to open the window.

Moments later Jack didn't even make it to the bottom of the stairs when a yell filled the Hotel.

JAAAACK YOOOOOU S.O.B.

Jack stopped at the front desk on his way out and paid the clerk for Tim's room and board for a week. He also arranged to have a maid check on Tim several times during the day and night for the next week to ensure that Tim would not have to venture too far for food, water, and relieving himself.

Jack drove the wagon out of town ten minutes later and headed for the Hidden Valley Ranch. He was nervous at the prospect of seeing Sue again.

The journey to Sue's was uneventful, the weather rather balmy for a winter day. A chinook had set in, and the warm air was such that Jack removed his winter coat as he travelled.

He stopped for a moment under the ranch sign and took in the view picturing it with no snow, trees, and bushes lush and green grass growing as high as his knees, cattle and horses grazing freely in the fields. He could almost smell the flowers and grass in the air. He *could* settle here.

His thoughts strayed to the last of the six outlaws and to whether he would make it back to try to live this dream. He quickly gave up this line of thought as he came back to the same point he had made with the sheriff. *He had to try!*

He continued up the road finding Sue standing on the front porch with her bare arms folded across her chest. She wore what looked like a summer blouse, all that was need for such a warm afternoon.

"Welcome back, Jack! You're a day early and alone. Is everything all right with Tim?" asked Sue, a look of genuine concern on her face.

"He's fine. It's a bit of a story though, so I'll get the horses settled and unload these supplies, and we'll have a talk," Jack explained.

He drove the wagon around the back and unloaded Sue's supplies, leaving his in the wagon under Sue's watchful gaze. She had tried to help, but he insisted that she let him do it alone. She should still be taking it easy, not lifting anything she didn't have to.

She wanted to ask why he was leaving some of the supplies in the wagon but bit back her questions, deciding to let him explain in his own time. She wasn't sure she wanted to know the answer, which she suspected anyway.

After the supplies were unloaded, Jack took the horses and wagon to the barn and got the horses settled with food and water. Only then did he return to the house to give Sue the explanation she was waiting for. Sue rose from the table as he entered into the kitchen and handed him a cup of coffee she had just poured for him.

"I've made us some supper, just leftovers. I figured you'd be hungry."

"Ah, Sue, you are a considerate woman. Thank you," he said as he accepted the cup and sat at the table.

"So . . ." Sue couldn't contain her curiosity any longer. "Soooo?" Sue was looking for answers.

"I'll just eat this fine meal first and then tell you all about it," Jack stated.

"You'll not get one bite until you start telling me what happened!" Sue said, raising her voice as she took Jack's plate away. Then she looked into Jack's eyes and saw the amusement in them, realizing he was teasing her.

She broke into laughter, Jack joining her, set the plate down in front of Jack, and sat demurely back in her chair.

Jack spent the next half hour explaining what had happened since he left a day ago and what his intentions were now in relation to the outlaw now on the run.

"Jack, it's not the time of year to go off into the mountains. It's just not safe. The railway loses men every year to avalanches up there. Please just let him go. You've done your best," pleaded Sue.

"I've got to try, Sue. It's not in my nature to just quit. I owe that much to my parents."

Sue looked down at the hands folded in her lap and came to a decision. "All right then. I want to help in any way that I can, so follow me," she said, rising from her chair. She headed for the door, stopping to get her shawl from a hook on the wall, wrapping it around herself. Jack followed somewhat mystified, not sure what kind of help she could be referring to.

They went to the barn, and Sue led Jack over to a large chest tucked away in the corner of the tack room. Opening the chest, she revealed it to be full of outdoor men's clothing, presumably her late husband's.

Sue removed and handed to Jack a full-length skin coat—the hair still intact—a thick pair of gloves, and a hat made of beaver fur.

"I'd like you to have these for your trip. The coat's caribou, the gloves and hat are beaver. They'll keep you warmer than anything you'd have bought in Calgary," Sue said as she reached out and stroked the fur of the beaver hat.

"Thank you, Sue," Jack said softly.

Sue suddenly looked up right into Jack's eyes, took the clothing out of his hands, and dropped them to the floor. She reached out and drew Jack into her arms, kissing him full on the mouth. Jack did not resist.

"Let's go to the house," Sue suggested.

Once inside, Jack said, "Well, Sue if it's okay with you, I was considering staying the night then leave fist light."

"You sure can." Sue smiled that he suggested such. "I will make us a good dinner. At the same time, I will do a lot of precooking for you. You will need food that will be already prepared heading in those mountains," Susan stated.

"Yes, but you don't need to do that. I can manage on the trail," Jack replied.

"Jack, we have all afternoon and evening, and it's the least I could do for you. All right?"

"Okay," Jack replied. "I will grab my supplies, bring them in."

The rest of the day and evening, Jack and Susan did just that, also getting better acquainted. Jack brought a bottle of red wine in while dinner was being served. Jack, being a gentleman as he was, even had Sue dancing with him, having a great time. Night had fallen, and two need to get some sleep. It was a long afternoon. Jack had tons of food precooked and packed ready for morning.

Susan, now thinking in her mind that Jack was going to sleep on the coach, decided to change those plans.

"Jack, listen. That couch is not very comfortable. Just to let you know, I have plenty of room for you if you care to sleep in my room," Susan stated with her cheeks blushing.

"Susan, I would like that. Thank you," Jack replied.

Once the fires were brushed up with more wood, both Jack and Susan retired for the evening.

The morning came all too soon for the newly made friends, and they rose quietly while it was still dark, each too wrapped in their thoughts. They did not do much talking while they dressed and saw to their morning routines. They were still a bit shy with each other now that the blush of passion had a new day shining on it.

Sue prepared them a hearty breakfast, and as they ate, they settled into a conversation, revealing small tales of their past to each other.

All too soon, it came time for Jack to leave. He wanted to be gone with the first light of day, which at this time of year was about 7:30 a.m. He figured he would have to ride hard for the first couple of days while the snow was not too deep to make up some of the miles the outlaw had gained on him. Jack, being well rested and having an extra horse with him, should be able to catch the outlaw within four or five days, as far as Jack's estimation went. If not, well then, he'd likely have to go over the pass and down the other side of the mountain.

"I've got to leave now, Sue," said Jack, sadness apparent in his voice.

"Jack, take both of the outlaw's horses so you have a pack horse and a spare to spell off the others. You will be able to move faster that way," Susan suggested. "Jack, you will come back to me, won't you?" Sue begged, tears beginning to stream down her cheeks.

Jack reached out and wiped the tears away, remembering when she had done the same for him.

"Hey now, I said I'll return. I promise. I have a lot of feelings for you, Sue." And he cupped her chin in his hand and kissed her gently on the lips.

"Jack, I think I am in love with you. Please don't *go*." Sue was in tears still.

"Susan, I never break a promise. I will return. I don't know when, but I promise I will be back." Jack once again kissed Susan one last time.

Jack turned away and mounted his horse, urging the horses into a fast pace to warm their muscles for the hard ride he intended. He didn't look back until the ranch was far behind, knowing if he did, he would likely turn around and ride back to Sue's arms.

His thoughts turned to his parents and all he had seen and done since their death. They would have loved Sue. She would have fit right in to their progressively minded family. And how he missed his mother! Tears of sorrow blurred Jack's vision, and he stopped the horse line abruptly.

"Damn!" Jack shouted to the forest ahead of him in frustration.

He wiped his eyes and, while doing so, made a promise to himself, speaking out loud to also make it a vow to God. "If I haven't found this varmint by my birthday, I'm giving up this journey, and I'm going back to that wonderful woman!" Jack's birthday was only five days away when he would turn forty-seven. And to Jack, it was a good time to settle down.

With a new resolve and sense of purpose, Jack picked up the reins and urged the horses on.

The snow started falling as Jack set the horses into a mile-eating trot. He found a steady pace that all the horses seemed comfortable with and posted along, keeping time. The miles melted away under the horses' feet, and Jack's thoughts returned to Sue, imagining the life he would share with her.

He came to a creek after some hours had passed and stopped the horses for a drink, having a quick lunch while he rested them and let them graze lightly on the browned grass.

The land around him was sparsely covered in snow, thanks to the recent chinook, which had melted most of the previous snowfall. He knew that this wouldn't last long. He had been warned that by the next afternoon, he would be into the mountains and that the snow pack there would just keep getting deeper the farther west he went.

After another seven hours of travel, Jack decided to set up camp for the night. It got dark at about 6:00 p.m. this time of year, and he didn't want to try travelling at night not knowing the area.

He got a good-sized fire going with brush lying close to his chosen campsite. Once he had the blaze going, he settled the horses for the night, deciding that hobbling them was the most promising way of keeping them close but would allow them to eat their fill. He melted water in a bucket for the horse to drink since eating snow was not good, for their only source of water. It was time consuming, but Jack hadn't seen a stream since his stop at lunch, and the horses were good and thirsty. They'd travelled a lot of miles that day.

Jack laid a waterproof skin out on the ground and set his rifles and handguns out in a row, methodically taking them apart and cleaning each one thoroughly. He didn't want any misfires if he needed one of them. The sheriff had cautioned him about wolves being about. The bears were in hibernation, but there were still a lot of wolves in the foothills. Prey was scarce now, and there had been some reports of attacks deeper in the mountains. He also sharpened each of his knives so they could split a hair.

He amused himself for some time, practicing his quick draw and throwing his knives at a dead tree lying at the edge of his camp. He sharpened his knives again and stoked up the fire, banking the coals for the evening. Once he had stored his guns back in their holsters and checked on the horses, he settled back on his bedroll and took a long pull from a bottle of scotch he had brought along.

He watched the night sky lit up with a million stars, the occasional spark from his campfire floating up and out into the darkness. A sense of peace came over him, and he drifted into a restful sleep.

About 4:00 a.m. he awoke, shivering in the cold night air. The fire had burned down to almost nothing, so Jack hurriedly climbed out of his bedroll and added some small pieces of wood, stirring them in amongst the coals.

After waiting a moment for the flames to catch, he added some larger pieces and soon had a roaring blaze washing it's warmth over him.

He took a quick look at the horses contentedly watching him as if to say, "City boy can't take the cold!"

He climbed back into his bedding and covered himself to his nose and was soon sound asleep again, not stirring until his internal clock woke him at 6:00 a.m.

After stoking the fire and watering the horse, Jack cooked himself a hearty breakfast of lightly cooked bacon—his favorite—and some biscuits Sue had added to his pack, washing it down with some campfire coffee.

He packed up his camp and set off to the west at first sunlight, moving slowly at first to allow the horse time to warm up. The pace he intended to set for himself over the next few days would be a gruelling one to be certain, but having set a date to return, he wanted to give it a good honest try to catch up and apprehend the outlaw.

Jack referred to the map the sheriff had given him throughout the day, noting the landmarks the sheriff had added with a sense of pride at his ability to find his way in the rugged wilderness of the Rocky Mountains. So far on this journey, it had been Tim that had led the way as Jack had never done much exploring on his own. Making it about fifty miles and not getting lost was a great achievement in Jack's eyes!

The next three days passed uneventfully for Jack. The snow, as promised, got deeper, the days and nights colder as the chinook moved off, and Jack began to feel a sense of impatience. He had one more day until his birthday, and he was nearing the midway point to the top of the pass. He should reach the cabin on his birthday if he could continue at the same pace, which looked entirely promising. He just hoped that he could catch up to the outlaw and put an end to his quest.

As he set up his camp for the evening, snow began falling. By far the heaviest he had seen so far. Soon the area he had cleared for his campsite was covered in snow up to his knees. He had to work hard just to keep an area clear for himself. The horses just stood looking forlorn as the snow rose higher and higher around them.

By 10:00 p.m., the snow was up to the horse's bellies and rising still. Jack struggled to keep the fire going and his bedding dry. He had constructed a small lean to from pine boughs, as Tim had taught him, to keep the weather off them. He had to make one for the horses too as they would not be in any shape to travel come morning if they didn't warm up some. Once he accomplished this, he settled back under his shelter and looked out into the swirling show.

It was time to end the journey. Come morning, he would push a trail through, back down the mountain, and call it quits, not even going to attempt to go to the cabin he was to stay. He'd done his best, but he would be a fool to try to go on with the snow getting worse.

As Jack mounted his horse, the echo of gunshots rang through the forest around him. His horse jumped sideways, causing him to fall to the ground, but he held tight to the reins.

"Whoa, boys!" Jack spoke to the horses, trying to calm them before they bolted away.

Another shot rang out and then another. This time, Jack was able to determine the direction the shots came from. It seemed that someone up ahead of him was in trouble or causing trouble of some kind.

Could he be so lucky as to have found the outlaw, just as he was ready to give up?

He mounted his horse and moved off in the direction the shots had come from. An hour passed, and he entered a heavily wooded area. After a few hundred yards into the bush, he spotted some movement in a clearing ahead.

He halted his horses, dismounting and carefully tying the lead horse securely to a tree. He didn't want them running off if there was gun play.

Taking his rifle from its scabbard, he moved forward, careful not to make any noise in the crisp snow.

At the edge of the clearing, Jack crouched down behind a fallen tree and surveyed the area before him.

A white male, with his back turned to Jack, was stripping the clothing off an apparently dead native male. Another native male was lying face down about forty feet away. The snow around the native's body and upper body was discolored in what looked like from Jack's distance like it was black. However, that was not the color that lay.

The man, who was stripping the native of his moose—and buffalo-hide clothing, suddenly looked up right in Jack's direction, affording Jack a good view of his face.

It was the outlaw! This was the very same man who had ridden, hell-bent for leather, past him after the murder of his parents! Cliff of which his name was found out in Calgary.

Jack gasped and held his breath, lest the mist give his position away, until the man looked away, continuing his grisly business. Jack wasted no time in lifting his rifle, taking aim at the outlaw.

His pride and conscience, however, would not allow him to shoot this man without at least trying to apprehend him.

Jack called out to the outlaw as he rose from his hiding place. Rifle still at ready, Jack yelled,

"Cliff, hold up there. Just stop what you're doing. Put your hands in the air!"

The outlaw, on edge and still alert for danger, didn't hesitate. He dove for cover behind the native's body, drawing his sidearm as he fired off round after round at Jack.

This made Jack back down behind the fallen tree.

The outlaw jumped up and ran for a small copse of trees in the centre of the clearing, which he took up post there.

From the safety of the fallen tree, Jack called out again to the outlaw, "Cliff, my name is Daniel Jack MacDougall. I think you know me by now. You've got two options. Throw out your weapons and come out with your hands raised, or we can shoot it out right here. I'm well-rested, warm, and well-fed. I'm guessing you're none of those. And no matter what happens, I will keep tracking you. I'm staying till you're dead, or you give yourself up to stand trial, so you decide now," Jack sternly announced.

A few moments went by when the outlaw called back to Jack. "Okay, okay, I give up. I'm coming out, so don't shoot!"

The outlaw appeared from behind the large tree, his gun belt held high in the air. He tossed it off to his right and walked slowly toward Jack.

This surprised Jack as he had fully expected this man to put up a fight.

Jack rose cautiously from behind the fallen tree and prepared to move toward the outlaw. He had to step over the tree, and as he did so, distracted for an instant, the outlaw dove toward his pile of plunder on the ground coming up to his knees immediately with his rifle firing.

Jack was not so lucky this time. The bullet clipped Jack's arm. *Damn that hurts*, Jack said to himself.

Quickly, Jack ripped of the caribou coat as he lay, hearing Cliff's voice say "I hit you, didn't I?"

Jack said nothing as he was mending his arm. *Thank god just a flesh wound*, Jack said to himself. Then Jack ignored even to try and stop the bleeding as he knew it was minor.

Jack now thought he needed to move from where he was.

Then he cleverly left his caribou coat beside the fallen tree. Jack then burrowed in the deep snow, working his way underneath.

Jack could still hear Cliff. "You alive, Jack? Talk to me." This started making Cliff think maybe he did get Jack.

Jack thought back on how he used to dig tunnels in the snow when he was a child.

Jack reappeared twenty-five feet from where he started. Cliff, now thinking Jack was no more, stepped out from his new post. Jack lay back cleaning out the snow on the rifle's attachments. Once knowing everything was in operation, he peeked up seeing Cliff walking cautiously toward Jack's coat thinking he was laying there.

Jack just waited off to the side as Cliff put another bullet in the caribou coat, which lay a yards in front.

Jack stood. "You looking for me?" Cliff turned to his right finding Jack standing there, rifle at his side pointing downward. Cliff, wasting no time, raised his rifle at Jack. And a gunshots rang through the forest. To Jack, it sounded like it echoed forever.

The two men stared at each other in disbelief. Jack stumbled losing his footing in the snow, and fell forward planting his rifle to steady his fall, while still gripping his hand gun that just fired its last shot.

Cliff was standing still in the knee high snow, and watched his rifle submerge beneath the snow around his feet. He then looked back at Jack and saw him rise, having found better footing to gain his balance. He saw Jack re-holster his hand gun but his mind hadn't had time to grip the significance of that action as Cliff only registered surprise that Jack would have drawn from his side, when the rifle was still in his hands.

A startling realization dawned as Cliff fell backward in an explosion of snow that engulfed most of his body. He placed his hand on the area where pain registered in his body where the buffalo hide that he had taken from the native lay open. Cliff lifted his hand and raised it over his face and stared at his blood dripping from his palm. Losing strength quickly, his arm fell limply to his side.

Jack worked his way towards Cliff; the closer he came the deeper the snow was. Cliff lay motionless but his eyes darted from side to side and then rested upon the tree tops watching the brisk winter wind blow through the trees as the pine cone at the top became so vividly clear.

Jack now stood at Cliff's side looking down into his eyes. The two enemies stared into each other's eyes as if taking a final measure. Cliff was barely capable of talking but managed to grit out, "Don't think I'm going to pull through this am I Doc?" He had a smirk on his face as Jack stared down at him.

Jack knelt at his side and pulled Cliff's shirt open and ripped a piece of material off and placed it over the wound. The cloth and surrounding area were immediately saturated and the blood sprayed through Jack's fingers in rhythm with every beat of the dying man's heart.

Jack looked back at Cliff and nodded solemnly, "I believe you're probably right. Believe it or not if there was something I could do I would try, but it's no different now then it was with my mother when she died in my arms." Jack pulled his hand away, "I'm afraid there is nothing more I can do."

With those words Cliff nodded and said wryly, "Well I guess we live by the gun we die by the gun."

"That's what they say," Jack replied.

"Well then let me do something for you", Cliff continued, struggling for breath, "That rifle down by my feet, dig it up and wipe the snow off it. There's an inscription engraved in the butt end. I believe that rifle was meant for you, it came from your parent's store."

Jack quickly dug around the area where Cliff's feet were and his hand snagged something solid. He reached in deeper and managed to pull out the rifle which he wiped off with his coat sleeve and sure enough there was writing engraved on it, it read:

TO OUR LOVING SON DR.DANIEL JACK MCDOUGALL HAPPY 46th BIRTHDAY FROM MOM / DAD was the inscription in the solid gold plating.

Tears fell from Jack's eyes as he thought about what a miracle this was as today was in fact his 46th birthday, December 18, 1907. Refocusing his eyes, he swiped the tears from his face and looked back at Cliff. He saw that Cliff was gone, his sightless eyes looking straight above at place he would not be going. Jack leaned forward and pulled his eyelids down. He then said softly, "May God have mercy on your soul."

Jack stood and started to make his way toward one of the natives that was closest. He knew logically what he would find, but for his own peace of mind he needed to check just in case one of them may still be alive.

He was about 10 feet away from the native man's body when the forest went quiet, deadly quiet. The wind stopped blowing the birds stop chirping, all Jack could hear was his own breathing. Then thunder roared and the mountainside felt like it was shaking as Jack stopped to listen to the unfamiliar sound and within seconds he realized that it was the sound of an avalanche.

"OH GOD NO!!" Jack yelled as he attempted to find whatever cover he could or anything to hold on to, but with the depth of the snow his steps were slow an clumsy and he was soon overtaken by a wall of snow over 20 feet high that ripped through the trees snapping them in half and adding to the debris hurtling down the mountain. Jack was thrown and struck from every angle by rocks, trees, and snow which tumbled him over and tossed him like a ragdoll for close to 30 seconds.

Once the moving snow died down again, it had brought Jack about 100 yards away from where he had been first caught in the maelstrom. Jack managed to slowly open his eyes only to be looking directly at a tree trunk that had been dislodged and now trapped against him. He tried to move but was only able to free one arm enough to clear some space close to his face so that he could breathe better. He realized that as well as the tree, he was seeing blue flashing lights.

Jack knew he was in trouble without even knowing the depth of the snow above him. He didn't know it but he lay buried under twenty feet of snow without any hope of burrowing out of this as he was unable to move due to the tightly packed snow trapping his arms and legs.

Hours passed and Jack was still getting what small amount of air was trapped in the snow but it was dwindling rapidly at this point, slowly Jack drifted off to sleep on sleep that he would never wake up from. Eventually freezing Jack completely as death set in.

Spring came in 1908 to Calgary, and Tim and the sheriff decided to try searching in the pass for some sign of Jack. They made their start from Sue's

Hidden Valley Ranch. Sue stood on the porch, the same spot that she had said farewell to Jack, and watched them as they rode off to the west, her hand resting on the swell of her stomach, full of the child that she had made with Jack.

Tim and the sheriff rode on through the days to the mountain pass, stopping at an area that with no doubt an avalanche had took its toll.

Tim began to feel a tingle on the back of his neck, like they were being watched. Tim's horse started pawing the ground *un*noticed. Tim was looking all around him, not knowing that ten feet below him his friend lay.

Must be losing it, Tim thought to himself.

"Well, Tim, there is no way that we will find anything to do with Jack out here. Jack would have been back easy a month ago," the sheriff stated

Both men returned to Calgary days later.

Sue was watching from her porch again as Tim and the sheriff returned. She read the expression of defeat on their faces and cried softly for the love she had lost. She would give Jack the child he had dreamt of, but he would never see him.

Tim continued on the ranch as Sue's lead hand and had the opportunity to tell Jack's children years later all about their father.

Susan West had twins: one boy she named Jeffrey and a beautiful girl Susan named Nicole, both very healthy and loving kids.

And Daniel Jack McDougall aka Doc Jack slept on in his snowy grave.

In the winter of 2009-2010, a series of avalanches had taken their toll in the Rocky Mountains of Alberta, which buried some five snowmobilers. A rescue team and helicopter was dispatched to the location in question.

After hours of hard labor, all five men were found alive. The search dog named Find-him was never in question of his searching capabilities. He did a great job. Then the dog continued his search, pulling away from his handler. This stunned the rescuers involved. Obviously not ready to go.

Find-him stopped at one last location. This attracted all rescuers as all men were found already. Just the same, they decided to gander a look under. To their amazement, they did indeed come across another body, which was frozen solid. This body was dressed in clothing only worn a century ago.

On the body, they also found two revolvers still in its holsters. A caribou coat was also pulled from this location, which gave a small but another clue to who this man may have been. The rescuers all agreed this man was not from this time period.

Finding such a perfectly preserved artifact was a rare gift to find. Archaeologists were indeed impressed when they arrived on the scene two hours later. The body was quickly removed. All rescuers that day were advised by a higher authority that "This body was never here."

The body was sent to a cryogenics research center, which is the study of freezing and unfreezing that of mammals, in hopes that one day, they will be able to freeze a human body with a disease of no cure.

Later, once a cure was found, this body could be unfrozen then cured of its fatal disease, giving back its natural life. These experiments have been in play for years as well, not just used to freeze an illness but also to protect certain humans from fatal war affairs—very well-designed, and I give them all the credit to continue as they do.

My name is Daniel Jack McDougall. *I was* born <u>December 18, 1863</u>. With great masterminds in the universe, our planet that is, I thank these that were involved in finding my body and soul where it laid for over one hundred and two years. I also thank those that returned me back to a living being .

Congratulations to all; I am here and living.

Thank You,

Doc Jacks

I am currently still in the care of some highly trained doctors, but have been visiting a hypnotherapist as well. I am having strong visions, almost graphic daydreams during my waking hours, as well as extremely vivid, realistic dreams at night that seem familiar yet I can't seem to make my conscious mind pull the pieces together.

Due to the years that I spent frozen in my solitary hibernation, my mind seems to have blocked out all details of the final days before my demise. I feel that the memories of those last few days, possibly months, contain vital information that I need to find peace with that chapter of my life

At this time, I am researching the people of the Blackfoot Native Tribes of Historic events. They have been kind enough to pass on their lore and in the telling of their stories; I strongly believe that I was living with the Blackfoot Tribe in the mountains in Alberta before my passing. I believe that in listening to the elders' winter counts of historical events involving their tribes over the last hundred years will help me to reconcile my dreams with real life events and solidify my memory of that time.

With these new facts surfacing, I may have more of a story to tell, to fill in the blank canvass that has been missing so far.

Be prepared for Book Two: The Final Days of Doc Jack.

Daniel Jack McDougall a.k.a. Doc Jack

Made in the USA
San Bernardino, CA
05 February 2016